T0398921

YANKEE DOODLE DANDY

THE BROADWAY LEGACIES SERIES

"South Pacific": Paradise Rewritten
Jim Lovensheimer

Pick Yourself Up: Dorothy Fields and the American Musical
Charlotte Greenspan

To Broadway, to Life! The Musical Theater of Bock and Harnick
Philip Lambert

Irving Berlin's American Musical Theater
Jeffrey Magee

Loverly: The Life and Times of "My Fair Lady"
Dominic McHugh

"Show Boat": Performing Race in an American Musical
Todd Decker

Bernstein Meets Broadway: Collaborative Art in a Time of War
Carol J. Oja

We'll Have Manhattan: The Early Work of Rodgers and Hart
Dominic Symonds

Agnes de Mille: Telling Stories in Broadway Dance
Kara Gardner

The Shuberts and their Passing Shows: The Untold Tale of Ziegfeld's Rivals
Jonas Westover

Big Deal: Bob Fosse and Dance in the American Musical
Kevin Winkler

"Pal Joey": The History of a Heel
Julianne Lindberg

"Oklahoma!" The Making of an American Musical, Revised Edition
Tim Carter

Sweet Mystery: The Musical Works of Rida Johnson Young
Ellen M. Peck

The Big Parade: Meredith Willson's Musicals from "The Music Man" to "1491"
Dominic McHugh

Everything is Choreography: The Musical Theater of Tommy Tune
Kevin Winkler

Yankee Doodle Dandy: George M. Cohan and the Broadway Stage
Elizabeth T. Craft

YANKEE DOODLE DANDY

GEORGE M. COHAN AND THE BROADWAY STAGE

ELIZABETH T. CRAFT

Oxford University Press is a department of the University of Oxford. It furthers the University's objective of excellence in research, scholarship, and education by publishing worldwide. Oxford is a registered trade mark of Oxford University Press in the UK and certain other countries.

Published in the United States of America by Oxford University Press
198 Madison Avenue, New York, NY 10016, United States of America.

Library of Congress Cataloging-in-Publication Data
Names: Craft, Elizabeth T., author.
Title: Yankee doodle dandy : George M. Cohan and the Broadway stage /
Elizabeth T. Craft.
Description: New York : Oxford University Press, 2024. |
Series: Broadway legacies | Includes bibliographical references and index.
Identifiers: LCCN 2023054942 (print) | LCCN 2023054943 (ebook) |
ISBN 9780197550403 (hardback) | ISBN 9780197550427 (epub)
Subjects: LCSH: Cohan, George M. (George Michael), 1878-1942—Criticism and interpretation. | Cohan, George M. (George Michael), 1878-1942—Influence. | Actors—United States. | Theatrical producers and directors—United States. | Composers—United States. | Broadway (New York, N.Y.)
Classification: LCC PN2287.C56 C73 2024 (print) | LCC PN2287.C56 (ebook) |
DDC 792/.092 2 23/eng/20240215—dcundefined
LC record available at https://lccn.loc.gov/2023054942
LC ebook record available at https://lccn.loc.gov/2023054943

DOI: 10.1093/oso/9780197550403.001.0001

Printed by Sheridan Books, Inc., United States of America

To my parents,

JOHN AND HEATHER TITRINGTON

CONTENTS

FOREWORD

Not too long ago writers on the Broadway musical regularly touted how rare it was for a single person to be responsible for both the words and the music. It seemed as though at some point in nearly every biographical profile of Cole Porter the profiler would offer a variation of the following: "Unlike other songwriters, Porter managed not only to compose the music, he also wrote the words." Other profiles would substitute names of other composer-lyricists such as Irving Berlin, William Finn, Jerry Herman, Frank Loesser, Stephen Schwartz, Stephen Sondheim, Meredith Willson, or George M. Cohan. The lyricists Alan J. Lerner and Oscar Hammerstein (among others) usually wrote both the book (the libretto) and the lyrics, but it's even less common for a lyricist-composer to write the book as well, as Loesser did for *The Most Happy Fella* and Willson did for *The Music Man*. With one exception, none of the double threats mentioned so far wrote the books *nearly all the time*, and none of the above were known to act, sing, dance, and star in their own show, although some might produce it.

The exception is Cohan (1878–1942), the subject of Elizabeth T. Craft's *Yankee Doodle Dandy: George M. Cohan and the Broadway Stage*, who starting right at the beginning of the twentieth century did *all* of the above and continued to do so for nearly forty years. It would take another hundred years for a major Broadway figure to arrive who could demonstrate a comparable number of Cohan's varied off- and on-stage talents, someone who created the words, the music, and the books *and* also performed on the stage as an actor and singer. This would be Lin-Manuel Miranda (b. 1980), who played an important character in *In the Heights* (2008) and the starring role in *Hamilton* (2015) and is also a rapper and filmmaker. Indeed, multitalented and multifaceted figures like Cohan and Miranda *are* rare. Even Halley's Comet comes around every seventy-six years. Interestingly, in addition to writing this pioneering first book, Craft, who teaches on the faculty at the University of Utah, has written articles on *In the Heights* and *Hamilton* by Cohan's multifaceted successor, so don't be too surprised if Miranda's name pops up before you're done.

Surprisingly, as she writes in the introduction, "this book is the first on Cohan in fifty years." Rather than attempting to achieve comprehensive coverage of Cohan's forty-plus shows, Craft combines biography, analysis, and cultural history, using a well-chosen selection of works that places her subject's "multifaceted contributions within overlapping historical and cultural contextual webs to examine his wide-ranging impact on Broadway and beyond." Her story begins shortly after the young Cohan's apprentice years as part of a vaudeville stage act with his parents and sister called the Four Cohans, with the first hit, *Little Johnny Jones*, an historical milestone from 1904 still remembered for two songs, "The Yankee Doodle Boy" and "Give My Regards to Broadway." The musical marked the creation of a new kind of "original, fresh, even daring" theatrical and musical entertainment, musical comedies that featured fast-paced American vernacular dialogue and musical language in urban settings, in contrast to the exotic and mythological settings, classically trained vocalists, and European musical styles and forms associated with operetta.

Within its loosely chronological thematic structure, Craft examines "the various identities that Cohan came to embody." First we meet "the flag-waving patriot" who wrote shows that featured songs like "You're a Grand Old Flag." This aspect of Cohan's persona would later include his famous patriotic song "Over There" composed in 1917, not for a show but in response to World War I. Cohan received a Congressional Gold Medal for the part his songs played in America's victory (the first artist so honored). In the next chapter Craft describes and dissects what constituted the Cohanesque style that "helped shape the emerging genre." In the chapter after that she examines Cohan's role as a businessman, especially in connection with shows produced by his longtime partner Sam Harris, before Cohan's controversial decision to side with management over labor in the Actors' Equity Association strike of 1919.

The repercussions of Cohan's anti-labor position lasted beyond the grave. While serving as the chairman of the committee formed to raise $100,000 to fund what eventually would become the only statue of a theatrical figure in Broadway's Times Square, Hammerstein wrote in a letter that he "found a great many people who didn't like George M. Cohan." The money was eventually raised and the statue went up in 1959, but shared dislike of Cohan led to a two-and-a-half-year delay. One of those people who didn't like Cohan was Hammerstein's collaborator in the 1940s and 1950s, composer Richard Rodgers. In the 1930s, Rodgers and his first lyricist Lorenz Hart had a series of unpleasant experiences working with Cohan on his only musical film, *The Phantom President* (1932) and in their stage musical *I'd Rather Be Right* (1937).

In the latter show Cohan acted, sung, and danced the pivotal role of Franklin Delano Roosevelt. In his autobiography *Musical Stages* Rodgers wrote that while the critical reception of this show was mixed, *Cohan* "got ecstatic notices," and that despite Cohan's condescending and unpleasant offstage behavior, Rodgers would nevertheless be "the first to admit that he fully deserved them." It needs to also be said that Cohan was by no means universally disliked or unpleasant, especially when he was not working *for* someone else's show as he was with Rodgers and Hart. His arranger Mike Lake, for example, wrote about what a great boss he was and that those who worked for Cohan usually idolized him.

Craft devotes Chapter 4 to Cohan's evolution in the late 1910s and 1920s "from hyper-patriotism to Irish American pride with a spate of Irish American–themed shows." Her examination of this new turn in subject matter clearly demonstrates how Cohan represented and promoted Irish American identity and the increasing acceptance of the Irish as Americans in the early twentieth century. Chapter 5 explores Cohan's self-promotion as a celebrity who invariably knew how "to broadcast his distinct personality" and to perpetually reinvent himself, even as his output became increasingly outmoded and nostalgic.

Perhaps the most memorable marker of Cohan's celebrity was the musical biopic *Yankee Doodle Dandy*, in which James Cagney emulated the speech and singing characteristics and especially Cohan's "stiff-legged" dancing style. This is the topic of Craft's final chapter. In his efforts to recreate these dancing idiosyncrasies Cagney studied diligently with John Boyle, who had choreographed dance numbers in Cohan's shows from 1906 to 1922. The biographical component was considerably fictionalized, but the narrative was packed with music from Cohan's entire career. Craft shows how the timing of the film's release in 1942, when the outcome of the war was uncertain, contributed to it becoming "an archetype of cinematic wartime patriotism and the primary entry point to Cohan for generations of audiences."

When George M. was still part of the Four Cohans (before *George M!* became the title of a 1968 biographical musical starring Joel Grey), at the end of a show Cohan invariably spoke to his audiences to express his gratitude: "My father thanks you, my mother thanks you, my sister thanks you, and I thank you." In this spirit I would like to share the following message to Elizabeth Craft for writing this excellent book: "My editor [Norm Hirschy] thanks you, Broadway scholars will thank you, general readers will thank you, and I thank you."

Geoffrey Block
Series Editor, Oxford's Broadway Legacies

ACKNOWLEDGMENTS

Even someone who seemed to do it all, like Cohan, could only do so because he had supporters and collaborators. Likewise, this book has been a collective endeavor. My work on this project began in the vibrant intellectual community of Harvard University's Department of Music, where I was incredibly fortunate to have the mentorship of Carol Oja and to work with Sindhumathi Revuluri and Kay Kaufman Shelemay. They have shaped my work and life indelibly. A memorable coffeeshop conversation with Suzannah Clark helped determine how I think about Cohan's tunes. I am grateful also for the other Harvard music faculty and for colleagues who offered camaraderie and early feedback, including Ryan Bañagale, Andrea Bohlman, William Cheng, Christopher Chowrimootoo, Louis Epstein, Andrew Friedman, Glenda Goodman, Frank Lehman, Hannah Lewis, Thomas Lin, Lucille Mok, Matthew Mugmon, Samuel Parler, Meredith Schweig, Anne Searcy, Michael Uy, and Micah Wittmer. Phone calls and emails, conference catch-up sessions, and visits with many have seen me through the end of the project as well.

I have been equally fortunate in the wonderful colleagues and friends I've found at the University of Utah, including Jane Hatter, Seth Keeton, Catherine Mayes, Sarah Sinwell, and for a time, thankfully, Stephanie Doktor. The communities of scholars I have gotten to know through the Society for American Music and Song, Stage, and Screen conferences have enriched my work in formal sessions and informal conversations alike. Michael Garber generously shared Cohan-related materials. Charles Hiroshi Garrett, Katherine Preston, Jessica Sternfeld, Elizabeth Wollman, and others offered support and encouragement along the way.

Norm Hirschy, editor at Oxford University Press, and Geoffrey Block, Broadway Legacies series editor, have been on this journey with me since this book was a conference paper and a few bullet points, and they've been wonderfully steadfast and patient. They've provided sage advice and remarkably quick responses to my questions. I am deeply grateful for the excellent feedback from the anonymous peer reviewers and from Geoffrey, who offered sharp, thorough comments on the manuscript. My thanks also to copyeditor Anne Sanow and the OUP production team and to Dominic McHugh, editor of *The Oxford Handbook of Musical Theatre Screen Adaptations* (2019), which contains an earlier version of Chapter 6.

Many libraries and institutions have supported this project. My sincere thanks to former curator Morgen Stevens-Garmon, former volunteer John Kenrick (who processed the Cohan Collection), Gavin Robinson, and others at the Museum of the City of New York; Sylvia Wang at the Shubert Archive; Brett Service at Warner Bros. Archives; Mark Horowitz at the Library of Congress; Amelia Bathke at The Players Foundation for Theatre Education; Jeff Ksiazek at the Ward Irish Music Archives; John Calhoun and others at the New York Public Library for the Performing Arts; Pamela Anderson and Carey Stumm at the National Archives and Records Administration; and the many who aided my research at the Harry Ransom Center at the University of Texas at Austin and Harvard University's Loeb Music Library. Librarians at Baylor University, Brigham Young University, the Enoch Pratt Free Library, Johns Hopkins University, Mississippi State University, and the University of Oregon helped me obtain sheet music, even during a pandemic. At the libraries of my home institution, I'm particularly grateful to Allyson Mower at Marriott Library and to Lisa Chaufty at McKay Music Library.

This book's research was supported, at various stages, by the Charles Warren Center at Harvard University, an Andrew W. Mellon Foundation Research Fellowship from the Harry Ransom Center, a Society for American Music Virgil Thomson Fellowship, and fellowships and grants from the University of Utah. My research was also supported by the Undergraduate Research Opportunities Program at the University of Utah, with funding awarded to Sofia Filip, Steffan Perez-Velez Solis, and Brynn Staker St. Clair. Destiny Meadows and Misti Webster provided top-notch research assistance as well. My thanks to Mat Campbell for preparing the musical examples, to Erin Maher for preparing the index, and to Eden Kaiser for her careful proofreading.

I am tremendously grateful to the support system of fellow scholars and writers who helped see this project through the COVID-19 pandemic and to its fruition. Fellow members of my longtime writing group—Louis Epstein, Frank Lehman, Hannah Lewis, and Matthew Mugmon—have lived with this project as long as I have, and they have been unfailingly generous with their feedback and enthusiasm over multiple drafts and stages. I have been buoyed by Zoom co-writing sessions with Joanna Dee Das, Rachel Carrico, Saroya Corbett, Adanna Kai Jones, Esther Viola Kurtz, and Kate Mattingly. So many of the ideas on these pages were worked through in our virtual gatherings. Joyful and generative writing retreats with Alice McKeon, and with Emily Mercado and Sarah Sinwell, came at just the right time. I am indebted to Joanna Dee Das, Charles Hiroshi Garrett, Sarah Gerk, Glenda Goodman, Larry Hamberlin, Jane Hatter, Kate Mattingly, and Catherine

Mayes for their feedback on individual chapters at various stages. Sheryl Kaskowitz provided expert feedback on the entire manuscript; I cannot thank her enough.

One of the great gifts of this project was lucking into the remarkable support and camaraderie of a stellar group of folks who have been as invested in George M. Cohan and this project as I am. I'm forever thankful that B. T. McNicholl found my dissertation and invited me to participate in La Mirada Theatre's Cohan extravaganza in 2019 and Cohan Lab readings in 2022, events that have provided a model for historically engaged performance brimming with vitality. Through these events, I've been fortunate to get to know Anne Marie Lofaso, a fellow scholar as well as a Cohan descendent. David Collins's website "George M. Cohan in America's Theater" helped spark this research, and he has been tremendously generous in sharing his personal collection and wealth of knowledge. Scott A. Sandage has been the book's patron saint: when my primary research site shut down to researchers in the wake of the pandemic, he shared the fruits of his own archival research as well as precious interviews with people who have since passed away, and he has been equally generous with his knowledge, insight, and encouragement. David and Scott generously read the manuscript and saved me from several errors. (Those remaining are, of course, my own.) With this group, research has never felt lonely, and their influence is felt throughout these pages.

Without my parents Heather and John Titrington, to whom this book is dedicated, this book would not have been written; they shared the values that inspired it and provided the practical necessities for its creation, most of all many hours with their grandchildren. I'm grateful for the love and support, too, of Anne and Bill Craft, Sarah and Jeff Flick, Susanne Edmunds, Adam Titrington, and all of my extended family. A special thanks to Neal, Carla, Clara, and Violet Young, who hosted me on trips to New York and shared in the daily ups and downs of my research there. Finally, my deepest love and appreciation go to my family: Josh, who has lived with this project day in and day out with an endless reserve of support, and Anna and John, my Yankee Doodle joys.

ABOUT THE COMPANION WEBSITE

www.oup.com/us/yankeedoodledandy

Oxford has created a website to accompany *Yankee Doodle Dandy: George M. Cohan and the Broadway Stage*. Material that cannot be made available in a book, namely audio and video recordings, is provided here. The reader is encouraged to consult this resource while reading through the book. Examples available online are indicated in the text with Oxford's symbol ▶.

INTRODUCTION

Some of my earliest and favorite childhood memories are from the Fourth of July in my small hometown in North Carolina, which put on a four-day celebration designated the official state festival. It was not until much later in my life that I learned that Independence Day wasn't universally considered the biggest and most important holiday in the United States. There were competitive games between local volunteer fire squads; activities for children, like sack races and trying to catch eggs dropped from the raised platform of a bucket truck; a street dance; a parade; and, of course, fireworks. And there was choral and band music—local groups put on a concert each year.

Was it there that I first heard Cohan's songs? Or perhaps from my *Wee Sing America* cassette tape, one I played so often I knew all the lyrics by heart? Wherever I learned them, the tunes and words of "Yankee Doodle Boy" and "You're a Grand Old Flag" were etched in my memory before I knew what Broadway was or had ever heard of a person named George M. Cohan. That's true for many—these songs, along with "Give My Regards to Broadway" have become like folk songs in US culture. They hardly seem to have been composed, they just seem to have always existed. Some people can link the songs to the man who wrote them. Perhaps they've seen the film *Yankee Doodle Dandy* (1942) about Cohan's life or have seen Cohan's statue in Duffy Square in Manhattan, the only statue of a Broadway artist in the broader hub known as Times Square. Among musical theater buffs, he is a legend, proclaimed the "father of musical comedy."[1] Generally, though, telling friends or acquaintances whom I am writing about, I am met with an uncertain look until I name a few songs and, if the titles do not ring a bell, sing a few bars. Cohan "is something of an unforgettable forgotten man," as biographer John McCabe wrote in 1973.[2] If anything, he is even more forgotten since then.

Yankee Doodle Dandy. Elizabeth T. Craft, Oxford University Press. © Oxford University Press 2024.
DOI: 10.1093/oso/9780197550403.003.0001

In his day, however, Cohan was famous, as the "Yankee Doodle Boy" from his hit song and as the "Man Who Owned Broadway" from his musical of the same name. As his career took off at the dawn of the twentieth century, Broadway—as theatrical center of New York and the nation—was coming into its own, and the genre of the musical had yet to coalesce from theater's manifold forms. Cohan, as this book demonstrates, was a key figure in the construction of each. With his timely stories, colloquial language, snappy tunes, and savvy sense of publicity, Cohan made the musical in the United States "American," a distinctly homegrown product representative of US society and culture, including its inherent debates and complexities.[3] Equally important, he helped create Broadway as a symbol beyond the physical place. The entertainment that Cohan helped sell and package in the metonym of Broadway was centered in New York but aimed at nationwide audiences and even exported abroad, unapologetically commercial and highly professional but deeply idealized—the American musical as we have come to know it.

"Never was a plant more indigenous to a particular part of the earth than was George M. Cohan to the United States of his day," Oscar Hammerstein II aptly wrote in a tribute to Cohan in 1957.[4] Cohan came of age as the US came into its own as a world power. Over the course of his lifetime (1878–1942), the nation went from being predominantly agrarian to a nation of cities, from relying on foreign investment to hosting the financial capital of the world, from being perceived as a cultural backwater to being a cultural force in its own right, with distinctively American or newly Americanized forms like jazz, Hollywood films, and musical comedies.[5] Cohan's Horatio Alger–like rise mirrors the sense of national ascendency; he started as a childhood performer with his Irish American family's troupe in the late nineteenth century and became a Broadway mogul by the 1910s. He grew up trouping the country, and as vaudeville became respectable and took off as popular entertainment, his family became famous as the Four Cohans. In the 1890s, the adolescent George charted a course for New York and the so-called legitimate stage, which was often defined in this period in opposition to vaudeville, encompassing musical works as well as spoken drama.[6] He established himself as a creative force, writing sketches and songs not only for the Four Cohans but also that were increasingly in demand with other vaudeville acts and music publishers. In addition, he took over the business side of his family's act.

Breaking onto Broadway in the first years of the twentieth century, Cohan captured the mood of the nation with patriotic, populist bravado and relentless motion. A 1909 *Los Angeles Times* article explained that with his multiple roles and "enormous output," Cohan "is a sign of the times—the embodiment of the aggressive, unresting, clean though perhaps slightly superficial spirit of American life at this rushing dawn of the twentieth century."[7] By the 1910s, Cohan was one of Broadway's most well-known and influential figures, a "luminary of the legitimate."[8] When the United States entered World War I in 1917, he provided sonic fuel in the form of the wartime anthem "Over There." His opposition to Actors' Equity Association in the actors' strike of 1919 was a major turning point in his career; it marked the end of his successful business partnership with Sam Harris and diminished his reputation. Still, he continued to write, perform, and produce through the Roaring Twenties and the Great Depression. He saw the United States enter World War II before his death in 1942. His career "spanned decades that seem like centuries," to borrow an evocative phrase from scholar Sunny Stalter-Pace about Cohan's close contemporary Gertrude Hoffman.[9]

Cohan was remarkable—then and since—for his multiplicity of talents and roles: he was a composer, lyricist, playwright, performer (who acted, sang, and danced), director (who also staged dance numbers), theater owner, and producer. No other figure in American theater has done more. He wrote or co-authored over forty shows, and he produced and "doctored," or helped rewrite, many more.[10] He published hundreds of songs. Performing from his childhood into his sixties, he was seen in countless theaters across the United States. When Cohan was still in his twenties, at the start of his career, one critic wrote, "There may be others who can act as well as he; some who can write plays equal to his; some who can stage them; some who can write songs, compose the music, and sing it when it is composed, and some who can dance as he does, but it would be hard to find any man of equal youth who can do all these things and do them as well as George Cohan does."[11]

Cohan's many roles fed on one another: as a playwright, he wrote the works that would display his performance skills to best advantage and promote his public persona. As a producer and theater owner, he ensured that they would be staged and under good conditions. He was also a celebrity with considerable agency in his self-publicity, a role stemming from his work as an artist and businessman, one that is worth examining in its own right. Indeed, many of the roles he played in American cultural life went beyond professional categories; he was an emblem of patriotism, a proud Irish American, a Broadway magnate. These identities were linked. Cohan's longtime stage director Sam Forrest commented when the Warner Bros. film about Cohan's life came out in 1942, "*Yankee Doodle Dandy* is only one of a number of titles the motion-picture people could have used for the story of Cohan. . . . George, who inspired the nation with his patriotic songs, is the personification, too, of the best of Broadway, the best of Irish-Americana." He reflected, "Maybe all that adds up to 'Yankee Doodle Dandy,' because it's all part of the Yankee heritage."[12] The title of this book, too, reflects the many dimensions bound up in Americanness and the appellation "Yankee Doodle Dandy."

Surmising a historical figure's thoughts is a tricky proposition, but I feel certain that the young George M. Cohan who burst onto the New York theater scene at the turn of the twentieth century would have found it surprising that a university professor and musical theater scholar would be writing a book about him over a century later. Then again, he would also be surprised there would be such thing as a scholar of musical theater, then called musical comedy. Cohan's was the world of popular and ephemeral entertainment; his foremost goal was profit, not posterity. While he gained prominence in the realm of drama as his career progressed, his heart remained in show business, and especially the lighthearted entertainment known as musical comedy, until the end, and its products—shows and songs—are at the heart of this book.

We rarely see Cohan's shows or hear his songs in their original contexts today, and there are some good reasons for that. The shows are of their time—topical in a way that later playwrights and lyricists, writing in hopes of having a hit with a ten-plus-year run, are not. The jokes often refer to events of the day, happenings of that year or even that month. Some, contextualized or reimagined, would, I suspect, hold up. They have not lost the snap and humor that made them popular. But many are of their time in more deleterious ways, in particular with portrayals of certain ethnic and racial groups that were harmful in their day and are offensive in ours. Some things are not worth reviving. Yet in their sound and style, from their most trivial details to their fundamental themes, these shows are time capsules.

Cohan's shows do not just tell us about a long-forgotten era, however. I was born roughly a century after Cohan, and I have found the parallels between Cohan's lifetime and my own striking. Both have been periods of rapid industrial or technological change, developments in communication, mass immigration, and urbanization, and the considerable anxieties and debate that have accompanied these shifts. In both periods, the identity of the nation has been at stake, and Cohan helped make the Broadway stage, and especially the musical, a site for negotiating meanings of Americanism—"reflecting, refracting, and shaping U.S. culture," as scholar Stacy Wolf puts it—amidst these shifts. His shows helped tell Americans who they were, what the United States was, to whom the nation belonged and who would be excluded, at a time when each of these questions was contested. To borrow the formulation of political scientist Benedict Anderson, Cohan helped imagine the community of the nation onstage. Sending touring productions out, traveling himself, and through his sheet music, recordings, and the press, Cohan shared his vision of the nation and its entertainment throughout the country.[13]

* * *

Yankee Doodle Dandy: George M. Cohan and the Broadway Stage is not a biography, nor does it make any attempt to be comprehensive in its coverage of Cohan's work for and on the stage. Rather, this book looks at George M. Cohan as a central figure of his day, placing his multifaceted contributions within overlapping historical and cultural contextual webs to examine his wide-ranging impact on Broadway and beyond. Cohan contributed to and shaped public discourse in myriad, linked ways: through his shows, his songs, his performances, his writings, and portrayals of him in the media. I examine all of these.

Despite his importance, this book is the first on Cohan in fifty years. It is also the first academic book on Cohan: I aim to be inviting and engaging to broad audiences but also enter scholarly dialogues and make my claims and evidence traceable using citation of my sources. Cohan has his place in musical theater histories, but the existing scholarship on him is otherwise scant.[14] The multifaceted nature of his career—one of the most remarkable things about him—is almost certainly also one reason his legacy in scholarship has suffered. In part, the sense that he has been good at many things but is not one of the "greats" in any single category has dogged him. He received no mention, for example, in Alec Wilder's 1972 book *American Popular Song: The Great Innovators, 1900–1950*, though he was added by Robert Rawlins to the third edition in 2022, and he does not appear in most volumes on American drama or lists of great American plays.[15] This is closely linked to the lowbrow reputation he embraced and the type of popular entertainment he promoted which, for decades, remained outside the main purview of scholarship in many fields and seemed to be in contradiction to its values. For Wilder, for instance, greatness and innovation were linked, so writing popular songs in existing musical idioms would not be sufficient to qualify him for inclusion; Cohan's tunes also lacked the sophistication Wilder frequently praised in other songwriters. With his many roles, moreover, Cohan eludes categorization; the breadth of his work spans contemporary academic disciplines and does not fit neatly into a single book. Yet to consider Cohan in only one of these categories, I argue, is to fail to grasp the nature of his accomplishments and public impact.

Although there is a growing body of work on musical theater and popular entertainment in the early twentieth century, comprehending and conveying performance in this period remains challenging.[16] Cohan turned out shows quickly, and the scripts and music that appear in archival collections, particularly from his early years on Broadway, were clearly made for practical use, not for preservation. The music is in orchestral parts and not full score, often peppered with scribbles and doodles of the various musicians who played it, and sometimes it is unclear which script was the "final," to the extent such a thing existed at all.[17] While reviews and extant scripts suggest a general consistency in what was performed, it is equally evident that texts were flexible; Cohan talked about adding in extra verses with local material in certain songs at each stop on tour, for instance.[18] It is fortunate that Cohan's scripts and music still exist at all, and indeed, the fact that they do is a testament to the changing profession. Many of Cohan's shows were preserved in bound volumes in the library of The Players social club, a project motivated by the desire to ennoble and elevate the theatrical profession.[19]

At the same time, scripts and scores alone do not capture what audiences saw, the essence of a theatrical work, or how the show functioned in society. I have sought to catch and convey glimmers of Cohan as a performer and the performance of his shows by perusing photographs; listening to and viewing the handful of audio recordings, film appearances, and fragments of surviving video footage; and reading through the various reviews and other reports. The digitization of the exploding print media from this time period has opened up new possibilities in this regard. Newly digitized newspapers, in big cities and small towns alike, and magazines that catered to theater fans have made it easier to look "beyond Broadway," to echo a phrase and call from recent scholarship. They have also made it easier to see Broadway—which, as Cohan adamantly pointed out, included the traveling productions of "the road"—through an ever-expanding range of lenses.[20]

Although Cohan was uniquely versatile and maintained a remarkable amount of creative control over almost every aspect of his productions, he worked in a collaborative art form. Many people helped create Cohan's shows and even his public image at various points in his career, generally with far less visibility. These included his longtime partner Sam Harris, other members of the Four Cohans, orchestrator/arrangers and music directors, directors and choreographers, press agents, and other personnel. One advantage of looking at Cohan as a public figure as well as a creative one is better grasping how the name and concept of "George M. Cohan" was deployed in marketing and the construction of his celebrity, with collaborators downplayed or highlighted in various settings and circumstances.

This book opens with Cohan's emergence on Broadway, as a young adult at the turn of the twentieth century. However, he had already at that point been part of American entertainment for over a decade. To grasp his boldness in claiming the mantle of Yankee Doodle and the ways in which he transformed Broadway, we have to understand Cohan's position as an Irish American and his theatrical upbringing within the racial politics of the day.

* * *

George Michael Cohan was born in 1878 to Helen Frances Costigan Cohan ("Nellie") and Jeremiah Cohan ("Jerry"), both children of Irish immigrants, among the millions who came to the United States in the nineteenth and early twentieth centuries as conditions at home spurred them to seek a living elsewhere.[21] The Cohan family, whose name was said to come from "O'Caomhan" by way of "Keohane," settled in the Boston area, an Irish immigrant stronghold, and the Costigans in Providence, Rhode Island.[22] (George's parents had pronounced "Cohan" with the stress on the second syllable, but by the end of George's life, it was "CO-han.")[23]

Jerry was among the many Irish Americans who established a career as a traveling performer. In the nineteenth century, such performers presented a range of fare including songs, dances, sketches, novelty acts, operas, plays, and minstrel shows in venues across the country. After they wed in 1874, Nellie, and then later their children Josephine ("Josie," born in 1876) and George, joined Jerry on the stage.[24] The Cohans got their start in variety-style entertainment, touring together with various companies. By 1890, they were billing themselves as a family act, earlier on as the Cohan Mirth Makers and later as the Four Cohans, the moniker by which they became famous. Traveling with his family's troupe from early childhood, George M. Cohan was exposed not only to much of the United States but also to a diverse and heavily racialized theatrical world.[25]

The Irish in the United States from the mid-nineteenth century into the early twentieth were nominally White, with the legal privilege Whiteness afforded, yet they were also considered racially distinct from so-called old-stock Anglo-Americans. As historian and American studies scholar Matthew Frye Jacobson discusses in *Whiteness of a Different Color: European Immigrants and the Alchemy of Race*, this period of mass immigration saw a "fracturing of whiteness," as various groups of European immigrants were racially defined as Celts, Hebrews, Slavs, and so on, creating a "system of 'difference' by which one might be both white *and* racially distinct from other whites." Understanding the thinking about race during this period, Jacobson explains, requires abandoning later twentieth- and twenty-first-century notions, including the anachronistic concept of ethnicity. "Conflicting or overlapping racial designations" circulated simultaneously: the Irish "were 'white' according to naturalization law; they proclaimed themselves 'Caucasians' in various political organizations using that term; and they were degraded 'Celts' in the patrician lexicon of proud Anglo-Saxons." After the Johnson-Reed Act of 1924 dramatically reduced the flow of immigration, these European immigrant splinter groups were "reconsolidated" as Caucasian, in a racial process of becoming White that was inseparable from the process of assimilation, or becoming American.[26] The life and career of George M. Cohan spans this ideological fault line.

Nativism was a constant undercurrent, with rising tides of anti-immigrant activity during periods of societal stress, in the "century of immigration" that constituted the political landscape of much of Cohan's life. Nativists objected to immigration on overlapping and intertwining religious, economic, cultural, racial, and political grounds.[27] Irish Catholics in the United States, the group to which Cohan belonged, were seen as undesirable and unassimilable citizens for their disadvantaged status, their religion, their perceived racial inferiority, and their politics, whether in Tammany Hall or in the campaign for Irish nationalism. An image appearing in 1889 in the magazine *Puck* serves as an illustration: it shows members of various nationalities being stirred acquiescently into a vessel of citizenship, while an Irishman bearing a knife and a banner of Clan na Gael (a secret, revolutionary Irish American nationalist organization), stands defiantly on the rim. The caption: "The Mortar of Assimilation—and the One Element that Won't Mix" (see Figure I.1).

The Cohan family were well aware of nativist attitudes, as demonstrated by a humorous anecdote that Jerry Cohan told about a performance of the family act for the Pilgrim Fathers society at Revere Beach, Massachusetts.[28] The Cohans' reception at this event for an audience of "well-behaved, sedate" Puritans, as Jerry recounts, was initially cool, with only "frosty smiles, and sometimes gentle applause" for their efforts. "We were sore, oh, so sore," he says. "But we didn't let up. No, we banged away at 'em till they thawed out." By the time George and Josephine did their "famous 'doll dance,'" the audience was enthusiastic, calling for so many encores and bows that Jerry had to make a speech. He recalled telling them that his family "was proud of applause and praise, coming with such sincerity from the hands and hearts of those whose ancestors made it possible to dwell in peace in this free land." And he added

> we, too, have some claim upon your regard, which you will acknowledge when I tell you, with pardonable pride, that Boston is my native city. My

Figure I.1 "The Mortar of Assimilation—and the One Element that Won't Mix," Puck, *June 26, 1889.*

> great grandfather was a soldier, a regimental surgeon, and served on many a bloody battle field in the war of the great rebellion. (Tremendous applause and emotion.) We might be enrolled as sons and daughters of the revolution (cheers and cries of "Yea, yea"), and we should, we would, but for the fact that my ancestor fought on the wrong side. He surrendered with Cornwallis to the continental army.[29]

Beneath the story's comedic veneer lie some dark realities: the exhausting nature of entertainment on the local circuit, the Cohans' desperate attempts to win applause in a disheartening situation, and, undergirding the encounter, the probable prejudice of "old-stock" Americans toward an Irish immigrant family of performers. But Jerry cunningly turns the tables by playing to his audience's partialities. He invokes discourses of nationalism in which citizens prove their worth through lineage and places his own family on equal ground before revealing the ruse.

Yet to see the nineteenth and early twentieth centuries only in terms of nativism would be to overstate the movement's impact. Faith in the power of assimilation and recognition of immigrants' contributions to society remained strong on the whole.[30] In the early twentieth century, Jerry felt confident enough in audiences' sympathies to offer his Pilgrim Fathers story to the press as humor. Even the above cartoon, in showing the Irishman as an exception, testifies as much to the prevailing notion that the equality of America would create good citizens as to the fears that a few might be unassimilable.[31]

Jerry Cohan was his son George's earliest and most profound influence, and Jerry's stage experience, like that of many late nineteenth-century Irish American performers, was rooted in ethnic and racial stereotypes of Irish and African Americans. He acted as Barney the Guide in MacEvoy's Hibernicon and performed with other Irish-themed companies, including his own. Hibernicons offered a pictorial tour of Ireland with songs and dances, combining the entertainment of variety and the moving panorama. Jerry's handwritten "Cohan Family Repertoire-Book" manuscript survives at the Harvard Theatre Collection, and that, along with his privately published volume of *Poems and Sketches*, give a sense of his Irish material. In these scenes, Irish characters speak in thick accents and employ funny mannerisms, conversing about a range of topics from life as a servant to love and spinsterhood, aspirations of wealth to drinking and politics.[32] They caricature the Irish immigrant but also take to heart his trials and struggles; as theater historian Michelle Granshaw has demonstrated, Irish-themed entertainment both reinforced stereotypes and allowed Irish and Irish American artists to "assert their perspectives about Ireland" and "construct Irish belonging." The Hibernicon also, as Granshaw discusses, influenced the next generation, including George, whose early stage experience also included Irish-themed fare.[33]

Irish showmen were also prevalent on the minstrel stage, donning a mask that functioned in multifarious and frequently contradictory ways. Purporting to draw upon Black dialect and music, blackface minstrelsy established modes of entertainment and put forth caricatures, like the Jim Crow and Zip Coon figures, that endured well beyond the nineteenth century. Stereotypes of Irish Americans and African Americans in minstrelsy and popular song shared certain similarities: both disclose a romantic nostalgia for what is perceived to be an earlier, simpler life alongside comically delivered commentary and mockery. The romantic notion of the Irish exile pining for "Erin" bore a resemblance to sentimental depictions of the plantation South, and the comic stereotype of the feckless, irrepressible Irish "Paddy" paralleled, in many ways, that of slave figure "Jim Crow." Jerry Cohan performed Irish material like the "Dublin Dancing Master" for the minstrel show, not only for the Hibernicon. While these representational types may have rubbed shoulders, however, any real-life cultural exchange was inherently unequal, and the performance of these caricatures served different functions for the White performers of the characters and the Black performers who, as they entered the realm of entertainment, had to contend with them. For Irish American performers, blackface performance served as both "a displaced mapping of ethnic Otherness and an early agent of acculturation," as American studies scholar Eric Lott writes. It could offer a means of immigrant self-expression, yet also, by reinforcing a Black/White divide, serve as a path to racial Whiteness; the perverse mask of Blackness, as scholar Michael Rogin put it, "passed immigrants into Americans."[34]

Arguably the most popular form of theatrical entertainment of its day, the "burnt cork minstrel show" served as Jerry Cohan's training grounds. With its varied and well-executed entertainment and broad audiences, Jerry considered it "the best school to make an actor."[35] A few decades later, it was "coon songs," another form capitalizing on stereotypes and musical styles of Black Americans, that helped pave George's path to success in the 1890s. But like many of his contemporaries, including his mentee Irving Berlin, George also shared his father's nostalgic view of minstrelsy and was slow to let go of it. In addition to occasionally writing minstrel sketches and performing in blackface, he and his partner Sam Harris launched their own minstrel company in 1908, which performed without much success for a couple of years before they concluded that "American minstrelsy was a dead issue."[36]

Minstrelsy may have been Jerry's proving grounds, but it was vaudeville that shaped the Four Cohans—including George. Variety-structured entertainment, musical theater scholar Larry Stempel writes, was "perhaps the only truly democratic mass medium of the period: It reached virtually all areas of the country and placed no demands of literacy on its audience."[37] Vaudeville—with its programs of song-and-dance, skits, acrobats, magicians, and more—was itself influenced by minstrelsy. It had been known as "variety" but was rechristened when it was "cleaned up" to appeal not only to working-class audiences but also to the middle class, women, and children.

The Four Cohans fit these changing needs perfectly. As scholar Nicholas Gebhardt has discussed, Cohan developed from his time in a family act and in vaudeville his kinship-like sense of theater with high value placed on mutuality, encapsulated in the signature closing that George developed: "My father thanks you, my mother thanks you, my sister thanks you, and I thank you."[38] Eventually, the Four Cohans became one of the most popular acts in the country, receiving top billing and commanding high sums, and George also honed his writing skills by preparing sketches for other acts. Vaudeville's mishmash of forms and democratic impulse fed into his later shows, especially his plays with music and his musical comedies.

George had the opportunity in his youth to soak in other theatrical entertainment as well, including melodramas and other plays, Gilbert and Sullivan operettas, Weber and Fields revues and other musical shows, and many of the famous performers of the late nineteenth century.[39] Among his significant theatrical predecessors and influences were the shows of Harrigan and Hart and of Charles Hoyt. Edward (Ned) Harrigan and Tony Hart, along with composer David Braham, staged tremendously popular comedic and contemporary ethnic-themed musical plays in the 1870s and 1880s. While, as he once wrote, the duo's shows were a bit before his time, Cohan was able to see a revival of *Reilly and the 400* and see "why the great Harrigan had been such a popular idol." He also waxed rhapsodic about Braham, recounting memories shared by his father, and suggested a connection between the Harrigan and Hart shows and his musical play *Forty-Five Minutes from Broadway* (1906).[40] Charles Hoyt was a playwright, director, and manager whose farces with music were popular in the 1880s and 1890s. Cohan was frequently described as a Hoyt successor, and while there were many differences between them, Cohan's shows shared with Hoyt's an emphasis on contemporaneous subject matter and real-life characters. Cohan followed in Hoyt's footsteps in his crossover financial and creative career, emphasis on entertainment rather than edification, and persona as "self-made dramatist" as well. Cohan purportedly treasured his souvenir paperweight from the 360th performance, in 1892, of Hoyt's highly successful musical *A Trip to Chinatown*.[41]

* * *

The chapters of this book are organized thematically around the various sociocultural identities that Cohan came to embody: the flag-waving patriot, the entertainer, the "man who owned Broadway," the Irish American, and the celebrity, with the last chapter dedicated to the film *Yankee Doodle Dandy*, which preserved a wartime version of Cohan's American identity on screen. There is a loose chronological arc to the book, but the chapters are not time-bound.

Chapter 1, on Cohan as a flag-waving patriot, shows how his early hyper-patriotic shows modeled—and occasionally challenged—Theodore Roosevelt's contemporaneous rhetoric of "true Americanism," which called for each American to possess a keen sense of national identity and civic responsibility. Focusing on *Little Johnny Jones* (1904) and *The American Idea* (1908), it examines the composition and boundaries of Roosevelt's and Cohan's visions of American society. Critics questioned whether Cohan's so-called flag-waving was entertainment or propaganda, but his tactics received ringing endorsement from the box office.

Critics struggled to describe what it was about Cohan's inimitable style that set him apart, and they resorted to simply adjectivizing his name: his songs, scripts, directorial and acting style, and dancing were "Cohanesque." Chapter 2, on Cohan the entertainer, unpacks this term, identifying and discussing Cohan's trademark characteristics and innovations as a playwright, director, composer, and performer. Taken as a whole, Cohan's stylistic traits helped shape the emerging genre that would come to be known as "the musical."

Chapter 3 focuses on Cohan the businessman, the so-called man who owned Broadway. It looks at his role as a producer and places it into dialogue with shows of his that thematized business, wealth, and masculinity, especially the play *Get-Rich-Quick Wallingford* (1910). The chapter also discusses Cohan's vehement anti-union stance in the highly publicized battles over the formation of Actors' Equity Association, a decision with career- and legacy-defining implications.

Later in his career, Cohan shifted from hyper-patriotism to Irish American pride with a spate of Irish American–themed shows, from *The Voice of McConnell* (1918) to *The Merry Malones* (1927). Chapter 4 shows that a variety of forces, including growing acceptance for Irish Catholics, Irish American support for Irish nationalism, and the events surrounding Ireland's 1916 Easter Rising and World War I, fused at a moment when Cohan had become safely established in his profession and impelled him to turn more fully toward representing and promoting Irish American identity. It demonstrates how Cohan's Irish American–themed shows helped to write the Irish into the influential model of Americanism he had already established.

Throughout his career, Cohan was a savvy self-promotor. Chapter 5, on Cohan as a celebrity, examines how he harnessed the mass-circulation press and burgeoning journalism dedicated to stars of the day to broadcast his distinct personality, Yankee Doodle persona, and fashioning of Broadway.

He thus established himself as a national and even international figure, one whose fame extended far beyond New York City. When his popularity waned and Broadway turned to new styles in the 1920s and 1930s, Cohan trafficked in nostalgia—in his shows, the print media, and radio programs—to bolster his flagging career and maintain his public visibility.

Cohan's celebrity made him an attractive subject for a film, and in the early 1940s, he signed a contract with Warner Bros. for *Yankee Doodle Dandy*, starring James Cagney as Cohan. Chapter 6 traces the development of this 1942 film, a highly fictionalized account of Cohan's life that became an archetype of cinematic wartime patriotism and the primary entry point to Cohan for generations of audiences. It demonstrates how the film navigated Cohan's stipulations and responded to the political climate by strategically linking Cohan's life story with histories of the American stage and of the nation.

The book's epilogue considers Cohan's longer-term legacy, his indelible impact on Broadway, and the constantly evolving role of his memory and songs in the American cultural consciousness and public sphere. The identities highlighted in the chapters of the book, and their attendant contradictions, have shaped the ways in which Cohan and his work have been seen since his death as well as during his lifetime. With changing historical circumstances, Cohan's songs and even his personal image have sometimes appeared in new guises, though—especially in the case of patriotism—in equally charged debates.

Cohan's shows drew upon the various strands of theatrical and musical entertainment that had come before, but they were also original, fresh, even daring—as was he. He was an Irish American who had the audacity to represent himself as the Yankee Doodle emblem of the nation, a vaudevillian who had the nerve to unapologetically climb the ranks and package his lowerbrow style as Broadway. The story of George M. Cohan is the story of a fascinating individual. It is also a story of early twentieth-century Broadway theater and of the United States itself—the America that Cohan lived in and the one he helped shape through his songs, shows, and role in public life.

THE FLAG-WAVING PATRIOT

> He's the most original thing that ever hit Broadway. You know why? Because he's the whole darn country squeezed into one pair of pants.
>
> —*Yankee Doodle Dandy* (1942)

> The American flag struck me as popular, so I used it. I believed in it; I thought it should be waved.
>
> —George M. Cohan

In the song "Go and Get a Flag" from the 1914 revue *Hello, Broadway!*, George M. Cohan (as composer and lyricist) poked fun at himself for flag-waving, a practice for which he had become well known and had been much criticized.[1] The show's subtitle of "A Musical Crazy Quilt" signaled its jollity and bricolage; it reveled in playfully mocking anything and everything on Broadway—including Cohan himself. In the jaunty number "Go and Get a Flag," Cohan's costar William Collier urges Cohan to include a flag-waving number to ensure box office success:

> Go and get a flag
> Because you need it, you need it, you know you do.
> Go and get a flag
> And always save it, and wave it, and they'll stand for you.
> Quit this Booth and Berret [*sic*] stunt and be a human being[2]
> Always pull the patriotic gag.
> Your play is alright in its way
> And this is all I've got to say—
> "For God's sake, go and get a flag."[3]

The song seems to accede to the view of disparaging critics that Cohan's flag-waving was merely pandering to the unsophisticated masses for commercial

Yankee Doodle Dandy. Elizabeth T. Craft, Oxford University Press. © Oxford University Press 2024.
DOI: 10.1093/oso/9780197550403.003.0002

purposes, even as it celebrates the stratagem. Yet in the revue, this song was "dutifully followed," as Cohan biographer John McCabe has noted, by the musically and affectively contrasting "My Flag," which sincerely praises the "Yankee Doodle do-or-die flag" and the nation.[4] These back-to-back flag-themed numbers testify not only to the importance of overt patriotism in Cohan's Broadway career but also to the complexities of this patriotism.[5]

Cohan's first so-called legitimate New York shows were *The Governor's Son* in 1901 and *Running for Office* in 1903, both expansions of vaudeville sketches for the Four Cohans. But he made his mark in 1904 with *Little Johnny Jones*, an exuberantly patriotic musical about an American jockey riding in the English Derby. In its first year, the show alternated Broadway stints with time on the road, with improvements made along the way; when added up, the performances constituted a strong total run.[6] In a 1914 sketch of Cohan in *Everybody's Magazine*, Peter Clark Macfarlane wrote that after the lessons he learned from *Little Johnny Jones*, Cohan "met [the] very evident desire for debauches of patriotic enthusiasm by designing flag songs and flag ballets and flag choruses, and indeed whole flag plays—'George Washington, Jr.,' 'The American Idea,' and 'The Yankee Prince'—in all of which, no matter what else happened, George or somebody else was there waving the flag."[7] Cohan's patriotic flag-waving brought mixed reviews—among them some vehemently scathing censure—from critics but a ringing endorsement from the box office.[8] It also earned him his reputation as the self-proclaimed "Yankee Doodle Comedian," or the "Yankee Doodle Boy" or "Yankee Doodle Dandy."

The stories, characters, and "Yankee Doodle" tunes of these shows reflected ideologies and debates of the day, aligning most closely—to a striking degree—with the discourse of Theodore Roosevelt, president from 1901 to 1909. In his landmark survey *Our Musicals, Ourselves*, musical theater historian John Bush Jones briefly compares these two figures, "America's Boosters," who "captured the public imagination as embodiments of the spirit of the age."[9] This chapter delves into—and expands upon—Jones's comparison: because Roosevelt and Cohan did not just embody their historical moment, they also shaped it. As historian Gary Gerstle has argued in *American Crucible: Race and Nation in the Twentieth Century*, Roosevelt's influential and pervasive ideology forged the "Rooseveltian nation" that held sway until the 1960s.[10] As a popular playwright, a celebrity, and an ethnic American, Cohan helped define notions of Americanness. Cohan's shows, songs, and rhetoric echoed Roosevelt's ideal of "true Americanism"—the citizen's keen sense of national identity, civic responsibility, and patriotism. Yet they also qualified Rooseveltian ideology in subtle but significant ways, pushing back on the tenet that for immigrants to be good Americans they must discard their former national identities.

While Cohan's shows and Roosevelt's discourse were blatantly patriotic, this hardly meant that either was insular. In fact, encounters between characters representing America and its "Others," both the foreigners outside national boundaries and the immigrants within, featured prominently in Cohan's flag plays, many of which were set abroad. The typical scenario: Americans run amok in London or Paris, where fortune-hunting British noblemen, in cahoots with title-hunting American parents, create hurdles for brash young Yankee heroes and their charming sweethearts. These tropes, silly as they seem, were not only highly entertaining but also spoke to current anxieties in contemporary language.

VISIONS OF THE NATION AND ROOSEVELT'S "TRUE AMERICANISM"

Historian Matthew Frye Jacobson has characterized American thinking at the turn of the twentieth century as filled with self-certainty and also self-doubt, "a paradoxical combination of supreme confidence in U.S. superiority and righteousness, with an anxiety driven by fierce parochialism."[11] The late nineteenth century had witnessed an upheaval wrought by industrialization, urbanization, and immigration. Thus, even as the United States entered the world stage as a rising imperial power at the dawn of the twentieth century, there was an undercurrent of worry. Aspects of life and livelihood that had seemed fixed, like work, gender, and race, had proved mutable. In the face of stark societal changes, various factions struggled to defend or adapt their visions of nationhood.

Roosevelt's idea of true Americanism must be understood within the framework of debates between two opposing, defining American ideals of nationalism: the racial and the civic. Racial nationalists, as Gary Gerstle explains, saw a nation unified by "common blood and skin color and by an inherited fitness for self-government," though the perceived boundaries of this common racial heritage shifted continuously. Civic nationalists stressed belief in "the fundamental equality of all human beings, in every individual's inalienable rights to life, liberty, and the pursuit of happiness, and in a democratic government that derives its legitimacy from the people's consent."[12] In the early twentieth century, as newcomers of different races and religions altered the make-up of the populace, these two poles were manifested largely in debates about the place of immigrants in the national polity.

On the one hand, nativists, subscribing to racial nationalism and seeing the nation's well-being as dependent on a Protestant Anglo-American composition, sought to heavily restrict immigration. On the other hand, pluralists advocated for a nation that would celebrate and be shaped by its newest newcomers. Intellectuals like Horace M. Kallen and Randolph Bourne articulated these views more fully in the mid-1910s, but they built on foundations laid by such figures as W. E. B. Du Bois, Jane Addams, and John Dewey.[13] Roosevelt's brand of nationalism was committed to civic ideals but also restrained by the limitations of racialized thinking.

Roosevelt proclaimed an "intense and fervid Americanism" to be the essential bedrock for combating the nation's challenges in his 1894 essay "What 'Americanism' Means," later reissued under the title "True Americanism." Citizens must be "Americans in heart and soul, in spirit and purpose, keenly alive to the responsibility implied in the very name of American, and proud beyond measure of the glorious privilege of bearing it," he exhorted. Remarkably in an era of debate over immigration, when many among the nation's Protestant elite took a nativist stance, Roosevelt embraced civic nationalism, welcoming immigrants, decrying "any discrimination against or for a man because of his creed," and "demand[ing] that all citizens, Protestant and Catholic, Jew and Gentile, shall have . . . their rights guaranteed them."[14] Roosevelt was particularly taken with Israel Zangwill's play *The Melting Pot* (1908), firmly believing not only in the equitability of accepting immigrants as Americans but also in the power of interracial mixing to produce a superior, united American people.[15] Yet this confidence had its limits, and the commitment to equity articulated by Roosevelt in his speeches and writing belied the racialized underpinnings of his ideology. In his view, the process of assimilation had to be regulated, and certain groups—namely those perceived as non-White—were excluded from full citizenship. Moreover, the national allegiance Roosevelt demanded of citizens—immigrants and native-born alike—was all-encompassing and permitted no other affinities.[16]

Roosevelt outlined three forms of false patriotism as antitheses to true Americanism: first, a spirit of parochialism, or having a local rather than broadly national allegiance; second, a lack of patriotism, and especially a preference for European ways; and third, immigration without Americanization. In other words, identifying with one's local community, as an expatriate, or as what was known as a hyphenated American—for example, as a German or Irish American with dual loyalties—was unacceptable. The latter two categories Roosevelt found particularly threatening. Those artists or social elite who were thought to be Europeanized, who looked too admiringly toward Europe or who chose to live there, represented to Roosevelt a "spirit of colonial dependence" and what he saw as the grave dangers of over-civilization. Similarly, Roosevelt held that immigrants must be undivided in their attachments. "We must Americanize [newcomers] in every way," he proclaimed, further asserting, "[The immigrant] must revere only our flag; not only must it come first, but no other flag should even come second. He must learn to celebrate Washington's birthday rather than that of the Queen or Kaiser, and the Fourth of July instead of St. Patrick's Day. . . . Above all, the immigrant must learn to talk and think and be United States."[17]

As historian Gail Bederman and other scholars have shown, Roosevelt's Americanism was highly gendered.[18] Roosevelt was an intentionally self-shaped model of the new man of his time; he was both swayed by shifting contemporarily notions of manhood and harnessed them for political gain. Characterizing the American expatriate as effeminate as well as un-American, Roosevelt warns in "True Americanism" of "the over-civilized, over-sensitive, over-refined" Europeanized man and the "undersized man of letters" who because of "his delicate, effeminate sensitiveness . . . finds that he cannot play a man's part among men" in the United States. Linking patriotism and robust masculinity, as historian Andrew Johnson notes, the essay was as much about gender as it was about immigrant assimilation.[19]

Roosevelt's America was not created unilaterally, nor was it uncontested. In *Rough Writing: Ethnic Authorship in Theodore Roosevelt's America*, literature scholar Aviva Taubenfeld has shown how several authors of diverse European backgrounds, including Danish-born reformer Jacob Riis and Irish American humorist Finley Peter Dunne, both took up and challenged Roosevelt's vision of America through literature. Roosevelt invited them to do so, in a sense, for he believed strongly in the power of narrative in nation building, calling for literature and art that "smack[s] of our own soil," and he perceived that America's own native-born writers were not fulfilling this need.[20] As Taubenfeld writes, this perceived cultural breach gave ethnic writers an opportunity to "reassert for the nation the values it wanted to believe defined it, creating in the process a place for themselves and their ethnic communities in America."[21]

In the pages that follow, I demonstrate how Cohan seized this opportunity on the stage. He contributed to discourse about immigration and nationalism and helped to create the soundtrack of the Rooseveltian nation, while also challenging some of Roosevelt's assumptions. He did so from a unique position as a third-generation Irish American who, increasingly throughout his early career, was seen as a flesh-and-blood emblem of the United States.

THE ROOSEVELTIAN IN THE COHANESQUE

During this period, George M. Cohan embodied Roosevelt's vision of immigrant assimilation and even one-upped Roosevelt's hypothetical true American gent. Not only did he revere the flag, but he also sang its praises, "pranc[ed] around [it]," and "drum majored with it as [the] leader," as reviewers described the staging of his song "You're a Grand Old Flag" in *George Washington, Jr.* (1906) (see Figure 1.1).[22] Not only did he celebrate the Fourth of July, he also claimed it as his birthday (a false claim I discuss in more detail in Chapter 5). Early in his career, one could almost forget Cohan was Irish American at all—on stage, he played the consummate American, without Irish inflections, and he carried that reputation with him offstage as well.

Both Cohan and Roosevelt were larger-than-life personalities with fascinating biographies, self-confident manners, and celebrity in their respective spheres. They each garnered extensive coverage in contemporary newspapers and even spawned their own adjectival forms: Cohan's shows were "Cohanesque" and Roosevelt's political policies and personal traits "Rooseveltian."[23] The two descriptors and the traits they indexed meshed remarkably well: the fast dramatic pace, snappy rhythms, singable melodies, colloquial language, patriotic themes, and "clean," wholesome morality of Cohan's shows seem in many ways a dramatization of Rooseveltian ideals.

Figure 1.1 Cohan waving the flag in George Washington, Jr. *From the collection of Scott A. Sandage.*

Like Roosevelt's, Cohan's vision of national identity was intensely masculine, somewhat xenophobic, civically minded but racially restricted, and, while confidently stated, riddled with contradictions and ambiguities. Cohan's heroes brim with the kind of overtly masculine nationalism and confident self-reliance that Roosevelt prescribed, proclaiming with loud enthusiasm their patriotic pride. Each man found room for certain immigrant characters in his imagined society of true Americans and excluded others based on racial difference. And through plots about Americans abroad and "international marriages," Cohan's shows demonstrated the Europeanization that Roosevelt regarded as among the nation's greatest threats and the evils of "Anglomania," a focus which also served to divert attention from Cohan's own Irish American heritage.[24]

Cohan called one of his early musicals, *The Yankee Prince* of 1908, "A Timely Satire on Titled Fortune Hunters," but this titled fortune hunting in the form of arranged international marriages featured prominently in the plots of all his early patriotic shows. An "international" or "foreign" marriage, in contemporary parlance, was between a high society American and titled European, usually a member of the British nobility.[25] The late nineteenth and early twentieth centuries saw hundreds of these unions, including that of Jennie Jerome and Lord Randolph Churchill, parents of Winston Churchill; and the much-publicized marriage of Consuelo Vanderbilt and the Duke of Marlborough. Common wisdom held that the member of the nobility was seeking wealth, and the Anglomaniacal American or her parents were jockeying for a title.

The combination of censure and admiration, of sensationalism and spectacle, generated by these marriages preoccupied turn-of-the-century journalists and authors. The unions and the leisure class that sought them not only filled newspapers' society pages but also formed the core of a slew of plays and books, including novels by Henry James and Edith Wharton.[26] An advertisement in the program for *The American Idea*, which premiered in 1908, reinforced and co-opted the title-chasing American stereotype: its cartoon drawing shows a masculine-looking raptor with a moneybag body (likely meant to be an American eagle) chasing a feminine-looking rabbit with a crown and collar to represent its noble status, while the text proclaims the clothing company's commitment to catching "the best styles" of any nationality (Figure 1.2).[27]

Many frowned upon the practice of international marriage, however, including Roosevelt. In a message to Congress, he denounced "that particular kind of multimillionaire who is almost the least enviable, and is certainly one of the least admirable, of all our citizens; a man . . . whose son is a fool

Figure 1.2 Advertisement for Rogers Peet and Co. clothiers in a program for The American Idea. *Cohan Collection.*

and his daughter a foreign princess."[28] In addition to these being seen as merely strategic alliances, critics were displeased about US money leaving the country and about the value the wealthy American elite placed on noble status, and the unions were frequently cast as unpatriotic.[29]

Through romance plots advocating true, pointedly American love, Cohan's shows reinforced concerns about these transatlantic unions and the European influence and moral decay they represented. The international marriages in his musicals are always arranged by corrupt relatives against the wishes of the bride- or groom-to-be. In *Little Johnny Jones*, the heroine Goldie's aunt goes abroad to arrange her marriage to the Earl of Bloomsbury, but Goldie wants to marry the American jockey Johnny Jones. Cohan's other flag plays followed suit with slight variations. In *George Washington, Jr.*, it's a US senator arranging his son's marriage to the snooty daughter of an English lord. In *The Yankee Prince*, the heroine's father eagerly pursues his daughter's marriage to the Earl of Weymouth while his folksy, unpretentious wife wants nothing more than to return to Chicago and leave English noblemen well enough alone. And in *The American Idea*, a German American and Irish American compete in arranging international marriages for their respective children. Cohan demonstrates in each show—to borrow the language of one—that a "Yankee prince of a guy" beats an English earl any day.[30] This basic fable was a holdover from the "Yankee plays" stretching back to the early years of the republic, described by Cohan's contemporary Constance Rourke in *American Humor* (1931), but Cohan put his own modern, urban spin on it.[31]

In Cohan's shows, the plot device of the international marriage generally enhances the broader scenario of Americans traveling abroad. Either London or Paris provides a suitably exotic setting for colorful scenery, like a scene set at Windsor Castle in *The Yankee Prince*, and allows for fun novelty numbers like "'Op in Me 'Ansom" in *Little Johnny Jones*, in which hansom cab drivers and sightseers sing about touring London (see Figure 1.3). Perhaps most important, though, the Europe-America encounter of these shows serves up ample opportunities for humor, sometimes at the expense of the wealthy Americans but more frequently at the expense of the Europeans.[32] In *The Yankee Prince*, for example, an American asks the waiter, "Hello, where did you come from?" "I was born here in London," answers the waiter. "Well I wouldn't go around bragging about it if I were you," the American retorts.[33] *Little Johnny Jones* features a similar exchange. The heroine Goldie, disguised as a French mademoiselle, asks another character, Anthony Anstey, "What makes the Americans so proud of their country?" "Other countries," he quips in response.[34] Other humorous scenes rely

Figure 1.3 Postcard depicting "'Op in Me 'Ansom" scene from Little Johnny Jones. *From the collection of David Collins.*

on cross-cultural miscommunication, as in this bit of wordplay in *George Washington, Jr.*:

> [SENATOR] BELGRAVE. What became of George?
> [LORD] ROTHBURT. Your son? He stopped to speak with a girl, I fancy.
> BELGRAVE. A girl you fancy?
> ROTHBURT. No, no, what bally rot! He stopped to see a girl, I fancy.
> BELGRAVE. That's what you said before. If you fancied the girl why didn't you stop to see her yourself?
> ROTHBURT. My word, but you Americans are obtuse! When I said he stopped to speak to a girl, I fancy, I meant that he stopped to see a girl HE fancied, I fancy.
> BELGRAVE. Oh, I see! You fancy he stopped to see a girl he fancied, I fancy.
> ROTHBURT. Exactly![35]

The meeting of Europeans and Americans—despite national rivalries, an innocuous and safe form of cross-cultural encounter—provides novelty and plentiful fodder for jokes while sending the clear message that traveling abroad may be fun, but life home in the United States is best.

The comparison of European and American people and lifestyles serves another important function. In a land of foreigners, specifically the grounds of relatively depoliticized, Western European "old immigrant" feeder nations like England or France, the importance of differences between Americans of various class and ethnic backgrounds fades, allowing Cohan to subtly assert the true Americanism of select immigrant Americans—namely his own group, Irish Americans. While Cohan's vision parallels Roosevelt's on the whole, it diverges slightly but significantly in that Cohan endorses a dual or hyphenated category of identity that is distinctly Irish American but nonetheless fully American. The traits that distinguish his characters as Irish, like their love of politics and drinking, also veer toward stereotypes of the "stage Irishman."[36] Still, on the whole, Cohan takes pains to depict them as upstanding Americans. We can see more closely how this inter- and intra-cultural encounter contributes to Cohan's vision of true Americanism, and the music that accompanied it, by examining two of his early patriotic shows: *Little Johnny Jones*, his 1904 breakthrough musical, and *The American Idea*, an ethnicized version of his by-then familiar formula.

LITTLE JOHNNY JONES, AND FRIENDS

Little Johnny Jones established the blueprint of Cohan's flag-waving shows and explored national identity through encounters between characters of different races, ethnicities, genders, and classes. In brief, the show's plot revolves around the thwarted love of the jockey Johnny Jones and his beloved, the heiress Goldie Gates. Jones travels to London to ride in the English Derby, while Goldie's aunt Mrs. Kenworth, a wealthy widow and the leader of the San Francisco Female Reformers, goes abroad to arrange Goldie's marriage to a British earl. Goldie intervenes, however. She, too, goes to London, disguising herself first as a French mademoiselle and then posing as the earl himself. Meanwhile, the dastardly villain Anthony Anstey has become betrothed to Mrs. Kenworth in order to reap her riches and quash her reform efforts. When Jones is accused of throwing the English Derby, it looks like not only his honor but also his chances with Goldie are lost. But The Unknown, the mysterious eccentric who turns out to be an undercover investigator, exposes Anstey as a crooked Chinese lottery operative and the agent behind Jones's setup. Music, comedy, melodrama, and patriotism merged in Cohan's unusual yet popular musical comedy formula.

Little Johnny Jones informed audiences about who qualified as true-blue Americans in both overt and more insidious ways. The playbill used the national label liberally, describing Johnny Jones as "The American Jockey" and Anthony Anstey as "an American gambler." Cohan, who played Jones, was billed as "the Yankee Doodle Comedian."[37] While the White, male characters Jones and Anstey represent two clear poles of hero and villain within Americanism, other characters' national claim is less certain. Strong women with civic and professional ambitions are in some instances celebrated and in others censured. And Cohan expresses even greater ambivalence about immigrant Americans, flirting with nativism in the hit song "The Yankee Doodle Boy" and dismissing certain ethnic American groups, yet also subtly advocating for the show's Irish American character, the politician and horse owner Timothy D. McGee.

While *Little Johnny Jones* draws its boundaries around true Americans most clearly along national and ethnoracial lines, it also reflects the same discourses of gender and class that underpinned Roosevelt's philosophies. Just as Roosevelt presented a new kind of American man in print, Cohan did so onstage. It was no accident that *Little Johnny Jones*'s hit patriotic song was "The Yankee Doodle *Boy*." While Roosevelt's effete cosmopolitans were over-refined, Cohan's heroes were brash and, some critics complained, vulgar.[38] These enterprising young men exuded the courage and confidence that Roosevelt desired from his true Americans.

Yet the women of Cohan's shows and Roosevelt's speeches and policies were not without agency and important civic roles. Roosevelt's views of women were hardly progressive, but he placed a high value on women's positions as mothers and combatants of so-called race suicide, a term that

Roosevelt brought into public discourse two years after sociologist Edward A. Ross coined it in 1901. This threat, for Roosevelt, took multiple forms, but prominent among them was the declining birthrate among native-born White Americans. In fact, one of the few known direct connections made between Cohan and Roosevelt in the press centers on this issue. Upon Cohan's second marriage to Agnes Nolan of Brookline, Massachusetts, the *Washington Post* proclaimed, "It was immediately reported in theatrical circles that 'Georgie' Cohan was simply carrying out the Rooseveltian idea of anti-race suicide." Nolan was one of eighteen siblings, and her father's job as a letter carrier was preserved when he was recognized by the president for his big family.[39] Roosevelt also, increasingly and under certain conditions, accepted women as members of the public sphere and contributors to the politics of reform.[40]

Little Johnny Jones, too, suggests in numerous ways that women are active and valued members of Roosevelt's coalition of true Americans, though with circumscribed roles. The heiress Goldie Gates, the reporter Florabelle Fly, and Goldie's aunt Mrs. Andrew Kenworth form a trio of lead female characters, each strong and driven in her own way. Traveling incognito with panache, Gates not only successfully adopts a French accent, passing herself off as a Mlle. Fauchette, but also dons male garb and a British accent to pose as the Earl of Bloomsbury, to whom she is supposed to be betrothed, all in order to thwart the arranged marriage and pursue her true—and American—love, Johnny Jones. Fly, described by another character as one of those "female newspaper men" and with a name evoking the famous contemporary journalist Nellie Bly, works diligently to scoop this sensational story that will trump her competitors, raise her salary, and "make every newspaper in American sit up and notice things."[41] The script leaves hazy precisely what things these newspapers—and the audience—are supposed to notice, but whether it's crime and corruption or the decay of America's title-seeking elite, her mission and Gates's are treated as generally admirable.[42]

The third female lead, Mrs. Kenworth, labeled as "a fanatic on the subject of reform," represents and mocks the female reformer, a prevalent figure of the day. Her upper-class snobbery in seeking a titled suitor for Goldie is framed negatively, and her fight against gambling, in particular the Chinese lottery, is depicted as silly and naïve. Conflating the domestic and civic, she calls the young ladies of the San Francisco Female Reformers her children, and they call her "Mamma." She is easily taken advantage of by Anthony Anstey, and the other characters also dismiss her. When Fly remarks that "she's proved a great subject for the press," for example, the Captain retorts, "A better subject for an insane asylum, I should say." And when Mrs. Kenworth proclaims, "I adore brave women who stand by their rights," Fly mutters sarcastically,

"Here's one who stands by her rights alright, alright, alright."[43] Whitney Wilson, The Unknown who turns out to be a detective, delivers a somewhat equivocal pronouncement on the matter in the show's final act:

WILSON [to Mrs. Kenworth]. I want to give you a little bit of advice.
MRS. KENWORTH. Yes, yes, go on.
WILSON. Give up this band of reformers and let the Chinamen alone. Don't dictate to anyone whom they should marry. Stay at home, do your knitting and sewing and let the rest of the world take care of itself.
MRS. KENWORTH. Why sir, I—
WILSON. Now don't mind me that was on my chest and I had to get it off—that's all.

The speech typifies Cohan's ambivalence, shared with Roosevelt, about women's place in national public life: no sooner does Wilson deliver his condescending, patriarchal criticism of female reformers than he disavows it by saying not to "mind [him]" and that it was just something he had to get off his chest. Thus Cohan's portrayal of the three female characters walks a fine line, championing women with spunk and even validating their roles as active citizens in the public sphere, but simultaneously suggesting that their roles are subordinate and can be pushed too far.

This brings us to the hero, Johnny Jones. The character is loosely based on the real-life jockey Tod Sloan, who rose to fame from lowly origins, and he epitomizes Cohan's true American—young and energetic, honest and forthright, and a bit cocksure.[44] In his first song, "The Yankee Doodle Boy," the Anglo-American Jones introduces himself as patriotism personified. "I'm a Yankee Doodle Dandy," he sings, "A Yankee Doodle do or die" (Figure 1.4 and ▶ Example 1.1).

The song became a blueprint for Cohan's musical theater flag-waving numbers, employing the style of music I call his "patriotic mode." Cohan had written patriotic songs before this, but now, he escalated his use of quotation and, as composer, lyricist, playwright, and actor-singer, indelibly associated the sound and stylings of the patriotic mode with himself. "The Yankee Doodle Boy" abounds with nationalistic signifiers. In duple meter and marked "Tempo di Marcia," the song is a march, and a motive resembling a military bugle call introduces each verse. The accompaniment is motored by a basic oom-pah motive, and slight syncopation in the eighth-quarter-eighth cakewalk pattern, which conductor Rick Benjamin notes could rightfully be called the "Cohan motif," adds a ragtime edge to the melody.[45] The trademark of Cohan's patriotic mode, however, is the stream of musical and lyrical quotations from popular American tunes that form the fabric of the song.

Figure 1.4 Beginning of the refrain of "The Yankee Doodle Boy." Published by F. A. Mills (1904).

Musicologist J. Peter Burkholder uses the term "patchwork" to describe this procedure, common in Tin Pan Alley songs, in which "fragments of several tunes," usually from the same genre, "are joined into a single melody."[46] Cohan popularized patchwork, but it was also used by many of his contemporaries, including popular songwriters Charles Harris and Harry Von Tilzer and classical composer Charles Ives, who in turn quoted Cohan's music.[47]

For "The Yankee Doodle Boy," the eighteenth-century song "Yankee Doodle" is the primary source, and in fact, Cohan's song is a sort of extended play on the popular Anglo-American tune.[48] As musicologist Raymond Knapp has pointed out, "The Yankee Doodle Boy" captured the spirit as well as the music and lyrics of its source: since "Yankee Doodle" was sung by the Revolutionary Era British to taunt Americans but was then embraced by its targets, it carries an air of "nose-thumbing patriotism" and "inverted chauvinism."[49] But Cohan also draws upon other well-known tunes, specifically "Dixie," "The Girl I Left Behind," and "The Star-Spangled Banner." The melody of the song's verse is essentially a series of quotations strung together with newly composed filler material. The ABAC refrain is a new Cohan tune with only one quotation, a musical and lyrical twist on "Yankee Doodle" in the first line of the "C" section that recalls similar quotations from the verse and propels into the song's final tag line, "I am the Yankee Doodle Boy." The song's borrowing is shown in Table 1.1.

Table 1.1 Borrowing in "The Yankee Doodle Boy."

Section	Lyrics (Italics designate lyrical borrowings)	Musical Borrowing
Verse 1	I'm the kid that's all the candy,	"Yankee Doodle"
	I'm a *Yankee Doodle Dandy,*	
	I'm glad I am,	[Newly composed]
	[Chorus:] So's Uncle Sam	
	I'm a real live *Yankee Doodle*	"Yankee Doodle"
	Made my name and fame and boodle,	
	Just like Mister Doodle did,	
	by *riding on a pony.*	
	I love to listen to the *Dixey* strain,	"Dixie"
	"I long to see the girl I left behind me;"	"The Girl I Left Behind"
	And that ain't a josh,	[Newly composed]
	She's a Yankee, by gosh.	
	[Chorus:] Oh, say can you see	"The Star-Spangled Banner"
	Anything about a Yankee that's a phoney [sic]	[Newly composed]
Instrumental interlude		"Dixie"
Refrain:		
A	I'm a *Yankee Doodle Dandy,*	[Newly composed]
	A *Yankee Doodle*, do or die;	
B	A real live nephew of my Uncle Sam's,	
	Born on the Fourth of July.	
A	I've got a Yankee Doodle sweetheart,	
	She's my Yankee Doodle joy.	
C	*Yankee Doodle came to London,*	"Yankee Doodle"
	Just to ride the ponies;	
	I am the *Yankee Doodle* Boy.	[Newly composed]

Many critics cited dramatic speed as the governing principle of Cohan's shows, but his flag-waving songs are driven by a more general sort of excess—of verve, of patriotism, and of referents both musical and lyrical. Cohan repeated the formula with songs like "You're a Grand Old Flag" (from *George*

Washington, Jr.), the first song written for a Broadway musical to sell over a million copies; "Yankee Doodle's Come to Town" (from *The Yankee Prince*); and "Any Place the Old Flag Flies" (from *The Little Millionaire*). Many critics disparaged the songs. One particularly acerbic review described them as "several bars of well-known patriotic or sentimental songs strung together with connecting links of lively and more or less original musical trash."[50] But audiences seemed to enjoy them. And indeed, why would they not? They were instantly familiar, made up of songs they already knew and loved. Patchwork also created a sense of commentary, as J. Peter Burkholder notes, by juxtaposing quotations with the composer's idiom. The cakewalk rhythm of the lines "I'm glad I am, / So's Uncle Sam" in the verse of "The Yankee Doodle Boy," for example, gives the impression that "the speaker is speaking in his own voice" in those phrases.[51] Cohan's use of borrowing thus highlighted the colloquial, up-to-date aspects of his own musical style. The songs' jaunty, unmistakably American messages and sounds perfectly fit the upbeat confidence of the day and Roosevelt's insistence that "love of country is one of the elemental virtues."[52]

That Johnny Jones has this "love of country" spoke to his good character, by Rooseveltian values, but his worth is not taken for granted within the musical's plot. Because of his comparatively lowly station and brash demeanor, Jones has trouble proving to Mrs. Kenworth that he is worthy of her niece's hand. And in the second verse of "The Yankee Doodle Boy," Cohan resorts to nativist rhetoric, giving Jones's parents Anglo-American names and citing their old-stock lineage to justify his position as a true American. "Father's name was Hezekiah, / Mother's name was Ann Maria, / Yanks through and through," Jones sings, adding later that "My mother's mother was a Yankee true, / My father's father was a Yankee too; / And that's going some, / For the Yankees, by gum." Cohan also throws in a militaristic claim to Americanness, asserting that "Father was so Yankee-hearted, / When the Spanish war was started, / He slipped on his uniform / And hopped upon a pony." The lines recall not only the lyrics of "Yankee Doodle," but also the self-perpetuated legend of Roosevelt and the Rough Riders. As if his message of true Americanism was not blatant enough, the verse concludes, invoking music and lyrics from "The Star-Spangled Banner," "Oh, say can you see, / Anything about my pedigree that's phony?"

The verse seems out of place, and it departs from Roosevelt's more inclusive stance. Perhaps it reflected Cohan's own ambivalence about what constitutes Americanness or aimed to pander to the segment of his audiences that shared such views. But one wonders whether it also harbored subversive implications, with this young upstart Jones—played by Cohan, another young upstart, blurring the lines between creator and character—boasting an impeccable pedigree. For Cohan himself could hardly claim such a lineage. By this reading, Cohan, as a hyphenated American, places himself on equal footing with old-stock Anglo-Americans by donning that guise, and the song, with its final provocative question ("Oh, say can you see anything about my pedigree that's phony?"), dares audiences to say otherwise.

The show's broader plot and other characters support this possibility, for, like Roosevelt, Cohan does not exclude *all* who are not "old stock" from his true Americans. This is not to say that the America that *Little Johnny Jones* depicts is pluralistic, or even that it affirms the equities of civic nationalism. In addition to ethnic Americans of European heritage, the show's characters include British and Chinese foreigners, and they are treated with xenophobic and, in the case of the Chinese, racist mocking. *Little Johnny Jones* portrays the English as competitors, ridiculing their customs. It dehumanizes the Chinese, who are played in yellowface by White actors, as laughable, potentially evil, and immutably alien.[53] As for those of foreign descent at home, the Chinese Americans are essentially ghettoized within the Chinatown of the very short third act; and the recent southern European immigrants are offensively dismissed, in absentia, as "dagoes" and therefore non-American.[54] In its exclusion of the latter group, Cohan's society of true Americans is debatably even more restrictive than Roosevelt's.[55]

Little Johnny Jones's Irish American character Timothy McGee, in contrast, not only proves to be a true American but also pushes at the strictures of Roosevelt's definition. Indeed, McGee seems to demonstrate how difficult it is for the immigrant to fully Americanize. Tellingly, while Jones and even the villain Anstey are labeled as "Americans" in the playbill, McGee is described as a "New York politician and horse owner," and in reviews, he is also referred to as an "Irish politician" or "New York Irishman."[56] He is identified as Irish within the script as well. He uses expressions like "be gorra" and fits the stereotype of the Tammany Hall politician, a type of whom Roosevelt was not fond.[57] And when Anstey is angry with McGee for his warm conviviality with Mrs. Kenworth, he mutters, "Damn that Irishman." But through McGee, Cohan carves out a space for the hyphenated yet truly American identity Roosevelt found oxymoronic. Cohan brings McGee into the American fold by demonstrating the Irish American's loyalty and integrity, manifest in his friendship with Jones, and by having him share in the exclusion of other groups, as when he and another character laugh at the very idea of a Chinese journalist.[58] Most of all, Cohan Americanizes McGee through the character's eventual alliance with Mrs. Kenworth. In the show's last scene, Wilson (The Unknown), speaking to Mrs. Kenworth, gives the final verdict on both McGee and Jones:

WILSON. I am tickled to death to see you with this man McGee.
(*At mention of his name McGee turns and swells up.*)
He's a good man—I know him. He's a Brooklyn Elk. You don't want to overlook this jockey Jones. They may have fixed that horse in England but they couldn't fix the jockey. He's the candy all right. I don't blame your niece for getting sweet on him.[59]

Cohan thus strikes a blow to high society and its European ideals, insisting that, regardless of class or ethnic background, Jones and McGee are true Americans and worthy of their wealthy romantic partners.

Little Johnny Jones and its over-the-top patriotic pride succeeded in putting Cohan on the proverbial theatrical map. His next show, the play with music *Forty-Five Minutes from Broadway* (discussed in the next chapter), continued to champion regular folks. It presented quiet, small-town life rather than excursions abroad, however, and abstained from patriotic braggadocio and flag-waving musical numbers. Yet in the few years after *Little Johnny Jones*, Cohan returned frequently to the topic of international marriage and the theme of American patriotism.

AMERICAN IDEAS, AMERICAN OTHERS

With *The American Idea* of 1908, Cohan made a slight but significant dramaturgical shift, ethnicizing his flag play formula. He borrowed a trope from *The Mulligan Guard Ball* (1879) by the famed performing duo Harrigan and Hart of two fathers, Irish and German, each appalled to learn that his own daughter wants to marry his rival's son.[60] (Edward Harrigan and Tony Hart, along with composer David Braham, staged tremendously popular comedic and contemporary ethnic-themed musical plays in the late nineteenth century.) Cohan placed the plot abroad, however, where the two fathers simultaneously try to outdo one another in a race to wed his daughter to a French nobleman. Thus, Cohan extended his celebration of patriotism and attack on international marriages to the rising ethnic upper class. The closest Cohan had yet come to having an Irish protagonist, the show was simultaneously a harbinger of his Irish American shows of the late 1910s and 1920s (discussed further in Chapter 4) and a throwback to an older brand of ethnic humor. By applying his morality tale on the international marriage question to immigrant Americans, Cohan reinforced a melting-pot model of assimilation and extended his mockery of the Yankee elite to the "Brooklyn 400" who sought to emulate them.[61] In addition, the show presented a big ensemble number called "The American Ragtime" that reveals the ways in which another form of racialized difference, Blackness, though frequently suppressed, also crept into the margins of Cohan's expressions of Americanness.

While his prior flag plays had been set in London or in the States, Cohan opted in *The American Idea* for a new European setting: Paris. Spending the summer there after working all winter, the audience learns, is "the American idea," and Brooklyn businessmen Dan Sullivan and Herman Budmeyer, along with their children, are among the Yankees abroad.[62] Each of their daughters is in love with the other's son, but the couples know their fathers would never approve. A tellingly named Stephen Hustleford is also among the Americans in Paris, and playing upon Sullivan and Budmeyer's rivalry, he comes up with an elaborate scheme to swindle them. He tells each that the other's daughter is marrying a French nobleman, prompting the other to compete, then engages the "crazy Frenchman" Pierre de Souchet to pose as a count. When a wealthy widow nabs Count de Souchet, Hustleford convinces Sullivan and Budmeyer, separately, that each man hoodwink the other by passing his son off to the other one as "Count de Phoney" and "Count de Bunk" respectively. As in *Little Johnny Jones*, it proves remarkably easy as well as humorous to masquerade as European nobility. In the end, the children decide to turn the joke on their fathers, who, resigned to the fact that their children will wed with or without their blessing, leave together to go "get loaded."[63]

Cohan continues to broadcast patriotism in *The American Idea* through word, song, and humor at the expense of the French. Encountering another American, Sullivan comments that "It's good to hear an American voice—every time these Frenchmen start to talk, it sounds like a fight in a frog pond."[64] The scenery included a room decked out with American flags—"the best expression of an American idea," according to Cohan.[65] Just as Jones sends his regards to Broadway in *Little Johnny Jones*, the Americans in *The American Idea* sing of their "longing for Long Acre Square."[66]

In addition, in the vein of earlier Cohan numbers like "I Want to Hear a Yankee Doodle Tune" and "You Won't Do Any Business If You Haven't Got a Band," they celebrate "The American Ragtime" (▶ Example 1.2). This number continues Cohan's patriotic mode and championing of all things lower-brow American over higher-brow European, taking a stylistic turn with distinct racial and cultural connotations. True to form, the verse of "The American Ragtime" eschews what Cohan saw as the "complicated music" of well-known highbrow opera like *Lohengrin* and *Faust* as well as a recent operetta (*The Merry Widow*) and melodrama with music (*The Candy Kid*), calling instead for "a Yankee march by Mister Sousa, or Arthur Pryor." Cohan also updates his paean to American music to match the trends of the day, however, defining ragtime, not the march, as the music "that pleases Uncle Sam." The song's catchy refrain praises this syncopated style for being lively, loose, and punchy, with "a patriotic swing."[67] The number was a hit. "Everybody likes ragtime, and that is one of the reasons why 'The American Idea' is proving so pleasing," reported the *Boston Globe*. In the "rattling finale" of "The American Ragtime," it continued, "the whole company goes prancing about the stage with Cohan-esque dash that makes everybody sit up and whistle."[68] The cast even donned red, white, and blue as ragtime was equated with American patriotism.[69]

"The American Ragtime" is a rare moment, amid the typically all-White Anglo and Irish American societies that Cohan depicts, in which he invokes in a more explicit, less sublimated way the nation's primary racial Others, African Americans.[70] For what makes it notable among Cohan's output, as musicologist Larry Hamberlin argues, is its "elevation . . . of African American music as emblematic of all Americans."[71] This was a few years before "Alexander's Ragtime Band" (1911) made Irving Berlin "the Ragtime King" and ten years before Gershwin declared that "The Real American Folk Song Is a Rag" (1918). In addition to the bits of syncopation and dialect, the line "E for soffa dil, E for soffa dil, oh!" betrays the racial associations of "The American Ragtime." This intertextual reference, which reflected a contemporary practice of nonsense-syllable singing documented by theater scholar Michael Garber, echoed in particular the "coon song" "Ephasafa Dill" (1903) and was used previously by Cohan in "Cohan's Rag Babe."[72] Dance contributed to the effect, with various couples cakewalking across the stage.[73]

In musical ideology, too, Cohan and Roosevelt shared common ground, for Roosevelt had subscribed to the opinion, espoused and propagated by Dvořák in the late nineteenth century, that the musics of African and Native Americans were fertile sources for a distinctly American style of music. "I want all of you to realize the importance and dignity of your musical work, of the development of music and song among you students," Roosevelt told the African American student singers of the Manassas Industrial School in 1906. Drawing on essentialist views on race, he continued, "I feel that there is a very strong chance that gradually out of the capacity for melody that your race has we shall develop some school of American music. It is going to come through you originally."[74] Yet there was heated debate over ragtime. As Edward Berlin writes in a history of the genre, for those cultural leaders who envisioned the development of American musical life following in the path of European art music, ragtime seemed to represent the "very antithesis—the sensual depravity of African savagery, embodied in the despised American Negro."[75] Many questioned whether ragtime could constitute—as one critic put it—"the one true American music."[76] In this light, Cohan's decision to call it just that, in line with statements by Roosevelt opening the gateway for such a claim, is a notable one, in particular coming from the Yankee Doodle Dandy himself.

At the same time, Cohan's version of ragtime is notably distanced from its racial origins, "cleaned up" for Broadway audiences. As Hamberlin points out, this "lively march" praising syncopation in fact has little of it.[77] Straight rhythms predominate in the verse, and while bits of syncopation pervade the refrain, the song gets truly "raggy" in only a few bars (Figures 1.5 and 1.6). While Cohan is content to draw upon elements of African American culture such as the cakewalk and to let the influence of African American music be heard as American, the music is moderated, and actual African Americans remain almost entirely absent.

"The American Ragtime" was not the first time Cohan had musically addressed Blackness and Americanness; in fact, Cohan's very articulation of Americanness was built on racialized moorings within the coon song genre popular at the time, which traded on racist stereotypes. His patriotic mode likely had its first voicing in the 1898 song "Patriotic Coon." In it, the singer promises to "be there" in battle, "fightin' harder than a white man" so he will be "honored by the nation" and "make [his] reputation / As de Dare Devil

Figure 1.5 Beginning of the verse of "The American Rag Time." Published by Cohan and Harris (1908).

Figure 1.6 Most syncopated line ("I've heard the Merry Widow . . .") from "The American Rag Time."

Patriotic Coon."[78] As in his later patriotic songs, musical and lyrical quotations feature prominently. The song gestures toward African Americans' attempts to gain belonging through military service, in this case in the Spanish–American War. It also perpetuates the worst stereotypes of African Americans, for instance that the song's subject has an advantage because "shots can't bring [him] pain." Like many other popular songwriters and Broadway theater figures, Cohan's artistic and financial success was built largely on a foundation of commodification of Black stereotypes and sounds, from coon songs and minstrelsy to ragtime—the Black, as performance studies scholar Brynn Shiovitz has put it, behind the red, white, and blue.[79]

Yet only one African American character actually appears in any of Cohan's flag plays: the minstrel-like Eaton Ham who works at Mount Vernon in *George Washington, Jr.*[80] Ham is exaggeratedly patriotic, as seen in the following exchange, and Cohan makes a pointed statement about African Americans' standing as true Americans:

HAM. (*As the flag is hoisted*) Good morning, Mr. Stars and Stripes, good morning! I salute you! I salute you!

PETE. Kind o'patriotic today, ain't you?

HAM. Patriotic every day, ain't you?

PETE. Yes, I guess all Americans are.

HAM. Well, I'm American. I know I'm unbleached, but I'm American just the same.[81]

The final line—which referenced performer and songwriter Ernest Hogan, billed as "the unbleached American"—is also revealing for its progressive, if tastelessly worded, implications. Yet Ham never escapes the part of comedic stereotype. *George Washington, Jr.* thus suggests that African Americans are true Americans, but with a limited role.

The scant public record regarding Cohan's racial ideology and treatment of Black performers sheds some light on his stage representations of African Americans but is equally complex and contradictory. In 1908, only a few months before *The American Idea* with its "American Rag Time" number, an article in the African American newspaper *New York Age* describes Cohan as an ally to stars Bert Williams and George Walker. Cohan was among the White theater professionals who attended a performance of their hit show *Bandanna Land*, after which he invited Williams and Walker to perform in a charity event he and Sam Harris were managing. When the other White performers saw that the duo had received top billing, one held a meeting trying to convince them all to drop out. The billing was not changed, however, and only a handful did. The event went forward successfully, and Harris reportedly paid top dollar for a box in support.[82] On another occasion, according to an anecdote in a 1923 book about Bert Williams (for which Cohan wrote a tribute), when Williams agreed to perform in an event with the theatrical social organization the Friars Club, he arrived to see all of the performers pairing up in dressing rooms. He stood off to the side until Cohan saw him, "greeted him warmly," thanked him, and said, "Come on, Bert, you're dressing with me," taking him to share the star dressing room.[83] In stark contrast, a 1911 magazine profile of Cohan shared a story about how he purportedly wrote the part of Eaton Ham to get back at an African American (whom Cohan described using a derogatory term) who "brushed him aside" while trying to get a streetcar seat.[84] Cohan's racial politics offstage, it would seem, were as inconsistent and changeable as they were onstage. Or perhaps they were depressingly consistent, with him as a benevolent ally of African Americans, at least his talented theatrical colleagues, only so long as his position of power remained unchecked.

With *George Washington, Jr.* as the exception, Cohan seemed to prefer to write African Americans out of his shows altogether. The European settings of the other three flag plays made it all too easy to do so while also helping to establish all of the shows' characters as Americans, even those of immigrant descent. In *The American Idea*, those White ethnic Americans are the story's focus—but are they the show's model patriots? *Little Johnny Jones*, *George Washington, Jr.*, and *The Yankee Prince* left no doubt, even from their titles, as to the show's protagonist and truest American, and Cohan played each of them. The issue is murkier in *The American Idea*, however, and interestingly, it is the only flag play in which Cohan did not perform. At first glance, it might seem that Sullivan and Budmeyer, whose feuding tactics dominate the pages of *The American Idea*, are its main characters, but they act more as comic relief than as heroes. "Go on, you blithering brewer," Sullivan taunts Budmeyer (the name was possibly a play on Budweiser). "Go on, Irish potato vender," the other retorts, each drawing on well-worn ethnic stereotypes.[85] And much of the show's humor comes from the parallel scenes as they are duped by Hustleford, who independently proposes to Sullivan and Budmeyer a scheme for besting the other. When each man asks why Hustleford would help them, Hustleford appeals to their ethnic loyalties to insure their gullibility. "Because my father was an Irishman, and I love the green flag," he answers Sullivan. "Because my mother was a German and I love the language," he replies to Budmeyer. In fact, it is Hustleford who sings the solo verses of "The American Ragtime," suggesting that this swindler may be the truest American of *The American Idea*.

As in Harrigan and Hart's works and in Cohan's earlier musicals, the Irish—even when minor characters—got pride of place among the various immigrant groups depicted.[86] Sullivan is the first character introduced in the show, and—unlike Budmeyer—he gets his own song. "Sullivan" celebrates an Irish name and heritage and is unmistakably similar in sound, form, and sentiment to "Harrigan" in *Fifty Miles from Boston*, which had premiered earlier in the same year. Citing contemporary personages like the composer (Sir Arthur Sullivan), the Tammany Hall politician ("Big Tim" Sullivan), and the heavyweight boxer (John L. Sullivan), the song stakes its claim that "there never was a man named Sullivan / That wasn't a damn fine Irishman."[87] The song is musically marked as Irish only by the slightest gestures, like the triplet figure at the beginning of the verse and a drone-like bit, repeated in the relative minor, as Big Tim and John L. are invoked in the refrain (Figure 1.7 and ▶ Example 1.3).

But there is no reason for copious markers of Irishness, for the song's singer and subject is not Irish but Irish American. And in fact, Cohan's message here is not that the Irish American is a good American but rather that he is a good Irishman. Sullivan notes just before the song that he plans to visit Ireland before returning to the States. Following the number, Cohan returns to making the opposite case—that Sullivan is a good American. Sullivan and Hustleford order "American style" cocktails, and Sullivan instructs the server to "tell them to put a flag in it."[88] Through the song and character of Sullivan, Cohan thus insists on the possibility of a patriotic American who is also proudly Irish. The message echoed across the footlights in the form of a

Figure 1.7 Famous Irish Americans in "Sullivan." Published by Cohan and Harris (1908).

"Sullivan night" at the New York Theatre, which drew members of the "clan" from as far as Boston and Rochester. Of the Sullivans mentioned in the lyrics, "Big Tim" was among those present, and John L. telegraphed his regrets.[89]

Ethnic pride and their fathers' displeasure notwithstanding, the audience of *The American Idea* is meant to root for the Sullivan and Budmeyer children's cross-ethnic romances. Cohan thus suggests that too strict an identification with one's ethnic heritage would impede assimilation, in this case by marriage. Through their unions, the Budmeyer and Sullivan children enact the melting pot ideal dramatized by Israel Zangwill in *The Melting Pot*, a play that opened in Washington, DC, only a month after *The American Idea*, with a captivated Roosevelt in the audience.[90] According to this model of acculturation, the so-called mortar of assimilation, crucible, or melting pot of the United States would forge a new people out of its diverse constituent—or, as sociologist William Newman once pithily explained it, "A + B + C = D."[91] That "D," according to proponents of the melting pot, was superior to its parts. As Gary Gerstle writes, Roosevelt described this very process as foundational to the nation's genesis in his history *The Winning of the West*:

> A single generation, passed under the hard conditions of life in the wilderness, was enough to weld together into one people the representatives of these numerous and widely different races [the backwoodsmen settlers]; and the children of the next generation became indistinguishable from one another. Long before the first Continental Congress assembled, the

> backwoodsmen, whatever their blood, had become Americans, one in speech, thought, and character. . . . They lost all remembrance of Europe and all sympathy with things European. . . . Their iron surroundings made a mould [*sic*] which turned out all alike in the same shape.[92]

In a speech Roosevelt gave at a Friendly Sons of St. Patrick's dinner, he praised his Irish American audience by placing Irish immigrants in this tradition, noting how "this masterful race of rugged character" had "planted themselves as the advance guard of the conquering civilization on the borders of Indian-haunted wilderness."[93]

In both Zangwill's play and Cohan's, however, the melting pot was not the frontier but rather marriage outside their culture. And, notably, marriage not to Anglo-Americans but to members of another immigrant culture—in the case of *The American Idea*, the two older immigrant groups of Irish and Germans rather than the newer southern or eastern European groups. While a German–Irish union may seem benign today, it was not so simple at the turn of the twentieth century, especially since it may well have also indicated a union of Protestant and Catholic religious traditions. The Sullivan and Budmeyer children of *The American Idea*, however, are fully Americanized, and they speak the language not of cultural heritage but of love. Charlie Sullivan is madly in love with Katie Budmeyer and Henry Budmeyer with Nellie Sullivan. Their storyline and their songs—"That's Some Love" and "Order Wedding Bells for Two"—prioritize romance over heritage. This was "melting-pot love," as described by literary scholar Werner Sollors, and it fit discourses of nationhood that emphasized *consent* over *descent*. By dramatizing romantic relationships "across boundaries . . . and often in defiance of parental desires and old descent antagonisms," immigrant authors also modeled consent-based national allegiance and citizenship, demonstrating their belonging as Americans. As Sollors and Aviva Taubenfeld show, Zangwill's play influentially enacted this premise, showing through the marriage of David and Vera that passion and procreation between different "races" would "forge the nation."[94]

This emphasis on romantic union as assimilation, of consent over descent, was particularly well suited to the burgeoning form of musical comedy, which typically revolved around a love story and often multiple romantic pairings. But with *The American Idea*, Cohan actually joins discourses of consent and descent through the dual family pairings. In the number "Brothers and Sisters," the girls sing, "I think my brother's awfully nice, / But your's [*sic*] is simply fine." The boys respond, "If you'll give me your sister / I'll be glad to give you mine." Later in the show, with hands joined, the four say together, "We're brothers and sisters and sweethearts and friends, and we're going to be husbands and wives."[95] When Sullivan and Budmeyer disinherit their daughters in the final scene, giving their sons the full inheritance, the children are able to respond, "Oh, what do we care!" Though Irish and German are joined, the unions are reciprocal and, in a sense, stay all in the now-extended family, while the intermixing of groups simultaneously guarantees the proper process of immigrant assimilation and the success of the American "race." *The American Idea* thus suggests several "American ideas"—of making enough money to summer abroad and of marrying or hustling for money, both under critique; of a nation whose essence, musical and otherwise, is inseparable from its racial constitution; of a patriotism compatible with pride in Irish heritage, challenging Roosevelt's notion of the good American immigrant; and, ultimately endorsing Roosevelt's vision, of a melting-pot pattern of assimilation.

MARKETING AND RECEPTION OF THE FLAG-WAVING SHOWS

The very mixed reception of Cohan's flag plays, a reception he found ways to shape and contribute to, contested but ultimately confirmed his legitimacy as an American playwright and composer. The programs, advertisements, and sheet music for Cohan's patriotic musicals abounded with national buzzwords and other signifiers, setting the tone for the reception of the shows and their author. In *Little Johnny Jones*, Cohan was billed front and center as "the Yankee Doodle Comedian," a tactical change from his first two Broadway efforts, *The Governor's Son* and *Running for Office*, in which the Four Cohans, "America's Favorite Family of Fun-Makers," received joint billing.[96] *George Washington, Jr.*, advertised as either the "great National Song Show" or "His Latest American Musical Play," was the patriotic extreme, with the flag design of its sheet music (Figure 1.8). But eagles and shields with the stars and stripes adorned a souvenir program of *The Yankee Prince*, which was said to open its first rehearsal with the singing of "My Country, 'Tis of Thee." And, building on its title, Cohan sponsored a contest for the best twenty-five-words-or-less statements of "what the American idea is" in conjunction with *The American Idea*.[97]

Cohan's flag-waving antics initially garnered critical responses divided between censure and (frequently qualified) admiration. *Life*'s theatrical critic James Metcalfe was Cohan's most vocal and acrimonious detractor. The magazine's theater guide listed *Little Johnny Jones* as "the apotheosis of stage vulgarity." This "vulgarity"—the rude, "smarty" behavior of

Figure 1.8 Cover of "You're a Grand Old Flag." Published by F. A. Mills (1906). UT Sheet Music Collection, University of Tennessee Libraries, Knoxville, Special Collections. (A color version of this figure is included in the color insert.)

Cohan's heroes—was Metcalfe's chief complaint, for it set a bad example for America's youth. Second in line, and related, he targeted Cohan's patriotic gimmicks and "commercializing of the flag." Metcalfe found his lyrics, for example, "mawkish appeals to the cheapest kind of patriotism."[98] His music, such critics complained, was equally "atrocious," as well as, they implied, unoriginal in its borrowing, for it was "patched up by Mr. Cohan from various patriotic, sentimental, and idiotic familiar tunes." "It began to be humorously remarked," a feature on Cohan later noted, "that the whole Cohan family was eating off the American flag."[99] For certain critics, Cohan's shows kindled hostility, related to class and cultural register. Cohan was, to Metcalfe and others in his camp, the "creator of the Star Spangled drama, the inculcator of the chewing gum standard of taste," with "a mind saturated with Tenderloin standards and Tenderloin ideals." His shows and their popularity illustrated their fears, prevalent at the turn of the century, about the masses' detrimental influence on the theater. "Persons who prate of the value of the stage as an educational institution," Metcalfe warned, "rarely stop to consider that the stage has possibilities of educating down as well as up."[100] In his intertwined racial, class, educational, and cultural status, Cohan presented a problem for such critics as Metcalfe, all the more so because he had the audacity to depict himself as the embodiment of Americanism (as Chapter 5 discusses in more depth).

Cohan fought back. He and Roosevelt—each subject to much criticism—shared a blanket disdain for cynics or critics, broadly construed, and for their intellectual tendencies. "It is not the critic who counts; not the man who points out how the strong man stumbles, or where the doer of deeds could have done them better," Roosevelt proclaimed in an oft-quoted portion of a 1910 speech. "The credit belongs to the man who is actually in the arena."[101] Cohan seemed to see himself as that man, with Broadway as his arena. Publishing his own bulletin on theatrical events called the *Spot Light*, he gained an outlet for taking on his detractors directly. He notoriously never forgave his hometown of Providence, Rhode Island, after its reviewer panned *Little Johnny Jones*, and he retaliated with a versified ABCs of theater cities. "A stands for Albany, good for one night. / B stands for Boston, for two weeks all right," it began. Each letter got a city and a line, then Cohan concluded:

> In the twenty-six letters the
> Alphabet's got,
> Not one stands for Providence,
> None in the lot;
> I wouldn't insult the
> Proud letter "P."
> I can't stand for "Prov.,"
> And it can't stand for me.[102]

In the following passage, republished by *Life* in a counterresponse from Metcalfe, Cohan borrows the gendered language typical of Roosevelt to respond to his most vocal critics:

The edict was passed; some dissented,
But the Davis–Dale–Metcalfe "combine
Of sissies" effete—circumvented
Demurrers; and whipped them in line.
Note—the stench of theatre destroyers
Is fed to the public as news
By these "lemons," who clinker the foyers,
To cook up their mess, for reviews.[103]

Labeling those critics who upheld more "refined" standards of taste as effete and sissies, Cohan tapped into the discourse, articulated by Roosevelt in "True Americanism," that warned those "citizens who pride themselves on their standing in the world of arts and letters" of the dangers of trying to emulate Europe. He thereby linked unmanliness, un-Americanism, the critic's "intellectual aloofness," and an emerging sense of—according to its deterrents, European-influenced—highbrow culture.[104]

To his detractors' chagrin, audiences—and indeed, many critics—did not punish Cohan for these deficiencies; rather, his flag-waving shows garnered favorable reviews, the all-American reputation he cultivated, and (some complained) a devoted fan base of "Cohanians." Critics less concerned with edification enjoyed the plots, music, costumes, and scenery. As early as 1906, he had been designated an "American dramatist," and by the 1910s, as Cohan turned to new themes and many critics found new depth in his work, there was lessening concern over the authenticity of his flag-waving tactics; commentators found that he could be "exploiter of the flag and our pioneer patriot" alike. Critic George Jean Nathan ridiculed, in his list of fads, "the idea that George M. Cohan was merely a song and dance fellow whose chief metier [*sic*] was waving the American flag."[105]

* * *

An emblem of a Rooseveltian America, Cohan personifies the idea of true Americanism in the characters he played and the music he wrote, capturing the period's anxieties about race and nation and also its hopes. Journalist S. J. Woolf wrote in 1933, "While he bucked and winged and waved the American flag he added the red and blue to the newly born Great White Way."[106] To do so, he adroitly navigated not only the art and business of Broadway but also his own racial and class status. By declaring theater entertainment and himself to be examples of Americanism par excellence, Cohan flaunted critics like Metcalfe. And by playing the old-stock American heroes he created, as well as through secondary characters like McGee and songs like "Sullivan,"

Cohan began to push against the Rooseveltian stance on Americanization, suggesting that Americanness and Irishness, the Fourth of July and St. Patrick's Day, were not incompatible. He thus opened a space, albeit one limited to his own immigrant group, for the patriotic hyphenated identity Roosevelt disparaged. In the end, it was Cohan's early, flag-waving, low-brow shows that brought him his most lasting fame. Yet as Cohan increasingly varied his output, interspersing other types of fare and moving away from flag-waving, other features too, critics agreed, set Cohan shows apart. Cohan had a distinctive, inimitable style, as a playwright, a songwriter, a performer—above all, an entertainer.

THE ENTERTAINER

• • •

DEFINING THE COHANESQUE

> He's not the best actor or author or composer or dancer or playwright, but he can dance better than any other author, write better than any other actor, compose better than any other manager and manage better than any other playwright.
>
> —William Collier about George M. Cohan

> I don't know whether you mean popular songs or not. But then of course so far as I'm concerned there are only two kinds of songs, popular or unpopular.
>
> —Cohan in a letter to critic Alexander Woollcott, apparently in response to a question about his favorite American song

While many critics initially saw Cohan as a one-trick "Yankee Doodle" pony, with the American flag as his sole (and cheap) trick, his fare was not limited to patriotic songs and shows.[1] Whether he was waving the flag or not, Cohan also came to be known for his inimitable musical and dramatic style, as a playwright, a songwriter, and a performer. Critics struggled to describe what it was about Cohan that set him apart, so they resorted to simply adjectivizing his name. His songs, scripts, directorial style, acting, singing, and dancing were "Cohanesque" or "Cohanian." His shows were full of "unbridled 'Cohanics.'" His characters spoke "Cohanese" and were always "georgecohaning" around the stage.[2] His shows were "Cohanistic" and his particular form of entertainment was "Cohanism," a term also applied to zingers from his shows.[3] By 1906, as Cohan sought to build on his success

Yankee Doodle Dandy. Elizabeth T. Craft, Oxford University Press. © Oxford University Press 2024.
DOI: 10.1093/oso/9780197550403.003.0003

with *Little Johnny Jones* (1904) in two new shows, *George Washington, Jr.* and *Forty-Five Minutes from Broadway*, these terms were cropping up regularly—undoubtedly welcomed and amplified by Cohan and his press agents.[4]

One reviewer of *George Washington, Jr.* imagined Cohan's unapologetic response to those who might criticize the show's minimal plot, "pert rather than witty" dialogue, or "simply Cohanesque" and bandlike music, with its "shrilling piccolos," "strident cornet," and so on: "Well, if you don't think much of it, why don't you come up here and try to do it yourself!" Defending Cohan against his imagined or real detractors, the critic, clearly a longtime Cohan admirer, asserts that no one can write "the Cohan dialogue" or his type of "noisy, patriotic song," or, "best of all . . . imitate that 'bend in the back walk,' that innocently upturned eye, those agile legs which in the merry dance take him all over the stage and yet keep time to the music." "He is himself," the reviewer declared, "and he has no double."[5] Not only was Cohan unique, this critic suggests, but he also made it look simple—and yet who could do as much as he did and so well?

This chapter explores Cohan's ideology of entertainment and the trademark characteristics that made him stand out in his day—as a playwright, as a songwriter, and as a performer dramatizing the songs and shows he had written. These include, as a playwright, the use of the vernacular and "real life" characters, increased emphasis on plot and steps toward musico-dramatic integration, the blending of theatrical genres, brisk pacing, and the use of intertextuality and self-referential or "metatheatrical" devices. His songwriting was marked by an aesthetic of simplicity, band and ragtime influence, and patchwork-style musical borrowing. And as a performer, he came to be known for energy balanced with reserve, command of delivery, speechlike singing, and idiosyncratic dancing. To illustrate Cohan's style and craftsmanship, this chapter examines a number of songs and dramatic works, focusing on his shows with music and exploring *Forty-Five Minutes from Broadway* (1906) and *Hello, Broadway!* (1914) in some depth; it was his musical comedies, broadly defined, that made Cohan's career, and he remained a "musical comedy man" at heart until the end.[6] Cohan's techniques as a songwriter, a musical dramatist, and a performer, joined with his American themes and style and widely broadcast doctrine of entertainment, not only marked his distinctive aesthetic but also helped shape the burgeoning genre of musical theater.

THE THEATRICAL CRAFTSMAN, OR, THE PROFESSIONAL LOWBROW

When Cohan made the leap from vaudeville to the "legitimate" stage, he entered an American theater that was heterogeneous and, in many ways, insecure about what national drama should look like and whether it could—and should—hold its own against Europe. Broadway theatergoers at the turn of the century could go see a comedic or dramatic play; an operetta, with cosmopolitan flair; an extravaganza, with dazzling spectacle; a musical comedy; and more. These categories themselves were varied and somewhat fluid. For musical comedies, a coherent plot was a possibility but not a prerequisite.

Cohan offered a style of theater that was undeniably American and notably well-crafted but, to the dismay of many critics, distinctly unelevated. His shows were unfailingly "clean," free of foul language or sexual suggestiveness, but their heroes—and writer—were seen as uncultured and unsophisticated. On a list of various "brow" categories ("high brow," "low high brow," "high low brow," and "low brow") circulated in various newspapers in 1911, George M. Cohan was on the "low brow" list, along with beer, toothpicks, and "Mellerdrammer" (this colloquialism evoking melodrama's reputation, in the early twentieth century, as a popular-price genre providing cheap thrills).[7]

Cohan emphatically claimed the turf assigned to him, carefully casting his contributions in opposition to capital-a Art. He was a "song and dance man" who sought only to entertain his audiences, as he repeated ad nauseam in interviews, programs, and speeches, some of which accompanied his early shows. "I don't pretend to be much of a comedian or playwright, and if I amuse you it is all I aspire to do," he told an audience for *George Washington, Jr.*[8] Such remarks helped to preempt criticism about his musicals' cultural value and define the merits on which his shows should be evaluated. (He may have been taking a page from the book, or more appropriately playbill, of his predecessor Charles Hoyt, who included a note on the program of *A Trip to Chinatown* saying, "The author begs to say that whatever this play may be, it is all that is claimed for it."[9]) Reviewers recognized Cohan's disclaimers as a "shrewd strategy," and more than one refused his implicit request. Cohan "disarmed all suspicion in his brief curtain speech by saying that he did not want anyone to take him seriously, either as actor, author or composer," a Providence, Rhode Island, reviewer (who particularly galled Cohan) wrote about a production of *Little Johnny Jones*. "He delivered his speech, however, from the corner of his mouth, which did not impart a tone of sincerity to his remarks."[10]

Contrary to many critics' hopes, Cohan failed to fade away like some unfortunate fad. Moreover, he found success as a playwright and actor not only with musical fare but with straight plays as well. By 1914 he was befuddling critics, not simply pleasing or vexing them. Peter Clark Macfarlane asked in *Everybody's Magazine*, "Is George Michael Cohan a joke or a genius? Or a high-brow in disguise?"[11] Even as he gained popularity and standing, however, Cohan continued to preach the doctrine of entertainment. "The musical comedy is intended to entertain, not educate," he insisted. He professed to an interviewer in 1919 a desire to write "a great American play," but when pressed to explain what kind, he answered, the kind "that the public will like." He also continued to place himself in opposition to the so-called highbrows, or at least, to tease them. Writing a newspaper article in 1924, Cohan described a scenario in which he, as "G. M. Hoakum," meets a certain "H. L. Highbrow" (a probable reference to literary critic H. L. Mencken). He finds himself pleasantly surprised by the encounter and concludes that "highbrowism and Hoakum are more or less synonymous," but cannot resist joking at the end that his highbrow readers will not understand since "as a general rule, [his] stuff is a little over their heads."[12]

Part of his lowbrow status was his lack of formal education, which Cohan claimed and highlighted. Reciting again and again his autobiographical story of growing up on the road as part of a theatrical family and acknowledging without regret the simplicity of his methods and aims, Cohan cast himself as a particular kind of dramatist: a self-made American song-and-dance man. In 1907 he claimed to have only read three books, all by Mark Twain, which he figured were likely "worth two hundred that I might have read haphazard." A 1914 article commented, "An audience was the first book George Cohan ever learned to read." Cohan described his musical chops similarly. "I could play four chords on the piano in F sharp," he claimed in his 1924 autobiography. "I'd vamp these four chords and hum tunes to myself for hours and hours at a time. I've never got any further than the four F sharp chords, by the way. I've used them ever since."[13] (Favoring F-sharp, a key signature made up primarily of the black notes on the piano, was common for self-taught pianists of the time; it was also said to have been the only key Irving Berlin could play in. Both songwriters used transposing pianos that allowed them to play a tune in one key and hear it in another.) These statements advanced the persona he projected of a self-made man interested in entertainment, not art.

While Cohan may have lacked education, he had no shortage of training. The product of a nineteenth-century society in which children commonly worked in the theater as in other realms, he had learned his trade through his work with the Four Cohans, and he was proud to know it inside and out.[14] He scoffed as much at dilettantism and amateurism as he did at elitism and advocated the apprenticeship model of his upbringing, continued until the theater's "technic, from the curtain line to the gridiron, is as familiar as ABC," as the best way to achieve success.[15] By the time he was a teenager, the world of variety theater was thoroughly familiar to him, and he cut his teeth as a playwright by writing skits for other popular vaudeville performers, while simultaneously developing his talents as a popular songwriter. "I didn't have time to make a serious study of playwrighting," he said in one interview, "because I always was too busy writing plays."[16] As his career progressed, Cohan gained a reputation for hard work and professionalism; as actress Peggy Wood put it, "He never stopped thinking of the theatre . . . that was one of the great reasons for his success."[17]

Indeed, if the goal of theatrical work was entertainment, the means were theatrical knowledge and labor. The process of creating theater, for Cohan, was "toil"—"real, downright, sleep destroying, nerve wracking labor"—with one main objective: profit.[18] He was drawn to playwrighting, as he told the press, by watching his father's "laborious efforts" to keep the family "supplied with new chatter for the stage." He hastened to add, "And I didn't know a thing about art then and don't claim to now."[19] This pragmatic and heavily gendered conception of his creative work also motivated the business side of his career, which would take off in the 1910s. Yet even as his managerial role increased, Cohan always remained a professional playwright, one whose skill, experience, and role as a producer eventually led him into work as a "play doctor," revising or "Cohanizing" the scripts of others as well as writing his own. He had a strong understanding of just what made theater work, acquired over years of experience.

Principles of the Cohanesque Musical Comedy

Cohan defined musical comedy, a nascent and flexible form in the early twentieth century, as "a combination of farce, comic opera, and vaudeville," and he outlined his school of thought about what makes a good one in a 1909 *Saturday Evening Post* article on the subject.[20] The plot, he wrote, "may be of the flimsiest sort, a kind of flexible backbone to which may be attached anything entertaining which relates to it." The themes should be "based on some eternal human quality," like avarice and vanity, and should lend themselves "to good-humored satire or burlesque," like the "international marriage habit" plots discussed in Chapter 1. The script should move quickly, with no long dialogues or quiet conversation, because "the audience must either laugh or applaud constantly." Musical numbers help ensure that they will: the first must be novel and gripping, "unique if possible," and the musical finale must be "the best thing in the act." Their lyrics should be "intelligent, never draggy, and always a part of the story." Either a song, dance, or some other feature must stand out and "compel comment." The setting "must have plenty of room and color," with large scenery and costumes that differ from other shows, yet none of it need be expensive. (*Forty-Five Minutes from Broadway*, he noted, cost only $4,400 to produce, while other managers were spending $40,000 to $50,000.) Finally, the shows should be "clean and wholesome," appealing to the women and children upon whom ticket sales depended.

Although guided by a clear set of principles, Cohan's works of musical comedy are not easily categorized and do not follow a set template. They were billed using several genre labels, sometimes even for the same show, including "Musical Farce," "Musical Frivolity," "National Song Show," and, frequently, "Musical Play."[21] Cohan used a range of structures: his earlier musical shows tended to have three acts and his musical shows of the 1920s had two, but *The Talk of New York* (1907), in addition to several of his plays, used four. Quantity of musical numbers, too, varied, and increased over the course of Cohan's career; his earlier musical comedies averaged around twelve, while his shows of the 1920s boasted about two dozen musical numbers apiece.[22] Musical selections were also frequently offered between acts. Interestingly, Cohan's "musical farce" *The Little Millionaire* (1911) and two of his plays with music—*Forty-Five Minutes from Broadway* and *Fifty Miles from Boston* (1908)—had no musical numbers in the second act. While the specific distribution of his musical numbers varied, they were often used at key structural points, for instance to open acts or as a finale at the end of a show, and they included solos, duets, and ensemble numbers, with plentiful dancing. Cohan also had a penchant for band and military drill scenes. Music served multiple functions within Cohan shows; scores included diverting novelty numbers with little connection to the show's content, but also songs that served to establish a mood or setting, advance the plot, and delineate or develop character.[23]

In fact, a significant overarching component was a strengthened relationship between music and dance and plot and character, or what musical theater scholars have come to call *integration*. Many critics perceived Cohan's shows to be doing something differently from others, using language of "unity" to describe a close relationship between music and story. One Chicago critic found *Little Johnny Jones* to be superior to most musical comedies because "it has more of a story than have they. . . . The musical numbers, too, grow out of the situations, and the whole piece thus takes on a consistency and unity which are wanting in the average musical comedy."[24] Cohan also sometimes described his work in terms of narrative cohesiveness and development. He noted, for instance, that as a dancer, he had "always made a point to have [his] dances tell a complete story—get somewhere."[25] Cohan's partner Sam Harris complimented the way Cohan wrote full parts for each character, avoiding "star vehicles" built around and catering to a single performer. Cohan was a "generous" playwright, Harris said, who "gives everybody a chance, instead of annexing all the fat for his own portion."[26]

Such comments buck the once-standard line in musical theater historiography that integration began with the watershed moment of Rodgers and Hammerstein's *Oklahoma!* (1943), bolstering scholarship that has identified other predecessors and eroded the perceived boundary between integrated and non-integrated musicals.[27] And just as musicologist James McLeary reveals about *Oklahoma!*, the integration in Cohan's musicals was a strategic way of publicizing the show as well as a formal development.[28] Many newspapers reprinted Cohan's own assertion that *Little Johnny Jones* "proved that a story can be consistently told with music, as well as without."[29] Later rhetoric surrounding integrated musicals would stress artistic aspiration, but for the anti-elite Cohan, coherence in musical comedy was simply the "common sense" approach, and good salesmanship besides.[30]

What did this proclaimed and perceived unity look and sound like for Cohan's early twentieth-century US theater audiences? Audiences of *Little Johnny Jones* would have seen novelty numbers like "'Op in Me 'Ansom," in which hansom cab drivers and sightseers sing about touring London, but also songs that, following a key principle of aesthetic integration, "express the characters who sing them."[31] Timothy McGee's number "They're All My Friends," for instance, characterizes McGee as a Tammany Hall type. While it doesn't sugarcoat machine politics, its major key, jaunty syncopation, and long notes emphasizing the lyrics "all my friends" also convey McGee's amiability; and the lyrics even include his name. Though it has had a robust life outside the show, "The Yankee Doodle Boy," too, serves an integral purpose within the show, characterizing the title character of *Little Johnny Jones* through music and lyrics as young and energetic, a bit cocksure, and the epitome of patriotism. While they may be enjoyed in other contexts, these songs were clearly written for these particular characters. Later on,

Cohan musicalized entire scenes, using a Gilbert and Sullivan-esque recitative. In his memoir, arranger and orchestrator Mayhew "Mike" Lake cites an example from *Little Nellie Kelly* (1922) in which a lengthy scene of dialogue was set to music, thereby emphasizing the scene's occurrences, improving its continuity, and reducing its playing time.[32]

Cohan's use of music to streamline a show illustrates yet another Cohanesque principle: the pacing must not drag. "An author should create five times as much material as he expects to use," Cohan wrote in his "Musical Comedy" essay. "One should have material enough for two plays when his curtain goes up, and then he may cut and cut during three or four performances until he gets the piece about right."[33] Scriptwriting, for Cohan, was the art of distilling the dialogue to its minimum in order to keep it moving. As a director, he was able to guarantee that this aesthetic goal would be enacted.[34] In his 1924 autobiography, he recalled his pre-curtain speech to the cast of his first Broadway show *The Governor's Son* in 1901: "Ladies and gentlemen, . . . don't wait for laughs. Side-step encores. Crash right through this show tonight. Speed! Speed! and lots of it; that's my idea of the thing. Perpetual motion. Laugh your heads off; have a good time; keep happy. Remember now, happy, happy, happy. Do you all understand? . . . And don't forget the secret to it all, . . . Speed! a whole lot of speed!"[35] (See Figure 2.1 for a photograph of Cohan directing.) We can hear in his memory of his direction and the repetition throughout his speech the nervousness of the young director, actor, and playwright trying to make it big, but also the importance of this key dictate. As new technologies like automobiles accelerated the pace of movement and transformed American culture, Cohan seemed to have his finger on the pulse of the nation.[36] In the next sections, I further unpack how Cohan's principles and rhetoric of musical theater were put into practice, first turning to a more in-depth example, *Forty-Five Minutes from Broadway*, and then analyzing another strand of the Cohanesque that runs throughout his work: metatheatricality.

"The Best Thing I've Done": Forty-Five Minutes from Broadway

One of the shows that exemplifies Cohan's dramatic impulses is *Forty-Five Minutes from Broadway*, which premiered on Broadway on January 1, 1906, after opening in Ohio and playing in Chicago. While *Little Johnny Jones* became his best-known show, *Forty-Five Minutes from Broadway*, which was his next show, is probably a close second. As Cohan tells it in his 1924 autobiography, it was his response to a challenge. Seeing promise in *Little Johnny Jones*, theatrical magnate A. L. Erlanger asked Cohan, "Think you could

Figure 2.1 Cohan directing a rehearsal of Popularity *(1906). Theater Biography Collection, Harry Ransom Center, The University of Texas at Austin.*

write a play without a flag?" "I could write a play without anything but a pencil," Cohan flippantly countered.[37] The show enjoyed a historic cast: it was written for the established star Fay Templeton, and it helped launch the Broadway careers of vaudeville favorite Victor Moore, who would play the character Kid Burns again in Cohan's sequel *The Talk of New York*, and of Donald Brian, whom Cohan had also cast in *Little Johnny Jones* and who shot to greater fame the following year in *The Merry Widow*. *Forty-Five Minutes* departed from Cohan's previous fare not only in eschewing flag-waving but also in being more a play with music than a typical musical comedy, with only a scant handful of songs. However, it continued and solidified many Cohanesque traits. Several years later, with over a dozen Broadway shows to his name, Cohan called it the best thing he had done (although ever the self-publicist, he may have also been trying to subtly promote its revival) and the most profitable.[38]

When the show opens, we learn that a certain Mr. Castleton has died, and his nephew Tom Bennett has arrived in New Rochelle, New York, from New York City to receive his inheritance. Bennett (played by Donald Brian in the original cast) brings along his citified, quirky friend and secretary Kid Burns (Victor Moore's character), an "ex-race horse tout and personified fable-in-slang," as one critic described him.[39] Bennett's betrothed and her snobby mother Mrs. Dean follow shortly thereafter. There had been rumors that there was a will, and that Castleton's housemaid Mary Jane Jenkins (Fay Templeton's character) was to be the inheritor, but none has been found, making Bennett the beneficiary. Villain Daniel Krohman means to get his hands on the inheritance one way or another, and he uses Mrs. Dean to get to the household safe. In the meantime, Burns finds the will in an old coat pocket, forcing him into the difficult decision of whether to share the document that will disinherit his best friend. At the end of the show, he reveals both the will and his love for Mary, saying that he could not expect her to marry him with this newfound wealth, and Mary, choosing a life with him over millions, tears up the will.

As silly as the story may seem to present-day readers (who, among other things, likely see no problem with Mary getting both the money and the man), as with *Little Johnny Jones*, its compelling plot and "real life" American protagonists stood out in its day. Here as in other shows, Cohan champions those outside of the social elite, showing that character is not concomitant with status. Kid Burns and Mary are lower- or middle-class characters who speak not in elevated language but in everyday English (in Mary Jane Jenkin's case) and a distinct urban slang (in Kid Burns's). A butler who speaks with an English accent describes Burns as the "strangest man I ever met" with "a language all his own." "A foreigner?" another character asks. "No, but he might as well be," the butler replies. "I can't understand a blessed word he says." When Burns arrives, we see what the butler meant: "Come here, Cutey," Burns tells him. "Slip around to the stable and tell that geek that minds the fillies to hitch up that sea going affair and meet that one o'clock rattler when she blows into this man's burg. Understand?"[40] Cohan's choice and pace of language—favoring rapid-fire dialogue over long speeches—fit Kid Burns and other similar Cohanesque protagonists, who were often energetic, jocular, young, urban, male, and either lower-class or challenging the attitudes of their upper-class parents, while adhering to his principle of speed.

The show highlights tensions between the residents of the growing metropolis of New York and its small-town neighbor north of the Bronx on the Long Island Sound, "only forty-five minutes from Broadway" as one of the show's songs tunefully proclaimed. Burns comments on New Rochelle's "jay atmosphere" and "rubes," referring to the town's lack of sophistication and country bumpkins.[41] Yet as Cohan explains in his "Musical Comedy" essay, while he aimed for satire or burlesque, it must be good-humored, without acrimony, "since it is the purpose of this kind of play to make friends, not enemies, and to cause even those it satirizes to laugh."[42] One reason residents of New Rochelle could likely laugh at Cohan's depictions of them was that their home was in fact a rapidly growing small city, not a rural outpost. Cohan also kept the ribbing light-hearted. The conniving Mrs. Dean praises whichever location is more convenient for her, so both locations receive their due as well as their digs. "Oh, what a splendid atmospheric change from the broiling sun of Broadway to the glorious salt air of New Rochelle," she says in one early scene, before later complaining of the "great sacrifice" she's made in leaving the stage and "the joys of Broadway, with its glorious cafes and social gatherings."[43]

Like many of Cohan's shows, *Forty-Five Minutes from Broadway* blended elements from several theatrical genres, with entertainment as the paramount goal. His early shows drew heavily on melodrama. The plot of *Little Johnny Jones*, as one of Cohan's harshest critics noted, included a kidnapping, a Chinese gambling den, and "other strenuous things which are usually associated with lurid melodramas."[44] *Forty-Five Minutes* hinged on a lost will and attempted theft from a household safe. As the less-than-impressed *New York Times* reviewer noted, its heroine did a lot of skulking about, eavesdropping.[45] A melodrama-influenced scene in *Forty-Five Minutes* is offered as an example of "Things that Act upon the Tear-Ducts" in the article "The Mechanics of Emotion," by Cohan and critic George Jean Nathan, in which they list various devices for effectively eliciting certain audience responses. In it, "the heroine drops a rose from her corsage after a disagreement with the hero" and "the hero subsequently picks up the rose, presses it to his lips, and stands with the flower in hand, looking in the direction whither the heroine has made her exit."[46] (An image of another melodrama-influenced scene is shown in Figure 2.2.) Yet *Forty-Five Minutes* also abounded

SCENE IN FAY TEMPLETON'S NEW PIECE, "FORTY-FIVE MINUTES FROM BROADWAY"

Figure 2.2 Scene in Forty-Five Minutes from Broadway *(1906) in January 1906 issue of* Theatre *magazine.*

with vaudeville-like humor—Victor Moore's background in vaudeville was put to good use—and musical comedy–style choruses.

Erlanger was supposedly worried by the small female chorus and lack of money spent on the women's costumes, but Cohan boasted about his departures from theatrical norms. "Some one has got to break away," he told an Indianapolis journalist. "They may say I'm crazy for framing up a show of the kind, but I know I'm not. People buy tickets, sit and laugh, . . . and that's the answer." The article reported that Cohan "knows people have begun to grow tired of straight comic operas, where pink and blue tights twinkle over shapely contours."[47] Opinions of Cohan's success in this realm varied. The *New York Times* critic deemed it "a case of oil and water," with disparate elements unable to mix. Although the Indianapolis critic likewise found it "strange to see such a queer form of entertainment"—describing it "like the opera glasses have something on the lenses"—he pronounced it "a good anomaly" and Cohan the "Davy Crockett of the theatrical forest."

Although *Forty-Five Minutes from Broadway* had only five musical numbers and a couple of instances of diegetic singing, far fewer than any of Cohan's other early shows, music was integral to the show and its storytelling.[48] Like *Little Johnny Jones*, the show linked song and story in ways that suggested principles of aesthetic unity and drew comments from critics, and again, Cohan helped guide the discourse about his work. He claimed in an interview that having comparatively few songs was intentional, a way to ensure "they can consistently be made a part of the story."[49]

The show's two songs by or about its heroine exemplify Cohan's attempts to have music arise naturally from and fit within the story. The first, "Mary's a Grand Old Name" in Act I, comes out of dialogue in which Mary and Kid Burns meet and connect over the fact that Mary was also the name of Burns's mother. One of Cohan's most popular songs, it is also one of his most integrated. In it, Mary tells of her mother, good and true, who gave her daughter the same name. Both lyrically and musically, it tells the audience about Mary and her values, extolling the value of the plain and ordinary. The name itself is a marker of old-fashioned virtue—society may prefer Marie, but while one who calls herself Marie may be "fair to see," the lyrics state, she cannot be trusted. The music reinforces the message (see Figure 2.3, ▶ Example 2.1). The verse of the song has a conversational feel, imparted by its slight syncopation, narrow range, and stepwise motion at the beginning of each line. The melody of the chorus's opening motive, "But it was Mary," simply articulates the home-key triad, and chromaticism is minimal throughout. In both verse and chorus, the word "Mary" almost always falls on the beat, on two half notes, and homophonic textures predominate. In short, the music "sounds

Figure 2.3 Beginning of the chorus of "Mary's a Grand Old Name." Published by F. A. Mills (1905).

so square," just as the name is said to. The song is a good example of Cohan's aesthetic of simplicity, but simple does not mean unartful. Where chromaticism is used in the melody, it supports the mistrustfulness of "Marie" and colors the "something there" before being "corrected" on the descending line "sounds so fair." Likewise, there are skillful touches in the lyrics, like the internal rhyme in the line "But with propriety, society will say Marie," demonstrating through a touch of witty wordplay the pretentiousness that stands in contrast to the lyrics that describe Mary.

The tune of "Mary's a Grand Old Name" is heard again at the end of the scene in which it is first heard as Burns finds and reads the will in his coat pocket. Looking after her, he comments, "She wants to do the right thing by everybody—so do I," and taking the will out of his pocket, vows, "And I'm going to do it, too." The music's return represents the lingering presence Mary has in Burns's mind and the inspiration she provides.[50]

While the regular gal Mary has a counterpart in regular-guy protagonists like Burns and others, her traditional qualities and unpretentiousness are highly gendered, marked as feminine virtue. Valorizing Mary and affixing her as Burns's romantic ideal, "Mary's a Grand Old Name" seems to follow in the tradition of many songs of the past inspired by an idealized woman and her name—from "Jeanie with the Light Brown Hair" (1854) to the then-recent "You're the Flower of My Heart, Sweet Adeline" (1904). The song and show suggest that Mary is the antithesis of the "New Woman" Maries of the early twentieth century and much more demure than the "female newspaperman" Florabelle and strong-willed Goldie of Cohan's last and simultaneously running show, *Little Johnny Jones*.[51] While she is a working woman, a domestic worker, Mary is hardly a rebel against social conventions. After all, in the end of the show, she sacrifices a fortune for a traditional marriage. At the same time, in contrast to many other songs idolizing a woman, "Mary's a Grand Old Name" is sung by the female protagonist herself, about her mother and the name she bestowed upon her daughter. In the original production, moreover, it was sung by the formidable Fay Templeton. This Mary, as embodied by Templeton, may have been plain and ordinary, but the actress playing her was no shrinking violet.[52] The agency of the performer thus complicates the message of the song's lyrics.

The other "Mary" song from *Forty-Five Minutes*, "So Long Mary" in Act III, provided yet another example of the way Cohan's "story guides into his songs" in his shows, as one critic noted. In this scene, Mary is set to depart, and the crowd bids her goodbye. "*Mary* is going away from New Rochelle. The setting is the railway station. A song is needed," the critic wrote. "Does [Cohan] put in 'My Little Dream Girl,' or 'The Maid with the Starlit Eyes,' or some such fool ballad with plenty of electricity? No; *Mary* is going away. Her friends come to the station to say good-by. 'So Long Mary' belonged right in that spot and no other, and 'So Long Mary' made a hit."[53]

As with *Oklahoma!* four decades later, this kind of discourse may reflect the ideals of the writers as much as the formal elements of the show. On one hand, for instance, the gently lilting figures of the melody and unpretentious lyrics of "So Long Mary" were well-matched to the character, and the names and places of the lyrics are specific to the show. It does seem to be a song written for this show and not simply put into it after the fact. On the other hand, the song does little to advance the plot, and while it shows Mary to be well-liked in New Rochelle, it provides no deep insight into her character or her feelings about the situations she has encountered. Although written for the show, one can easily imagine playing the song in other settings, and indeed, it was a hit. That song along with "Mary Is a Grand Old Name," one newspaper reported, were "played in all the hotel restaurants and whistled on the streets."[54] Versatility and popularity outside the theater's walls were equally important functions of early twentieth-century theater music.

Yet another key function in the total package of Cohanesque theater, one discussed in Cohan's "Musical Comedy" essay, was to offer spacious, colorful scenery and interesting stagecraft, and setting Act III (including "So Long, Mary") in the New Rochelle train station provided ample opportunity. The act featured several train-related effects: the train is seen departing as the curtain goes up, it arrives back on stage later in the scene, and we hear bells and whistles. A popular feature in shows of that theatrical season, the stage effect of a train in motion was, as one commentator wryly put it, "a more reliable manufacturer of fictitious enthusiasm than any device that it is possible to put on the stage."[55] The train is one of many contemporary technologies pictured in *Forty-Five Minutes*—the plot also hinges on a fraudulent telephone call and Mary's turning on the household phonograph to sound the alert of an intruder—and it is also reminiscent of the steamship and rocket used to great effect in *Little Johnny Jones*. From the transformation scene of *The Black Crook* (1866), and from operatic works like those at the Paris Opéra before that, through the crashing chandelier of *The Phantom of the Opera* (1986) and beyond, these kinds of spectacular effects have been a regular facet of musical theater, despite, like Cohan's flag-waving, frequently eliciting scoffs from the theatrical highbrow.

Forty-Five Minutes from Broadway also contained multiple jokes referencing the theater and its conventions, hinting at a practice that was to become a Cohan trademark. When someone asks Kid Burns, "Are you speaking to me, sir?" he responds, "What did you think I was doing—a monologue?"[56] Sometimes these jokes were enriched by knowing something about the performers delivering them, as in later in the act, when someone comments that it's too bad that Mr. Bennett is going to marry an actress. "Why? Because she's an actress?" Mary responds. "There are lots of good actresses. There are more bad plays than there are bad actresses, I think."[57] This joke likely carried more weight for contemporaneous audiences than it does on the page because of the circumstances of its delivery at the time, given that the show had been written to feature Templeton, who was a big catch for the young playwright. There may have been some tension between the playwright and famous comedienne, who, as one reviewer noted, was "not as prominent as might be expected."[58] Cohan later told a humorous anecdote about Templeton requesting another number in the show. He put her off, saying that he would write one later and "to sit easy in her saddle" in the meantime. Six months later and still without her new number, she telegraphed him,

"I'm saddle sore."[59] Whether or not any such gossip reached the audience, they would have been well aware of who Cohan and Templeton were, and one can imagine her pointed delivery of the wisecrack. As Cohan continued to develop as a playwright, these wink-and-nod theatrical in-jokes increased, and in the 1910s, he found they were perfectly suited to a new (for him) genre: the musical revue.

Metatheatricality and Hello, Broadway!

A hundred years after Cohan's first Broadway shows, in the early twenty-first century, a crop of musicals took what seemed like a fresh approach after the earnestness and narrative absorption of mid-century Rodgers and Hammerstein and the passionate, epic theatricality of late twentieth-century megamusicals, with characters explicitly acknowledging being in a show and even mocking generic conventions.[60] In the Tony Award-winning 2001 musical *Urinetown*, the show's narrator figure Officer Lockstock breaks the fourth wall to welcome the audience to *Urinetown*—"Not the place, of course. The musical." Then he lets the audience in on what they can expect, referencing its structural and literary workings. Urinetown the place, he shares, is a "place you won't see until Act Two. And then . . . ? Well, let's just say it's filled with symbolism and things like that."[61] Scholars and commentators found it Brechtian.[62] An early twentieth-century theatergoer, however, might have called it Cohanesque.

Like *Urinetown*, Cohan's shows reference, poke fun at, and celebrate theatrical conventions. His shows draw attention to their own devices, as when Cohan opens Act II of *The American Idea* (1908) with the chorus singing about being the merry musical comedy chorus, commenting that "this is supposed to be a Hotel in Paris, / But it is scenery owned by Cohan & Harris," and tease the audience, as when the Prince in *The Royal Vagabond* (a "Cohanized Opera Comique," 1919) threatens to disappear before his coronation, and his tutor retorts, "And disappoint the poor boobs that paid railroad fares to come and see the entertainment?"[63] Increasingly throughout his career, this metatheatricality became associated with his style, seen as one of those things that made a show Cohanesque. "He lays bare the hokum of plot with the frankness of a [Ferenc] Molnár," one critic wrote, referencing the contemporaneous Hungarian author whose plays appeared regularly on Broadway.[64] Sometimes, as biographer John McCabe notes, Cohan's metatheatrical moments also served to "disarm criticism" of cliché or old-fashioned theatrical devices.[65] Cohan could have his cake and eat it too, so to speak, engaging in well-worn tropes, well aware of their ability to manipulate audiences' emotions, with a conspiratorial wink, implicitly telling his audience, "I don't think you would *really* fall for that."[66] Cohan's metatheatricality was not confined to his stage works. Many of his writings, including newspaper columns and his 1924 memoir, were also introduced in a self-referential way, with him talking about how he came to be writing the project in the first place.

As many scholars of musical theater have discussed, musicals are highly intertextual and reflexive.[67] They frequently adapt—and are thereby understood in reference to—other sources, and they are rife with songs about entertainment, shows within shows, and in-jokes. Cohan's shows were no exception. His play *Get-Rich-Quick Wallingford* (1910) adapted a popular series of stories by George Randolph Chester, which first appeared in the *Saturday Evening Post* in 1907. He also continued or re-created his own works: in addition to the aforementioned *Forty-Five Minutes from Broadway* sequel *The Talk of New York*, *The Honeymooners* (1907) reworked his 1903 show *Running for Office*, and the failed play *Popularity* (1906) was reworked into the musical comedy *The Man Who Owns Broadway* (1909). His shows were highly topical, referencing current cultural and political events. A quip in *The Royal Vagabond* (1919)—to "go a little slow with that 'flu' stuff; it'll be an epidemic in a minute"—even referenced the ongoing influenza pandemic.[68]

As musical theater scholar Adam Rush notes, we can see the concept of metatheatricality as yet another subtype of intertextuality.[69] Used in musical theater literature to describe both a genre and technique across many times, places, and types of theater, for whole "metamusicals" like *A Chorus Line* and wink-and-nod moments like those in *Urinetown*, the term risks being too big of an umbrella.[70] Nonetheless, the latter usage, which Rush describes as the practice of citing and parodying musical theater's generic conventions and cultural reputation without using specific examples, seems most apt for capturing Cohan's idiosyncratic way of referencing the theater within his shows.[71]

In the mid- to late-1910s, Cohan found the highly intertextual, topical revue to be a good fit for his increasingly metatheatrical approach. Likely motivated by Florenz Ziegfeld's success with the *Ziegfeld Follies* and the Shubert brothers' with *The Passing Shows*, Cohan jumped on the bandwagon with three revues of his own: *Hello, Broadway!* of 1914 and the *Cohan Revues* of 1916 and 1918.[72] While musical comedies were driven by plot, revues by various producers tended to be given coherence by style, tone, and pacing: Ziegfeld's productions, for example, exuded elegance.[73] Cohan's revues, especially his first, were—what else?—"characteristically and consistently Cohanesque."[74] They stood out for their metatheatricality; for being, even more than other revues, chock-full of insider references to other shows; and for featuring the talents of one or more charismatic figures. In the case of *Hello, Broadway!*, Cohan came out of one of his many retirements to play the co-lead alongside his friend and fellow actor and director William Collier.[75]

"This Entertainment is a Musical Crazy Quilt Patched and Threaded Together with Words and Music by Mr. Cohan," announced the program of *Hello, Broadway!*, setting expectations for what was a new genre for Cohan while also, as always, emphasizing entertainment.[76] The show celebrates and spoofs theatrical conventions and breaks the fourth wall throughout. The opening number introduces the "musical comedy cops" who are "just an excuse for their singing a song" and "save many a show today," as the chorus explains.[77] (Cohan used singing policemen and metacommentary about them in other shows as well, including *The Rise of Rosie O'Reilly* in 1923.) Elsewhere in *Hello, Broadway!*, one character calls for lights; another tells someone who feels that they can't say something to "sing it" instead; and yet another takes his part out of his pocket and starts reading aloud, including the stage direction, "Exit Ambrose in a business-like manner."

Throughout *Hello, Broadway!*, the characters chase about a hat box said to contain the plot. In one bit about the box, the character George Babbit "The Millionaire Kid," son of the "Soap King" Bolivar Babbit, explains that its contents are a "big surprise for the final curtain." George Babbit was played by George Cohan.

> [BOLIVAR] BABBIT. Well, I hope you've at least told the audience what's in it.
> GEORGE [BABBIT]. Told the audience what's in the hat box! Well, I should say not!
> BABBIT. Oh, my boy, you must tell the audience. You may have a perfect right to hoodwink the people in the play, but you must always take the audience into your confidence. It's against all dramatic laws to do otherwise.

Another character backs the older Babbit up, saying that he "heard a college professor say the same thing." George insists they're wrong, though, saying that the audience "love[s] to be fooled." The debate continues: Bolivar Babbit invokes the dramatic critics, saying that they would agree his argument is a sound one, then George asks the audience directly, "You do love to be fooled, don't you?" George wins out, and the surprise is saved until the final scene, when the hat box is revealed to be empty. "What became of the plot?" one character asks. "There never was a plot," George responds.[78] Cohan's humor here lies in the gibes at the perceived high-art dramatic establishment of the professoriate and critics, as he invites the audience to take his side.

In addition to referencing and poking fun at general theatrical tropes, *Hello, Broadway!* also spoofed or "burlesqued" specific, real-life Broadway figures and shows through character names, scenarios, and dialogue. Reviewers compared it to the earlier shows of the Weber and Fields Music Hall, which parodied current Broadway hits (in 1898, for instance, *Cyrano de Bergerac* became *Cyranose de Bric-a-Brac*), but different "in that it is not a succession of travesties, but a confusion of them."[79] This exchange featured titles of shows, and a film, playing on Broadway in 1914. (Titles are set in boldface.)

ELSIE. Believe me, boys, I've seen **Life**; I've had **Experience**.
GEORGE. We know the rest of the story.
BILL. Yes, you were put **On Trial** for stealing **My Lady's Dress**.
GEORGE. And they claimed you were **Under Cover** with **a Pair of Silk Stockings**.
BILL. And they threatened to send you to **Cabiria** if you didn't **Kick In**.
GEORGE. But you used **Diplomacy** and were pronounced **Innocent**. We know all about it.
ELSIE. And that all happened this season.[80]

Cohan had so many shows running in quick succession or even simultaneously that yet another play from earlier in that season that was referenced in *Hello, Broadway!* was one of Cohan's own, *The Miracle Man*. At the close of the show, George—the character and "the author"—is handcuffed; "you're a thief" who has "stolen every play in town," his fictional father exclaims.

For readers today, the references and therefore also the humor are opaque. For in-the-know contemporary theater fans, though, *Hello, Broadway!*'s burlesques and topical, intertextual, inside-baseball–style humor, geared toward New York theater's biggest fans, must have been hilarious, offering an experience similar to that of the off-Broadway *Forbidden Broadway* revues spoofing Broadway shows that began in the 1980s. Several critics commented on the show's rather narrow target audience or "interpretive community," as scholar Stanley Fish has theorized it.[81] These were "shoes for the cobbler's children," as one critic described the theater's trend toward intertextuality and metatheatricality, sparked by Cohan and including *Hello, Broadway!*, in shows in the 1914–1915 season: "fun apparently made for the fun-makers; confidentially and almost criminally intimate sprees" for members of fraternal social clubs with ties to the theater community.[82] Critics surmised that *Hello, Broadway!* was likely "to prove rather mystifying to the average person in New York, and certainly to the out-of-town visitor who is not an Elk, a Lamb, a Player or a Friar" and wondered if future audiences would understand even two-thirds of the show. Yet these revues did have some success on the road, and more than one out-of-town critic argued that *Hello, Broadway!* held up just as well for audiences unfamiliar with many of the shows being burlesqued.[83]

Hello, Broadway! contains meta-songs, like the tribute to Cohan's fellow songwriter and mentee "Those Irving Berlin Melodies," and even a meta-production number, "Down by the Erie Canal," in which the song's staging and theatrical context are commented upon. The ragtime-tinged verse of the latter introduces the refrain as the kind of number every Broadway show must have: a "tin pan song," "usually sung by the female star," that "the orchestra murders . . . o'er and o'er," that "the management features . . . near and far," and that is encored repeatedly, by guarantee of the ushers and, if need be, the "trick" of having hired applauders in the gallery.[84] As critic Channing Pollack noted in *Green Book Magazine*, it satirized sentimental popular ballads and the ways in which theatrical performance helps them become bestsellers as sheet music and recordings. Providing a detailed description of the staging, Pollack explained how after Louise Dresser sings the refrain, "a boy in the gallery sings it—then a man in an upper box, then the musicians in the orchestra pit, and then bells distributed through the auditorium play it." When the chorus comes on stage, "blue cloth streamers transform the stage into a raging deep, upon which float gondolas full of singing girls and across which rushes a canvas railway train." Next comes Cohan, who Pollack describes as "Hazel-Dawn-like," referencing an actress of the day who played violin onstage. After Cohan "saws the melody from a violin," Pollack writes, "the chorus returns to repeat the number, with various conventional maneuvers and an accompaniment of banging tambourines."[85] Gondolas, a railway train, banging tambourines: dance director Ned Wayburn (credited in the program with the staging of the number), Cohan, and their collaborators clearly pulled out all the stops. Simultaneously mocking and celebrating, Cohan's self-referential numbers about entertainment carried an "implied flip, sarcastic message," as musicologist Michael Garber writes, "You and I are . . . part of a clever, up-to-date cognoscenti."[86]

The shows Cohan parodied were rife with ethnic and racial stereotypes, just as many of Cohan's "flag plays" and other shows were. *Hello, Broadway!* follows the pattern of Cohan shows before and after it, in which the Irish are treated more favorably, if with hints of cliché, while characters of other races and ethnicities are portrayed more offensively. Self-reflexively introducing the song "Broadway Tipperary," the singer explains that he had just heard someone singing the very popular "It's a Long, Long Way to Tipperary," reminding him that "a musical show is not a musical show nowadays without a Tipperary song." Cohan's song reminds the audience that "there's quite a bit of Tipperary . . . right here on old Broadway."[87] In contrast, African Americans are depicted through the theatrically popular, culturally degrading lens of blackface minstrelsy: Cohan and co-star Collier "black up" and perform the number "Two Dandy Darkies," recycling well-worn tropes from the urban Zip Coon caricature and evoking nostalgia for the song and dance of the vaudeville venue of "Tony Pastor's back in '82."[88]

In other places in the show, Cohan's deployment of ethnic and racial stereotypes takes a more self-reflexive turn, reifying common stereotypes while also highlighting their absurdity. One of the 1914 shows burlesqued in *Hello, Broadway!* is *Mr. Wu*, a lurid melodrama imported from London with an abhorrent depiction of the eponymous Chinese character, played in yellowface by actor Walker Whiteside, who swears vengeance on the family of the man who has courted and betrayed his daughter.[89] The script of *Hello, Broadway!* is equally derogatory in its language and portrayal of Wu, hearkening back to the Chinese villains of *Little Johnny Jones*, and the song "Look Out for Mr. Wu" is an exaggerated portrayal of all the worst stereotypes of the inhumanly evil Chinese villain. At the same time, by its over-the-top depiction and laughable situations, *Hello, Broadway!* renders the play *Mr. Wu* ridiculous. The Mr. Wu of Cohan's revue finds out about his daughter's beau from the cake of soap she's been given from his family's business, and Wu comments that the man's friend is "probably in some manager's office now trying to dispose of the melodrama I sold him" (the one supposedly in the hat box).[90] In another scene, a comic bit with the character Bum Lung (played by actor Martin Brown, for whom this was not the first yellowface role), and Bill (played by Cohan's co-star William Collier) draws attention to the constructed nature of ethnic stage stereotypes:

BUM LUNG. Yes, me. Huh! Heap Big Me!
BILL. Heap Big Me! That's Indian talk, you damn fool! You're playing a Chinaman.[91]

While not reproving these racist caricatures, Cohan's metatheatrical treatment highlights the shallow and interchangeable nature of ethnic stereotypes as performed by White actors who would play multiple of these "types" without really understanding, or even remembering, the difference.

"THE TUNES ARE PRETTY GOOD, TOO": COHAN THE SONGWRITER

If any number can capture George M. Cohan's musical philosophy, it is "I Want to Hear a Yankee Doodle Tune" (1903) (▶ Example 2.2).[92] The song is a precursor to the many patriotic showtunes to come. It is also an oddity in Cohan's output: written before he had established himself as a permanent fixture on Broadway, it is one of his few songs not created for one of his own shows, yet also one of only a handful that he recorded. And it is a manifesto. "I've always hated this overrated, pretentious music, complicated, / And compositions that have conditions, and intermissions that please musicians," the verse begins. The singer asks for "a tune that's worth a whistling," with a "dash of rag and go"—a "Sousa strain" rather than a "Wagner pain." "What I'm stating, is advocating," the verse concludes, "the popular melody school." A quotation from John Philip Sousa's *Washington Post March* propels listeners into the chorus with its titular sentiment: "I want to hear a Yankee Doodle tune." Cohan juxtaposes the "Yankee Doodle tune" with European, operatic, highbrow music, singing, "Now you can have your William Tell, and Faust and Lohengrin as well." The anti-elite sentiment, replete with its nod to commercialism (the song "may be trashy . . . but gets the cashy") and impudent humor ("Wagner" is pronounced using the American, rather than German, pronunciation) have Cohan written all over them, as does the music, which delivers the Sousa-esque march that the lyrics describe with a pattering and speak-song–friendly melody.

Before Cohan was known on Broadway, he was making his way as a songwriter. His songs—whether from shows or independent entities—were sold and heard as sheet music for home consumption, phonograph records, and, later, on the radio throughout his lifetime. During the time between Cohan's first published song in 1894 to his last, and his death, in 1942, popular music styles in the United States changed drastically, and Cohan was part of the transformation. As discussed in Chapter 1, he contributed his own subtype, patriotic songs like "The Yankee Doodle Boy" and "You're a Grand Old Flag," and helped bring the rhythms and spirit of ragtime, watered down as it may have been, into the musical language of mainstream American musical comedy. Yet Cohan also wrote in other styles and types of the day—ballads, "juvenile songs" about children, "philosophical songs," and Irish-themed songs.[93]

Even those who liked his shows were not always so fond of Cohan's songs. A critic of *Little Johnny Jones* disparaged the "dozen and a half 'musical numbers' whose distinguishing feature is ginger. In fact there is more ginger than music." Critic Walter Pritchard Eaton acknowledged Cohan's versatility, "mighty mind," and promise (if less than fulfilled) as a playwright but wrote scathingly of his work as a composer. "As a musician, of course, Mr. Cohan has always been a joke. . . . He tosses 'Yankee Doodle,' 'Dixie,' a Sousa march, a few yards of ragtime, a stock waltz or two into a pot, sets it on the stove and waits till it comes to a boil. Then he skims off the waste matter which rises—and, lo! that scum is a Cohan overture, or march, or waltz, or 'patriotic song,' or anything you choose, according to the tempo employed by the conductor." A critic who positively reviewed *Hello, Broadway!* exasperatedly wished, "If only he would not write his own music. . . . His invention and fertility both forsake him when he tries to write tunes." Cohan has "small skill with melody or rhythm," the reviewer went on, "he repeats himself endlessly," and he "remains an artless and elementary practitioner" of ragtime.[94] Over a century later, Cohan's reputation for unoriginality as a songwriter persists. In the 2021 film *Being the Ricardos*, a character compares Desi Arnaz's patriotism to "George M. Cohan, who loved America so much he wrote the same song five times."[95] Michael Lasser calls them "a showman's songs with little depth or reflection" in his 2019 book *City Songs and American Life*. "They thumped along in a toe-tapping way and expressed their clear, simple emotions in familiar, effortless chatter."[96]

By the end of his lifetime, however, Cohan had also received validation for his songwriting, even from some members of high-art elite. In a Lotos Club dinner honoring Cohan in 1930, *New York Times* music critic Olin Downes credited Cohan with having the "spirit of art," which he deemed more important than artistic technique, and proclaimed that "Mr. Cohan is writing real American music, genuine, full of power. . . . So many of his good songs are replete with touches of genius, that I look at them and realize what a simple thing genius is."[97] In a 1943 issue of the League of Composers' periodical *Modern Music*, which went to print just a few months after Cohan's death, American modernist composer Elliott Carter, reviewing the film *Yankee Doodle Dandy*, tipped his hat to Cohan the songwriter as well: "James Cagney, who vivaciously takes off Cohan, stiff legs and all, in the musical film *Yankee Doodle Dandy*, puts across many of those brash, gay little numbers and keeps them from being too embedded in Hollywood plush. The tunes are pretty good, too."[98] It is for those tunes, like "You're a Grand Old Flag" and "The Yankee Doodle Boy," that Cohan remains best known today.

Patchwork-style borrowing, march influence, an elementary use of ragtime, and perhaps above all, simplicity: the same traits have made Cohan's songs seem unoriginal and vapid to some and fresh, enjoyable, or classic to others. The oft-remarked-upon Cohanesque simplicity of Cohan's songs is a double-edged sword. Elliott Carter's compliment, backhanded as it was, is remarkable not only because the realm of modernist classical music inhabited by composers like him stood so far apart from the popular music world, but also because it put such a high value on complexity. Songs written to be sold to amateurs for performance in the home, on the other hand, needed to be accessible. Cohan's certainly were. One of Cohan's orchestrators, Don Walker, admitted that while the lyrics and melodies were "untouchable," he found himself bored by Cohan's harmonic structure—which may, in some cases, have been supplied by a collaborator but which had to be okayed by him—"for he had only the one, that one being the simplest harmony possible, the most unrefined, the supremely obvious."[99] In part, this reflects the fact that Walker worked with Cohan in the 1930s, when musical tastes had changed, yet his songs stood out for their simplicity and related traits even in their heyday.

A cynic might suggest that the simplicity of Cohan's songs is explained by his minimal training as a musician and composer. All he recounts in his autobiography is two weeks of lessons with a "fiddler friend" of his father's who issued the verdict, "Impossible to teach this boy any more. HE KNOWS IT ALL."[100] Other newspaper accounts name a particular teacher from George's childhood, a Mr. Von Olker who was musical director of the Providence Opera House, though Cohan recalled sending notes to his teacher that he was sick in order to use the money for "soda water and a show."[101] In yet another case, as recounted by John McCabe, Cohan recalled that "every time Dad hired someone to lead the small orchestra which always toured with us, he would give the leader an extra five dollars to teach me the violin." He noted that these instructors, who he said were primarily clarinetists, not violinists, "weren't terribly good."[102] We should take these Cohanesque anecdotes with a grain of salt, however. Given his reported performances on violin as well as his abilities at the piano—even if a transposing one—he likely had more training than he let on.[103] Perhaps his interactions with Von Olker and with the musicians the Cohans regularly interacted with on the road sparked his interest and laid a foundation for his work in the musical side of theater.

Like many composers of popular song and musical theater who had little musical training, limited time, or both, Cohan had musical collaborators.[104] At least when he was starting out, Cohan later claimed, he did not know how to "put down the music." "Once I had a good melody in my mind," he explained, "I would hold onto it until I had hummed it over for the publishers, or had got some orchestra leader to put it down for me."[105] A 1909 cartoon and 1919 account describe him humming his melodies to a musical

Figure 2.4 Cohan "humming the melody of a new song" to Gebest in "Creative Genius at Work" cartoon in August 1909 issue of Munsey's *magazine.*

secretary, as the position was called, for the tunes to be notated (Figure 2.4).[106] For the majority of Cohan's career, Charles J. Gebest was his musical right-hand man, working with him for decades, beginning with his first Broadway show *The Governor's Son* in 1901.[107] In 1922, Cohan brought Mike Lake onboard as his arranger and orchestrator, though Gebest continued as musical director and conductor. And helping to orchestrate a series of 1933 Cohan radio programs was an early job of famed Broadway orchestrator Don Walker, who worked in part with Cohan's accompanist John McLaughlin.[108] Lake, who praised Cohan's melodies and managerial skills alike in his 1983 memoir, described their process: Cohan would write the tune and "crude accompaniments limited to 'ear' chords," and Lake would supply the "proper" harmonies and orchestration. Cohan still had input, however. "When George would encounter any strange harmonization," Lake recounted, "his face would pull down into a grimace, one eye would close and we knew without his saying a word that the chords were out. At least for the time being." Although stubborn, Cohan could occasionally be convinced.[109] Still, the story evinces the harmonic simplicity of Cohan's music as his distinct aesthetic preference.

As with his playwriting, Cohan's songwriting was motivated by profit and powered by labor. When Cohan published his first songs in the late nineteenth century, the sheet music industry known as Tin Pan Alley was becoming big business. In 1891, the song "After the Ball" by songwriter Charles Harris (also first notated by an arranger) sold over a million copies—a staggering number. The ambitious teenaged Cohan saw an opportunity; he recalled in his autobiography traipsing around to different publishing houses, initially with little success but a heart "set on being a popular-song writer."[110] Once the young songwriter got going, he churned out material, publishing dozens of songs in the mid- to late-1890s that reflected and capitalized on shifting stylistic currents. The waltz was a well-established song type newly popular in the 1890s, and Cohan wrote several, including his second published song "Venus, My Shining Love" (1894), which Cohan described in his autobiography as "still the best song I ever wrote," and "My Little Polly's a 'Peach'" (1896).[111] "Excelling all other ladies," the Venus of the former is an idealized love who would be at home in songs of earlier decades. The lyrics are peppered with "ne'er," "twixt," and other poetic (or affected) terms and phrases.[112] Polly, on the other hand, while praised in equal degree, is a more down-to-earth and up-to-date sweetheart, who the singer hopes will "jump on a trolly" with him to "get spliced," slang for marrying.[113] Cohan also jumped on the new trend for "coon songs," syncopated, ragtime-influenced tunes with stereotyped, derogatory lyrics about Black characters; "Sally" (1894), was billed as a "comic negro song," and "Hot Tamale Alley" (1896) was performed by vaudeville actress and "coon shouter" May Irwin, who was also credited as lyricist.

For an ambitious songwriter at the turn of the twentieth century, "the pinnacle of success," as a manual from the day stated, was having a famous comedian sing your song or writing for Broadway shows.[114] "Venus" was performed by Harry Leighton and "Polly" by Harry Dietz, and their images graced the sheet music covers. Even better, it seemed, for a songwriter with writing skills and a wealth of theatrical experience, was to write songs for one's own shows, and most of Cohan's published songs from his success with *Little Johnny Jones* in 1904 onward were from the scores of his shows. Not all, however.

Two of the exceptions, both written in the 1910s—the World War I rallying tune "Over There" (1917) and the self-referential meta-song "That Haunting Melody" (1911)—illustrate key Cohanesque traits of his songwriting. One of Cohan's best-known songs in his lifetime and since, "Over There" helped spur American soldiers to war, and in supporting wartime morale, it earned Cohan a Congressional Gold Medal for patriotic service in 1936. After publishing the song with William Jerome Co. and earning several months' worth of royalties, Cohan sold it to publisher Leo Feist for $25,000—at that time the highest price by far paid for a popular song. At least one version of the sheet music displayed the famed check on the back cover.[115] The song's origin story, as told by Cohan's daughter Mary, has become legend. Sunday, April 8, two days after the United States formally declared war on Germany, she recalled, "Dad called us all together," saying that he "had just finished a new song and he wanted to sing it for us. So we all sat down and waited expectantly because we always loved to hear him sing. He put a big tin pan from the kitchen on his head, used a broom for a gun on his shoulder, and he started to mark time like a soldier, singing: 'Johnnie, get your gun . . .' "[116]

When journalist Walter Winchell later remarked on Cohan's "gift for fine simplicity," "Over There" was the song he gave as an example (▶ Example 2.3).[117] The song is formally conventional, with a verse-chorus structure and thirty-two-bar ABAC chorus. Typical of Cohan's patriotic songs, it borrows from existing songs; the opening "Johnnie, get your gun" used the rhythm of an 1886 minstrel song by this title.[118] Cohan sets the phrase to a pattering, drum-like rhythm, repeated with slight variation before the melody broadens to longer notes on the lines, "Hear them calling you and me; / Ev'ry son of liberty." Cohan varies the rhyming pattern in the third line, creating an added sense of urgency with the familiar melody: "Hurry right *away*, no *delay*, go *today*." The verse builds tension with five repeated notes on the fifth scale degree of the dominant chord, winding up for a return home to the tonic at the start of the refrain, whereupon we hear the song's iconic bugle call: "Over there, over there, / Send the word, send the word over there." Jaunty syncopation accompanies the phrase "the Yanks are coming," with melodic emphasis on the wrong syllable—"ming" rather than "come"—but to a youthfully enthusiastic effect. The last line of the chorus introduces new material by inverting the bugle call after a brief descent (see Figure 2.5). An emphatic B-flat, the home note, drives home the message that "we won't come back till it's over over there." Cohan's repetition of the word "over," with two different meanings, risks sounding clunky but comes across here as clever and determined. The arranger's artful touches in the sheet music version, like the piano part marching downward as the singer sounds the bugle call "Over There," show

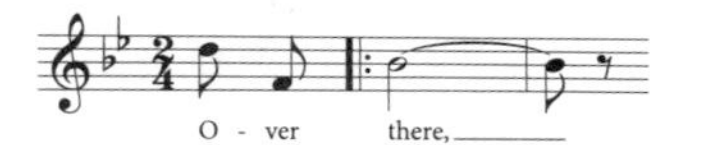

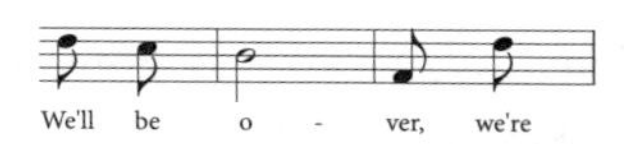

Figure 2.5 Bugle call and its inversion in "Over There." Published by Leo Feist (1917).

up in multiple recorded versions, and the bugle motif lent itself to interludes and countermelodies, as in recordings by Arthur Fields and Enrico Caruso. "All I wrote was a bugle call," Cohan said, in his often self-effacing way, but with a grain of truth; the song's effectiveness lay in its construction around that simple, powerful musical gesture.[119]

Another trick in Cohan's songwriting toolbox was to combine self-reflexivity with patchwork quotation to create a song about a song. "That Haunting Melody," for example, is about a song that made "an awful hit" with the singer. The "haunting melody" pervades its eponymous number. Cohan uses the four-bar melodic hook—which is also emblazoned on the sheet music cover (Figure 2.6)—much as he borrowed snippets from preexisting tunes in his patriotic songs, skillfully interweaving the hook throughout the song. After a striking introduction in the relative minor of the song's major key—an unusual choice in Cohan song arrangements—the singer begins, "Tell me, have you ever heard this melody?" and then hums the catchy tune. The "haunting melody" returns once more in the verse then takes center stage in the refrain: it kicks off the first line and is repeated three more times for good measure. The surrounding melody captures the love-hate relationship with a captivating hook—at one point in the verse, the conversational range expands to octave-wide exclamations that the singer has "nearly gone insane" from the lingering tune even as they continue to love it. In the refrain, a line beginning in minor, which is also heard in the song's introduction, suggests the singer's frustration as they exclaim, "What is it from?" The singer "can't help but hum" it, and by the end of the song, the listener will undoubtedly be humming it as well.

The sheet music for "That Haunted Melody" does not mention a related show, announcing it only as "Geo. M. Cohan's Latest Song." Cohan had garnered enough fame that it is his image, as composer, that is emblazoned on the cover. The song was used, however, in a Shubert-produced show called *Vera Violetta* in 1911, the year the song was published. In the show, it was performed, in blackface, by an up-and-coming Al Jolson, and it became Jolson's first recording.[120] As conductor Rick Benjamin and musicologist Gillian M. Rodger have pointed out, there are vast differences between the song as presented in the sheet music and the recorded performance popularized by Jolson, to which he brings a crude racial dialect, variations on the melody and rhythm, a proto-scat singing in lieu of humming, and, as Rodgers puts it, a sense of "grotesque comedy."[121] In both versions, the sheet music (a more faithful rendition of which can be heard on Benjamin's album *You're a Grand Old Rag: The Music of George M. Cohan*, ▶ Example 2.4) and Jolson's performance (▶ Example 2.5), the clever self-referential or

Figure 2.6 Cover of "That Haunting Melody." Published by Jerome and Schwartz (1911). Courtesy of the Levy Collection.

meta-compositional nature of the song and Cohan's treatment of the "haunting melody" gives it the witty lyrical and musical flare that had come to be known as Cohanesque.

Cohan repeated the meta-song formula a few years later with "There's Only One Little Girl" (1916), and he continued to publish songs, those from his shows and independent of them, through the end of his life. Yet he gained arguably more renown for another of his many roles; from his youth and into his last working years, when his work as a playwright had mostly ceased, he was a performer.

FROM SONG AND DANCE MAN TO "AMERICA'S FIRST ACTOR": COHAN THE PERFORMER

Perhaps the most important aspect of his Cohanesqueness, Cohan's activity as a performer is also the most ephemeral. Cohan represents a rare case in which the author of the scripts and scores was also, frequently, a performer of them. As his career progressed, he also performed in works by others, and by the end of his career, he was arguably more renowned as an actor than a playwright or composer. Unfortunately, we cannot see Cohan's stage performances today. Still, we can get a glimpse of his way of entertaining through reviews, photographs, anecdotes, and his own writings, as well as a few audio recordings, film appearances, including in the 1932 talkie *The Phantom President*, and fragments of other video footage.

In his role as an actor, just as in his role as a playwright, Cohan firmly relegated himself to the realm of entertainment—a "song and dance man," he called himself. In his 1924 autobiography, he sets up a trajectory of being dismissed and then finally accepted as first a dancer, in 1908, with his performance in *The Yankee Prince*; then a dramatist, in 1913 with *Seven Keys to Baldpate*; then as a songwriter, in 1917 with "Over There." Finally, in 1923 with *The Song and Dance Man* (a play and not a musical, despite the title) "comes the big laugh of the story—the real punch to the tale. The actors admitted that I was a *good actor*. Gosh darn it! Why did they keep me waiting so long?" With this, Cohan writes, "my dreams had all come true. My highest ambition satisfied at last."[122]

Like many of Cohan's stories, there's a kernel of truth amidst the embellishment. He *did* earn wider and more highbrow recognition as an actor in the twenties and thirties for his "polished naturalis[m]," as one scholar put it, and critics even deemed him "America's first actor."[123] A 1930 review of Cohan's performance in a revival of *The Song and Dance Man* captures this characterization well: "As an actor Mr. Cohan has art that conceals art," the reviewer writes. "He is so natural that he never seems to be acting."[124] This distinguished status was cemented by two particularly notable appearances in works that he did not write: the play *Ah! Wilderness* (1933) by Eugene O'Neill; and the musical *I'd Rather Be Right* (1937), with music by Richard Rodgers, lyrics by Lorenz Hart, and book by George S. Kaufman and Moss

Hart. On Cohan's performance in O'Neill's *Ah! Wilderness* (1933), *New York Times* drama critic Brooks Atkinson wrote that Cohan was "quizzical in the style to which we are all accustomed from him, but the jaunty mannerisms and mugging have disappeared. . . . Ironic as it may sound, it has taken O'Neill to show us how fine an actor George M. Cohan is."[125]

Yet some early reviews complicate this teleological account of reaching the pinnacle of acting success after evolving over his career from farce comedian to the finest actor. A reviewer of a Buffalo, New York, performance of Cohan's first Broadway show *The Governor's Son*, in May 1900, before the show went to New York City, noted that Cohan had "an ability as an actor that is not too often seen on the more pretentious regular stage," presaging that Cohan's vaudevillian influences and personal style would bring something new to Broadway, whether desirable, as suggested here, or deplorable, as *Life*'s theatrical critic James Metcalfe and Cohan's other detractors believed. The Buffalo critic praised Cohan, as an actor, for his nonchalance, comical expressiveness, and overall "command of effect." The playing of the show as a whole, the reviewer states, is "remarkable for its reserve and quietness. One would think that James A. Herne had staged the piece, so repressed is the acting."[126] Given that Herne was known for forays into realism while Cohan was from the world of vaudeville and drew heavily from melodrama and farce, this seems at face value a surprising comparison, though Cohan later cited Herne's *Shore Acres*, which played in New York City in 1893, as one of his most significant influences.[127] While Cohan and his productions were sometimes stereotyped as bombastic, reviews make clear that he did not overact. Rather, as John McCabe puts it, "What Cohan was doing, at a very early age and at a time unaccustomed to it, was underplaying," projecting "pert blandness, an ingratiating comic reserve."[128]

Critics of the time commented, and the few recordings we have further attest, that Cohan sang and danced with a "disregard of all the rules except his own." Observers commented on the way he talked and sang from the side of his mouth.[129] He was not much of a vocalist when judged by traditional standards like range, rich tone color, and lyricism, but he knew how to put over a song. Cohan did very little studio recording; in fact, while he would get involved in radio later on, he recorded on only one date in the acoustic era: May 4, 1911, for Victor Records.[130] Given the constraints of the studio and his lack of experience in that setting, we cannot take it as representative. Still, it gives us some sense of his delivery, bearing out what commentators of the day said in reviews and articles. By 1915, theater critic Burns Mantle could talk about Cohan "singing in his old time fashion through his old time nose," and indeed, Cohan's nasal tone is in full aural display in the 1911 recording of his song "Hey There! May There!" (1903). At the end of each line of the verse he snaps to the word's closing syllable, if it can be sustained at all, as in the case of "r" and "n," and holds them, apparently as a stylistic choice, breaking the traditional rules of good singing (▶ Example 2.6). Especially in his recordings of "philosophical songs" such as "I'm Mighty Glad I'm Living, That's All" (1904) (▶ Example 2.7) and "Life's a Funny Proposition After All" (1904) (▶ Example 2.8), we hear the speak-singing for which Cohan was well known. The accompaniment carries the pitches of the melody, while Cohan hardly hits one. His declamation of the lyrics is chantlike, largely on approximately the same pitch, with slight movement upward for emphasis and regularly dropping downward at the end of lines, though he speaks loosely in the music's notated rhythm.

Cohan's dancing drew more praise, even if it was equally idiosyncratic. In fact, by his telling, he escaped being pigeonholed as a dancer only by force of will.[131] He danced throughout his career, from the "Lively Bootblack" skit of his youth to his star role in *I'd Rather Be Right* at near sixty years old. As he rose through the ranks, he became a "crackerjack dancer," as he explained in "The Practical Side of Dancing" in the *Saturday Evening Post*, but the public did not appreciate the advanced steps—they liked the unusual, so he became an "eccentric" dancer, moving across the stage floor in an individualistic, even grotesque, manner.[132] He also became known for his "lively caper across the stage with his fast-swinging cane."[133] For the Cohan biopic *Yankee Doodle Dandy* (1942), Jimmy Cagney was trained by Johnny Boyle, who had worked with Cohan, and Cagney tried his best to imitate Cohan's dancing, including his signature move of running up the side of the scenery or proscenium arch.[134]

Even Richard Rodgers's widow Dorothy Rodgers, who decades later was still none too happy with Cohan for his rudeness toward her husband and changing lyrics in *I'd Rather Be Right* without permission, had only positive things to say about Cohan's "very nimble, very graceful" dancing.[135] It is on full display in the approximately one minute of footage of Cohan performing on stage that we have today, a segment of 16mm film from *I'd Rather Be Right* (1937) that has no sound and, thanks to changing standard speed in film equipment, appears sped up. Cohan, as Franklin D. Roosevelt, struts across the stage in his tailcoat and top hat, in front of the chorus, with his torso bent ever so slightly forward and making good use of the trademark cane that points as well as twirls (see Figure 2.7). At five feet six, he is shorter than most of the other performers, though the hat gives him a bit more height. His motion will seem contained—just a jaunty, stylized walk, a turn or a bit of footwork here or there—then he will throw back his head and torso,

Figure 2.7 Cohan as President Franklin D. Roosevelt in I'd Rather Be Right *(1937). Photo by George Karger/Getty Images.*

kick up a leg straight in front of him or up past his hip on the side; or strike a lopsided "ta-da"-like pose. The star of the show, he clearly commands the stage.[136]

* * *

Cohan had a distinctive style, as a playwright, songwriter, and performer, and a strong sense of what Broadway entertainment should be. His fingerprints are all over American musical theater, in its energetic pacing; blending of genres; metatheatrical strand; and cocky, masculine protagonists who cannot really sing but can put over a song, and who caper as much as dance. The contradictions inherent in his vision of entertainment are those of Broadway, particularly its musicals: modern and fresh but nostalgic, realistic but metatheatrical, and anti-elite but professional and commercial. In addition to shaping Broadway artistically, Cohan also contributed to the business of theater behind the scenes, as a businessman. In all of these roles, he brought a craftsperson's approach and ideology: know your trade, work hard, please your customers. Perhaps this is what allowed him to become—literally as well as figuratively—one of the men who owned Broadway.

THE MAN WHO OWNED BROADWAY

> And now he has opened The George M. Cohan Theatre—a monument to Yankee grit and Yankee wit, a *national* theatre in the name of the first American "Yankee Doodle!"
>
> Opening this house of Cohan . . . George M. Cohan seems to have fulfilled his "The Man Who Owns Broadway."
>
> —Wendell Phillips Dodge (1911)

Romantic love was the primary driving force in musical theater and popular song of the early twentieth century, and Cohan's shows and songs were no exception; but for Cohan, money was a close second.[1] In his first Broadway production, *The Governor's Son*, Cohan imagined and philosophized about having it in the musical number "Then I'd Be Satisfied with Life" (1902) (▶ Example 3.1). It's unusual to meet a man truly satisfied with life in this greed-filled world, Cohan explained in the verse, but he himself doesn't need much to be fulfilled. Reaching the song's chorus, he delivered his modest list: "All I want is fifty million dollars," it begins. Sealskin garments, partridge for breakfast, a champagne fountain, a mansion built of gold, and an heiress for a wife—the lyrics paint a vivid picture of Gilded Age opulence set to a conversational, meandering melody, and one can imagine Cohan's dryly humorous and largely spoken deadpan delivery. The song was seen as a highlight of the show, so Cohan repeated the sentiment and musical style in his next show the following year with "If I Were Only Mister Morgan" (1903). Speaking directly, though ambivalently, to the pressing economic issues of the day, these songs referenced Carnegie, Vanderbilt, and Rockefeller as well as Morgan—the wealthy business giants whose names every American was sure to know—and alternately proposed profiting from or busting the trusts that were currently occupying politicians and newspaper headlines.[2] They

Yankee Doodle Dandy. Elizabeth T. Craft, Oxford University Press. © Oxford University Press 2024.
DOI: 10.1093/oso/9780197550403.003.0004

teasingly touted satisfaction with the ordinary life before indulging in fantasies of extraordinary affluence.

When Cohan performed and published these songs, this kind of wealth was wishful thinking for the young entertainer. A few years later, however, he had moved from the wishful to the wealthy, and his 1908 song "M-O-N-E-Y" from *The Yankee Prince* takes a less whimsical, more direct approach. "I wonder what we wouldn't do for money," the singer comments. It's the "wherefore and the why," the driver of human behavior from politics to the pulpit, for those who have it and those who don't, the song's lyrics explain. The tune is lighthearted, but the motoric eighth notes of the melody reinforce the sense of capitalism's ceaseless grind (Figure 3.1).[3] In the sheet music for "M-O-N-E-Y," the song itself was sandwiched between an advertisement for the Cohan and Harris "Yankee Doodle Music Publishers," the new entity that would sell all Cohan songs, and a list of the by then extensive Cohan and Harris productions.[4] By the following year, when he premiered the show *The Man Who Owns Broadway*, it seemed like an apt descriptor for Cohan himself.

As a creator and performer who also became one of Broadway's most powerful producers and businessmen, in conjunction with partner Sam Harris, Cohan occupied an atypical, even singular, position. His obituary in the *New York Times* said, "For all the money he made, Mr. Cohan was always predominantly the artist rather than the business man," commenting on how he rarely went to his office, preferring instead to be on the go—he quipped that his office was in his hat.[5] Fellow producer and manager A. L. Erlanger, on the other hand, made the tongue-in-cheek comment at a 1910 dinner honoring Cohan that his "real career" was "parting the public from its money."[6] Cohan never stopped being a creative figure or, despite semi-regular announcements of his retirement from acting, a performer. These were the identities

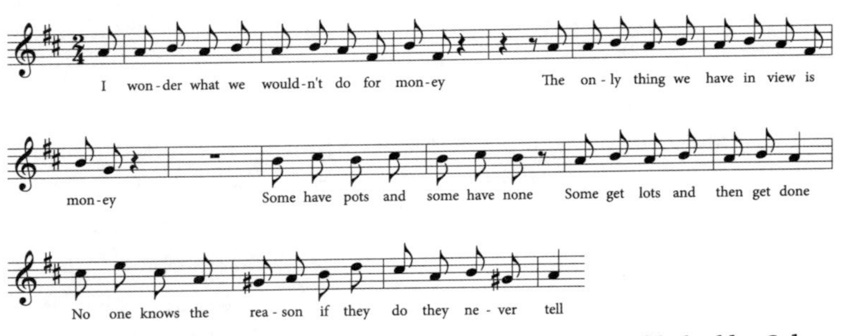

Figure 3.1 Beginning of verse of "M-O-N-E-Y," voice only. Published by Cohan and Harris (1908).

he held closest to his heart; his role as a businessman sprang from them. They were also, however, inseparable. As we saw in Chapter 2, his work as an artist was motivated by the "M-O-N-E-Y" he also wrote and sang about.

This chapter examines how Cohan helped shape contemporary public discourses about wealth and business, both as a Broadway magnate and as a creator of plays and musicals, amid a rapidly transforming US economy and theatrical industry. While themes of money and class pervade Cohan's shows throughout his career, in the decade from around 1909 to 1919 business came to the fore and Cohan's authorial perspective on these themes shifted. In shows like *Get-Rich-Quick Wallingford* (1910), Cohan staged national anxieties about big business capitalism while also celebrating it. He also modeled, in his shows and public discourse, a "regular fellow" masculinity and homosociality suitable for business's highly gendered realm. Eventually, the tension in Cohan's roles as Broadway performer and businessman, "regular fellow" and magnate, came to a head with the famous actors' strike of 1919 and his notorious, vocal opposition to the Actors' Equity Association. In this atypical, highly publicized battle between business and workers, Cohan's unique position made him a lightning rod.

THE PRODUCER AND THEATRICAL BUSINESSMAN

In many ways, the story of the late nineteenth- and early twentieth-century United States is an economic one. More specifically, it is a story of the rise of modern capitalism and the tensions between business and labor, as industrial and technological developments remade the nation. Formulations of historians capture not only differences in interpretations but also the multiple, sometimes contradictory impulses of the period itself: the "age of reform" and a "search for order" overlapped with the "era of big money" and a nation "standing at Armageddon."[7] The traditional periodization of the Gilded Age and Progressive Era suggests a shift from economic excess to reform. Yet these labels can obscure the many continuities from the late 1890s to the 1910s, when Cohan established his career and the United States adjusted to the economic and social transformations of moving from a predominantly rural, agrarian society to an urban, industrial one.

It was a period of great economic inequality; the wealthy and well-to-do owned the vast majority of the nation's wealth, and New York City was rapidly becoming the financial capital of the world as many lived under the poverty line. The United States was supposed to be free of Europe's rigid class barriers, and Cohan exemplified the promise of upward mobility, but it was more mythology than reality for most in the lower economic rungs, including most of his fellow Irish Americans. As historian Nell Irvin Painter writes, business, which was more successful at "portraying their interests as those of Americans as a whole," valued hierarchy and order and offered the promise of prosperity, promoting the idea that capital and labor shared interests. Those advocating for workers offered democracy and equity but also the threat of disorder, made evident in widespread strikes.[8] As Cohan was ascending in wealth and class as dizzyingly quickly as the skyscrapers popping up around him, the nation weighed these competing visions.

As the business of business was changing, so was the business of theater. The changes were part and parcel of the many technological, economic, and social upheavals of this turbulent period—from the electric lights that gave Broadway the nickname "the Great White Way," to the expansive rail system that actually constituted "the road" for traveling stage performers, to the developments in sound and film recording technology that held both promise and the peril of replacement for those performers.[9] As businesses merged to form powerful conglomerates, the industry of theatrical "combination companies" traveling from and to New York underwent a similar process on a smaller scale. At the turn of the century, as Cohan was making the leap from vaudeville to the so-called legitimate theater, New York saw the rise of the Theatrical Syndicate (known simply as "the Syndicate"). Together, this group of six producers—A. L. Erlanger, Marc Klaw, Charles Frohman, Al Hayman, Samuel Nixon, and J. Fred Zimmerman—owned many of the venues nationwide and were able to control booking and also contracts of top performers. Centralization under these "new-style businessmen," as theater historian Sean Holmes describes them, offered significant advantages, bringing order to what had been a chaotic, risky way of doing business. However, the Syndicate's monopoly structure, with ever-growing power in a few hands, had significant downsides as well, and they were brought to light in the well-publicized battle between them and rival producers the Shubert brothers and disputes between producers and actors in the first and second decades of the twentieth century.[10] Cohan, in partnership with Sam Harris, navigated relations with the Syndicate to become a theater magnate, one of the best known and powerful of the day.

George "Get-Rich-Young" Cohan, A Man Who Wouldn't Be Standardized

Cohan's life story echoed the rags-to-riches Horatio Alger–type tales one could find on bookshelves and newsstands in the early twentieth century.

As Chapter 5 on Cohan's role as a celebrity discusses further, he—and his press agents—readily packaged it that way for public consumption. It made a good story, in line with American aspirations of the day. In this case, it also happened to be true. Cohan did not come from wealth. His mother Nellie later described their circumstances without the rose-colored glasses that frequently accompanied her and her husband's recollections: "It was a joke, our pennilessness. . . . I could sew adequately and thus the children were always well dressed. But lack of money always bothered us. . . . It was a very hard life. Sometimes we didn't have streetcar fare and we carried the children for miles in our arms to the theatre." But she also acknowledged the joy in their life in the theater, continuing, "Still, somehow, when we got to the theatre, and we put the children to sleep in a drawer or a trunk, it was worth it because my husband . . . loved what he was doing so much that we all caught fire from him."[11] Cohan, too, adored his father, who may have been a fine actor but was, according to his son's estimations, not much of a businessman; George thought that Jerry's timidity and "gentle manner" meant he was sometimes taken advantage of, and in the 1890s, the teenage George took over the business matters for the Four Cohans.[12] When his mother died in 1928, she left almost all of her estate's value to her son, saying that whatever property she and Jerry had owned came from his generosity.[13] By the early 1910s, Cohan was a millionaire, and when he died, the net estate was appraised at $827,384 (over thirteen million in 2023 dollars).[14]

In keeping with his all-American, anti-highbrow public image, Cohan embraced the commercial aspects of theater. He was never shy about being motivated by money, and he was strategic in acquiring it. He described himself as "enormously ambitious," stating that "making millions was the pinnacle of my hopes."[15] He played a long game, betting on the success of his work and potential for advancement from early on and purportedly brought the royalty plan to vaudeville; his skit "A Romance of New Jersey," performed by the Russell Brothers in 1902, was said to be "the first variety act ever sold on a royalty basis." They "thought I was crazy," Cohan said, when he offered sketches to actors on a royalty basis rather than for a lump sum.[16] Upon taking over the business matters for the family vaudeville act, as Cohan tells it, he strategically chose performance opportunities that did not have the best pay but did offer opportunities for exposure, especially with more "high-class audiences" in more "legitimate" venues.[17] Profits were generally divided among a work's creators, so Cohan's ability to do it all artistically, as a playwright, composer, and lyricist, helped him monetarily, as did his work as a performer. Cohan also wanted financial control and buy-in, though; "I always had an idea that I would produce my own plays and get along without managers," he explained. Coming through the ranks, he eschewed the advances of managers and producers, biding his time and treading carefully among the emergent powerhouse conglomerates of the theater business. "When I did start out," he said, "I wanted to start out for myself."[18]

While actor-managers were more common in the nineteenth century, the theatrical business became increasingly specialized, centralized, and complex in the early twentieth century. Cohan both contradicted and participated in these trends. As critic Howard Barnes later put it, Cohan was "a man who won't be standardized"—he "deliberately refused" to specialize.[19] Yet his conception of theater as commercially driven entertainment and his experiences "barnstorming" and navigating the vaudeville circuits with his family also prepared him well to adapt to the new business practices taking hold in New York's theater industry. Remarkably, given how rare it was to find success in so many different endeavors, Cohan's game plan to move into legitimate theater and gain across-the-board artistic and financial control paid off. Being a producer and manager had many advantages for the young playwright and performer. It gave him the clout to get the most favorable treatment for his own shows. Having fingers in many pies, proverbially speaking, also meant that Cohan was able to diversify his income and distribute risk, thus maximizing his earnings. "George Get-Rich-Young Cohan," a newspaper called him in 1912.[20]

Cohan and Harris Present

Straddling the artistic and business sides of theater would not have been sustainable without Sam Harris (1872–1941). The Jewish American Harris also had " 'up-by-your-bootstraps' origins," growing up on New York's Lower East Side.[21] He had worked as a prizefight promoter before establishing his career in theater. Both relative newcomers in the New York theater scene, Cohan and Harris teamed up for *Little Johnny Jones* (1904), launching a partnership that would last until the actors' strike of 1919 (Figure 3.2). Harris was described in an obituary as "a playwright's producer," one who sought to support the ideas of the artists he worked with.[22] Harris focused on the financial side of producing and Cohan on the artistic side. This arrangement allowed Cohan to continue his creative and acting work and gave Harris the advantage of an in-house writer providing a steady stream of strong shows. The two shared theatrical tastes and interests, valuing well-written American plays and musicals that did not necessarily promote a star performer—like those penned by Cohan. The two men were also a good match temperamentally. Harris reportedly got along well with everyone, whereas in his youth Cohan

Figure 3.2 Cohan and Harris in 1904, with handwritten caption "First Photo taken together." Theater Biography Collection, Harry Ransom Center, The University of Texas at Austin.

had the reputation of being, by his own description, "a cute little guy"—clever but insufferable.[23] Harris insisted, however, that Cohan was considerate and generous. In sum, as theater scholar Alisa Roost writes, Harris was an "ideal" partner for Cohan.[24] Beyond their professional work, the two were linked personally. Both previously divorced, they married two sisters, Agnes and Alice Nolan, each of whom had been chorus girls in *Little Johnny Jones*, in 1907 and 1908. After several years producing Cohan works, they expanded to produce works by other playwrights, often doctored by Cohan, as well.

Although their business partnership ended in the wake of the successful actors' strike of 1919, with Cohan temporarily retiring from the theater, they went on to produce shows separately. In 1937, their professional lives intersected again; they coproduced Cohan's play *Fulton of Oak Falls*, and Harris produced *I'd Rather Be Right*, a musical by George S. Kaufman and Moss Hart with music by Richard Rodgers and lyrics by Lorenz Hart, in which Cohan played the lead.

Together, Cohan and Harris focused on advertising as a means of building their business. *It Pays to Advertise*, the title of a 1914 Cohan and Harris–produced and Cohan-doctored play by Roi Cooper Megrue and Walter Hackett, was not only a catchphrase of the day but also describes one of the partners' earliest guiding principles. Cohan grasped the importance of advertising early on. In fact, the business tactic also became an aesthetic feature of his songwriting, the patchwork approach to borrowing that would come to mark his patriotic songs. Edward B. Marks recounted, in his memoir of the song publishing business, the young Georgie Cohan trying to sell him and his business partner Joe Stern a song. After many lackluster efforts, Cohan "came into [the] two-room tune factory with that flashy Irish grin all over his face. 'I've got a new one for you, boys,' he said. 'The Songs that Maggie Sang.'" "No more Irish," Marks and Stern responded in chorus, until they looked at the song and found that Cohan had created a song from the songs in their catalogue. In the style of the heroine-focused songs of the day, Cohan's waltz-song describes in the verse a girl with a grand piano and fine voice who sings all the latest Tin Pan Alley tunes, then strings together in its chorus musical and lyrical quotations from several examples, including "Sweet Rosie O'Grady," "Down in Poverty Row," and "Elsie from Chelsea." In many cases, Cohan did not even need to change the key. "We took 'Maggie' as a house ad," Marks wrote. "Selling a copy was like selling a half a dozen other tunes."[25] The cover displayed all the tunes quoted and a few others (Figure 3.3).

Cohan later described "turn[ing] advertising upside down" with the early Cohan and Harris shows. Paradoxically, they did so by going back to "old-school" advertising, "plaster[ing] the town" with lithographs and billboards and running half-page ads in newspapers.[26] "Cohan Well Boosted," *Billboard* magazine reported in 1907, noting that Cohan had become famous for the way his press agents advertised his shows. The article described the most recent example, the publicity around *Fifty Miles from Boston* at the Colonial Theatre in Chicago. Cohan's general press representative Edward W. ("Eddie") Dunn, who was dubbed "energetic" and "ubiquitous" by the press, and the manager of the Colonial Theatre succeeded in negotiating to hang "a monster banner"

Figure 3.3 Cover of "The Songs that Maggie Sings." Published by Jos. W. Stern (1897). Reproduced from the Ward Irish Music Archives, Milwaukee, WI.

for the show stretching across State Street.[27] According to another anecdote, Cohan and Harris offered a theatrical manager who had come to visit them a return ticket back to Philadelphia, but when he went to use it, he discovered it was in fact not an actual railway ticket but a "very clever ad" that "entitled the holder to one continuous laugh over the Cohan Comedy Line to see *Forty-Five Minutes from Broadway*."[28] Such stunts also reaped secondary benefits of the ensuing publicity they received when newspapers covered them.

Cohan, Harris, and Dunn also put out their own house organ, a company newsletter called the *Spot Light*, beginning in 1905.[29] As Cohan writes in his autobiography, describing his characteristic bravado, their press agent had "dug up a mailing list three thousand miles long, so we claimed 'the largest free circulation of any theatrical publication in the world.'"[30] The *Spot Light* included news of theatrical productions, first and foremost Cohan and Harris's, as well as poems by Jerry Cohan, quips by George, and other humorous anecdotes. While the more established and powerful Syndicate came to be aligned with the New York paper the *Morning Telegraph*, Cohan and Harris's paper was akin to bulletins like the "Keith News" of the Rhode Island Keith Theatres and house organs in other industries.[31] Later, the Shuberts challenged the Syndicate by putting out their own. Cohan also used the *Spot Light* to take on "unfriendly critics," who would then respond in their various publications. The strategy was successful, as Cohan notes, in keeping his name before the public and racking up free advertising.[32]

Cohan and Harris also prioritized "the road," cultivating national networks of audiences across the United States. Despite Cohan's close association with Broadway, as theater scholar James Fisher observed, his shows tended to fare better on tour than in New York.[33] To Cohan, the economics of the road made more sense. "Many producers don't care how their shows go until they get to New York. But for my part I'd rather see a show go well in Hartford [Connecticut] than here, any day," Cohan wrote in 1909, explaining that the better terms, or higher percentage of the gross receipts, that producers received on the road significantly outweighed the additional traveling costs when playing to capacity houses.[34]

A show thus did not need to have a record-breaking New York run to have record-breaking profit. The firm's biggest money-maker was reportedly *Forty-Five Minutes from Broadway*, which premiered in Columbus, Ohio, then played in Dayton and Indianapolis, and spent twelve weeks in Chicago before kicking off a ninety-performance Broadway run on January 1, 1906.[35] The show dramatized urban-rural tensions, but it did so in a way calculated to appeal to both demographics. It had a lukewarm response from New York critics, but returned to Chicago and then New York again, and Cohan reported with satisfaction in his 1924 autobiography that "a solid year was divided between the two cities." They then organized and sent out road companies, making it the third Cohan show on the road at that time.[36] The show's popularity, especially on the road, along with its low production costs and overall feasibility gave it a high profit margin and made it a good choice for the stock companies that formed or became more active in cities and towns across the United States as touring productions declined.[37]

Cohan and Harris boasted of their "hard and fast rule against sending out inferior companies."[38] "I practice and preach giving the best everywhere, New York or Podunk," Cohan wrote in a *Green Book Magazine* article in 1915.[39] In advertising, too, Cohan and Harris promised their "small-town audiences" that they would get the same experience as in the Cohan Theater in New York. In an advertisement for *Little Johnny Jones*, they claimed to have the largest musical comedy on tour and boasted to newspapers that "it has not been cut down for 'the road,' but remains intact as to company, scenery and costumes, exactly as presented in New York City."[40] An advertisement for *It Pays to Advertise* stated that "Messrs. Cohan and Harris desire to say that the production in Butte [Montana] will be identically the same in every respect as at the Cohan theater."[41] Advertisements for performances with Cohan in them promised, in big, bold type, "Geo. M. Cohan (Himself)."[42] Even as the increasing costs of moving scenery and props, the competition of cinema, and the ability for audiences to travel further to see entertainment with automobiles shrank the business of traveling companies, Cohan and Harris continued to invest in theirs.[43]

Cohan and Harris also set their sights abroad. As early as 1904, *Billboard* reported that Harris was making arrangements for a Cohan production in London, and many similar reports followed. Most of these arrangements do not appear to have come to full fruition, but in 1913, *Get-Rich-Quick Wallingford* played at the Queen's Theatre. *Broadway Jones*, *Seven Keys to Baldpate*, and *Little Nellie Kelly* were among those that followed in England.[44] Australia, too, saw multiple Cohan productions. Cohan's sister Josephine and her husband went there for six months in 1912 to help bring George's shows there.[45] Cohan's productions made it further from the largest English-speaking theatrical centers as well; in 1913, for instance, productions of Cohan shows were also staged in Panama and Trinidad by the Morton Musical Comedy and Opera Company.[46] Sheet music as well as theatrical productions circulated abroad; for instance, one could get the "The Yankee Doodle Boy"—trumpeted as an "international success"—in Dutch translation, spreading Cohan's conception of American identity beyond national borders.[47]

"All O.K. with K. and E.": Navigating the Syndicate and the Shuberts

Success as producers in the first decade of the twentieth century meant choosing between establishing good relations with the Syndicate or challenging it; the up-and-coming Cohan and Harris chose the former, while simultaneously maintaining their independence. Cohan put the state of affairs into song in "I'm All O.K. with K. and E."—referring to Syndicate leaders Klaw and Erlanger—in his 1909 musical *The Man Who Owned Broadway*. The number is sung by a minor character, the theatrical manager and producer Bill Robinson, introduced as the man who discovered the show's hero, Broadway star Sydney Lyons, in Toledo. Like many of the real-life Broadway moguls of the period, Robinson is a rags-to-riches can-do man who went from newspaper boy to "the only manager delivering the goods on Broadway," as he sings in his self-aggrandizing solo. The song comments on the hierarchies and politics of the theater industry in surprisingly explicit ways. Advertising himself, Robinson claims to have bested Frohman, Hammerstein, Belasco, Fiske, and other prominent producers and that he'll "paralyze the Shuberts / For [he's] all O.K. with K. and E." (Figure 3.4). Lyrically, the song used a favorite Cohan device of playing with letters and initials, one he also used in "When We Are M-A-Double R-I-E-D" (from *The Talk of New York*, 1907). Musically, "I'm All O.K. with K. and E." moves between minor and major, with minor passages (e.g., "I'm the only showman . . . ") conveying the threat looming in the character's power for those who would dare to cross him and major passages (e.g., "And I'd like to wager two bits . . . ") to describe Broadway, his relationships with prominent actors, and being "in" with Klaw and Erlanger.

While the appellation "the man who owns Broadway" is supposed to apply to the star actor Lyons, this number suggests that it is actually the theatrical manager and producer who owns Broadway. This self-referential, navel-gazing look at the theater industry was a precursor to Cohan's revues,

Figure 3.4 First chorus of "I'm All O.K. with K. and E.," voice only. Published by Cohan and Harris Publishing (1909).

and despite the fact that Harris was mentioned in the lyrics, audiences may well have seen Robinson as a stand-in for Cohan and Harris themselves. The song's sheet music was published in the mass-circulation *New York Journal*, reaching even many of the New Yorkers who did not see the show or purchase the sheet music independently.[48]

The Syndicate was not a corporation; it was a loose collective of managers who also retained their individual interests. And while Cohan and Harris were not founding members, they were considered Syndicate allies, especially early on.[49] According to their remarks at a dinner honoring Cohan in 1910, Syndicate heads A. L. Erlanger and his partner Marc Klaw saw something in this young man who had his pulse on the times and "always want[ed] to run something."[50] Erlanger put money in Cohan's first show *The Governor's Son*, and Cohan wrote *Forty-Five Minutes from Broadway* at his request. They coproduced the show: as Erlanger recalled, Cohan "tried to make me believe he was a bad businessman" and told Erlanger that "he would take half the risk" in the production. "Well, he took half, and $250,000, just to show me he wanted to treat me on the square!" Erlanger quipped. When Cohan and Harris formed their partnership, Cohan and Harris Attractions, they leased office space in Klaw and Erlanger's New Amsterdam Theatre. Letters flew from one part of the building to another as Cohan and Harris booked tours on Syndicate routes and, when they felt the terms needed to be more "equitable" (i.e., more profitable for them), asked Klaw and Erlanger to intercede.[51] The *Spot Light* newsletter reinforced their solidarity. "Abe Erlanger and Sam Harris now and forever," Cohan wrote in a 1906 issue.[52] Cohan and Harris also coleased the Gaiety Theatre in New York with Klaw and Erlanger. Outside of New York, they coleased multiple theaters with Syndicate member Samuel F. Nixon, and in 1907, they joined Nixon in becoming officers of the newly expanded Ohio circuit, then renamed the "Nixon, Cohan, and Harris Circuit."[53]

While Cohan and Harris profited from their close association with the Syndicate in more obvious ways, Klaw and Erlanger also benefited from having Cohan and Harris Attractions—and, more specifically, Cohan the playwright, songwriter, and performer—in their theaters. Correspondence and legal records demonstrate that Klaw and Erlanger had a share and were involved in Cohan shows besides *Forty-Five Minutes from Broadway*.[54] Writing to Klaw in 1908, Erlanger reported that he had been working very hard on rehearsals of *The Yankee Prince*. "George was splendid; he took every suggestion," Erlanger noted gleefully, deeming the show "the best thing that Georgie has ever done" and reporting shortly thereafter that the show was making a good profit. After the show's out-of-town performances, it opened in New York at the Syndicate-owned Knickerbocker Theatre, which Erlanger felt confident would "get into line with the Cohan show." In another instance the following year, he commented on how much money "Georgie Cohan" was making for their theaters.[55] The relationship between the two partnerships, then, was mutually beneficial. Working out a misunderstanding in 1907 about what Jerry and Nellie Cohan were to be paid on a vaudeville tour of *Running for Office*, Erlanger offered to pay the difference between what he had promised theater managers ($750 per week) and what Harris apparently thought the Cohans were supposed to be paid ($1,200 per week), insisting that he could not possibly have written the number down wrong but that his "policy always has been never to make a profit out of a partner."[56]

Even as they maintained their good relationship with Klaw and Erlanger, Cohan and Harris sought to position themselves as leaders and ambassadors in the industry in their own right. The *Spot Light* was ample in its complimentary reports and cheering words about many productions and theater professionals. To ring in 1906 and mark their arrival as a significant force on Broadway, Cohan and Harris hosted a New Year's dinner for the members of their three current companies, *Little Johnny Jones*, *Forty-Five Minutes from Broadway*, and those of the newest show, *George Washington, Jr.* (Klaw and Erlanger, who were among the 250 guests, surprised Cohan with a "big silver loving cup").[57] They also hosted multiple philanthropic events, inviting the Shuberts, to whom they were always scrupulously polite, as well as members of the Syndicate. By 1917, they were reaching out to their fellow producers for charitable causes so frequently that Lee Shubert complained to his brother about it.[58]

Having established themselves, Cohan and Harris sought to expand their domain and operations still further and to control every aspect of their work in the sprawling entertainment business. By 1908, Cohan and Harris boasted a roster of what they called "hustling executives," in line with the business ideals of the day.[59] They expanded into the music publishing business, and they began acquiring and opening their own theaters in New York and Chicago, with two bearing Cohan's name.[60] *Variety* surmised that they were likely "heeling," or arming themselves, "in the event of a split with Klaw & Erlanger at some future time."[61] Every producing manager, however, wanted a few theaters so that he would have a place to put their shows quickly, without having to share profits with theater managers, as Cohan explained in a later magazine article.[62] By 1914, Cohan and Harris rivaled Klaw and Erlanger for the number of New York City theaters under their control.[63] They continued to have some fealty to "K. and E.," turning down a proposition from the Shuberts "on account of [their] long relationship" with the former,

Figure 3.5 Image of Cohan in a parade celebrating the opening of the Friars' Club, May 22, 1916. Library of Congress, Prints and Photographs Division, LC-DIG-ggbain-21739.

but they did business with and sought to maintain a nominal friendship with the latter as well.[64] Beyond that, they took new positions of leadership. Cohan became "prompter" of the Green Room Club and later "abbot" of the Friars' Club, both associations for theatrical professionals (Figure 3.5). After the United States' entry into World War I, he became president of America's Over There Theatre League, formed to send entertainment to troops abroad. Harris led an effort to bring together the theatrical managers to address the problem of cut-rate tickets, those sold at prices below face value, and he led the formation of a new lunch club for theatrical managers, where they would be able to discuss business matters privately.[65] They had gone from being up-and-comers to leaders in the industry—men who owned, both literally and metaphorically, at least a significant piece of Broadway.

COHAN'S U$ OF A: CAPITALISM AND MANHOOD ONSTAGE

Not only was Cohan a savvy, prosperous businessman himself but he also dramatized wealth and business on the stage. As Frank Glann put it in his 1976 dissertation, "Making money, having money, wanting money, inheriting money, stealing money, business and money, and the uses of money"—money is foundational to Cohan's plots.[66] Business, too, is everywhere in Cohan's shows, in all its meanings: characters getting into one another's business, or being told not to; stage business, referring to onstage action without dialogue; and business as commerce and profession. Cohan's stance on capitalism and commerce, however, shifted over the course of his career, tracking cultural trends and, to some extent, the changes in his own professional and class status. As an image of Cohan and Harris's team of "hustling executives" in the *Spot Light* suggests, the realm of business was male, and Cohan's mid-career shows of around 1909 to 1919 offered a compelling vision of masculine identity in the professional realm.[67]

For all of their emphasis on money, Cohan's early shows exhibit a remarkable amount of ambivalence about having it; who it is shared with (for instance, the "international marriage" threat discussed in Chapter 1); and the means of obtaining it, especially via business. On the one hand, Cohan often championed lower-class heroes and heroines and carved out space for lovable comic characters who are solidly middle class. Among the protagonists who come from means, a common trope is that they are willing to disavow their fortunes for love. On the other hand, for all his emphasis on character over class, his shows teemed with wealthy or upwardly mobile characters. Even if the protagonist does not start with money and is willing to forgo it, in the end, he or she generally does not have to and wins both love and fortune.

Business in Cohan's early shows is often used as a euphemism for dastardly deeds. Protagonists with colossal fortunes are at risk of being taken in by "bunco steerers" selling shares in phony gold and copper mining schemes or other unscrupulous conspirers. "I'm a business man," the villain Anthony Anstey says in *Little Johnny Jones* (1904), explaining how he has arranged to profit from marrying off his fiancée's niece to a British nobleman. Blackmail, to him, is simply a "business proposition."[68] In these shows with conniving "businesspersons," there's frequently an undercover newspaperman or -woman or detective on the scene to ensure that justice prevails. Gilded Age–style wealth and corruption meet Progressive Era–style investigative journalism and reform.

Cohan's treatment of money and business shifted, however, around the 1910s, as he became one of the men at the top, rather than one of the ones striving to get there, and his work as a producer came to equal and began to meld with his work as a playwright. As one critic put it, "Mr. Cohan keeps developing. He not only sings of Broadway, but he is getting to be a sort of song-bird and prophet of that frank materialism characteristic of a certain side of New York, and, indeed, of America."[69] Among the plays that Cohan either wrote or those he coproduced and doctored (or "Cohanized") that dealt with themes of "frank American materialism" were *Get-Rich-Quick Wallingford* (1910), *Broadway Jones* (1912), *It Pays to Advertise* (1914, by Roi Cooper Megrue and Walter Hackett), *Hit-the-Trail Holliday* (1915), *A Tailor-Made Man* (1917, by Harry James Smith), *A Prince There Was* (1918), and *The Meanest Man in the World* (1920, by Augustin MacHugh), and most of these fit the category of farce.[70] By 1924, John Corbin of the *New York Times* could observe that Cohan, along with two of the playwrights whose work Cohan had produced and doctored, now "presided over" a "prolific school of business comedy." As theater scholar Michael Schwartz writes, these "business farces" "celebrated the 'can-do' salesman hero." They were among many Broadway offerings helping to create and affirm the identity of the emerging professional managerial class.[71]

It was not new for economic issues to find their way onto the stage; in many ways, they lent themselves to dramatization. As historian Charles Ponce de Leon observes, "urbanization and the spread of market exchange had made economic relations distinctly theatrical."[72] One of the shows for which George's father Jerry Cohan was known, for instance, was *"The Molly Maguires," or the Black Diamond of Hazleton*, about labor relations and an allegedly violent secret society of Irish miners who were executed in 1877, the year of an anthracite coal strike.[73] The early twentieth-century business-related shows that Cohan wrote and coproduced likewise referenced and spoke to major socioeconomic concerns of his day. They did so from his vantage point as someone whose position and perspective had largely shifted from precarity to wealth, worker to manager.

Cohan's business farces and musical comedies were among the shows thought to appeal to a growing and increasingly important, if often stereotyped, audience demographic: "that contingent of the community known as the 'tired business man,'" as a *Theatre Magazine* critic put it in their review of *The Man Who Owns Broadway* in 1909. The critic continued, "The element that demands the frothiest of entertainment after a strenuous day amid the busy marts of trade, has again been provided for. Cohan and Harris are the managers who cater to these jaded mental conditions."[74] The tired businessman was presumed to come to the theater not wanting to think but quite interested in seeing musical comedies or revues with attractive female figures.[75] While Cohan's shows were short on the latter compared to shows like the Ziegfeld Follies, they did serve up the kind of light amusing fare that was thought to appeal to the tired businessman and his ilk. With male-heavy casts of characters and themes often dealing with business and wealth, they did not offer an escape from business concerns so much as, with their energy and thrills, "force 'the tired business man' to forget that he is tired," as one review put it.[76] Staging both business and manhood, Cohan put forth the rosy view that capitalism, so long as it was employed in the right spirit, would benefit the many and not just the few.

In his 1912 play *Broadway Jones*, for example, the eponymous hero inherits his uncle's chewing gum factory and plans to sell it to the chewing gum trust, but he changes course after learning what it means to the people working there and that the trust simply intends to close it. Although the good of the workers is often invoked in the script, the workers themselves are barely shown, and when they do appear, they are not portrayed in a very positive light. The show's true heroes are the factory's new owner Jones; the company's chief accountant and Jones's love interest Josie; and the advertising company manager and scion of the company's owner, Jones's friend Wallace.[77] Through shows like this one, Cohan spoke what historian Nell Irvin Painter calls the "persuasive idiom of prosperity," invoking identity-of-interests thinking to suggest that capital and labor were not antagonists but rather had shared interests; functioning properly, the hierarchical social economy would lead to profit for all.[78] *Broadway Jones* also emphasized a mistrust of big capitalism, championing the so-called little fellow of the business world against the evil conglomerates who would not hesitate to employ "low, contemptible tricks" to squeeze him out.[79]

Shows like *Broadway Jones* also offered a strong sense of how to navigate the changing workplace and society as a "regular fellow," helping to construct a new, twentieth-century masculinity. During Cohan's lifetime, gender roles were among the many areas of rapid cultural change. Outside of the theaters, and sometimes within them as well, advocates fought for women's suffrage, and the "new woman" challenged Victorian ideas of womanhood. Notions of manhood, too, were shifting, and the Victorian ideal of civilized manliness coexisted with a new ideal of physical, aggressive masculinity.[80] Striking a balance between the two poles, Cohan construed manhood as "regularness," and he imbued his male characters, who were by far the majority in his plays and musicals, with heaps of it.[81] Being "regular" connoted down-to-earth friendliness, unpretentiousness, moral decency, and robust heteronormativity. An increasingly popular trait in the early twentieth century, audiences could find it touted in theater program advertisements, such as for clothing or cars, as well as depicted onstage.[82] Cohan complimented this popular quality in others—Theodore Roosevelt was, in his opinion, a "regular fellow"—and the press saw it in him.[83] One journalist described Cohan as "the apotheosis of what the district calls 'regular,'" adding, "When a thing is not regular, Mr.

Cohan does not want to have anything to do with it." "George M. Cohan Is Voted Stage's 'Most Regular Guy,'" another announced.[84]

As Cohan's flag-waving shows had demonstrated, the regular fellow version of manhood that he propounded was tightly bound to national identity. "Are we Americans gents or gentlemen?" he opened his July 1915 installment of his serialized feature "The Stage as I Have Seen It" in *Green Book Magazine*. The trouble, he explained, lay in "difference of standards of gentleness and manliness" between England and the United States. In his opinion, a gentleman need not "wear a wrist-watch" or "tuck his handkerchief up his sleeve" but "should be a regular fellow who lives every day so that he could look any damn man in the face and tell him to go to hell."[85] Many of Cohan's male heroes and secondary comic characters fit this description to a T—they are confident, full of vim and vigor, unconcerned with formalities. "Regular fellow" masculinity, for Cohan, also extended to business practices and social life: as a producer, he wanted what he called "regular people" as actors in his companies.[86] One of the venues in American society for reimagining and enacting manly identity was fraternal organizations. Cohan's characters regularly mentioned their membership in the Elks, Knights of Columbus, and the like, and Cohan himself belonged to several such groups geared toward comedians, performers, and theater professionals.[87] Cohan's business farces demonstrated how to wield masculinity in the professional realm.

Get-Rich-Quick Wallingford

The most successful of Cohan's business comedies of the 1910s, and his show with the longest Broadway run overall, was *Get-Rich-Quick Wallingford*. Premiered in 1910, the show was based on a few of the stories from a popular series by George Randolph Chester that appeared in the *Saturday Evening Post* beginning in 1907; Cohan's version took many elements from the original but was, unsurprisingly, highly Cohanized.[88] In addition to running on Broadway for a remarkable 424 performances, *Get-Rich-Quick Wallingford* toured the United States; was produced in the United Kingdom, Australia, and France; and was made into a 1921 silent film. One critic reasoned that "Shakespeare's audiences liked to eat and drink, so they were amused by a sort of Gargantuan eater and drinker. Mr. Cohan's audiences like to make money, and it is natural that they should be amused by a man who makes it with absurd easiness and a light heart."[89]

The treatment of business in Cohan's *Get-Rich-Quick Wallingford* was both lightly satirical and celebratory. It tells the story of two "confidence men" (or con men)—Col. J. Rufus Wallingford and Horace "Blackie" Daws—who try to take in the small Iowa town of Battlesburg with a spurious plan to manufacture covered carpet tacks. In the end, they each fall in love, experience a change of heart and stroke of luck that allow them to go legitimate, and find that they have actually grown a happier, more prosperous Battlesburg. (For those familiar with the 1957 musical *The Music Man*, which is set in the same time period, similarities abound.) Business begins, as in many of Cohan's earlier shows, as a form of chicanery, but in the end, the con men—thanks to the help of the talented, newly discovered desk-clerk-turned-general-manager Edward Lamb—are running a real business.

The show demonstrates notions of business, of urban/rural relations, and of gender and masculinity typical of Cohan's shows and reflective of discourses and tensions of the day. The orientation of the show is clear even from reading the list of the cast of characters, which introduces most of them, especially the men, by their job or profession: Lamb is the head clerk, Willie the office boy, Harkin the newspaper reporter, and so on. Set in middle America, *Wallingford* opens with a town debating its future. Should Battlesburg continue on its conservative, sleepy path or should its leaders "do something with their money," developing the town?[90] An opera house, a modern hotel, a rapid transit traction line—the play invited audiences of the rapidly changing 1910 United States to just think of the possibilities. Enter Blackie, representing a man looking for a "wide-awake town for manufacturing purposes." In other words, a capitalist. Some of the characters are skeptical—rightly, as it turns out—but Blackie paints an impressive, even heroic picture of Wallingford as head of the Mexican Rio Grande Rubber Company, San Diego Blood Orange Plantation Company, Locos Lead Development Company, and more. The waggish names ought to clue Battlesburg's citizens in, but instead, the list of companies has the intended effect of impressing them.

Wallingford and Blackie hoodwink the town partly through appeals to capitalistic patriotism. Touting Wallingford's fabricated list of achievements, Blackie tells the men of Battlesburg that they have "not only brought him to his present proud position, but have also contributed to the wealth of the nation."[91] When Wallingford arrives at the hotel in town, he asks to have his "parlor decorated with American flags." The local newspaper reporter, buying in to the ruse, describes Wallingford's plans to develop Battlesburg as a "brave and patriotic struggle." And when the town's leaders are rendered speechless by the underwhelming business proposal at hand, covered carpet tacks, Wallingford flatters them for their "brilliant, active American minds." Not all capitalism is patriotic, however. Wallingford's patriotic spirit is also something that is said to distinguish him from the typical business mogul. Comparing Wallingford to J. P. Morgan, Blackie says, "Yes, Morgan's done some great stunts with money, but he's not patriotic. You see, Wallingford doesn't care about money; he has the good of the country in his heart." The ambivalence expressed about whether real-life tycoons were truly American reflected concerns of the period and the range of opinions audience members were certain to have.

Get-Rich-Quick Wallingford included one non-White character, Wallingford's Japanese valet, played by actors who are the first known Asian Americans to appear on Broadway and its subsequent touring productions. The part was originally performed on Broadway by an actor listed as Daniel Gold, which according to newspaper interviews was the stage name for Du Gle Kim, who came to the United States in the very early twentieth century.[92] Cohan's own Japanese valet, Yoshin Sakurai, also played the role, touring across the United States in 1911 and 1912, and an actor listed as "S. Sakaki" played the part in several performances in 1912. (Sakurai's was previously thought to be the first appearance of an Asian American actor in mainstream theater, but Kim preceded him.)[93] Within the show, the presence of the Japanese valet, a longtime "symbol of the nouveaux riches," was a marker of Wallingford's ostensible wealth, helping to impress Battlesburg; he appears again in the final act, still the loyal valet.[94] The character of Yosi is both dehumanized, as when he is called "the Jap," and challenges stereotypes, as when a townsperson makes a rude comment assuming he is Chinese and he retorts, "in good English," "Go on, you big stiff."[95] The character and the actors who played him call attention to the overwhelming, constructed Whiteness in this imagined world and many others from Cohan's pen. Both the character of Yosi and the valet–actor Sakurai serve as a reminder that American capitalism and the wealth and status of the elite, including Cohan himself, were dependent upon the labor of the nation's large immigrant population.

Having had a flop with his first play, *Popularity*, in 1906, Cohan was proud with *Wallingford* to have a yearlong Broadway run in a play "without a song or a note of music."[96] However, he is overstating the absence of music. Like many "straight plays," *Get-Rich-Quick Wallingford* has music—both sung tunes and instrumental music—and here they are used in intentional, consequential ways. Singing proves a critical strategy for bringing the businessmen of the town into Wallingford's scheme and keeping them there. In the meeting in which Wallingford ropes the town leaders into joining his enterprise, they are heard singing "The Star-Spangled Banner." Blackie explains to a confused listener that "the Colonel always insists on patriotic songs being sung by the board of directors."[97] When his business partners later start to get wise and come to him demanding an accounting of funds spent, Wallingford gives them an earful, shaming them for their mistrust until they are begging his forgiveness, and then he reunites them musically through the invocation to sing their hymn of homosociality: "Let's sing the Corporation song and we'll all forget it." They launch into "Dear Old Pals," a late nineteenth-century music hall tune by G. W. Hunt that circulated, in a slightly different version, as a "sociability song" in the twentieth century (Figure 3.6).[98]

Secular communal singing, as ethnomusicologist Sheryl Kaskowitz writes in her book on the song "God Bless America," is a powerful "vehicle for the forging and contesting of community ties."[99] It creates, as political scientist Benedict Anderson has written in his landmark book on nationalism, a sense of "unisonance," which he defines as "the echoed physical realization of the imagined community."[100] Community singing was part of the entertainment and social practices of the early twentieth-century United States, and the burgeoning community singing movement of the 1910s sought to harness its democratic potential.[101] But here, this affective power is being used duplicitously—and, in the case of "The Star-Spangled Banner," in stark contrast to the sincerity of Cohan's displays of patriotism in his flag-waving shows. This perhaps explains why Cohan does not have the men sing one of his own patriotic tunes. He was not shy about plugging his work, but having "You're a Grand Old Flag" sung in this context would cheapen it.

Calling attention to patriotism and song as merely commercial strategies for winning people over—one of the very things Cohan had been accused of in the past—would undermine Cohan's vision of American patriotism were it not for Wallingford's about-face in the end of the show. With his

Figure 3.6 "Dear Old Pals" from Rodeheaver's Sociability Songs. *Published by Rodeheaver (1928).*

decision to lead a straight life, however, both Americanism and business are redeemed. The show's climax comes in the third act, when Wallingford and Blackie are about to have to leave town and the two women they have fallen in love with, but they get a buyout offer from a real businessman offering them "a legitimate fortune."[102] Conflict resolved and couples united, the show could end—but it does not.

A fourth act serves as a paean to industrial development and capitalism.[103] It opens with ragtime being played on the piano at a party at Wallingford's residence. Together with a trolley car effect in the background, it sets a scene of modernity, city life brought to rural Iowa. New technologies had previously been unusual in Battlesburg—a telegram sent to Blackie's sweetheart's house is the first to come there in years—but now they have automobiles, a taxi company, the "best traction line in the western country."[104] A detective who knew Wallingford and Blackie in their days as crooks has come to see whether the rumors of their going legitimate and making millions are true. It is. With Lamb as general manager, they have consolidated, buying out the Eureka Tack Company, and they control the US tack business. It is not enough for Wallingford and Blackie to have millions, though; countering concerns about the concentration of wealth in a few hands, which Cohan himself had expressed elsewhere, they point to how the wealth has spread. "There's the proof," Wallingford says, pointing to the town in the distance. "The most prosperous town in the Middle West," and, Blackie adds, "They've all got coin." In a nod to New York theater, Harkins, a former newspaperman who bought a small theater with his newfound money, reveals that it has been upgraded from the Bijou Theatre, with moving pictures and illustrated songs, to the Wallingford Opera House, which gets "all the leading shows" straight from the top Broadway producers.[105] The play includes the moral that a man is a "damn fool . . . for being a crook," but, as this scene shows, honest capitalism is a shining success, the mechanism for building cities of dreams, replete with fine entertainment. As the revelers say goodnight, men from the tack company emerge from the house singing the company song, the music of the "regular fellow" businessmen transforming the nation.

On stage, Cohan could depict national anxieties about capitalism with humor and put forth a vision of shared, transformative prosperity, in which rural and urban, lower and upper classes, labor and capital alike had a happy ending—or could be written out of the story. In real life, however, reconciling competing interests proved to be more challenging. In 1919, any remaining ambivalence melted; when a theatrical battle between capital and labor ensued, Cohan took the side of capital.

Figure 1.8 Cover of "You're a Grand Old Flag." Published by F. A. Mills (1906). UT Sheet Music Collection, University of Tennessee Libraries, Knoxville, Special Collections.

Figure 4.2 Cover of "Nellie Kelly I Love You." Published by M. Witmark and Sons (1922). York University Libraries, Clara Thomas Archives and Special Collections, John Arpin Collection, JAC004811.

Figure 4.3 *Cover of "Born and Bred in Brooklyn." Published by M. Witmark and Sons (1923). Courtesy of the Levy Collection.*

Figure 4.4 Little Nellie Kelly *flyer. Theater Biography Collection, Harry Ransom Center, University of Texas at Austin.*

Figure 4.8 Cover of "Molly Malone." Published by M. Witmark and Sons (1927). Vocal Popular Sheet Music, Maine Music Box Collection.

Figure 5.6 Back Cover of the Spot Light, *July 4, 1906. Eda Kuhn Loeb Music Library, Harvard University.*

Figure 5.9 Cover of "For the Flag, For the Home, For the Family (For the Future of All Mankind)." Published by Vogel Music (1942). Theater Biography Collection, Harry Ransom Center, The University of Texas at Austin.

COHAN THE ACTOR-MANAGER BECOMES COHAN THE SCAB: THE ACTORS' EQUITY ASSOCIATION STRIKE OF 1919

In early August 1919, Cohan's *The Royal Vagabond* was playing at the Cohan and Harris theater in New York. A big success, the show had been running for about half a year. It was a spoof of *opéra comique*, with the kind of pervasive metatheatricality that had become a Cohan specialty and a story about a revolution to overthrow the monarchy in the exotic land of Bargravia. Outside, a real-life revolution was being staged. On August 6, 1919, the members of the Actors' Equity Association ("Equity") voted to strike any manager in the Producing Managers' Association (PMA), of which Cohan was a member and Harris was president, "or who refuses to recognize our association or issue its contract."[106] Twelve productions were shut down the following day. A few years earlier, before Equity was a union, Cohan and Harris seemed to be among the managers open to negotiations.[107] As a star actor as well as a manager, moreover, Cohan could have been expected to be one of the most sympathetic of the producers. By the end of the strike, however, Cohan had become the public face and voice of the opposition.

Cohan's public writings bear out that as his duties and clout as a Broadway producer had grown, his perspective shifted. He performed less and talked about retiring from acting. "The actor" became someone with a third-person, rather than first-person, pronoun. In a 1910 *Saturday Evening Post* piece called "The Actor as a Business Man," Cohan described the actor's "superstition" that the businessman is always trying to get the better of him and his assumption that the manager is richer than he is. "But when the actor becomes a manager," Cohan added, "he soon forgets that he has ever been an actor—and if he has been the loudest in his abuse of owners he now becomes the most exacting in his treatment of actors."[108] Cohan left unstated whether he was reflecting upon his own experiences, but he had clearly come to understand and identify with the concerns of the manager. In 1917, Cohan put this idea into a humorous song called "Since I Became a Manager," an interpolated number performed by Raymond Hitchcock in the revue *Hitchy-Koo*, Hitchcock's first effort as a producer. The song, *Variety* reported, "related how since becoming a manager, Hitchcock, as an actor, would never roast a manager again. The song probably expressed Mr. Cohan's feelings in the matter as fully as it did Mr. Hitchcock's and it must have been an easy lyric for Cohan to write."[109]

The 1919 strike was simultaneously improbable and had been in the making for some time. The mistreatment of actors was not new. The conditions that Equity sought to address in its proposed standard contract—like actors having to pay their transportation to and from New York to a tour's opening and closing, to rehearse shows without compensation, and (for performers who were not stars) to purchase their own costumes—were long-standing, and if anything, the actors' plight had improved under the centralization that occurred with the rise of the Syndicate.[110] Moreover, despite labor unrest and organizing being common at the time—strikes or unions were among the current-day topics mentioned in Cohan's shows, and there were many strikes in summer 1919 alone—actors were hesitant to pursue collective action, which they associated largely with the industrial working class. Equity asserted upon its formation in 1913 that it was not a labor union. However, it warned that it may need to become one in the unlikely event of "flagrant injustice on the part of managers."[111]

The impetus for Equity, then, was a combination of factors: for the typical actor, economic problems; and for better-positioned stars, a loss of power in the shifting economic structures and a general sense of decline and overcommercialization of the theater.[112] The managers, hardly a united or even a collegial group, were uncoordinated and uneven in their response to actors' demands. Over years of being unable to settle upon and enforce a standard contract, Equity became less resistant to the idea of unionization and affiliated with the American Federation of Labor (AFL). In discussions with the new PMA in May 1919, they "abandon[ed] the politics of conciliation," as historian Sean P. Holmes puts it, and demanded a closed-shop agreement, which would allow for employment of Equity actors only. When negotiations broke down, they did the previously unthinkable: they called for a strike.[113]

Cohan was placed in an unenviable position. The actors' strike made it untenable for Cohan to fully hold identities as both an actor and manager, a "regular fellow" and a mogul—not least in the eyes of many of his fellow theater professionals. His decision to oppose Equity and the closed shop, however, was swift and his stance unyielding. As one author expressed it, Cohan the manager turned on Cohan the actor.[114]

Leading up to the strike, discussions between Equity and the PMA had been going poorly, and Cohan satirized the situation in sketches for Lamb's Club Gambols held in May and June 1919. At that point, the situation could still elicit chuckles—the entertainment newspaper the *New York Clipper* reported audience members' delight at each—but the sketches also give a glimpse into how Cohan viewed the dispute and the impasse setting in.[115] "Actors and Managers Dinner," performed at the May event, shows Equity leader Francis Wilson and a group of unnamed Equity members meeting with several major managers, most played by actors but a few, including Sam Harris and, undoubtedly, Cohan, played by themselves. In it, Cohan paints the managers and actors alike as petty and ridiculous; the sketch ends with a free-for-all fight that even the policemen and firemen who have come to investigate end up joining. The managers are competitive and bicker amongst themselves, and the actors, represented by Equity leader Francis Wilson, are unreasonable, with outlandish demands and no interest in compromise, as evident in this bit:

KLAW. Then here's another preposition. Suppose we give you Christmas and New Year's weeks for vacation purposes and cut out the Thanksgiving matinees and guarantee you 52 weeks work every six months. Would you then be willing to play an extra matinee on Good Friday?

WILSON. Boys, will you play an extra matinee on Good Friday?

ALL. No, no, no!

WILSON. Good! You see, Mr. Chairman, the boys are anxious to do anything they can to help you out.

Harris offers the most generous and preposterous proposition: "Suppose we agree to make the productions and stand all losses and turn over 85% of the profits to the Actors Equity, would you gentlemen be willing to divide these profits with the Salvation Army if we agree to cut out all rehearsals, pay for your costumes and give you four weeks' extra salary the last Saturday night of the season?"[116] It is also refused.

In the sketch, Cohan acknowledged and poked fun at his unusual and uneasy position. "Come on, everything's all right. You've got just as much right here as any of the other managers," Harris coaxes Cohan as they enter. But Cohan responds that he's "not a regular manager." Harris reassures him that he is a regular manager, a good one at that, and a great actor as well, but then, as an aside, says that stroking Cohan's ego is "the only way I can get along with him. I have to bull hell out of him to keep him from raising his royalties," reminding the audience of Cohan's third role, as creator of the content they stage.[117] While Cohan was comfortable enough in his relationship with Harris to joke about it, he was also clearly aware of the way his multiple positions meant that he did not quite fit with the other Broadway businessmen.

The sketch also points to the way that negotiations between Equity and theatrical producers were theatricalized, in the lead up to the strike and even more once it began. Unlike for other organizing workers, the actors *were* the commodity they were producing. That fact made the strike challenging, but it also served as their chief advantage.[118] Picketers ad libbed for bystanders, and the *Times* reported, "There never has been a strike in which picketing was done with such style."[119] They made the strike theater, earning audiences' sympathy.

But as an actor himself and a shrewd advertiser and self-promoter, Cohan—and the Cohan and Harris company—employed the same strategy to try to counter the striking actors. Cohan created good theater out of the event even in his autobiography, published years later, recounting that he had just started out on a vacation but rushed back upon hearing the news of the strike from Harris.[120] Whether or not this was the case, the strike should not have taken him by surprise; in fact, the PMA had named Cohan to an emergency committee to "protect the interests of actors and managers" only a few days before.[121]

When *The Royal Vagabond* at the Cohan and Harris Theater was delivered a strike notice, Sam Harris was reported, by various accounts, to have either struck or thrown out by the collar the deliverer Harry Lambart.[122] That evening, a crowded house sat waiting until 9:00 p.m. until, in what one paper called "the most dramatic happening of the evening," Sam Forrest, stage director for the firm, and Harris appeared; Forrest said, "In calling this strike the actors did not take into consideration these boys and girls of the chorus, nor did they consider the inconvenience of the public. The striking actors are all players receiving two or three hundred dollars a week. They have no grievance against this management. We have played fair." Then Forrest reportedly turned to the chorus, asking, "Have you any grievance?," to which chorus members shouted "No!" He asked if they had always been treated fairly by the management, and was answered by cries of "Yes!"[123] Equity had not originally included chorus members in its organization. It would add a Chorus Equity Association, but in the meantime, they were available to step into vacated roles.

The following evening, *The Royal Vagabond* reopened. Cohan claims to have entered the theater that morning to find the stage director James Gorman rehearsing with a cast that now included many newly promoted understudies and chorus members, at which point, realizing they were still short of covering the parts, he joined Sam Forrest in jumping into the show.[124] The *New York Times* reported that despite not knowing all the lines, Cohan "walked away with the honors of a hilarious evening," holding to the script and reading lines even while "taking running jumps at the proscenium arch."[125] At some point in his fill-in run, he substituted new lyrics to rib his opponents—from the reporter's recollection, "In a kingdom of our own, /

We're going to sit upon a throne, / With a prince and princess on our knee— / And they won't be members of the Equity."[126] He also used the stage and the spotlight it offered in his role as a manager. He delivered a speech from the stage, saying somewhat paternalistically, and very much in line with anti-union discourse of the time, that he aimed to "deliver the actor from the agitators under whose influence he has fallen."[127] Not every manager could step in, steal the show, and keep a full house each night; to the actors of Equity, Cohan was not just a manager refusing their demands, he was also a scab, betraying the cause.

Cohan's status as star actor as well as manager made him a lightning rod from the outset. On August 1, in Equity's first meeting since affiliating with the AFL, James William Fitzpatrick of the White Rats Actors' Union of America (which was merged with Equity in the AFL under a new umbrella organization) reported a mysterious omen at the former White Rats clubhouse: a "large, beautiful picture" of Mr. Cohan, "without a single bit of outside influence brought to bear . . . fell from the wall and was smashed into a thousand pieces." *Billboard* noted that Cohan "came in for more criticism in one afternoon than has been leveled at him in all of his previous life."[128] Picketers sang a parody of "Over There" with the lyrics "Over fair, over fair / We have been, we have been over fair."[129] When Cohan said that he would run an elevator before doing business with Equity, a sign famously appeared in a window in response:

WANTED
ELEVATOR OPERATOR
GEORGE M. COHAN
PREFERRED[130]

Eddie Cantor quipped, "Somebody'd better tell Mr. Cohan that to run an elevator he'd *have* to join a union."[131] Equity leader Francis Wilson singled him out in a letter, printed in *Variety*, pleading with him to recognize Equity in line with the "*real* George Cohan."[132] Instead, Cohan resigned from the PMA and became president of the rival organization or "company union" the Actors' Fidelity League, making him even more of a target of strikers' ire. Fidelity (which Equity nicknamed "Fido") declined the $100,000 Cohan offered. Still, to Equity actors, it was as if Cohan thought he could simply reclaim his performer hat to ostensibly represent their cause while funding the group seen as the opposition from a manager's coffers.[133]

The strike had become as bitterly personal as it was ideological, cementing Cohan's hostility toward Equity and its members. Members of theatrical clubs, friends, and even relatives were divided; Cohan's brother-in-law

Fred Niblo, though in Hollywood at that point, was among the members of Equity.[134] Cohan's daughter Mary recounted later that Cohan's car was followed, shots were fired at their house once, and her father hired guards to protect the family.[135] A *Variety* writer penned an article in Cohan's defense, claiming that until the strike, Cohan had been on a pedestal in the theatrical community. "Why pick Cohan?" he asked. "The only one of the mob who is on the other side of the fence who ever really did something for the actor. Why not take a slam at Belasco, Al Woods, the Shuberts or some of the other eggs you are battling."[136] Those other eggs, however, had not confused their roles in the unfolding drama.

David eventually won out against Goliath. But even after other managers, including Harris, accepted defeat and acceded to the strikers' demands, Cohan continued to be a vehement detractor of Equity and the "closed shop." This is one of the many seemingly paradoxical things about Cohan. After all, he was an actor himself, one who had come up through the ranks and had experienced many of the bad conditions Equity sought to quell. He had a reputation for treating his employees well, at least comparatively speaking, and for generosity within the theatrical community.[137] When he became president of Fidelity, he promised to see "that the actor is not only given a square deal by the manager but a squarer deal than the Equity Association ever dreamed of getting for him or could ever hope to obtain," and the contract that Fidelity drew up—and for which Cohan sought to take full credit in an impassioned open letter "To All Members of the Acting Profession"—included the majority of the provisions Equity had demanded and, according to Cohan, more.[138]

Cohan's anti-Equity stance and extreme reaction undoubtedly reflected a number of factors. He may have had some lingering resentment from when a strike by the White Rats vaudeville performers union nearly derailed the opening performance of his first Broadway show in 1901 or from frustrating encounters with the already-unionized stagehands or musicians thereafter.[139] As a manager—and moreover one who was frequently also director, star, and, for other playwrights' work, "play doctor"—he was accustomed to having a great deal of authority and control, and he may have felt the stipulations of the Equity contract burdensome. More than that, he likely felt them unnecessary or unseemly in show business as he liked to envision it—an idealized, largely bygone world of direct commitments between employer and employee in which one's word was one's bond. "We all know what we want," he told the press, "a return to the old days," with "friendly relations with our managers and our associates, and . . . no weapons over our heads."[140] As he intimated earlier in "The Actor as a Business Man," he also felt that the actors underestimated the skill and knowledge of the manager. The members of the Equity council "imagine that they can run the business end of the theatre; that the showman, the business man, is in no way needed," he wrote in a Fidelity publication in 1920.[141] As Sam Harris put it coercively and perhaps with a grain of truth, they objected not to the actor and his demands but to Equity's methods and leadership, whom Cohan, at least privately, deemed "radicals."[142] Both reacted most strongly to the threat of the closed shop, which Cohan claimed was an affront to individuality and personal liberty.[143]

Cohan also found Equity as hypocritical as they found him. To him, the fact that chorus members, who were often considered lesser than other actors, were not initially included was an indication of Equity's true values. He wrote in a Fidelity publication in 1920, "All the wild talk about the 'Big fellows' fighting for the 'Little fellows' was a lie. If the big fellows had any feeling at all for the little fellows, why did they walk out of the Cohan & Harris Theatre in New York without even saying [g]ood-bye to the forty-odd chorus girls and boys who were playing in 'The Royal Vagabond'?"[144] (Chorus members were not the only group left out: Black actor Bert Williams went to the theater and dressed as usual; despite his star status, no one had told him about the strike.[145]) Cohan made the same point in his autobiography. As with Cohan's public rhetoric on many topics, it is difficult to untangle his own feelings and reasoning from what he felt would be persuasive in the court of public opinion; still, it is reasonable to assume that these comments spoke at least to some extent to both.

Last but not least, Cohan's treatment during the strike seemed to threaten his sense of identity as a member of the theatrical community and as a very powerful man who was also a "regular fellow." He resigned from the Lambs and Friars' theatrical social clubs because he felt he was being pilloried there, in the communities and physical spaces that most symbolized these identities. When he was asked to reconsider, he stated, in a speech printed in multiple newspapers across the United States, "You are too late. I am in the fight to a finish and whatever the results, I will leave with my manhood."[146] It did not help that Cohan was notoriously stubborn. Equity became *the* union representing stage actors and professional theater, on and beyond Broadway, but although Cohan went on to act again, he never became a member of Equity. He would remark, biographer Ward Morehouse noted, that he was "the only scab on Broadway."[147] While Cohan was able to work without an Equity card, the battle tarnished his career and his reputation. For someone who sought to so carefully manage public images of himself, Cohan was unable and unwilling to erase the image of himself as Broadway scab.

* * *

Understanding Cohan's role as a Broadway businessman, in tandem with his other work, not only furthers our knowledge of the early twentieth-century theater industry but also is critical to understanding his shows, his unique position in the actors' strike of 1919, and his legacy. Strategically navigating a shifting theater industry, Cohan remarkably managed to become a leading producer as well as a leading creative figure and performer, a financial force on Broadway as well as an artistic one. Together, Cohan and Harris savvily worked with the Syndicate and emerged as leaders and power brokers in their own right. Their story complicates the common historical narrative that has focused on the Syndicate versus the opposition, first and foremost the Shuberts.[148] They courted the businessman as an audience member and portrayed him onstage, helping to shape the shifting and contested notions of capitalism and masculinity. The balance of Cohan's roles was changing, away from acting and toward work as a producer. The actors' strike of 1919, however, forced Cohan's hand: he touted his position as actor, stepping into *The Royal Vagabond* and leading a competing actors' union, while keeping the sensibility of a manager.

In the wake of the strike, Cohan and Harris amicably parted ways, both ideologically and in their business partnership. In the short term, Harris pragmatically continued in his role as president of the PMA, which was no less challenging after the strike had ended, aiding in "building up the Association to the place it must occupy" and cajoling managers who had a willfully different interpretation of or refused to follow Equity contracts.[149] Cohan, president of Fidelity until May 1920, continued the fight against Equity's closed shop and for what he described as "his right as an American citizen, the right to live as he sees fit, under the law."[150] As his career took a sharp turn and as new trends eclipsed his once cutting-edge style of theater, he would mine a different aspect of his identity, as an Irish American, and the power of a different sort, as a celebrity, to sustain his work.

THE IRISH AMERICAN

> For the last 25 years of his life George M. Cohan ordered his press agent . . . to send every Cohan song to [the operetta composer] Franz Lehar. . . . Lehar wrote him that he thought "Over There" was "pretty good" but that his favorite was "H-a-double r-i-g-a-n Spells Harrigan." . . . "I often wish," wrote Lehar, "that I could express my sentiments for Vienna as lovely as you do for Ireland." . . . "Thanks, but forgive me for disagreeing," replied Cohan. "You belong to the world and I only to Broadway—the long green side of the street."
>
> —Leonard Lyons, newspaper column (1948)

Premiered only two years apart, in 1916 and 1918, George M. Cohan's sister songs "You Can Tell That I'm Irish" and "You Can't Deny You're Irish" offer the same ambivalent sentiment, each to a lilting waltz: no matter how an Irishman may try to hide it, his Irishness shows through.[1] The name ("Mac something or other"), accent ("touch of the brogue"), mannerisms ("swing of the walk" and "wink of the rogue"), and physical features ("eyes," "cheeks so red," and "cute little turn of [the] nose") all give it away.[2] By the time of these two songs, Cohan had achieved fame as a flag-waving patriot, playwright, songwriter, performer, and Broadway magnate. Now his Irishness, long sidelined, seemed to burst through.

As we have seen, George M. Cohan was well versed in various racial theatrical stereotypes, including the range of representations of the Irish seen in various genres of nineteenth-century stage entertainment. In his youth, touring with the Four Cohans, he performed Irish reels, waltz clogs, and his specialty Lively Bootblack skit, and as he began writing his own material, Irish works were a popular subgenre and a path clearly open to him.[3] As was typical of vaudeville, Cohan relied heavily upon ethnic stereotypes for comedic purposes, including in the Irish comic song "Hugh McCue (You -

Yankee Doodle Dandy. Elizabeth T. Craft, Oxford University Press. © Oxford University Press 2024.
DOI: 10.1093/oso/9780197550403.003.0005

Mick - You)" (1896) written for Maggie Cline and sketches like "The Dangerous Mrs. Delaney" (1898) performed by the Elinore sisters, and "Hogan of the Hansom" (1899), performed by Walter Le Roy and Florence Clayton. They featured stereotypical characters like the "pugilist" Hugh McCue; the newly wealthy, uncouth Mrs. Delaney and her more proper daughter; and Hogan, the Irish hansom driver who "loike[s] fish on Froiday" and speaks in an "oily brogue."[4] And in 1905, Cohan published "The Irish American," a march and two-step. Yet these pieces, primarily written just as he was starting out and intended for other artists, were the exceptions that proved the rule. On the whole, Cohan's early Broadway shows included a small number of Irish characters relegated to supporting, comic roles who were portrayed positively but tended to be played by actors other than members of the Four Cohans. With great care and savvy, Cohan cast himself as a paragon of mainstream America.

In the mid-1910s, however, he became more outwardly invested in Irish American politics and culture in his personal life and took a somewhat abrupt, if not entirely unprecedented, turn in his theatrical work to musicals brimming with Irish American pride. During the late nineteenth and early twentieth centuries, the Irish in the United States had made some headway in economic, social, and political terms. But World War I led many to question so-called hyphenated Americans' loyalties, and the postwar period brought a resurgence of nativism and anti-Catholicism. Around this time, from 1918 to 1927, Cohan wrote a spate of Irish American–themed shows—*The Voice of McConnell* (1918), *Little Nellie Kelly* (1922), *The Rise of Rosie O'Reilly* (1923), and *The Merry Malones* (1927)—works that kept his career afloat as his earlier brand of theater began to go out of style even as they worked through contemporary issues facing Irish Americans in the United States. In the last of his Irish American–themed musicals, *The Merry Malones*, Cohan played an Irish American character for the first time—a significant departure from his earlier hyper-American roles.

These shows attracted some criticism at the time for their formulaic nature, and scholars, following suit, have tended to dismiss these musicals as derivative or to give them only a passing glance.[5] Indeed, with *The Voice of McConnell*, Cohan capitalized on its well-known star, Chauncey Olcott, and the vogue of the Irish tenor; and with *Little Nellie Kelly*, *The Rise of Rosie O'Reilly*, and *The Merry Malones*, he rode the wave of Cinderella tales. The songs from these shows, historian William H. A. Williams wrote in his book on images of Ireland and the Irish in popular song, "failed to break new ground, and they arrived just at the point when the Irish genre of popular songs had passed its peak."[6]

Yet Cohan put his own stamp on each formula, and several of the shows had strong reviews, long runs, or both. Moreover, as he had already defined and, for many, embodied what it meant to be a patriotic American, Cohan was particularly well positioned to write the Irish more fully into that definition. His advocacy for the Irish within his shows frequently came at the expense of other groups whom he depicted more negatively. His Irish American heroes and heroines, meanwhile, sang, danced, and married their way to full acceptance in US society.

COHAN THE IRISHMAN: NEGOTIATING THE POLITICS OF EARLY TWENTIETH-CENTURY IRISH AMERICA

By the turn of the twentieth century, the Irish in the United States included approximately 1.6 million Irish-born, 3.4 million second-generation, and uncounted multitudes of third-, fourth- and subsequent-generation Irish Americans among the total US population of 76 million.[7] Although hardly a homogeneous bunch, as a diasporic population Irish Americans occupied a moment in which full social acceptance and participation in national life seemed within reach, yet most still felt a strong sense of Irish identity.[8] Many, especially among the growing numbers of American-born Irish, began to gain access to white-collar occupations and to enter the ranks of the middle and even upper classes. They sought respectability as well as economic gain, and the designation "lace curtain Irish" arose to describe newly middle class social climbers.[9] As Irish Americans gained clout, the worst stereotypes of them began to recede, helped by the activism of Irish groups like the Ancient Order of Hibernians, who "declare[d] war" on the "Irish comedian" in the early years of the twentieth century.[10] Prejudice toward the Irish and anxiety about their influence did not entirely dissipate; however, the Irish began to improve by comparison in the public eye as new groups from southern and eastern Europe, who were perceived as even less-desirable Americans, outnumbered the Irish among new immigrants.

Still, Irish Americans were not fully accepted by the so-called old stock, and in the mid-1910s, Irish nationalism and World War I tested Irish Americans' loyalties.[11] The movement for independence in British-ruled Ireland had long drawn Irish American support, and events in 1916 roused nationalistic sentiment anew. When the Irish Republican Brotherhood, having obtained arms from Germany with the aid of a small group of supporters in the United States, seized several buildings in Dublin and declared the establishment of the Irish Republic, it received front-page coverage in the *New York Times* for two weeks.[12] The British forces ultimately prevailed, but the harsh government response, which included martial law and executions of leaders of the uprising, engendered sympathy for the nationalist cause on both sides of the Atlantic. "In the wake of the insurrection," historian Kevin Kenny explains, "Irish-American nationalism became a mass movement for the first time since the 1880s."[13]

Irish American support for the Irish revolutionaries was highly charged during this period.[14] Even before the United States entered it, World War I spurred questions about ethnic Americans' allegiances, especially with a small group of German and Irish Americans pressuring the government to uphold true neutrality and cease partiality toward the British. Historian Thomas J. Rowland notes that 1915 to 1916 represented the height of the Wilson administration's campaign "to purge the 'hyphen' in American society."[15] "Anti-hyphenism"—the desire for immigrants' complete assimilation and demand for their total loyalty—was not new (see the discussion of Theodore Roosevelt's rhetoric on immigration in Chapter 1). It took on new vehemence in the context of war, though, with Irish Americans joining German Americans as a target. President Woodrow Wilson warned in his 1915 address to Congress, "There are citizens of the United States, I blush to admit, born under other flags but welcomed under our generous naturalization laws to the full freedom and opportunity of America, who have poured the poison of disloyalty into the very arteries of our national life."[16] At a 1916 "Irish race convention," which led to the establishment of a new organization called the Friends of Irish Freedom, speakers strove to walk the line, perceived now to be a divisive one, between American patriotism and Irish nationalism. One orator, a first-generation immigrant from New England, expressed pride that he was American by choice rather than by birth, asserting that "Americanism is not a question of birth. It is a question of psychology." Another speaker insisted, "I am no less an American because I love the land that gave me birth."[17]

When the United States entered World War I in 1917, Irish American organizations seized the chance to demonstrate their loyalty and good citizenship by actively supporting the war.[18] Cohan proved a model patriot. He wrote the popular war song "Over There." He hosted and performed in war benefits, served refreshments to men in uniform at the Knights of Columbus service station in Times Square, and helped send entertainment to soldiers abroad as the president of the Over There Theater League. And he acted in the Red Cross benefit tour of the play *Out There*, playing an American soldier alongside Chauncey Olcott's Irish soldier—which, incidentally, reveals how quintessentially American Cohan was perceived to be.[19]

Despite their wartime efforts to prove allegiance, Irish Americans faced increased prejudice after the war.[20] A revived, reorganized Ku Klux Klan targeted Jewish and Catholic as well as Black Americans. Some states sought to close Catholic schools, and increased support for immigration restrictions—including from President Coolidge, who declared, "America must be kept American"—culminated in the Johnson-Reed Act of 1924, which curbed immigration and privileged northern and western European immigrants by setting annual quotas based on the dubious logic and contrived calculations of the current population's "national origins."[21]

Anti-immigrant rhetoric and the broader upswing in anti-Irish and anti-Catholic sentiment elicited a unified defense by Irish Catholics.[22] By the 1920s, Irish and Catholic Americans (heavily overlapping groups) were not without political recourse. Irish groups banded with Germans and Scandinavians—considered more established, "White" immigrant populations—to protest when national origin quotas were announced in 1927, and the renewed anti-Catholicism of the 1920s prompted an organized response from the church leadership and its members.[23] As historian Lynn Dumenil has shown, a subset of American Catholics—those who were upwardly mobile, English speaking, and seen as more assimilated—exercised considerable agency, emphatically denouncing anti-Catholicism and employing organized activism to battle in a "war over the right to define what it meant to be American."[24]

Cohan's stance in this "war" was cautious and more concerned with cultural than political nationalism.[25] In his early career in the 1900s and early 1910s, Cohan appears to have steered clear of Irish American and Catholic associations and politics, with the exception of the Catholic Actors' Guild, which was founded in 1914 and of which his father Jerry was the first vice president.[26] He did not intercede in Irish nationalist affairs. In contrast to composer Victor Herbert, for example, who became president of the newly organized Friends of Irish Freedom in 1916, Cohan's name does not show up among the leadership of such organizations or even on attendance lists.[27] This is not surprising: Irish Americans' senses of identity, including their perceived affinities with Ireland and interest in the movement for Irish home rule, varied widely. As historian William M. Leary Jr. notes, "To some Irish Americans, although they were born abroad, affairs in Ireland meant little; to others, although they were third-generation Americans . . . these affairs meant everything."[28] Moreover, to identify closely with Irish organizations, and Irish nationalist groups in particular, would have countered the all-American image Cohan was creating for himself as he established his career.

Yet in the mid- to late 1910s and 1920s, Cohan became more involved in Irish and Catholic organizations, and he seemed to become more invested in Irish American politics and culture. Characteristic of Cohan, when he spoke about Irish nationalism in public, it was tongue-in-cheek: asked in 1921 about what he would do after retiring (one of many planned retirements), Cohan joked that he "might go over to Ireland and free it."[29] His name was linked to Irish nationalism through events held in theaters bearing his name, however: one of the meetings of the so-called Irish race convention of March 1916 was held in the George M. Cohan Theatre in New York City's Times Square, and following the Easter Rising that April, sympathizers again found a home in the Cohan Theatre in New York as well as at Cohan's Grand Opera House in Chicago.[30] While it is unclear whether he actually had any role in authorizing the theaters' use, many would have perceived that he did.[31] In fact, the *Gaelic American* later reported in its obituary of Cohan about the "historic meeting" of the Irish Race Convention, claiming that the theater "was turned over to them by the greatest actor, producer and composer America has ever known."[32]

More significantly, in the early twenties Cohan helped form the American Committee for Relief in Ireland, organized to combat suffering and starvation, and performed in a benefit for the cause. This organization was an apolitical humanitarian effort, one endorsed by President Harding and Vice President Coolidge, and Cohan's role in the Committee and its benefit was noted in Irish American newspapers as well as the major New York papers.[33] And in 1925—the year after the Johnson-Reed Immigration Act—he joined the well-established American Irish Historical Society, whose goal it was "to make better known the Irish Chapter in American History" and who protested the national origins quotas.[34] Perhaps, one might speculate, the Immigration Act of 1924 spurred Cohan's further alliance with Irish and Irish American interests, or maybe the process of writing his autobiography, published a year later, spurred a deeper interest in his own roots. He may have also been seeking new social and professional affiliations after the fallout from losing his well-publicized battle against the Actors' Equity Association. While Cohan's feelings on these matters are impossible to document, his affiliations demonstrate clear choices to express Irish American identity, primarily through politically moderate, socially sanctioned organizations. That the content of Cohan's work shifted toward Irish American themes around the same time hardly seems coincidental.

Of course, Cohan's motivations were never fully political or social. The shift in his shows' subject matter should also be understood in light of a changing Broadway, with new modes of business and aesthetics that put Cohan increasingly at risk of becoming hopelessly old-fashioned, with profits at risk. Taking up Irish American characters and themes may have seemed, in part, a new route to commercial success in an era that saw the tremendous popularity of certain Irish stars and shows with Irish American heroines. Still, cultural products considered to be Irish had to negotiate the politics of representing an Irish America that, although flourishing in some ways, was embattled in others, and that—on the whole—was not yet seen as equal in standing as American citizens. In three of Cohan's four Irish American shows (*Little Nellie Kelly* of 1922, *The Rise of Rosie O'Reilly* of 1923, and *The Merry Malones* of 1927), Cohan told of Irish American lasses climbing to higher social echelons through virtue, romance, and good fortune. In his play with music *The Voice of McConnell* of 1918, the hero to be integrated into respectable American society is male, newly arrived, and an Irish tenor to boot.

HEAVENLY VOICE, REGULAR GUY: *THE VOICE OF MCCONNELL*

The Voice of McConnell opened at the Manhattan Opera House on Christmas 1918 to highly favorable reviews. It told the story of the meteoric rise of a fictionalized Irish tenor unmistakably meant to evoke the celebrated John McCormack, who was "a mega-superstar in the days before we knew about mega-superstars" as music commentator Miles Hoffman put it.[35] McCormack successfully crossed boundaries of genre and audience as a singer of opera and Irish ballads, and he became an American citizen in 1919, in the months after Cohan's show closed. Chauncey Olcott, who played the McCormack-inspired character Tom McConnell, was a popular Irish tenor and actor in his own right, known for performing Irish heroes in romantic melodramas featuring a handful of sentimental songs. Both the subject and star, therefore, were apt choices for a musical presumably designed to attract both more "mainstream" Broadway theatergoers and Olcott's more heavily Irish following.[36] In the show, McConnell achieves acceptance as an American through his down-to-earth masculinity and heavenly voice as well as his romance with an Irish American member of the social elite, the vivacious young heiress Evelyn McNamara. The storyline allowed Cohan to capitalize on Olcott's and McCormack's well-established reputations while also showcasing three newly composed Irish-themed songs.[37] The show merged aspects of the star Chauncey Olcott's usual melodramatic fare with the snappier musical comedy style of Cohan as playwright and composer, and critics hailed it for its novel mixture of Irish and American elements.

Cohan Americanizes the McConnell character largely through contemporary gender discourse, specifically Cohan's "regular guy" model of American masculinity. In *The Voice of McConnell*, it is McConnell's regular-guy attributes that mark him as fittingly American even as he is immanently Irish. The first twelve pages of *The Voice of McConnell*'s script are dedicated almost entirely to establishing Tom McConnell's manliness, his so-called regularness, and his discomfort with fame and its trappings. McConnell doesn't want a valet and tries repeatedly to get rid of the one assigned to him. He has no use for the robe he is asked to wear, which makes him "feel like a fairy queen in a comic opera," or the flowers bestowed upon him. "If there's anything I hate on top of the Lord's green earth it's to see a man receiving flowers," he exclaims.[38] Cohan gets in a gibe at a rival genre, the purportedly fantastical and feminine "comic opera," while characterizing McConnell as a manly, no-frills fellow. At another point, McConnell laughingly remarks, "'Tis like a king I am sitting here with me meals served in this palatial room. . . . By gad, I'd look more natural at a lunch counter behind a beef stew." McConnell is depicted as a recognizable, likeable Horatio Alger–style everyman—if he can strike it rich in the United States with his preference for beef stew over room service, so can anyone.

Even as McConnell is depicted as an American-style regular guy, his name, dialect, and mannerisms declare him to be unmistakably Irish. His brogue and witty repartee emphasize his Irishness while also ingratiating the character to the audience and providing material for jokes. When record executives court him, for example, he is ready to sign with the first, a Mr. Jackson from the American Phonographic Company, until learning that the competitor's name is Sullivan. "I don't know but what I'd give Sullivan a lot of consideration at that. This other fellow doesn't impress me very much," McConnell says, displaying his Irish affinity as he reassesses the situation.[39] When he asks a visiting reporter to talk to "his impresario" while he steps out for a few minutes, he adds, "He'll give you a much better story than I could. Sure, I never told a lie in me life." One can imagine Olcott delivering this quip on the stereotype of Irish blarney with a mischievous, tongue-in-cheek inflection, and he laughs along at his own joke. And in case the affectionate teasing was too subtle, the script of *The Voice of McConnell* also celebrates the Irish outright, declaring them "wonderful people!"

Like Americanness in Cohan's early, patriotic musicals, Irishness is celebrated in *The Voice of McConnell* through jokes, banter, and song but defined largely by its Others—by what, and who, it is not. It is not, for example, Protestant. For McConnell, and most likely for his creator, Cohan, Irishness denotes Catholicism. In an early scene, McConnell admonishes his valet

Hendricks for ordering an orange for his breakfast. "Don't you like the taste of orange, sir?" Hendricks asks. "It isn't the taste, it's the color of the damn thing I can't stand." McConnell replies. The ham and eggs served to him "on a Friday!" are sent away in another fit.[40]

If Cohan hints at an internal Protestant–Catholic rivalry among the Irish, he trumpets tensions with other ethnic and national groups. In Act II, McConnell learns that not everyone is "quite ready to hail [him] as a great singer," especially the envious Italian opera singers. "Italians, is it!" he responds. "Ah, sure those foreigners have no use for an Irishman at all, at all," and everyone onstage laughs.[41] This may have obliquely referenced the "friendly rivalry" said to have existed between John McCormack and Enrico Caruso, but even more revealing is the joke's commentary on foreignness.[42] The punch line cleverly acknowledges McConnell's own outsider status in a tongue-in-cheek manner while facetiously setting a firmer boundary between the Italians (who remain absent onstage) as "foreigners" and the Irishman as something else. Cohan thus removes the designation of foreigner from McConnell and bestows him with some kind of companionable, if not equal, status with the insider group of Anglo-Americans.

Cohan defends the aesthetic value of the Irish tenor in a similar manner, championing the singer and his genre's not-quite-highbrow status.[43] We learn that Mrs. McNamara—widow of "one of the wealthiest Irishmen in America," mother of the love interest Evelyn, and a great fan of McConnell's—"nearly struck" someone who said that McConnell "might possibly appeal to the general public, but . . . was far from being a great artist." McConnell replies:

McCONNELL. Oh, sure I never pay any attention to these Italians.
EVELYN. Oh, he's not an Italian.
McCONNELL. No?
EVELYN. No, he's a Canadian.
McCONNELL. A comedian?
MRS. McNAMARA. (*Laughing*) No, he's an old friend of ours. He belongs in Montreal.
McCONNELL. Does he? Why didn't you tell him that. (*All laugh*)[44]

This Canadian detractor's implication is, of course, that McConnell's performance is low- or middlebrow, not intended for the culturally sophisticated and certainly not great art. This musical elitism is shown alongside a more general class snobbery. Douglas Graham, who has designs on Evelyn and whose father made the remark above, tells Evelyn at the McNamaras' party that McConnell is not a guest but "a paid entertainer" and that "once you spoil a beggar of this sort, he never knows his place again." While these are partly the aspersions of a jealous lover, they also represent exclusive social structures that limited opportunities for class mobility for Irish immigrants and members of the lower class. But others' acceptance of McConnell and praise for his vocal performance expose these opinions as wrongheaded snobbery. Moreover, by placing these views with characters identified as Canadian, it depicts them as un-American.

Nonetheless, it is not every Irishman who can join in the McNamaras' party and even vie for Evelyn's heart. The social boundaries separating the household's Irish servants from the upper-class McNamaras are unquestioningly maintained. It is McConnell's liminal status as a singer that puts him in a separate category: both his position as a singer and the songs he sings are integral to his Irish identity and his Americanization within the show's plot. The very quality of his voice—for which the play is named—features prominently as the element providing him access to a certain realm of American society while continually marking his difference from those who inhabit it.

Multiple remarks in the script complement, and fetishize, McConnell's voice, attributing almost magical qualities to it. The show opens the morning after McConnell's triumphant New York debut. McConnell's valet and manager sort through the "sensational" reviews, and a waiter, who is clearly marked by the script's dialogue as another ethnic type, raves about the concert as he delivers breakfast. "What a voice!" he exclaims. "I was up top—(*Pointing as if indicating gallery*)—No can afford downstairs, you see. But I know a voice, monsieur, when I hear a voice. I am musician—not great musician, but I know."[45] A comment from the McNamara's butler, who clearly shares McConnell's heritage, perhaps unsurprisingly relates these qualities to McConnell's Irishness: "Did you ever hear such a voice?" the butler asks. "'Twas like every note was from heaven! But he's from Ireland, so 'tis the same thing."

The exceptional, purportedly Irish nature of McConnell's voice distinguishes his exotic difference while also providing a way to enter America's musical world and overturn its established order. Over the course of Act I, McConnell's manager Severard tells the story of how he "discovered" McConnell three years prior, singing in "an obscure little church" on the outskirts of Dublin, after learning of this "unusual tenor" whose voice "had that peculiar quality that seemed to jingle like American dollars."[46] He then sent McConnell to Italy for further training before bringing him to the United States. This account objectifies McConnell's voice as a find, a resource to be tapped, and evinces the voice's exotic appeal for American audiences. Severard is even described by a record executive as "some little Christopher Columbus." If McConnell's voice is an acquisition, however, it is also a force to be reckoned with—it will "stand America on its head, critics and all," as Severard puts it.

The Voice of McConnell's songs, and even the very act of singing, are plainly coded as Irish. "Sure, I've been singing all my life. I love to sing. Show me the Irishman who doesn't," McConnell proclaims early in the show.[47] Yet despite the centrality of McConnell's voice, music occupies relatively little of this "comedy with songs," as the play is billed.[48] There are only a handful of songs in *The Voice of McConnell*, each sung by McConnell and presented diegetically (i.e., with the singer aware he is singing), most often either in an onstage performance or trying out material that might be performed.[49] At a basic level, this concert-within-a-show framing device distances McConnell from the songs he sings. The audience recognizes that, within the show's onstage world, he is a professional performer; the words and melodies he sings are not his. Yet Cohan simultaneously blurs the boundaries between character and song, even in the selections McConnell sings as a hired performer. In the case of "Mother Machree," Chauncey Olcott, the actor who played McConnell, was also the song's cocomposer and frequent performer. And two other songs—"Ireland, My Land of Dreams" and the later number "When I Look in Your Eyes, Mavourneen"—are composed, according to the plot, by Evelyn McNamara and Tom McConnell for one another; McConnell sings the former at the party and sings the latter directly to Evelyn as a gift. The familiar stereotype of the singing Irishman justifies McConnell's performances as wholly natural, driven by personal relish in the act of singing rather than by commercial gain.

Still, McConnell's Irishness, especially as expressed through song, is imposed as much as it is embraced. In one illustrative scene, McConnell and Mrs. McNamara construct a list of songs for the upcoming party, many of which had been performed or recorded by Olcott, McCormack, or both. Each time McConnell makes a suggestion—both of them tenor numbers by an English composer—Mrs. McNamara replaces it with a more distinctly Irish selection. "Ah, Moon of My Delight" (1896) from a song cycle by Liza Lehmann is discarded in favor of "A Little Bit of Heaven" by Ernest R. Ball and J. Keirn Brennan, with lyrics about how Ireland got its name, sung by Olcott in *The Heart of Paddy Whack* (1914) and recorded by McCormack in 1915. "O Vision Entrancing" from the 1883 opera *Esmeralda* by Arthur Goring Thomas is replaced by the Olcott favorite "Mother Machree," which had also been recorded by McCormack.[50] This scene reveals the inseparability of McConnell's musical and ethnic identity for his Irish American admirers.

The numbers on the McNamaras' list tend to romanticize Ireland in a nostalgic, sentimental tone, in keeping with other Tin Pan Alley tunes and a tradition stretching back to antebellum parlor music and Thomas Moore's early nineteenth-century *Irish Melodies*, and they betray their Irish character through language and musical style. For example, "Ireland, My Land of Dreams," McConnell's first solo in the show, paints a vivid dreamscape of journeying to the "Home Sweet Home" of "Dear old Dublin."[51] The initial pentatonic melodic ascent of the verse's first bar gives a faint and fleeting suggestion of Gaelic folksong (Figure 4.1).[52] Marked "tenderly," the refrain's lyrical melody, with its climbing phrases, lingering high notes, and occasional chromaticism, contains plentiful opportunities for emotionally touching moments from Olcott. Common *topoi* like home and nature take on an Irish hue: the singer dreams of "sweet colleens" there to greet him at his homecoming and of "roam[ing] the wildwood" with his father. The song's imagery, evoking a pastoral land in a simpler time, must have appealed to turn-of-the-century city audiences coming to grips with urbanization. As William H. A. Williams has noted, a romanticized Ireland also represented "yearning for the unattainable," perhaps most of all for those Irish American listeners who were well aware of the great disconnect between the real Ireland, with all its problems, and the "mythical Ireland" of song.[53]

Yet even in this song steeped in Irishness, Cohan could not help but include a quote from one of his most famous songs. One admiring reviewer noted that "as though to tag [the song] as his most precious own, Mr. Cohan has woven into it the most haunting short passage in his biggest song hit

Figure 4.1 Beginning of the verse of "Ireland, My Land of Dreams." Published by M. Witmark and Sons (1918).

'Over There.'"[54] Indeed, for a brief but noticeable two bars of the verse, Cohan quotes both melody and lyrics of his popular World War I song, with the accompaniment echoing the distinctive bugle-call motif (see the last three measures in Figure 4.1). While Cohan regularly quoted well-known melodies in his patriotic songs, here the moment seems an odd topical disruption to the song's veneer of reminiscence. Given the opposition among some Irish Americans to the United States entering World War I, this may have served as a subtle assertion of Irish Americans' wartime patriotism. Or perhaps the quotation was simply a measure for Cohan to save time, cross-promote his musical wares, or, as the reviewer suggests, leave his musical signature. Whatever the purposes, the clearly audible snippet infuses a notable sonic emblem of American patriotism into the song's lush Irish sentimentality.

Irishness was, as Cohan depicts it, inescapable—both imposed by others and inherent to one's character. In the number McConnell performs as an encore at the McNamaras' party, an upbeat waltz called "You Can't Deny You're Irish," traits of the Irish are treated affectionately but nonetheless shown to be immovable markers of ethnic difference. The first verse states that "The Italian can pose as a Frenchman, / While the Frenchman Italian can be," and so on, but "an Irishman hasn't a chance" of "pass[ing] for something [he's] not." The refrain explains that Irishness shows in all the Irishman's features so "[he] can't deny it, / There's no use to try it, / The whole world knows!"[55] McConnell introduces the song as one that "was popular in Ireland a few years before [he] left home," bestowing upon the tune a sense of folk authenticity.[56] But the message only makes sense for the Irish abroad, members of the large diaspora. For beneath the "rollicking roguery" (as one reviewer described it) lies an emphatic and pointed statement about assimilability: one's Irish heritage, the song asserts, cannot be hidden or erased.[57] By extension, if the Irish are to enter Yankee society, it will not be by passing as Anglo-American or by discarding their Irish heritage. Rather, the song celebrates Irish pride but invites the Americans into the club. In fact, it does so almost literally: McConnell asks the party guests to "join in the chorus," and the catchy, singable tune lends itself to group performance. "Just between us Irish, / If ev'ry one was Irish, / Then we'd be in clover, / The war would be over, / The whole world gay," McConnell sings, bringing his American listeners into the imagined Irish "us." Never mind that the war was over by the show's premiere, or that Cohan himself had urged America's involvement with "Over There"—the essential sentiment is that the Irish are a carefree, peaceable people who, by extension, are also worthy of American citizenship.

While music nudges open the gateway for McConnell to become Irish American, and his regular guy characteristics confirm his eligibility, marriage seals the deal. Evelyn is much younger, wealthier, and perhaps a bit too coquettish—she "makes a regular business of breaking men's hearts," according to her mother—but she is suitably Irish and also, crucially, American. McConnell proves worthy of her by his dogged, creative persistence as well as by diplomatically resolving the show's main conflict, a jewelry theft by an adventuress attending the party as the guest of the young, unknowing Harry McNamara. The songs Evelyn and McConnell compose for one another and that McConnell sings—"Ireland, My Land of Dreams" and "When I Look in Your Eyes Mavourneen"—further confirm their musical connection and mutual compatibility. But while the singer yearns for Ireland in the former, he finds all he needs in his sweetheart's eyes in the latter. The Gaelic-derived term of endearment mavourneen ("my darling"); a mention of "Irish eyes of blue"; and an extraneous "sure," typical of Irish dialect, are the only markers of Irishness.[58] The fairly vacuous lyrics of love move toward universality, and the lyrical music is devoid of ethnic coding. McConnell sings the song after he has placed a ring upon Evelyn's hand, music and marriage thus signifying his full assimilation, as an Irish American, into US society.[59]

The Voice of McConnell ran in New York for only thirty performances before going on the road, but reviews were positive. Critics perceived the show, like its principal male character, to walk the line between what was Irish and what was American. The *New York Times* proclaimed upon its opening, " 'The Voice of McConnell' is Brisk and Rich in Humor, Not All Irish" and complimented Cohan on achieving broad appeal, stating, "One of the marks of Mr. Cohan's triumph . . . is that, although the play is Irish, one does not have to be Irish to enjoy it."[60] The *Sun* described the show as "Tuneful Irish American Drama."[61] What did this mean? In part, a blending of comedic style and dramatic pace, according to a reviewer who commented on Olcott's blend of "Irish wit and charm" with "something of the traditional Cohan speed."[62] The show was thought to demonstrate "the Irish penchant for romance, intrigue, repartee and free-handed generosity," with "rapturous allusions to Ireland and the Irish," but the setting and, accordingly, costumes were changed from the typical Olcott drama.[63] In addition, some of the show's themes were distinctly American. "The element of shrewd business instinct," a common feature in Cohan's shows of the period, was seen as "characteristic of a no less indigenous product than the *Saturday Evening Post*."[64] In other words, the hybridity of genre, style, and subject matter set it apart from the Irish theater associated with Olcott as well as from Cohan's previous output.

One critic viewed the result as a clear improvement upon the shallow stereotypes of Olcott's usual fare, pronouncing *The Voice of McConnell* "credible although Celtic." Olcott, the review explained, "is still the incorrigible blarneyer and balladist of yore, but he is not a stuffed effigy out of a museum of old-fashioned plays; he is alive and wears citizen's clothes." *The Voice of McConnell*, it concluded, "is glibly amusing, and its Hibernianism is adroitly modified by American assurance."[65] The Irishman was no longer a stock character, but a contemporary, Irish American citizen. Cohan won praise for creating the new genre that presented this updated type. "There is not in our theatres to-day any more complete or perfect example of the Americanization of Irish humor, sentiment and melody than that afforded by the comedies and songs of George M. Cohan," wrote John H. Raftery in the *Telegraph*.[66] The play, announced the *Sun*, "is entitled to rank in the forefront of the whole body of Irish American drama—of which Mr. Cohan is the sole creator."[67] While Cohan certainly was not the sole creator of Irish American drama—one need only think back to Harrigan and Hart, for example—it is notable that he was perceived to be. He had launched a new chapter in his own work and for representations of Irish Americans in theater.

IRISH AMERICAN CINDERELLAS: *LITTLE NELLIE KELLY* AND *THE RISE OF ROSIE O'REILLY*

Cohan returned to Irish American protagonists a few years later with *Little Nellie Kelly* (1922) and *The Rise of Rosie O'Reilly* (1923), both of which told tales of lower-class ingénues, in this case Irish Americans, sought by wealthy young American men. In the meantime, the show *Irene* (1919), with music by Harry Tierney, lyrics by Joe McCarthy, and book by James Montgomery, had become a "runaway hit."[68] Cohan had also produced the successful heroine-centered *Mary* (1920) and *The O'Brien Girl* (1921), both by Otto Harbach, Louis A. Hirsch, and Frank Mandel. Perhaps it was these other models that steered Cohan toward writing his own similar stories. The rags-to-riches formula centering on a charming, wholesome heroine became a common one—so much so, in fact, that musical theater historian Gerald Bordman labeled the 1921–1924 period on Broadway "The Cinderella Era."[69]

Years earlier, Cohan had written about the age-old popularity of Cinderella stories in a 1914 article co-authored with drama critic George Jean Nathan entitled "Plotting Against the Public." The piece asserts the sure way to box office success and audience members' hearts is to recycle common plots and themes. And the "*Stammvater*" (or progenitor) of them all, Cohan and Nathan explain, is "Cinderella." "Give the public [this tale]," they write, "and the line at the box office window will be pretty sure to extend round the block." "Keep the fundamentals of the plot, and change the externals," they add, "and it is ten to one you will ride in limousines the rest of your life!" Why Cinderella? Because it is the "one big story of the world's loves, ambitions, troubles, heartaches, disappointments, with, at its conclusion, the world's ever-throbbing dream to realize its dream of dreams."[70]

Many of the 1920s Cinderellas, and *all* of Cohan's, were clearly, markedly Irish. Using this blueprint, Cohan explores whether a poor Irish American Cinderella can, indeed, marry a wealthy American prince and live the American dream, as well as what routes from rags to riches are open to these Hibernian Cinderellas' brothers and the Irish beaus vying for her heart. In each show, Cohan promotes the assimilability and uprightness of his lower-class Irish American characters—the basic impulse is that Nellie and Rosie are, indeed, rightfully American. However, the message is more complicated in both cases. In *Little Nellie Kelly*, Nellie ultimately marries within her class and ethnicity, suggesting a tight-knit, upwardly bound (Catholic) Irish American community in line with what historian Timothy J. Meagher describes as a "militant American Catholicism" operating as a "parallel society" to that of the Protestant mainstream.[71] *The Rise of Rosie O'Reilly*, on the other hand, promotes Irish American ascendance to and reconciliation with the WASP elite, but the story is treated as fairy tale and gently parodied.

Advertisements and sheet music for *Little Nellie Kelly* and *The Rise of Rosie O'Reilly* shaped audiences' impressions before they even made it to the theater and after they went home. These elements of branding clearly signified Irishness while also liberally applying the term "American." The sheet music covers are replete with Irish stereotypes (see Figures 4.2 and 4.3). Symbols like the shamrock and the colors red and green were cemented in their association with the Irish by the turn of the century, and both sheet music cover designs drew on this familiar iconography.[72]

Nellie's red hair and bright red and green outfit shout her heritage loudly. Rosie's pink and darker green hues are more subdued, but lest there be any doubt, shamrocks frame the list of available tunes from the show. Yet the green and red were not used consistently; the shows were marketed as American as much and as frequently as they were Irish. Boasting "a regiment of singing and dancing Americans," the advertisement for *Little Nellie Kelly* shown in Figure 4.4 replaces green with blue to create a red, white, and blue color scheme. The back of the flyer evokes American patriotism and Irish

Figure 4.2 Cover of "Nellie Kelly I Love You." Published by M. Witmark and Sons (1922). York University Libraries, Clara Thomas Archives and Special Collections, John Arpin Collection, JAC004811. (A color version of this figure is included in the color insert.)

character in immediate succession, with the phrase "A Singing and Dancing American Chorus Never Equalled [*sic*] on the Musical Stage" followed by "Not Since the Days of Harrigan and Hart has a Musical Show Warmed the Cockles of the Heart as Does 'Little Nellie Kelly.'"[73]

Figure 4.3 Cover of "Born and Bred in Brooklyn." Published by M. Witmark and Sons (1923). Courtesy of the Levy Collection. (A color version of this figure is included in the color insert.)

Ads in the *New York Times* lean toward patriotism, billing *Little Nellie Kelly* as the "New American Song and Dance Show" and, later, the "Best American Musical Play in the Whole Wide World," with star Elizabeth Hines, "Our Own Little American Girl."[74] *The Rise of Rosie O'Reilly* is described almost

Figure 4.4 Little Nellie Kelly *flyer. Theater Biography Collection, Harry Ransom Center, University of Texas at Austin. (A color version of this figure is included in the color insert.)*

identically as "the *Great* American Song and Dance Show."[75] Given the careful positioning of these shows, sometimes as Irish *or* American and at other times as both, it seems that Cohan was still determined, at this stage in his career, not to have his shows—or himself—pigeonholed as Irish. Tacking on the label "American" to describe the star, chorus, and show, especially in the shows' marketing, was almost certainly intended to attract mainstream musical-going audiences accustomed to Cohan's flag-waving fare. It also, however, underscored that Nellie Kelly and Rosie O'Reilly were no modern-day Bridgets (a female Irish stereotype of yore)—they were as American as they come, and the shows were designed as much for the Joneses and Millers as the Kellys and O'Reillys.

Similarities abound between *Little Nellie Kelly* and *The Rise of Rosie O'Reilly*, from the characters and settings to parallel musical numbers. In each, following the Cinderella formula, a young millionaire falls in love with the eponymous lower-class girl, despite the disapproval of friends or family members. Both Nellie and Rosie are salesgirls—albeit at very different levels, with Nellie an employee at the posh shop of DeVere and Rosie the proprietor of a humble newsstand—and both are characterized as virtuous, working-class, Irish American girls with hearts of gold. Each plot has an element of crime, and in each, an Irish American boy falls under suspicion. In *Little Nellie Kelly*, a strand of pearls is stolen, and a boy from Nellie's neighborhood in the Bronx, Jerry Conroy, becomes the prime suspect. In *The Rise of Rosie O'Reilly*, Rosie's younger brother Buddie faces arrest for his (unwitting) involvement in bootlegging. Each heroine's home neighborhood is even celebrated with a hallmark dance: "The Hinky Dee," the newest craze from the Bronx, in *Little Nellie Kelly* and "The Brooklyn" in *The Rise of Rosie O'Reilly*.[76] The stories end differently, however. In *Little Nellie Kelly*, we learn that "there's only one boy in the world for Nellie Kelly"—not the wealthy Jack but rather the Irish American childhood friend Jerry. In *The Rise of Rosie O'Reilly*, on the other hand, the millionaire Bob Morgan "wave[s] goodbye to a great American fortune" to be with Rosie, though in the end, Bob's father decides not to disinherit his son after all and even sets a wedding date for the happy couple.[77]

Nellie and Rosie exemplify the Irish American girl of Tin Pan Alley—a ubiquitous, if vaguely defined, type closely descended from "the true-hearted, pure Irish colleen of the old parlor ballads but with a bit more up-to-date zip and personality."[78] While their class status is evident from their occupations and neighborhoods, their Irishness is signaled, as in *The Voice of McConnell*, in the shows' eponymous titles. Names had long been a significant marker of Irish heritage in Cohan's shows and songs, and in *Little Nellie Kelly*, main characters Nellie and Jerry shared the names of Cohan's parents, and Nellie's father, Captain John Kelly of the New York City Police Department, sings a paean to "The Name of Kelly." The *New York Times* commented in its review, "This time it is Nellie that is the most wonderful name in the world and it is Kelly with a capital K that stands above all others of the long string of Irish patronymics Mr. Cohan has celebrated on our stage."[79] He celebrates yet another in *The Rise of Rosie O'Reilly*, in which Rosie sings that there's "A Ring to the Name of Rosie." The heroines' names, with their rhyme (Nellie Kelly) and alliteration (Rosie O'Reilly), are not only attractive on a marquee, but also eminently singable and recognizably Irish.

Apart from her name and red hair, however, the Irishness of the Irish American girl of popular culture was sometimes difficult to detect. The fully, resolutely Americanized daughter was a trope in songs, literature, and theater about the lace curtain Irish.[80] So it is perhaps unsurprising that Cohan's heroines, too, show few traces of their Irish heritage. Although Rosie and Nellie represent two variations of the Irish American girl in their class status—Rosie is poor, from the "deep slums," while Nellie is slightly better off—both are at least second generation and neither speaks with a brogue.[81]

They are described extensively, but the traits mentioned are vaguely good and not attributed to Irishness. In the catchy waltz song "Nellie Kelly I Love You," for example, Nellie is described by American colloquialisms: she is "ev'ryone's pal, ev'ryone's gal" and "wholesome and plain, right as the rain (▶ Example 4.1)."[82] And their grace and poise, it is implied, make them at home in any social situation.

The male characters of Irish heritage in *Little Nellie Kelly* wear their green more openly. Nellie's father, Captain Kelly of the New York Police Department, for example, fits the familiar stereotype of the Irish cop. This common theatrical character had a footing in reality. As cities built up their infrastructure and personnel in the urbanization of the early twentieth century, the Irish were readily available to fill the ranks, and political machines like Tammany Hall further helped populate squads with their supporters. Consequently, they became disproportionately represented on police and fire squads.[83] Captain Kelly possesses other stereotypical Irish traits as well. He is clearly well established in the new country, having attained the position of captain, but also connected closely enough to the old country to have retained a touch of brogue. He is a man of action, a charmer, and, even as a policeman during Prohibition, inclined to the bottle. When he first storms onto the scene, he has been called to break up a supposedly raucous party.

KELLY. What's going on here? What's this wild party I've been hearing about? Where's the bootlegger? I demand you hand the bootlegger over to me at once.

JACK. You must be mistaken, sir. There's no bootlegger here.

KELLY. Are you sure of that?

JACK. Absolutely.

KELLY. (*Making a wry face*) My God have I got to go without a drink?[84]

His song "The Name of Kelly," much like "You Can't Deny You're Irish" in *The Voice of McConnell*, is a hearty sing-along inviting the onstage party guests—and offstage audience—to join in the celebration of Irishness. It has few musical markers of Irishness on the whole. However, near the end of the verse as Captain Kelly asserts the Kellys' good name and, in the second verse, their ties to Irish royalty, an openly spaced and accented chord, rolled in the bass part, sounds just enough like bagpipes to signal a sense of Celtic difference (Figure 4.5).[85] The harmonic rhythm and patterns shift here, signaling Ireland's exoticism as well as adding musical variety and preparing the chorus. Although this name song follows a contemporary trend, it stands in notably stark contrast to others' more derogatory comic "Kelly" songs such

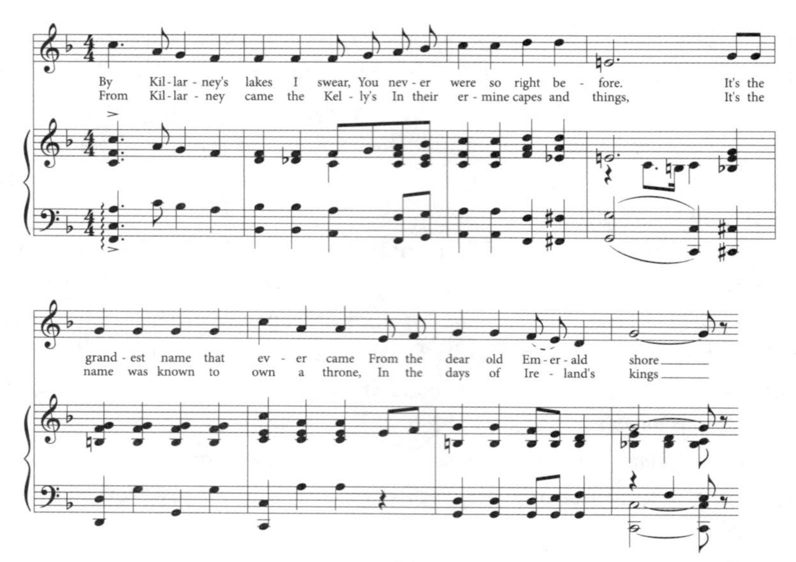

Figure 4.5 End of the verses of "The Name of Kelly." Published by M. Witmark and Sons (1922).

as "If I Knock the 'L' Out of Kelly (It Would Still Be Kelly to Me)" (1916) and "Officer Kelly (Don't You Think That It's Time to Wake Up?)" (1924).[86]

For Jerry Conroy, unlike Tom McConnell or Captain Kelly, it's not an accent that gives away his Irishness—like Nellie, he is presumably at least second generation—but rather his temper. One reviewer describes Jerry as "the young Irishman who would defend anything so long as there was a little fight in connection."[87] The reviewer overstates the matter in his eagerness to discern the Paddy stereotype; Jerry is not pugnacious. He is, however, hot-headed. Having been accused of stealing a pearl necklace, he goes with Captain Kelly to give an account of what he witnessed to the private detective assigned to the case.

KELLY. Well, we're here to tell him all we know. (*Turning to Jerry*) Aren't we, Jerry?

JERRY. (*Crossing Nellie to C[enter]*) Sure we are. I'll tell all I know and I'll tell him a few more things, too, if he tries to make anybody think I'm a crook. Nobody's going to hang anything like that on me and get away with it, I'll tell you that right now.

KELLY. (*Stands left of Jerry trying to keep him quiet*)

NELLIE. (*Comes down to right of Jerry*) Now, don't lose your temper, Jerry.

KELLY. Sure, I've already explained to Mrs. Langford that your hands are as clean as a hound's tooth.

JACK. Yes, there's nothing to get excited about.

JERRY. There isn't, eh? (*Crossing to Jack*) Well, maybe there isn't for you, but there is for me.

JACK. Nobody's directly accused you.

JERRY. (*His temper rising*) No, and nobody better accuse me, do you understand that?

Jerry apologizes to Nellie a moment later for breaking his promise to her and "losing [his] head," explaining that he "saw something just now that got [his] Irish up."[88] After being pressed, he reveals that he was hurt by seeing Nellie alone with Jack. But Jerry's anger also reflects the power dynamics at play as he, a young, lower-class Irish American, is suspected of stealing from a wealthy, older Yankee woman.

The plots of both *Little Nellie Kelly* and *The Rise of Rosie O'Reilly* hinge on an unlikely crossing of paths across ethnic and class divides. In the former, this happens when Jack hosts a party for the shopgirls at DeVere's clothing shop. In the latter, Rosie and Bob meet when he goes "slumming." A common urban practice of the late nineteenth and early twentieth centuries, slumming, as historian Chad Heap writes, "served as a mechanism through which affluent whites could negotiate the changing demographic characteristics and spatial organization of modern U.S. cities."[89] The extended opening number of *The Rise of Rosie O'Reilly* thematizes this experience explicitly. Jimmy, the millionaire Bob Morgan's friend and the show's narrator, explains that he first heard Rosie when "We were all out slumming / And we heard the strumming / Of the jazz band."[90] A single expedition to the other world of the Brooklyn slums, the lyrics suggest, offered the upper-class visitor unparalleled excitement in the form of a range of novel exotic and modern stimuli, from jazz music to chop suey, topped off with a whiff of danger. As Heap has written, slumming also offered upper-class White Americans "an opportunity to shore up their own superior standing in the shifting racial and sexual hierarchies by juxtaposing themselves with the women and men that they encountered."[91]

Yet in Cohan's musicals, cross-class encounter with the Other—albeit the not-*too*-Other of the Irish—in fact reveals for the progressive young Yankee protagonists the moral chasms of the upper echelon. When his friends rebuke him for hosting a party for the DeVere staff, Jack responds that the shopgirls are "unspoiled, all real, honest, wholesome girls, who are not only interesting, but appreciative of any little attention that's paid them," adding that "they're not only a relief but a revelation."[92] These traits of genuineness, honesty, and wholesomeness constituted not only the Cinderella prototype but also the female version of the "regular guy" and the model American that

Cohan had so frequently championed. And Irish American, lower-class Nellie and Rosie, Cohan asserted through his Cinderella shows, were its paragons.

But can Nellie, Rosie, and the rest of the Kellys and O'Reillys truly assimilate into American society, according to Cohan's shows? And how? The paths to full acceptance into American society vary for the characters depending on their generation, gender, and class. In *Little Nellie Kelly*, for example, Captain Kelly is still very much Irish but belovedly so. His route to the American middle class has been through a police career, and it seems to have brought him a stable, if modest, family life in the Bronx. *Little Nellie Kelly* further presses his assimilability through his gallantry with Genevieve Langford, Jack's wealthy aunt whose life, we learn, Captain Kelly saved many years ago. They share close conversation, flirtation, and a foxtrot, and in the final scene, they are paired. Mr. Kelly, extending his hand, says, "Mrs. Langford, you're a queen." Taking it, Mrs. Langford replies, "Mr. Kelly, you're a king."[93] The language and staging suggest social equality. Yet Captain Kelly is married, so Cohan is able to hint at his worthiness as a partner across class and ethnic lines without following through with the more daring statement of marital union.

Nellie's pathway in American society and the plot of *Little Nellie Kelly* hinge on her choice of beaus. Will she join the elite world of Anglo-American Jack Lloyd or stay in the Bronx with Irish American Jerry Conway? For other Cinderellas of the era, there would have been no question—as musical theater historian John Bush Jones put it, they "almost always [went] for the gold as well as the guy (frequently synonymous)."[94] But Nellie is no fortune seeker; she "has a fine sense of the real things in life."[95] The show's script gives every indication she would not only fit in with the elite but would also be an asset to them. Yet despite there being no objections to the match, it becomes clear that shared cultural bonds will trump the strength of Jack's infatuation. Jack tells Nellie that hers is "the loveliest name in the world" because it's *her* name, while Jerry loves it "because it was [his] mother's name" and spells out other similarities in the "mother song" "You Remind Me of My Mother" (▶ Example 4.2).

For Jerry, whose place in American society is least certain among the Irish American characters, Nellie occupies a civilizing role. Jerry reminisces to Nellie about her reaction when he "slipped [his] arm around [her] waist" when they went to Coney Island on the trolley:

> JERRY. (*Earnestly*) Gosh! I thought you were going to get sore at first, but you didn't. You just turned around and looked me square in the eye and—what did you say?
>
> NELLIE. (*With mock severity*) Jerry Conroy! Behave yourself, young man!

JERRY. (*Laughing*) That's exactly what my mother used to say to me, whenever I did something to make her laugh. You certainly made an awful hit with me that day, Nellie.[96]

This dialogue echoes social commentary, from within the Irish Catholic community and from popular culture, that women "not only held the family together," as historian Hasia R. Diner explains, "but they propelled the family out of poverty and into the respectability of the middle class."[97] Nellie has the option to enter the upper class by marriage to Jack Lloyd, but Jerry's path of assimilation and social uplift is through her. By choosing Jerry's "cottage neat and cozy" over Jack's "mansion rich and rare," Nellie not only upholds the value of love over wealth—a common theme of Cohan's shows—but also helps maintain a distinct Irish American community.[98] In the end, she also inherits the clothing shop where she works.[99] Thus, it is a Cinderella story after all: through business—another sacred American institution—rather than marriage, Nellie can have both love and social mobility and be both fully Irish and fully American.

Only a year later, in *The Rise of Rosie O'Reilly*, Cohan did an about-face with a similar story. Although the match in question, between a parentless newsstand girl and a millionaire's son, is even less likely than Jack and Nellie's, Cohan bows to the trend of the day and gives the two a happy ending, with plans for a June wedding. The show's subtitle, however, is "Poking Fun at Cinderella," and even as Cohan depicts Rosie and her brother Buddie overcoming class and ethnic barriers, he acknowledges the utopian aspect of the rags-to-riches story through a strand of self-referential commentary running throughout the musical. This metatheatricality, which characterized many Cohan shows, saturates *The Rise of Rosie O'Reilly*. In addition to supplying humor, the show's various self-reflexive moments undermine the optimistic messages of social mobility and reward for virtue at the heart of the Cinderella story. The audience never forgets that they are seeing a fantasy and a satire, that Cohan is "poking fun at Cinderella." Buddie marvels at his luck to Cutie, his sweetheart and sidekick: "Pretty soft for us when you figure it out, eh, Cutie? Picked up by a crowd of millionaires, dressed up, educated, fussed over, taken to the Hippodrome, the race track, to church, and everything. I wonder if anything like this could happen in real life?" "Not without songs and dances," is Cutie's rejoinder.[100] For the real Buddies, Cuties, and Rosies of the world, Cohan admits, a rise from slums to mansions is only a fairy tale.

The Rise of Rosie O'Reilly lacks overt Irish pride, signifiers, and songs, but Cohan promotes the Americanness of Irish Americans through negative depictions of other ethnic groups. The lack of any ethnic markers of Irishness in the main characters allows them to be subsumed into the White in-group, while members of other immigrant groups are heavily and grotesquely stereotyped. Now-offensive ethnic nicknames and expressions pepper the script as Cohan describes an underworld where "a square deal hasn't got a Chinaman's chance."[101] The only named member of the show's bootlegging gang is Hop Toy, described on the cast list as "a Chinese crook." Even the Irish policemen are "Micks," but Casparoni, the show's main villain, is "the darned old Wop" and he and his wife "naughty Dagoes."[102] Casparoni, who along with his wife speaks in broken English with strong accents, is almost comically awful. He plots to kidnap Rosie when he learns he could get a ransom from Bob Morgan, and, in a now-repugnant scene in which his wife Bella tries to prevent his evil doings, he responds by threatening her with grotesque violence. Occurring three times in all, the scene becomes farcical through repetition: it paints Casparoni, and even Bella, as ridiculous as well as evil. Offensive stereotypes of Italians, Chinese, and other racial minorities were hardly rare on the early twentieth-century musical theater stage, and Cohan had drawn upon them before. Here as elsewhere, he uses them not only to poke fun at generic conventions but also to draw a firm racial boundary, emphasizing and cordoning off the Whiteness of his Irish American characters.

Cohan's Cinderella shows were, to some extent, derivative and formulaic; he recognized a lucrative trend and jumped on the bandwagon. But he used the formula self-consciously and, according to many critics, skillfully, particularly in the case of *Little Nellie Kelly*, which later became the inspiration for a 1940 Hollywood film starring Judy Garland.[103] The *New York Tribune* commended Cohan: "Mr. Cohan has not hesitated to take the standard props of the successful musical comedies of the last two or three years, the shop girl, the rich young man, the *modiste*, the mansion, the country estate, and the other familiar appurtenances. But, just as one of his songs points out, that it's 'All in the Wearing,' so too, may it be said, that it's all in the treatment."[104] Critics and audiences alike found Cohan's "process of glorifying the Irish-American girl" an "amiable" one.[105]

The shows were especially popular in Boston, "the hub of things Celtic as well as things cultural," as one newspaper put it, and where "Miss Kelly has many vehement friends and relatives," as another stated.[106] How much of an Irish American following Cohan inspired is difficult to determine, but the press certainly believed it was substantial. Yet *Little Nellie Kelly* also ran for an impressive 276 performances on Broadway. The critic John Farrar commented on the show's New York City appeal in the magazine the *Bookman*:

> To be truly successful ["the comedy-drama with music"] should include a mother song and a sprinkle of flag waving. . . . True, there are no flags, as I remember, in that masterpiece "Little Nellie Kelly"; but there is that heart wringing ballad, "You Remind Me of My Mother," and the entire story is about a policeman and his daughter, which brand of Irish patriotism is quite the same thing for New York City as a Yiddish ballad or the actual red, white and blue of the flag.[107]

At least for some, Irish and American pride had become interchangeable theatrical commodities.

"FOR THE HONOR OF THE FAMILY": *THE MERRY MALONES*

The Merry Malones was Cohan's penultimate musical and his last explicitly Irish American one. During the show's dress rehearsal in Boston in September 1927, the actor playing the father John Malone, Arthur Deagon—who had also played Captain Kelly in *Little Nellie Kelly*—collapsed onstage and died.[108] Cohan, who had last performed in musicals on Broadway in the 1910s, stepped into the role and continued to play it throughout the show's run, playing an overtly Irish character for the first time in his Broadway career (Figure 4.6). The Yankee Doodle Dandy of yore became a Malone.

The Merry Malones continued the pattern of Cinderella shows. This time, the virtuous Irish American heroine is Molly Malone of the Bronx, and she falls in love with Joe Westcott, a drugstore soda water clerk who turns out to be—not surprisingly—the son of a billionaire. Upon learning his true identity, she initially refuses both Joe and his fortune, but love and riches prevail. The show also partook of other Cohan tropes. Richard Watts of the *New York Herald Tribune* described it as "the most Cohan-esque entertainment conceivable," explaining that it "overflows with all of the materials that have made the Cohan name eminent—the flags, the sentiment, the hokum, the persistent kidding of the plot, the Irish-American family humor, all managed with the most skilled of showmanship."[109] The reviewer's mention of "Irish-American family humor" notwithstanding, this was, in fact, the first time Cohan had depicted the complete Irish American family and not just parent-child pairs, like Mrs. McNamara and Evelyn in *The Voice of McConnell* or Captain Kelly and Nellie in *Little Nellie Kelly*. Themes of class, social standing, and the aspirations of the lace curtain Irish thus came to the fore, and Cohan reasserted Irish pride while challenging old-stock Anglo-American superiority.

Figure 4.6 Cohan as John Malone in The Merry Malones, *White Studio (New York, NY). Cohan Collection.*

Introduced in the domestic setting of the family living room, the Malones are clearly part of the so-called lace curtain set. They have a piano in the parlor and a cook named Annie, yet they aspire to rise even higher on the social ladder. The father, John, hopes Molly might end up with Tony Howard, a suitor whose family has wealth and influence. And Molly's younger sister Delia boasts about having "an important engagement with a member of the

O'Sullivan family. You know, the famous rubber heel folks," referencing the real-life O'Sullivan Rubber Company.[110] Ironically, while Mr. Malone is sorry to miss out on the prospect of Tony Howard as a son-in-law and Delia is boasting of rubbing elbows with the well-heeled (pun intended) set, Molly—who is unimpressed by wealth—is unwittingly falling for a man whose wealth dwarfs that of the Howards and O'Sullivans. Like Cohan's other Cinderellas, she gains riches by her refusal to seek them.

Molly Malone is the "angel of the house" and, like Nellie and Rosie, the girl next door for every neighborhood boy.[111] She is the girl who "the boys all adore" and "the girls are all for," as proclaimed in "Molly Malone," a tuneful light waltz that we learn has become a popular song in the Bronx.[112] "Molly Malone" has a long history in song and there were multiple songs of that name in Cohan's day, so his premise that a Molly Malone of the Bronx had inspired a popular song required little suspension of disbelief on the part of the audience.[113]

Those outside of her neighborhood find Molly equally winning. In a scene in Act I, Molly and her would-be beau Joe go, masked, to a high society masquerade ball, where a gaggle of men sing Molly's praises, simultaneously seeking to unmask her, in the song "Charming." The scene of a female star surrounded by adoring men, along with dancing that was reported to be one of the show's highlights, must have had a spectacular, Follies-esque effect. The verse begins in a minor key, creating an ominous tone as the men tell her she's "caught" and ask her to reveal her identity. The threat implicit to Molly as she pleads in the second verse for the men to "please desist" also gives it a disturbing undertone.[114] The refrain, in the relative major, imbues her with an ineffable attractiveness. Able to "captivate" and "fascinate" men beyond their own understanding and even their will, she fits long-standing stereotypes of the female Other—mysterious, irresistible, and frequently dangerous. Lest Molly come off purely as a siren and lose her wholesomeness, however, Cohan also casts her as a caretaker figure "safely guarding o'er" the men, again invoking the ideal of women as a motherly, civilizing force. This section of the refrain includes a blaring musical quotation of the hymn "Adeste Fideles," followed by the familiar first three notes of "Over There" (a quotation seen already in this chapter in "Ireland, My Land of Dreams") (Figure 4.7). "Adeste Fideles" may have carried connotations of Irishness. In a 1908 article, music historian W. H. Grattan Flood argued for its Irish roots, and the hymn was used at events like the St. Patrick's Day parade of 1926 and in performances by Irish tenor John McCormack, who opened his historic first radio broadcast with the song in 1925.[115] As we have seen in other instances of Cohan's musical borrowing, quotations—especially of

Figure 4.7 Section of refrain of "Charming," voice only. Published by M. Witmark and Sons (1927).

well-known tunes—have the ability to convey multiple meanings and associations. It is likely that Cohan drew on the popular hymn and the war song for their respective associations, with religion and Irish pride for the former and with patriotism and Cohan himself for the latter, as well as their familiarity and popularity.

As in *Little Nellie Kelly*, Cohan depicts the ethnic Irish character most vividly through the older generation. Mr. Malone, who bears striking resemblance to Captain Kelly, works for another stereotypically Irish institution, the political machine, as a district leader for the Democratic Party, and he also shares Kelly's fondness for drinking. Both Mr. and Mrs. Malone are characterized as intrinsically and proudly Irish; they use Irish expressions, and the actors playing them probably spoke with some degree of brogue.

The three children, presumably either second or third generation, are far less overtly Irish. They speak in American colloquialisms and sing standard Broadway fare, like the waltz "The Easter Sunday Parade" and the jaunty, ragtime-inflected "Our Own Way of Going Along." Yet the sheet music iconography, with its red and green color scheme, reminds us that Molly and her siblings, like Nellie and Rosie before them, are still recognizably Irish. Molly has flaming red hair and holds a shamrock like a flower (Figure 4.8). And the siblings' song "Fight for the Honor of the Family" exemplifies the family loyalty associated with Irishness, explaining that the siblings may bicker constantly, but should an outsider "strike a spark, bite or bark," they will come together to "fight for the honor of the family."[116]

As in Cohan's earlier Irish American–themed shows, the Malones share the stage with and are depicted in contrast to members of other ethnic groups and social classes. An Italian organ grinder and their clearly Jewish neighbors Isidore Rosinsky and his overbearing, busybody wife Rebecca are similarly characterized by ethnic stereotypes, but the idiosyncrasies of the

Figure 4.8 Cover of "Molly Malone." Published by M. Witmark and Sons (1927). Vocal Popular Sheet Music, Maine Music Box Collection. (A color version of this figure is included in the color insert.)

Malones, as the more fully drawn and loveable protagonists, are treated as more normative and American than those of other ethnic characters. The Malones' interactions with their cook Annie set them apart from the lower class, particularly the so-called shanty Irish who stood in contrast to the lace curtain set.

Farthest above the Malones on the socioeconomic ladder is Joe's father Mr. J. W. Westcott, a self-described "red-blooded Yank" and a billionaire who "makes and breaks governments and Kings."[117] At the show's opening, we learn that he has arranged his son Joe's marriage to the well-to-do Annabelle Van Buren, seeking to consolidate the two families' wealth. With his Yankee ancestry, thundering rage, and dynastic aspirations, Westcott serves as a foil for the loving, jolly Malones. He also draws attention to their ethnic differences. In a party scene, when the butler announces, "Mr. John Malone with an urgent message," Westcott responds with an aside to the audience, "Another vote for Smith." When Westcott decides he'll talk to Malone, he adds, "If his name is anything to go by, he'll have a bulging hip." Pointing out the presumed Irish allegiance to Irish Catholic politician Al Smith (which Cohan himself shared) as well as the popular image of the Irish as drinkers, with flasks in bulging hip pockets, Westcott's comments carry a tinge of disdain.[118] Here as elsewhere, Cohan draws attention to perceptions of ethnic difference while simultaneously reifying this difference, further stereotyping the Irish even as he celebrates them. After all, Malone fits the stereotype, and the audience gets a hearty laugh at these one-liners.

Although clearly aware of their outsider status in the Westcott's cultural orbit, the Malones assert social parity through pride in their Irish pedigree. When Molly spurns Joe Westcott, Mrs. Malone disapprovingly remarks at her shunning high society. But Mr. Malone proclaims, "More power to her. And why wouldn't she? It's no more than the name of Malone deserves. My great-grandfather's grandfather was an Irish king."[119] Mr. Malone's solo "God is Good to the Irish," like "The Name of Kelly," encapsulates this sentiment of Irish pride in song and dance. It is introduced with a song that Mrs. Malone "used to sing to [Molly] when [she] rocked her in the cradle," as Mr. Malone recalls. The script indicates the music cue, "Horn note: Irish Come All Ye," and Mrs. Malone launches into a sung rendition of an Irish nursery rhyme recited while bouncing a child on one's knees: "Gib gib my little horse / Gib gib again, sir / How many miles to Dublin town / Three score and ten, sir." While Cohan's version leads with "gib," one also commonly finds "chip," "hupp," or "trot," raising the possibility, at least, that Cohan was recalling the song from his own childhood.[120] The musical number continues with what is described as a "short Irish reel" with the male chorus, and then Mr. Malone launches into the boisterous number "God Is Good to the Irish."[121]

The blending of musical elements in "God is Good to the Irish" musically characterizes John Malone as proudly Irish but also proudly American. The song contains both semantic and musical Irish tropes. Its lyrics cite a plethora of characteristics commonly attributed to the Irish: they are "full

Figure 4.9 Beginning of the verse of "God Is Good to the Irish." Published by M. Witmark and Sons (1927).

of the divil," "must frolic and frivol," would "rather have fun than have gold," and are altogether "dancing and singing and happiness bringing."[122] The verse begins in the jig time signature of 6/8 with a bagpipe-like drone accompaniment—the score shows that woodwinds and strings play grace notes and held chords. In the sheet music, this sound is approximated for the more percussive piano by chords repeated every half measure (Figure 4.9). These common signifiers instantly conjure up Irish traditional music for the listener. The refrain then shifts into a more American-style 2/4 time signature, with an oom-pah and then arpeggiated bass line and a sprinkling of syncopation. In the second phrase, however, the grace note–inflected drone accompaniment returns, as if capturing the Irish-tinged "lilt of a tune" the lyrics describe (Figure 4.10). This back-and-forth of musical representations, one way that Tin Pan Alley songwriters structured ethnic songs, provided variety while speaking musically to different audiences.[123]

Malone's "God is Good to the Irish" has a counterpart in "The Yankee Father in the Yankee Home," as sung by J. W. Westcott. A Yankee to Westcott is an old-stock American, one who can trace his roots back for generations, to the European immigrants who first colonized the United States. Cohan uses the song to poke fun at Westcott and his ideals. Westcott sings in the verse:

> My Granddad built the old homestead,
> His dad lived on a crust of bread.
> I know my geneology, [*sic*]
> Ev'ry branch of the fam'ly tree.
> My dad came from the good old stock,
> I was born near the Plymouth Rock.
> The Yankee school and the will to rule
> Have made me what I am
> A damned fine Yank.
> But I've got my dad to thank.

Figure 4.10 Beginning of the refrain of "God Is Good to the Irish."

In the song's refrain, Westcott asserts his belief, reflective of attitudes prevalent in the 1920s, that "the Yankee father in the Yankee home / Is the backbone of the nation."[124] The staid musical language—with square, even rhythms and plodding accents on "Yankee home"—characterizes its sentiment as equally stodgy. Playful triplet figures, with a chromatic turn on scale degree five and drop to scale degree one, mockingly punctuate Westcott's pompous statements. And, it is worth noting, the song is on the shorter side, with no second verse. The overall effect is so overdone as to constitute caricature.

This fits in with the overall treatment of Westcott's character. He is the villain, to the extent that the show has one; the audiences' sympathies lie with his son Joe, Molly Malone, and the Malone family. Yet he is also a metatheatrical interlocutor with the audience, commenting on the show as a show, like Jimmy in *The Rise of Rosie O'Reilly*. During the masquerade party scene, Mrs. Van Buren asks, "Would you call [the party] a real success?" "Not unless it runs all season," comes Westcott's witty response—a joke for the audience's benefit that Mrs. Van Buren ignores.[125] Shortly afterward, Westcott sees that his daughter has been dancing with the private detective. Others dismiss an affair as impossible, but, delivering the lines from the footlights, Westcott complains to the audience, "Listen. The way the author has mixed things up in this play up to now, it wouldn't surprise me if the heroine jumped into the orchestra pit and married the trombone player." And in the end, when the curmudgeonly elder Westcott changes his mind and approves the match of Joe and Molly, he exclaims, "They ought to put [Molly's] name up in electric lights," a tongue-in-cheek joke given that the name of Malone was, indeed, on the theater marquee. It is rare in theater that the villain and comic relief are one and the same. Here it functions to render Westcott and his beliefs laughable and absurd. With *The Merry Malones*, Cohan thus returns to the overly nationalistic, borderline nativist sentiments expressed by some of his earlier shows, but now with gently mocking, comic critique.

Still, Cohan had not entirely left behind his flag-waving gimmicks and patriotic verve. In the opening scene of Act II in *The Merry Malones*, a parade marches onto the stage, described as follows:

> Policemen, holding and walking with bicycles beside them, enter first, followed by drum major and band, national flag bearers, Chamber of Commerce Banner Bearers, district flag bearers, members of Chamber of Commerce, and bearers carrying banner marked "Welcome Westcott." Line up on both sides of stage with band in center spotted. The band will play a medley of Cohan songs, finishing with "Over There."[126]

The somewhat flimsy pretext for the parade, within the script, is to welcome Joe Westcott to the Bronx. More to the point, it provides an excuse for spectacle, for the flags that some critics deplored but Cohan audiences loved, and for Cohan to plug his own songs, culminating with the patriotic wartime hit "Over There." In this scene, in particular, Cohan occupies multiple, layered subject positions. As author of the script, he is creator of the parade scene; he is also composer of the diegetic band music being played onstage, and what's more, the notion of a parade band playing a Cohan medley would have been—and still is—entirely plausible. Finally, as an actor, he is John Malone, who tells the parade to move on. Thus Cohan reminded audiences that he was still the premier patriotic American as well as the proud Irish American. In *The Voice of McConnell*, *Little Nellie Kelly*, and *The Rise of Rosie O'Reilly*, he had shown the Irish to be American in various ways. In *The Merry Malones*, he was, himself, a vehicle for that lesson, showing George M. Cohan, Yankee Doodle Dandy himself, to be Irish as well as American.

"ON EASY SPEAKING TERMS"

Cohan's Irish American–themed musicals, especially the final three, continued the stylistic traits that had come to constitute the Cohan brand: the breakneck dramatic pace; hummable tunes, some of them integrated within the show's plot; mixing of elements from varied genres; metatheatricality; and heavy reliance on dance. He also continued to stick up for the little guy or, in the case of Nellie, Rosie, and Molly, the little gal. An Australian newspaper reviewer of *The Merry Malones* saw the show as a commentary on the "millionaire menace" in the United States.[127] With his musicals of the 1910s and 1920s, Cohan continued to take on class snobbery, the elite Protestant establishment, and a perceived breach in the national democratic values of hard work and social equality.

Yet as this chapter has shown, Cohan made a discernible turn in protagonists and subject matter, using his dramatic and musical styles and even moral messages for a new purpose. In an era when the McConnells, Kellys, O'Reillys, Malones, and their ilk were still under fire from nativism and anti-Catholicism, Cohan, in many ways an unlikely advocate, placed them literally center stage. While his shows were conceived and received first and foremost as commercial entertainment, their sociopolitical messages were also clearly discernable. A passing comment in a 1924 *Time* magazine article about *The Rise of Rosie O'Reilly* states little but reveals much: "George M. Cohan is responsible for this obvious 'defy' to the Ku Klux Klan. He has been responsible for several others from the same mould [*sic*] in the past few seasons."[128] And Brooks Atkinson found it worth noting in his *New York Times* review of *The Merry Malones* that despite "poisonous 'wisecracks' between the children, doors slammed to indicate domestic short temper, and so on," the Malones "expand with warm-hearted Irish hospitality." He unpacked the musical's implications in coded, overlapping terms of class and ethnicity:

> When their middle-class pride is offended by the supercilious disdain of the Westcotts, the Malones become a clan; threaten one of them and the entire family turns up in fighting mood. Among the sophisticates it is the fashion to snarl over the stupidity of such American families as the Malones, to lay at their doors the blame for the intellectual sluggishness,

> the moral hypocrisy of a great nation. Mr. Cohan is not alarmed. The Malones keep him on easy speaking terms with his audiences.[129]

If the Malones kept Cohan on easy speaking terms with his audience, it is equally true that Cohan helped keep much of his audience on speaking terms with the Malones. He promoted Irish Americans through song, dance, humor, and romance, and also through regressive stereotypes, particularly at the expense of other ethnic and racial groups. Depicting a range of Irish American characters—male and female, first and second generation—he grappled with the dual, contested nature of so-called hyphenated Irish American identity during this period. His shows also subtly critiqued the social strictures and prejudice Irish Americans faced. As the Yankee Doodle Boy publicly claimed an identity that was Irish as well as American, bolstering his late career with popular trends and appealing to Irish American fans, he incorporated that into another role that was sustaining his career: that of Cohan the celebrity.

THE CELEBRITY

> As a distributor of mirth, music and general good cheer, it is safe to say that George M. Cohan has no equal on the stage to-day. Cohan is quite the most dominant, popular and conspicuous figure we have had in the amusement field for a decade.
>
> —theatrical manager Michael B. Leavitt (1912)

> Reputation generally rests upon the first thing a person does well. He can't live down a good thing any easier than he can a bad.
>
> —George M. Cohan (1909)

In Cohan's musical *The American Idea* (1908), the characters take a step back from their scheming to comment on society's predilection for "F-A-M-E"—"the merriest game that we play," something everyone wants and hustles to get but then sometimes regrets having.[1] The very topical number, with elements of a list song, offers multiple examples, including politicians, sports figures, performers, and more. Actress Lillian Russell attained fame with her "looks" and boxer Jim Jeffries with his "hooks." A whole verse and chorus are dedicated to writer Elinor Glyn and her scandalous new romantic novel *Three Weeks*, with the repeated refrain of "fame, fame, fame, fame" changed to "shame, shame, shame, shame." Each of the names cited was apparently quite familiar to listeners of the day; none required explanation or even a first name. The lyrics approach the subject of fame with a jollity that yields to skepticism before eventually erupting into full-blown critique, concluding that "we're all to blame" for Glyn's—and presumably by extension other notorious celebrities'—claims to fame. The music undermines the message, however, with its unwavering playful lightness (Figure 5.1 and ▶ Example 5.1). The tune is in a major key and a brisk, buoyant 6/8, and both the melody and the verse-chorus structure rely heavily upon repetition. In the show (as

Yankee Doodle Dandy. Elizabeth T. Craft, Oxford University Press.
DOI: 10.1093/oso/9780197550403.003.0006

Figure 5.1 Beginning of the verse of "F-A-M-E." Published by Cohan and Harris Publishing (1908).

opposed to the rendition in the published sheet music), the song culminates in dance, with accompaniment continuing until the performers frolic their way off stage.[2] The song revels in a twentieth-century notion of celebrity as a slightly dirty pleasure while enacting its own message; it entertains the audience even as it implicates them.

Cohan could have included his own name among the celebrities listed in the song. From the moment he bounded onto the Broadway scene at the turn of the century to his death, he was a megastar of his day, during a period when the very nature of celebrity was being reshaped by changing technologies, business practices, and notions of individuality.[3] In the early 1930s, even as Cohan's career waned and Hollywood eclipsed theater in American popular culture, a theatrical editor for the Associated Press commented that Cohan was one of only three theatrical figures whose names, in AP offices throughout the country, automatically made the news section rather than the theater column. (The other two were David Belasco and George Bernard Shaw.)[4] The nature of Cohan's appeal may have changed over the course of his lifetime—from evoking youthful rebellion to nostalgia—but the fact of it did not. When he died on November 6, 1942, the *New York Times* obituary, amidst wartime reporting, was granted six columns and six photographs, taking up the majority of page twenty. The sheer space devoted to celebrating his life speaks to a level of fame that has since dissolved.

As scholar and celebrity theorist Sharon Marcus notes, celebrity is derived from interactions between the public, the media, and the person.[5] Cohan seemed to understand this dynamic intimately. A savvy self-promoter, he took an active, deliberate role in the construction of his public persona, courting the public and seeking to influence media narratives. The attention to advertising that helped his career as a producer and manager, discussed in Chapter 3, also helped fuel his celebrity; as music publisher Edward B. Marks observed, "He knows how to sell himself to the public as shrewdly as he sold his song to us."[6] The public was the only audience that mattered to him, as he often told them through articles in the newspapers and theater magazines of the day. "Persons who desire to remain in public life must keep their names before the public," he wrote in 1915 in *Green Book Magazine*. "Let the world know you are on deck and kicking." He admitted to being "more or less a three-sheet for myself," referring to a common size of poster in entertainment advertising to describe his focus on self-promotion.[7] He was sounding the same tune over a decade later in 1932, talking about his lifelong "persistency in advertising" to publics both at home and abroad: "George M. Cohan is the only commodity I've had to sell, and I have not hesitated to spend money to sell it from one end of America to the other and in countries across the water."[8] While he was accustomed to "being a near-spectacle," he also claimed to be a "bad mixer," not particularly good in social situations, and confessed, "Personally, if I were out of the show business, I would try to keep my name to myself."[9] Even his reliance on self-advertisement and reluctance over fame were packaged for public consumption, contributing to the Cohan persona. Cohan was hardly the first or only such celebrity; indeed, he followed in the path and adapted the lessons of predecessors like actress Sarah Bernhardt, impresario P. T. Barnum, and band conductor John Philip Sousa.[10] Still, Cohan was remarkable in the degree and nature of his celebrity and the way he consciously cultivated a fresh, youthful twentieth-century persona tied to patriotism and Broadway.

This chapter examines Cohan the celebrity, demonstrating how he harnessed the mass circulation press and burgeoning journalistic attention to celebrity to establish his compelling "Yankee Doodle" patriotic public persona. As "Broadway's press agent," Cohan also promoted Broadway and linked his own fame to it. But his celebrity went far beyond New York; he cultivated and relied upon the national and international media. In the 1920s through to the end of his life in 1942, after his unsuccessful stand against Actors' Equity Association and as styles on Broadway changed, Cohan cashed in on celebrity through the Irish American shows discussed in Chapter 4, writings in the print media, performances in films and radio programs, starring roles in other playwrights' shows, and his standby—popular songs. He continued to harp on the familiar themes of patriotism, by that point threaded with Irish American pride, and Broadway, but now largely through the lens of nostalgia.

PRINT, PERSONALITY, PUBLICS: COHAN AND THE LANDSCAPE OF CELEBRITY IN THE EARLY TWENTIETH-CENTURY UNITED STATES

While fame and self-promotion predated Cohan, his lifetime marked a key point in the development of modern celebrity culture, profoundly shaping his career in the entertainment industry. Trains and steamships could transport celebrities themselves around the nation and the world, and telegraphs, telephones, and typewriters could transmit information about them. Audiences spending more time and money on leisure could see photographs of their favorite stars in addition to seeing them on the stage or, with the development of film, on screen. They could hear their voices on phonographs and, later, the radio. And they could read about them in their daily "penny press" newspapers and favorite magazines. Cohan's shows reflected the expansion of the press and the professionalization of journalism; reporters were frequently among their characters.[11]

Affordable forms of printing and distributing print media and the rise of advertising as a means of funding meant that newspapers and magazines proliferated in the late nineteenth and early twentieth centuries, expanding their readerships to reach large popular and niche markets alike and shaping the dimensions of modern fame. "Newspaper publishers," writes cultural historian Leo Braudy, "were the new impresarios."[12] A wealth of theater publications, too, sprang up. "Every trade and occupation to-day is represented in the public print by some organ devoted to its interests, and the theatrical profession is no exception," wrote Michael B. Leavitt in his 1912 memoir *Fifty Years in Theatrical Management*.[13] Trade publications like the *New York Clipper* (1853–1924), its loftier competitor the *Dramatic Mirror* (1879–1922), and *Variety* (founded in 1905) reported almost exclusively on entertainment and the dramatic arts. There were publications put out by producers, like Cohan and Harris's the *Spot Light*, which was both a house organ and a press sheet to be sent to dramatic editors; and those put out by unions or other organizations, like *Player*, the "official organ of the White Rats of America," an association of vaudeville performers. Such publications were valued for contributing to theater's professionalization, "perform[ing] a stupendous part in the task of elevating the dramatic art."[14] Niche theater publications also fed a public interest in the theater's stars. As Cohan launched his career at the turn of the twentieth century, improvements in photography and print prompted "an explosion" of illustrated magazines, including theater magazines, that promised readers, as one put it, "*just what you most want to know* concerning the theatre and its people."[15] Many theater fans and professionals collected the articles and photos in scrapbooks.[16]

As Cohan's case exemplifies, celebrity could be cultivated through engagement with the public and the media, but not singlehandedly; he worked with that increasingly important figure in the early twentieth-century theater business, the press agent.[17] Press agents were a new position, developed in parallel with the rise of popular print media, but they took over many of the duties of the "advance agents" who would travel ahead of a touring show to advertise and prepare for its appearance. As Garrett D. Byrnes of the *Providence Journal* described it, "The theatre-editors of newspapers always know when Mr. Cohan and one of his shows are headed for town, for into the office comes Charley Washburn, the actor-manager-producer's adept press representative. Washburn always has a supply of big press sheets concerning his employer. Across the top of the sheet in big red letters is the caption 'Ready reference for newspaper editors.'"[18]

Cohan and Harris employed a team of publicists, including a New York press representative and those serving as "advance" for various productions.[19] Edward W. Dunn, Walter J. Kingsley, and Charles Washburn seem to be the press agents who worked most closely with Cohan over the course of his career.[20] In a poem called "Lo, the Press Agent" from the 1917 volume *The Broadway Anthology*, Kingsley described these unsung heroes who were "called upon to make the show, / To save the show," but never given the credit of even "the slightest jester or singer or dancer / Who mugs, mimes, or hoofs in a hit." Kingsley describes their remarkable power behind the scenes, abasing and elevating, affixing laughter to gossip so it would take root in New York City and spread to the road, working like a "submarine / Submersible beneath the sea / Of publicity."[21] As Kingsley's poem describes, press agents or publicity promotors sold celebrities as well as shows, discovering them and leading their rise to fame until their names shown in incandescents on Broadway. Especially given the overlap in Cohan's roles as creator, producer, and frequently as star, publicizing Cohan's shows and Cohan himself were much the same job.

Press agents, many of whom had come from careers in journalism, sought to keep their clients in the public eye, largely by generating material for the print media. Actress Laurette Taylor wrote in her 1918 memoir that the press agent's business was "to coax some *sacred* anecdote from you to be blazoned forth as a reason why 'you are you.'"[22] In his book on *Press Agentry*, Washburn advised being truthful with the press—or at least tipping off the editor if a story is a fake—but described creating or capitalizing upon situations that would generate news stories in order to promote theater persons and their endeavors. This might seem "a trick," but "it's a trick era," he wrote.[23] These were often packaged as public interest stories. In 1928, for example, theater columnist Whitney Bolton reported what he described as "the sweetest story that ever came out of Broadway and the unlovely Forties." Billy Bryant, owner and producer of a showboat and a longtime admirer of Cohan, had reportedly been trying for twenty years to license a Cohan show—even one of the oldest, one he could afford. He had been consistently rebuffed by secretaries and play brokers until Eddie Dunn—a Cohan press agent—arranged for him to meet with Cohan himself. Learning of the back history, Cohan told Bryant to take any of his twenty-nine shows without royalties and without strings attached, to adapt as he wanted, and moreover, Cohan promised to come perform for a couple of weeks himself.[24] In a follow-up to the story, Bolton reported that Bryant's musical adaptation of *Broadway Jones* inspired Cohan to write one of his own, named after Bryant—*Billie* (1928)—and for his part, Bryant continued to perform Cohan shows, and to make sure the press knew about it, for years.[25] Cohan blamed (or credited) his then-press agent Charles Washburn for a later episode of the story, appearing in papers in 1936: "You give a press agent a pencil and no telling what he will do," Cohan commented, telling of how Washburn wrote a "tear-jerking letter" purportedly from Cohan to Bryant proposing to "play hookey [*sic*]" and leave the "hardships" of "the Broadway of today" to perform on the showboat.[26]

The Bryant story was effective for multiple reasons. For one, even though a press agent was involved, it was deemed to be plausible—although only barely so. Bolton wanted so much to believe it that he insisted that "the first person who says this is a press agent yarn is off my speaking-to list for life."[27] For another, it was well-timed; it appeared only a month after the hit musical *Show Boat* opened on Broadway. It also could be packaged as business news as well as a public interest story. In allowing a showboat producer to use his shows, the Cohan organization was changing a "life-long policy," *Billboard* reported.[28] Finally, it reinforced the traits for which Cohan was known. Publicity turned what may have otherwise been seen as a purely economic arrangement—and one that could potentially be seen through the lens of decline, as Cohan stooping to a lower level in the entertainment hierarchy to make money and keep his shows relevant—into a heartwarming example of Cohan's generosity, anti-elitism, and authentic roots as a trouper.

While Cohan's celebrity was helped along by talented press agents, he was also a skilled self-publicist in his own right. His sense of humor and perceived openness made him a media darling. "He is the delight of the newspaper men because he always can be counted upon to say something quotable," wrote Byrnes in the *Providence Journal*. Another journalist marveled that an interview with him "became something else . . . infinitely more pleasant." As he explained, "You don't interview George M. Cohan; you talk to him and he talks to you. And the result is no bunkum from either side."[29] Cohan had a facility with language, honed as a playwright, that lent itself to interviews and to writing guest pieces: "His remarks, like the lines he writes for the stage," Byrnes reported, "have a zip and a pithiness."[30] Although press agents surely assisted with the written material, it is probable that much of the writing was indeed Cohan's; he wrote frequently under his own byline and in his own distinctive style.

Cohan became known for his propensity for publicity, even beyond the United States. In 1912, a Dutch newspaper wrote about a particular scheme that they had previously reported as news—a man from Wilkes-Barre, Pennsylvania, had come into some money and used it to be a "millionaire for a day" in New York City, including attending Cohan's musical *The Little Millionaire* and being a guest of Cohan's at a supper party—revealing that Cohan had come up with the whole scheme to advertise two of his shows. Cohan is "very keen on publicity and does everything possible to be mentioned in one newspaper or another at least every day," the article stated, noting that it is no easy feat to get that much free advertising.[31] Cohan faced similar charges in the United States. On the front page of one issue of the *Spot Light*, he responded to a critic with the front-page column "Am I an Egotist?," in which he denied egotism but claimed his success and defended his self-promotion in no uncertain terms.[32] Multiple newspapers reprinted Cohan's article verbatim, amplifying his self-publicity.

Interviews with and stories about Cohan sold because he was thought to have the highly valued quality of personality. Cohan defines "personality" in a song by that name in *Billie* as the "art of attracting attention." It is not a practiced skill, the song explains; rather, it is innate and distributed by nature, and only some are given the key to unlock it. Not unlike the charm that Cohan ascribed to his 1920s Irish American heroines, Billie's personality is "unexplainable," "unattainable," but ultimately the "golden key to success." The lilting 6/8 melody, with the word "personality" introduced offbeat for emphasis, musically suggests the graceful, easy mannerisms, "in a wink or the wave of an arm," that give the bearer her captivation (Figure 5.2). A second verse that was included in an early script before being cut drives home that personality is one's "own and original style" while also

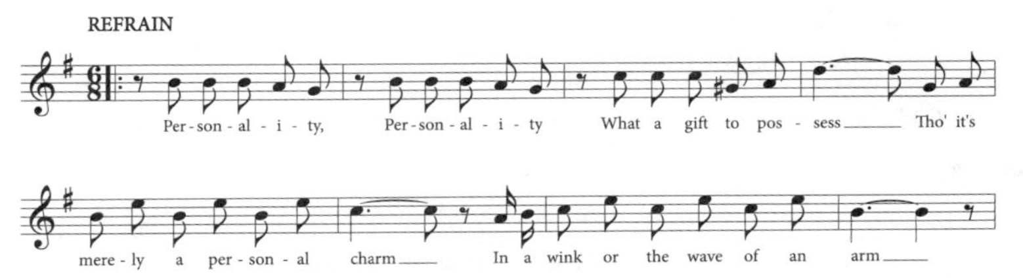

Figure 5.2 Beginning of the refrain of "Personality," voice only. Published by M. Witmark (1928).

commenting on its potential as a "spendable" commodity. "Oh, how eas'ly the public responds / Even richer than government bonds," Cohan writes.[33]

Cohan's was not the first song dedicated to "personality," which was a ubiquitous topic of the day, but it aptly captures contemporary discourse about it.[34] Referring to "the peculiar array of faculties, instincts, and dispositions that made each man or woman unique," personality, as historian Charles Ponce de Leon has written, overtook character as the ideal in the twentieth century.[35] Though possible to cultivate, a vivid or magnetic personality was also considered a gift (as Cohan describes in his song), and celebrities like Cohan had it. "It is curious how he dominates every group, large or small, of which he is a part. It isn't that he *tries* to do it. It's his personality. There's just something electric about him," an anonymous friend told *American Magazine* in 1919. "If he went into a room full of people, not one of whom knew who he was, it would be the same. Don't ask me why. As near as I can tell, it's because every nerve and fiber of him is *alive*." Mary Mullett, the article's author, found the most common description of Cohan to be "a real live wire."[36] Cohan's personality was discussed as an entity apart from the man himself; one newspaper article, for instance, proclaimed Cohan's personality "the real star" of *Yankee Doodle Dandy*, the biopic about his life.[37]

Cohan first became known, as he rose to fame, for being young, cocky, and a bit rebellious. His distinctive personality had polarizing effects. Many hated it—*Life* magazine critic James Metcalfe, who particularly disliked Cohan's flag-waving shows, complained that there was "no reason for his obtruding his personality on the stage" though he regretfully acknowledged "the fact that there seems to be an admiring following for his cock-sure vulgarity in bearing and manner of speech."[38] In contrast, Oscar Hammerstein II, who was Cohan's junior by seventeen years, was one of Cohan's young fans. "Here was the kind of young American we all hoped to be when we grew a few years older," wrote Hammerstein in his 1957 tribute, remembering that he and his friends called Cohan "slick" and noting that "higher praise had we for no one." The parts Cohan wrote for himself, Hammerstein noted, were "young men of poise, authority, and quick wit," and Cohan was "a smooth article on the stage." Hammerstein recollected that he sang "out of the side of his mouth. This habit, accompanied by a kind of droop of the eyelids, made him seem so sophisticated, so casual, so above it all! He danced in a slight crouch and had a trick of letting his head wag loosely on his neck with a kind of jaded relaxation. . . . He used only [dance] steps which he could perform with such consummate ease that, as you watched him, you felt almost as if you were doing the dancing yourself."[39] Cohan's appeal to young men, as theater scholar Michael Schwartz writes, was similar to that of later icons like a James Dean or a Marlon Brando.[40]

Cohan's fashion choices fit a public image built on youth, the informality of the everyday, and abundant energy combined with insouciance.[41] A 1907 *Chicago Tribune* article on "How Actors Dress Off the Stage" reported that Cohan "care[d] little for his personal appearance off the stage" and that "he started the fad of wearing soft felt hats which are known as 'George Cohan hats.'"[42] (Advertisements attest to the "Cohan hat" trend. For example, Figure 5.3 shows

Figure 5.3 Advertisement for "The 'George Cohan'" hat, Arkansas City Daily Traveler, *September 27, 1907.*

the first image in an "all-star cast" line-up of six hats fashioned on the styles of star actors.) Hammerstein remembered Cohan's look in detail fifty years later: "His trousers had a razor-sharp crease. His shoes were not only snugly fitting buttoned shoes, but they had gray cloth tops. A cane was one of the constant props he used on the stage, and how slickly he used it! His top hats, straw hats, and derbies (gray or brown) were worn at a slickly tilted angle." The early photo of Cohan shown in Figure 5.4 captures the effect, with Cohan's cool, direct gaze; casual stance; and cigarette. In addition to hats, fans could seek out Cohan

Figure 5.4 George M. Cohan (1904). From the collection of Scott A. Sandage.

cigarette cards, hand mirrors, playing cards (he was the three of hearts in a special "The Stage" deck), and at least one doll.[43]

His celebrity status was also evident in the frequency with which he was imitated by vaudeville performers and caricaturists, as well as by everyday fellows like Hammerstein and his classmates. In what historian Susan A. Glenn has described as a "mimetic moment in American comedy," vaudeville acts mimicking individual celebrities were common.[44] The instantly recognizable hallmarks of Cohan's personality, like his nasal voice, drawling way of speaking out of the side of his mouth, distinctive strut, and trademark curtain speech ("my mother thanks you, my father thanks you, my sister thanks you, and I thank you") lent themselves to imitation, making him a favorite choice. In her memoir of their "all-star" wartime benefit tour of the play *Out There* by J. Hartley Manners, Laurette Taylor recounted that a man offered $500 to the Red Cross in return for an imitation of Cohan. "Anybody can give a bad imitation of 'The Yankee Doodle Boy,'" she wrote, "and I did."[45]

Cohan appreciated these imitations, calling them "the sincerest form of flattery," and recognized that they were a mutually beneficial arrangement for the imitator and imitated.[46] Sometimes theatergoers could even see the imitation and the real thing back-to-back. Shortly after actress Elsie Janis performed in New York the same week as *Little Johnny Jones* was playing, Cohan gave her a plug, reporting to the press, "Elsie Janis is giving imitations of me on the New York roof. Elsie Janis is the best photographer I ever had."[47] Writer Faith Baldwin, a friend of Janis's, wrote Cohan a few years later, "I saw you for the first time last night, but I almost felt as though I knew you because I've seen Elsie Janis imitate you so many times both on and off the stage"; the letter was printed in the *Spot Light*.[48] Gertrude Hoffman, another acclaimed Cohan imitator, was cast in Cohan's 1907 summer show *The Honeymooners*, in which she performed imitations (although not, in this case, of him) in the third act.[49] By then, the Cohan imitation had "become as common as wet skirts in a rainstorm," and by 1911, Cohan had been "imitated to weariness by the youth of the stage," Minneapolis and Boston newspapers reported.[50] Even the "real thing" was seen as a construction. What the youth were imitating, the *Boston Transcript* critic said, was the Cohan who was "an impersonator of himself." His celebrity personality, according to the critic, was only one of the "manifold emanations of [Cohan's] being."[51] Cohan's distinctive personal traits lent themselves to cartoons as well, where a hat, cane, and forward-leaning stance could signal it was Cohan even without the face (see Figure 5.5a).

In short, Cohan exuded personality both onstage and off, in ways that engaged the public and the media alike, whether or not they found it appealing.

Figure 5.5a and Figure 5.5b Cartoons of George M. Cohan in The Little Millionaire *in* Stage Folk: A Book of Caricatures *(1915) and the* St. Louis Dispatch *(1906). National Portrait Gallery, Smithsonian Institution; gift of the children of Al Frueh—Barbara Frueh Bornemann, Robert Frueh and Alfred Frueh Jr.*

Celebrity journalism also, however, sought to give the public glimpses of the "real self" behind the curtain. Cohan satisfied these demands and created a niche for himself while keeping his current personal life remarkably private by tying his autobiographical narrative to patriotism and theater. He became known not only for his distinctive personal characteristics but for being the embodiment of the nation and of Broadway.

YANKEE DOODLE COHAN

Another cartoon, also by Al Frueh, captured Cohan's first and most enduring self-fashioning, as the emblem of the nation (Figure 5.5b).[52] By carefully aligning himself with the United States offstage as well as on, Cohan, an unlikely candidate as a third-generation Irish vaudevillian child actor, established a life-long identification as *the* Yankee Doodle Boy from his hit song. By 1934, a retrospective article on *Little Johnny Jones* could declare that "George M. Cohan is looked upon as a kind of national institution."[53] As Chapter 1 discusses, Cohan played markedly American roles, sang patriotic songs, decorated the stage with flags, and marketed his shows in ways that highlighted themes of American identity and pride. Cohan further bolstered his patriotic persona in interviews and articles. In a facetious article called "Save the U.S. Actor," written by the actor William Collier and edited by Cohan, for instance, each actor was likened to an American president—Cohan, unsurprisingly, to George Washington.[54]

Cohan's Fourth of July birthday was a convenient token of authenticity. Documentation reveals, however, that this was a stretching of the truth, part of the Yankee Doodle persona. Cohan's birthdate has been a matter of dispute: after biographer Ward Morehouse uncovered a baptismal certificate naming July 3 as Cohan's birth date, theater scholar John McCabe, in the next book on Cohan, argued that "the baptismal certificate hardly settles the matter," suggesting that the date was a "clerical error." He mentions (though does not cite) a diary entry by Jerry and the fact that Jerry and Nellie always celebrated their son's birthday on the fourth.[55] The birth registry from the city of Boston, however, shows that it was, indeed, the third, and an entry in Jerry's diary, which was posted for private auction in 2011, actually marks July 3, 1883 "George's birthday."[56]

When did Cohan's birthday "become" the fourth, then, who changed it, and why? The *New York Clipper*, in 1897, stated that he was born July 3, as does reporting about George's marriage to Ethel Levey in 1899. An article as late as 1906 reports on July 4 that Cohan "was twenty-eight years old yesterday" and that he had received presents and a dinner in his honor from his family, friends, and business associates.[57] However, as early as 1895, a blurb in the *Boston Globe* has his birthday as the fourth. After Cohan played the title character in *Little Johnny Jones* in 1904, singing the "I'm a Yankee Doodle Dandy . . . born on the fourth of July," mentions of Cohan's own birthday as the fourth became more common. By 1906, the article reporting his July 3 celebration notwithstanding, George had settled on July 4. He broadcast it in a special edition of the *Spot Light* on July 4, 1906, a "Birthday Number" for "Yankee Doodle Cohan," where the back cover featured Uncle Sam holding up a portrait of George M. and saying "That's my boy!" (Figure 5.6). In the same year, using duplicate text that must have come from a separate handout supplied by a press agent or Cohan himself, publications from *Billboard* to *Town and Country* proclaimed him a "Yankee Doodle comedian" and the "real live nephew of Uncle Sam" born "the morning of July fourth."[58]

Figure 5.6 Back Cover of the Spot Light, *July 4, 1906. Eda Kuhn Loeb Music Library, Harvard University. (A color version of this figure is included in the color insert.)*

Cohan continued to publicize and embrace the fourth as his birthday. Writing on "My Beginnings" for *Theatre Magazine* in 1907, Cohan stated that the event of his birth, "if not one of national importance, was associated with one that was such."[59] He attributed the shape of his career to being "born under the Stars and Stripes," and he even chose it for the date of his wedding to Agnes Nolan.[60] He also listed the fourth as his birthdate on his draft registration card in 1918.[61] It is likely that by that point, few remembered that he had actually been born before and not after midnight. Cohan's emphasis on his birth and upbringing—which he would draw upon many times in interviews, articles, and his 1924 autobiography—fit efforts to self-consciously present authentic-seeming life stories that were part of the developing culture of celebrity stretching back to the late eighteenth century.[62]

Article after article enforced the idea, put forth by Cohan, that he was uniquely equipped to represent the nation. Just as he was quintessentially American, so were his subjects. "Young America, as one finds him in the street, is the type of character George M. Cohan tries to represent," an article in *Theatre Magazine* reported. "Who could have a better opportunity for studying the many-sided American from all sides," the author asked, "than one doing a 'continuous' turn all over the country almost from the time he was able to walk on the stage?"[63] Cohan wore the mantle of Yankee Doodle dramatist well. He wrote in 1915, "I got every inspiration of my life from American sources. I never saw anything in Europe I wanted to bring home. American life is good enough for me to write about, because it is the real, honest-to-goodness life. American characters are the best in the world; American people are the best in the world, I think; I believe in the Stars and Stripes as I have written and sung of them, and I never aspire to write about anything but America."[64]

Cohan sought not merely to describe Americanism as a creator of theater and even to embody it as a performer, but also to claim it as his personal identity. He enacted, in effect, his own plot of *George Washington, Jr.* (1906), with his "rechristening of himself as the junior of the Father of His country through emulative loyalty."[65] To appreciate Cohan, his rhetoric suggested, was not just to be any old celebrity fan, it was to be a patriotic American. Cohan's patriotism, which was by all accounts sincere, was thus also strategic, and several commentators, both then and since, recognized the ways in which Cohan was advantageously equating himself and his ideas with Americanism.[66] One reviewer of *The American Idea* (1908) complained: "Mr. George Cohan is suffering pathetically, even ostentatiously, from delusions of grandeur. Evidently, he regards himself as what the sociologists call a type. Now the humblest and quietest of us—and Mr. Cohan is hardly that—is entitled to his own notions, his own ways and his own tastes. He may even put them, if he has the aptitude and can find the means, into a musical play. But it is another thing to label all this 'American' and to proclaim it accordingly."[67]

Yet even if his perceived flag-waving hurt his position with certain critics, it also bolstered his reputation for nonconformity, often a positive trait of celebrity; helped keep his name in the pages of newspapers and magazines; and ultimately helped him with the public—the ticket-buyers and ultimate arbiters.[68]

The public perception of Cohan as quintessentially, or perhaps excessively, American overshadowed but did not erase his perceived racial status. Journalists often remarked upon his racial background, whether recognizing him as Irish or—as was not uncommon—mistaking him for Jewish, due to similarities between "Cohan" and the common Jewish name "Cohen." Their comments demonstrate why it was advantageous for Cohan to construct a broader, patriotic persona. *Life*'s Metcalfe wrote in 1906: "One curious feature of [Cohan's] career is that his real name is said on good authority to be Costigan. It is not unusual for a Hebrew to exchange a patronymic which betrays his race for one which will conceal it, but for anyone bearing such a good old mouth-filling name as Costigan to change for a distinctively Hebrew appellation is strange indeed. However, Mr. Cohan is very shrewd in a business way and, considering present conditions in the theatre in America, he was perhaps wise in his choice."[69] From this account emerges hints of Metcalfe's and his magazine's known anti-Semitism, expressed in his obvious distaste for the "present conditions in the theatre"—that is, the prevalence of Jews.[70] Metcalfe also links Cohan, as a member of another immigrant group, to the endemic stereotype of Jews as greedy, exploitative, and too powerful in business, suggesting that Cohan would even go so far as to change his name to improve his bottom line. Soon thereafter, *Life* corrected its factual error, though not its noxious undertones, explaining that Costigan was Cohan's mother's name.

A common joke was that Cohan benefited from the confusion, allowing him to capture the Jewish as well as the Irish audience.[71] Cohan and his publicists also capitalized upon the jokes themselves, using the currency of ethnic humor. In one telling, Cohan flipped the joke. When Otto Harbach asked, "George, why do you give so many Irish titles to your shows—*Little Nellie Kelly*, *The O'Brien Girl*?" Cohan responded, "It brings the Irish into the theatre. The Jews come anyway."[72] Such jokes were frequently told for theater insiders, many of whom were Jewish. For example, the sketch he wrote for an event for the Lambs Club, a theatrical social organization, included this bit about Cohan and his business partner Sam Harris, who was Jewish:

BOY. (*At door*) Cohan and Harris have arrived.
[HOTEL] MANAGER. Cohan and Harris! Great Scot, aren't there anything but Jews in the show business!

[THEATER PRODUCER ARTHUR] HOPKINS. Pardon me! Cohan and Harris are not both Jews. One of them may be a Jew, but Sam Harris is as good an Irishman as ever lived.[73]

These accounts illustrate how Cohan deployed humor to navigate ethnicity and the politics of show business. They also suggest how ethnic and national identity could be leveraged, shaped to the circumstances in order to appeal to various audiences.

BROADWAY'S PRESS AGENT

As Broadway became a physical place and a commercial entity in the early twentieth century, Cohan imbued it with symbolic cachet.[74] In a 1915 article, he referred to himself, tongue in cheek, as "Broadway's press-agent."[75] It was an apt descriptor: he spoke and wrote frequently about Broadway in the press. More importantly, New York City settings and Broadway types abounded in his shows, and the word "Broadway" itself appears in four of his show titles and over a dozen of his songs. Titles such as "Too Many Miles Away from Old Broadway" (1901), "Give My Regards to Broadway" (1904), and "Too Long from Long Acre Square" (1907), among others, indelibly etched the heart of New York and the theater industry in the popular imagination.

Cohan's Broadway songs also inextricably linked it with American identity: Broadway, as "All Aboard for Broadway" (1906) asserted, was "the Yankeeland." In many cases, Cohan juxtaposed Broadway with foreign lands, as in the best-known of these songs, "Give My Regards to Broadway." Sung in *Little Johnny Jones*, in a scene set in London where a ship is departing for the United States (see Figure 5.7), the song's lyrics present the scenario of one American bidding goodbye to another who is returning home. He asks his friend to:

> Give my regards to Broadway,
> remember me to Herald Square,
> Tell all the gang at Forty-Second street,
> that I will soon be there;
> Whisper of how I'm yearning,
> To mingle with the old time throng,
> Give my regards to old Broadway
> and say that I'll be there e'er long.[76]

The lyrics reference specific places in New York: Coney Isle and the Waldorf Hotel in addition to Herald Square and Forty-Second Street. However, with language mixing informal ("old pal") with elevated, almost archaic language and a jaunty, mostly harmonically straightforward tune colored by a half-diminished chord that lends the words "Broadway" and "yearning" a wistful pang, the affect is of a broader sort of patriotic longing. In recordings of Cohan singing "Give My Regards to Broadway," from events in 1939 and 1940, he further emphasizes the song's yearning quality by slightly delaying the arrival of that word, which is written to be sung on the first beat (▶ Example 5.2).[77]

While Cohan wrote *about* Broadway, it was never only *for* Broadway. He found that rural audiences as well as urban had "a yen," as he put it, for songs and stories about New York.[78] Indeed, as discussed in Chapter 3, touring was essential to Cohan and Harris's business model, and as theater scholar James Fisher surmises, it contributed to the national celebrity of "this quintessential New Yorker."[79] Cohan's Broadway was thus pitched at audiences on the road as much as it was to New Yorkers. He frequently used the concept of Broadway in contrast to rural or suburban America, as in *Forty-Five Minutes from Broadway*, set in New Rochelle, New York, and *Broadway Jones*, about a Broadway type who finds his purpose in Jonesville, Connecticut. In the song "You Can Have Broadway" (1906), a character dreams of leaving Broadway for a country cottage but, given the opportunity, cannot cope with rural life

Figure 5.7 George M. Cohan in Little Johnny Jones. *Theater Biography Collection, Harry Ransom Center, University of Texas at Austin.*

and ends up going back to the city (▶ Example 5.3). Cohan's Broadway did not only romanticize the city and the theater, then; it also spoke to contemporary anxieties about urbanization and national identity in ways that could appeal to a range of audiences.

Cohan hitched his wagon to Broadway just as he did to patriotism, symbolically and strategically linking his public persona to both. He anthropomorphized Broadway, as in the song "Give My Regards to Broadway," and he sang and wrote as if Broadway were a personal chum. When he retired from the stage in 1920, he wrote "dear old friend Broadway" a heartfelt letter, a sentiment he put into song with "'Tisn't Easy to Say Goodbye Broadway" published in 1924. Further linking Broadway to American identity, Cohan wrote that it was Broadway who "whispered in [his] ear" to keep waving the American flag because "it [would] do [them] both a lot of good."[80] Cohan's Broadway, although frenetic and hedonistic, was also imbued with a sense of the mystical, as in this passage from *Broadway Jones* (1912), which biographer John McCabe evocatively describes as a sort of catechism:

> JOSIE. What is Broadway? . . . A street?
> JACKSON [JONES]. Sure, it's the greatest street in the world.
> JOSIE. Some people say it's terrible.
> JACKSON. Philadelphia people.
> JOSIE. And some people say it's wonderful.
> JACKSON. That's just it. It's terribly wonderful!
> JOSIE. I don't understand.
> JACKSON. Nobody understands Broadway. People hate it and don't know why. People love it and don't know why. It's just because it's Broadway.
> JOSIE. That's a mystery, isn't it?
> JACKSON. That's just what it is, a mystery.[81]

Selling Broadway was profitable. As Cohan put it, Broadway, "that little street," made him millions.[82] By writing about Broadway in his shows and songs and by stressing his upbringing in the theater in the press, Cohan positioned himself as its premier representative and spokesperson. Eventually, Cohan was given yet another nickname to add to his "Yankee Doodle" soubriquets: "Mr. Broadway."[83]

Cohan's ability to give an expert's view into the workings of Broadway theater provided yet another rich source of material for the press. As he shifted into a more managerial role around 1909 and into the 1910s, he kept his name in front of the public with articles for the *Saturday Evening Post* on the workings of musical comedy and the actor's changing position in the theatrical business; and for the *New York Tribune* about stock theatrical character types and plots, what qualities of a play script appeal to producers, and actors who unscrupulously seek to steal the spotlight.[84] It gave him a hook besides himself, something else upon which to pull back the curtain besides his own private life. The *Green Book Magazine* serial "The Stage as I Have Seen It," for instance, promised heaps of "'inside' information about stage affairs" in addition to "Cohan's *own* life story of his life and work."[85] Much later, in the 1930s when he was reflecting on his long career, Cohan wrote for the *New York Times* on "what ails the theatre" and what its future would hold.[86]

By the end of his career, Cohan's relationship with Broadway had shifted. In a *New York Times* article written in 1936 while his play *Dear Old Darling* was touring, he sought to correct the notion that he had forsaken Broadway. He wrote that Broadway had seemed "the beginning and the ending of the world" when he first arrived in 1893 with his family's variety act, but that "we've lost the Broadway we used to know," at least the friendship part. "Broadway today," he added, "is the symbol for The Stage." Indeed, he had helped create it as such. Now he mused about what it meant. Thinking over the "old [Broadway] titles," he realized, "The Four Cohans thought of the road and appreciated that Broadway stood for more than a row of incandescents—it stood for the stage." He closed by invoking the trains that carried trouping performers across the country: "Ticket and parlor car seat, James—Broadway!"[87] Emphasizing that Broadway stood for the stage nationwide, not only in New York, the article also shows how Cohan's perspective had become increasingly oriented toward the past. After his battle with Equity and subsequent separation from Harris, as he aged and as Broadway styles changed, nostalgia became the dominant lens through which he sold his songs, his shows, and himself.

THE THROWBACK

By the mid-1920s and increasingly in the 1930s, George M. Cohan was marketed as the past. His hit songs were republished as "Songs of Yesteryear" as early as 1924.[88] They appeared in the *Stage* magazine's "Fond Recollections Number" in August 1938. Cohan had spent much of the 1920s saying his sentimental, widely publicized goodbye to Broadway onstage, in print, and in song. "George M. Cohan Leaves Broadway," newspapers across the country proclaimed at the end of the 1921 theatrical season.[89] What would his next move be? Upon closing up shop, papers reported, Cohan was planning to buy a baseball team, to produce shows in London, "to raise beets and turnips" at home in Great Neck, New York.[90] The *Vancouver Daily World* took a more skeptical tone, declaring "George M. Cohan Is a Fiend for Free Publicity" in the headline of an article reporting that Cohan's announcement that he would never produce again was estimated to have "netted him nearly 30 feet of publicity in New York City alone," which "at average space rates" would cost $2,500.[91]

This was not Cohan's first retirement, nor would it be his last. He "Sarahbernhardted" it, as one paper put it in reference to Bernhardt's many so-called farewell tours, several times throughout his career, announcing that he was stepping down from acting, producing, or theater altogether.[92] Biographer John McCabe described it as "the one absolutely predictable pattern of his life."[93] He never did quit; he continued to write, perform in, and produce shows up until the rapid decline of his health in 1942 and subsequent death in November of that year.[94] Yet after his post–Equity battle farewell of 1921, he never fully regained his former standing as Broadway's fresh young upstart or as one of its biggest moguls, either. Instead, he maintained his cultural relevance by trafficking in nostalgia: in the print media, in radio programs, in the roles he played on stage, in his songs, and as America's "First Actor," seen now as one of the treasures of American theater.

By the 1930s, the world of musical theater had changed rapidly since Cohan's arrival on the scene in the aughts. Cohan had precipitated many of the changes—for instance, helping to bring the most recent Black popular music style, ragtime, into musical comedy, and declaring cultural independence from Europe—but the developments he helped set in motion continued on without him. The second half of the 1910s was a pivotal time not only for Cohan, as he went from the peak of success to *persona non grata* in theatrical society, but also for the nation, with World War I, the influenza pandemic of 1918, and labor unrest beyond Broadway. The United States' entry into World War I transformed American musical life and accelerated the push away from Old World authority. Jazz emerged from its regional roots in Black communities to become a national craze, with White as well as Black fans and, increasingly, musicians; by the mid-1920s it had replaced ragtime as the up-to-date vernacular music of Broadway. With the development of sound film in the late 1920s, vaudeville faded, theater increasingly competed with this new recorded form, and a new genre—the film musical—arose, with many artists and stars moving between Broadway and Hollywood.[95]

In many ways, Cohan continued to develop as a playwright, composer, and performer. In addition to embracing Irish American protagonists and themes, he demonstrated the depth and range of his acting abilities and experimented with genre and form by taking metatheatricality to the hilt with *The Musical Comedy Man*, the show he began working on in 1940, in the years before his death.[96] Yet he showed little interest in the new popular trends transforming the stage. Responding to a *Forum* magazine debate about whether jazz was music, Cohan wrote a letter to the editor musing about jazz, its relationship to popular song, and, more broadly, "where popular melody belongs in the scheme of music." He said he planned to do "some research work along 'jazz lines,'" concluding, "Maybe, for the first time, I'll write out-and-out jazz music just to see what happens."[97] He did not.

Cohan had slightly more interest in Hollywood but was ultimately disappointed. Several of his shows were adapted into silent films in the late teens and early twenties, and he acted in a few, but he did not return to make a sound film until 1932, at which point he appeared in *The Phantom President*, with songs by Richard Rodgers and Lorenz Hart.[98] While he expressed curiosity about movies just as he had about jazz, he did not ultimately care for the experience. "I'm used to running all over the stage, but here they put you in one spot and tell you to act," he "ruefully" told one reporter.[99] He disliked performing a work written by others, in which he was not permitted to improvise. "For years I've hardly written or sung a line which wasn't my own. Now if I try to change a word they say, 'Text, please.'"[100] He reportedly did not care for Rodgers and Hart's songs for the film, and he found that Hollywood had no use for him as a songwriter. (These were issues that resurfaced when he performed in works by others, especially in the Rodgers and Hart show *I'd Rather Be Right* five years later.) After his experience in *The Phantom President*, Cohan decided that while acting in "talkies" was "an interesting and educational experience," he did not feel at home there. "I suppose it is just a case of every dog liking his own kennel. And the stage is my kennel," he told the press.[101] By 1934 he was less tactful: "If I had my choice between Hollywood and Atlanta," he quipped, "I'd take Leavenworth" (at that time, the nation's maximum-security federal penitentiary).[102]

Radio helped maintain Cohan's national presence in the 1930s. Cohan was not enthusiastic about radio, in particular its sponsors and "commercial talk."[103] Still, he disliked it less than film and found it more akin to show business, "just a new slant."[104] In addition to frequent guest appearances and interviews, he headlined a Gulf Oil–sponsored series of Sunday night programs for a few stints in 1933 and 1934, filling in for primary star Will Rogers. Cohan wrote and performed in a revue format that mixed old songs and new, woven together by quasi-sung verse. Taking listeners "down through Memory Lane," his programs contributed to the nostalgia that was ingrained in the medium of radio from its outset and also came to be characteristic of American musical theatrical entertainment.[105] They capitalized on his celebrity, especially with older audiences, and introduced him to younger radio fans for whom, as a *Variety* article put it, his "yesteryear's tradition may be a bit obscure."[106] The programs offered reminiscences of both a past time lost to modernity and past shows that, due to theater's ephemerality, could never be reseen. They hit all of Cohan's old themes—Broadway, Irish pride, and patriotism, which, as he explained in one show, was what the listeners most requested.[107] He even included minstrel songs and "coon songs" stretching back to the 1890s, joining other radio artists who, by resurrecting these numbers, prolonged the longevity of their offensive imagery.[108] For his songs and shows of the 1920s, he seemed to assume listeners' familiarity, but for earlier fare, songs "so old they're almost new," he explained their significance.[109] In a newly written bit to introduce his song "When We Are M-A-R-R-I-E-D," he sang, "Did you ever see a play called *The Talk of New York*? / It was the talk of New York in its day. / For it was then quite up to date / Way back in nineteen hundred and eight."[110] Radio was not only a time capsule back to earlier shows, however. Many of the numbers Cohan included were originally sung by other performers, so radio provided the chance for listeners to hear Cohan performing them for the first time.

In keeping with his self-constructed persona as a genre-bending, anti-elite cultural renegade, Cohan exposed the workings of radio, broke its ostensible rules, and poked fun at them as he had in theater, in his characteristic humorously self-reflexive style. In one, he describes the NBC building in New York, in another the process of creating a radio show.[111] In yet another, he begins by interrupting the announcer to say that he will be singing the whole program that night. Each time the announcer tries to plug Gulf oil, Cohan jumps in to insist on doing it in song.[112] And in a fourth, he sings of all the topsy-turvy things he will do when he has "a little broadcast station of [his] own," like having Al Jolson doing *Hamlet* and Will Rogers singing "Mammy" songs and putting the sponsors in front of the microphones. An announcer interrupts to charge Cohan with changing the script and "kidding" the sponsors, and he insists that Cohan apologize to the audience. Striking the familiar theme of being a lowbrow among highbrows, Cohan claims not to know the word "facetious" and volleys one of his own, "fancifuleetus."[113] It was all very Cohanesque, to borrow critics' favorite explanation of his metatheatrical devices, and reminiscent of his earlier shows.

Cohan's broadcasts not only revived his reputation for patriotism but also gave it new dimension as he helped radio fulfill a civic mission in the context of the Great Depression. He could function as a unifying figure, as when Prohibition was repealed and he offered a toast "from coast to coast" both "to those who made the fight" and "those who fought against it."[114] He advanced the agenda of the New Deal, premiering a series of songs in support of the NRA (National Recovery Administration) and Roosevelt administration. These included "The N.R.A. Song" (see Figure 5.8), a jaunty song in the style of other Cohan "spelling songs" like "F-A-M-E"; and "Santa Claus of the U.S.A.," about FDR as the national Santa, sending "little bundles" marked NRA from his desk at the White House.[115] It is unclear to what extent the songs and their content were Cohan's idea. Although he later became disillusioned with FDR, Cohan was a proponent early on and wrote another song in support of Roosevelt in 1934, "What a Man!" At the same time, many radio performers had pledged to lend their services to the NRA, and at least the first of Cohan's songs was reported to be "at the suggestion of" government officials.[116] Moreover, Cohan made clear in his broadcasts that his shows were subject to the whims of radio executives. Regardless of how invested Cohan was personally in the New Deal songs, his Yankee Doodle image made him an ideal choice to help demonstrate commercial radio's patriotic potential, all the while bolstering his own reputation.[117]

In newly published songs as well as those for the radio, Cohan retooled his flag-waving style. Drawing upon his patriotic reputation in service of national events, he supplied "Thomas A. Edison: Miracle Man" (1929) for the "Light's Golden Jubilee" celebration of the anniversary of the invention of the lightbulb and "Father of the Land We Love" (1931) in honor of the two-hundredth anniversary of George Washington's birth. With World War II on the horizon, he premiered "We Must Be Ready" in April 1939; with the borrowing typical of his earlier patriotic mode songs, the tune was "threaded with remembered strains of 'Over There.' "[118] He again borrowed from "Over There" in two additional songs responding to World War II, "This Is Our Side of the Ocean" (1940) and "For the Flag, For the Home, For the Family (For the Future of All Mankind)" (1942). The stars and stripes sheet music covers recalled the cover of "You're a Grand Old Flag" and other hits from *George Washington, Jr.*, but the image of the elder Cohan that adorned them looked pensive and distinguished (Figure 5.9).

During the 1930s, Cohan returned to other familiar topics with even more palpable nostalgic sentiment, as in the song "When New York Was New York (New York Was a Wonderful Town)" (1937). The song was marketed explicitly for its nostalgia; the sheet music was released in the Jerry Vogel Memory Lane series. Described as a "lament," the song is a waltz with melodic rhythm

Figure 5.8 "The N.R.A. Song" (1933). Sam DeVincent Collection of Illustrated American Sheet Music, Archives Center, National Museum of American History, Smithsonian Institution.

Figure 5.9 *Cover of "For the Flag, For the Home, For the Family (For the Future of All Mankind)." Published by Vogel Music (1942). Theater Biography Collection, Harry Ransom Center, The University of Texas at Austin. (A color version of this figure is included in the color insert.)*

and oom-pah-pah accompaniment that calls back the time of "your Dad and my Dad." Music, subject matter, and sentiment all unmistakably invoked, for audiences who remembered the tune, "Sidewalks of New York" (1894) by Charles B. Lawlor and James W. Blake, whether from its heyday or perhaps as a carousel tune or as the campaign song for politician Al Smith in the 1920s (Figure 5.10 and ▶ Examples 5.4 and 5.5).[119] With lyrics written in past tense, "Sidewalks of New York" is already infused with nostalgia for the days "we would sing and waltz."[120] O. O. McIntyre had said in his widely read newspaper column many years before that the song "smacks of the days that are gone—when New York was New York."[121] Perhaps Cohan had come across the column, for he puts the idea into music, pairing a nostalgia for a musically simpler time "before we went jazz mad" with a longing for an earlier time and place when New York, though less "great," felt more like a "town," before it started "losing its heart and its soul."[122] With lyrics in the first person and Cohan's image on the cover, the song is sold on his celebrity, as songwriter, and presented as his personal sentiment, capturing the bygone days of Broadway.

Cohan also stoked nostalgia and contributed to the historicization of American theater—with himself, of course, front and center in that history—through the written word. Joining a bevy of critics and theater professionals both fostering and taking advantage of public interest in the stage and popular music industry, he published his autobiography *Twenty Years on Broadway and the Years It Took to Get There: The True Story of a Trouper's Life from the Cradle to the "Closed Shop"* in 1924, first as a magazine serial then as a book.[123] From 1924 to 1925, Cohan also wrote a widely syndicated column, and a few years later he wrote the sweeping serial *Broadway as It Once Was, Is and Will Be: As Seen and Foreseen by George M. Cohan* (in 1930).[124] These firsthand accounts of theater's bygone days offered a Cohanesque form of nostalgia: casual, jocular, self-referential, a "combination of self-glorification and self-satirization," as a review described his

Figure 5.10 Beginning of chorus of "When New York Was New York (New York Was a Wonderful Town)," voice only. Published by Jerry Vogel Music (1937).

autobiography.[125] The latter reinforced all the Yankee Doodle mythology, though with a self-aware kidding, as in this passage: "I was born. Not just ordinarily born, but born on the Fourth of July. (There he goes again.)"[126] Cohan took a full three-quarters of his autobiography to get to his first Broadway hit, *Little Johnny Jones*, in 1904. This served to shape the plot around his striving for success and personal development, but it also further aligned his personal history with that of the stage and the nation, a pattern continued in the 1942 biopic *Yankee Doodle Dandy*. "The years of his youth and early manhood were the changing years of the American stage, and few men had more to do with the change than he. Therefore the history of his progress . . . is a valuable version of the often-told history of the American stage," one reviewer wrote, adding, "There is no such book more basically American."[127]

Cohan's most successful efforts in his later career, but also those that seemed to leave him most conflicted, were his performances in the Eugene O'Neill play *Ah, Wilderness!* in 1933 and the musical comedy *I'd Rather Be Right*, with book by Moss Hart and George S. Kaufman, lyrics by Lorenz Hart, and music by Richard Rodgers, in 1937. Both invoked a kind of nostalgia and, like the shows Cohan wrote for himself to act in, were chances for Cohan to align his onstage and offstage identities, shoring up his public persona. *Ah, Wilderness!* was a "nostalgic comedy" set in 1906, in which Cohan played a small-town father. Brooks Atkinson's *New York Times* review carried the headline "In Which Eugene O'Neill Recaptures the Past in a Comedy with George M. Cohan." Atkinson found Cohan's performance in *Ah, Wilderness!* the "ripest" and "finest" of his career, "suggesting . . . that his past achievements are no touchstone of the qualities he has never exploited."[128] The work and Cohan's performance returned audience members to the moment of his heyday, but now through a different, more mature lens. According to O'Neill, one of the things that attracted Cohan to this part—Cohan had turned down a previous role in an O'Neill play—was the fact that the first act takes place on July 4.[129] *I'd Rather Be Right* offered audiences a different type of return to the past, to Cohan's days as a "song-and-dance man." Playing a singing, dancing FDR who boasts of his "personality," Cohan delighted audiences and critics with his energy and ability to perform as he had thirty years earlier, even bringing in "a few of the old Cohan steps."[130] It, too, was set on the Fourth of July.

Aligning himself with patriotism, with Broadway, and with memories of the past, Cohan constructed a decades-long celebrity career that encompassed and drew upon his many professional roles. He shaped the contours of early twentieth-century celebrity. Yet he also contributed to discourses of celebrity by writing about star performers in shows, depicting and often performing celebrity on stage as well as exemplifying it in American society.

STAGING THE BROADWAY STAR

Cohan was not the first and hardly the last to find the world of entertainment, one he knew well, good subject matter for his shows, and he wrote several about performers. The diversity of those shows is notable. In the first, the flop play *Popularity* (1906), as well as in the hit musical Cohan made from it, *The Man Who Owns Broadway* (1909), Cohan staged the Broadway celebrity star. The play with music *The Voice of McConnell* (1918), discussed in Chapter 4, centers on a star Irish tenor. The play *The Song and Dance Man* (1923) includes a rising ingenue who becomes a major star, but the titular role and focus is the anti-star, a down-and-out trouper whom Cohan himself played. And at the time of his death in 1942, Cohan was working on a new show called *The Musical Comedy Man*. Both *The Man Who Owns Broadway* and *The Musical Comedy Man*, written over two decades later, comment on the nature of theatrical celebrity, while also critiquing the position of musical comedy and its performers within contemporaneous cultural and social hierarchies. In the latter, a meta-musical, the playwright-composer-star protagonist clearly represents Cohan himself.

The Man Who Owns Broadway

Reworking and thereby, to Cohan's mind, redeeming his unsuccessful play *Popularity*, *The Man Who Owns Broadway* joined a star actor hero with a by-then familiar storyline, of swindlers after a wealthy family's fortune. The titular "man who owns Broadway" is popular actor Sydney Lyons. When Sydney's friend Tom Bridwell, son of a wealthy Manhattanite, calls Sydney in to help thwart his sister Sylvia's unwanted arranged engagement, Lyons ends up recognizing two swindlers who have ingratiated themselves with Tom's father and are engaged to father and daughter respectively. Sydney and the audience also learn that Sylvia has in fact been attending Sydney's show every night and has fallen in love with him. The swindlers try to bribe Sydney to keep silent, but he is too upstanding to be bought; he helps save the day and, of course, ends up with the girl. Stylistically, the show is typically Cohanesque in its use of metatheatricality, with Sydney commenting on theatrical conventions throughout. "My boy, the villains are never handcuffed 'till eleven o'clock. That's been going on for years and years," he says in one scene to explain to his friend Tom why they cannot be arrested immediately, and a group of characters sing about the situation being "A Nice Little Plot for a Play." Sydney promises to "stick to musical comedy as long as George Cohan will write them for me."[131] The show ends in a show-within-a-show scene in which Sylvia declares her love to Sydney through song from a seat in one of the boxes.

The Man Who Owns Broadway celebrates the Broadway star, challenging older stereotypes that had long kept actors at arms' length from high society, "feted as performers, excluded as individuals," as historian Benjamin McArthur put it.[132] Sydney Lyons is shown to have impeccable character and is even said to have the endorsement of the moneyed, business elite. "I've always heard him spoken of in the richest terms and by very prominent men. He's quite well liked in Wall Street," Anthony Bridwell says.[133] Sydney is shown to be a favorite with the ladies but wins over the men as well. A paragon of manhood, he stands up for himself but is not pugnacious, and he has an excellent sense of humor. When challenged at the party, he throws aside his hat, cane, and coat, seemingly preparing for a fight, but begins to waltz instead. In another instance, Sydney pokes fun at himself and Broadway, telling Anthony Bridwell, Tom and Sylvia's father, "I really am a great actor. If you don't believe me, ask my manager." "Do you dance?" Bridwell asks. "Can't dance a step," Sydney responds. "Do you sing?" Bridwell asks. "Can't sing a note," Sydney responds. "What do you do?" Bridwell asks. "I'm in musical comedy," Sydney delivers the punchline. Despite thinking highly of Sydney by the end of the show, Bridwell is still not ready to have him as a son-in-law; he admits to not liking actors, "as a class." Sydney, laughing quietly, poignantly responds, "Yes, actors are a pretty bad lot. These clowns have no calling except to amuse, make you forget, ring happiness out into the world, promote charities and swallow the insults of the very people for whom they make life worth living. Yes, actors are a bad lot." In the end, however, Bridwell's qualms are dismissed and the happy couple is united. The show documented a change that was already well underway regarding how actors were perceived among the elite as well as the lingering prejudices reflected in Bridwell's comments. Writer Margherita Arlina Hamm commented the same year as the musical that "the actor today" is in many cases "a social lion before whom all kneel in homage."[134] Through Bridwell's eventual support for the union, Cohan proposed that the Broadway star was not only a social lion but also marriage material.

The show also depicts the workings of celebrity—the press, the public, and most of all, the fan, with a romance that is the realization of fan fantasy. Sylvia has been silently worshipping Sydney Lyons from afar, "thro'

[her] opera glasses," as she explains in her solo "I'm in Love with One of the Stars."[135] She has been crying over his photograph, the quintessential material artifact of early twentieth-century celebrity, which she describes as the "the one consoling thing I possess on earth—the one secret within my heart." She has also been attending his show nightly; she sings his songs, could recite his plays, and even "talks about [him] in her sleep." Yet like most fans, she is a daydreamer whose fandom, like that of most fans "hover[s] between full activity and utter passivity," as celebrity theorist Sharon Marcus describes.[136] Indeed, when Sylvia's brother learns of her infatuation and tells of his plans to invite Sydney to their home, Sylvia asks him not to. The star actor is invited nonetheless, and he proves to be as wonderful in person as she has imagined him from his performances. Ultimately, he returns her affections, saving her from an unwanted marriage. Cohan thus stages, albeit in his characteristically "clean" way, the fan fantasy of sexual intimacy with the celebrity performer, making the show, which was thought to appeal to the tired businessman (discussed in Chapter 3), perhaps equally appealing for the businessman's wife.[137] While Cohan did not act in this show, the metatheatrical line mentioning him in the script and his headshot on the sheet music reminded audiences that the star of the musical was as much its creator, George M. Cohan, as it was the character Sydney Lyons or actor who portrayed him.

The Musical Comedy Man

With Cohan's last, unfinished show *The Musical Comedy Man*, which was in the works as early as 1939, he returned to the protagonist of the professional performer, a star actor who is also a playwright, songwriter, and producer: in short, it is quite clear that the lead character Joe Callahan is a doppelgänger for Cohan.[138] The show is highly autobiographical: in it, Callahan grapples with a decision about acting in another's play versus writing his own—a conflict with an unmistakable parallel in Cohan's own career. It is also infused with bits of nostalgia, in the form of a medley of some of the old Cohan tunes and a philosophical number called "Life Is Like a Musical Comedy," akin to earlier songs in this vein like "Life's a Funny Proposition After All," with the poignant sentiment that in life as in a show, lights are on and out again "before you know."[139] Unlike his radio revues or popular songs of the thirties, however, it was quite experimental. Unfortunately, Cohan died before he could complete it.

In the show, a major female playwright who is famous in her own right, akin to Rachel Crothers or Lillian Hellman, has written a play with Callahan in mind, and she visits him to convince him to take the role, offering the chance at success in a "legitimate drama," which by this point in Cohan's career was no longer used in opposition to vaudeville, as it had been when Cohan was breaking onto Broadway, but now emphatically excluded musical comedy. He is insulted at her hierarchical distinctions between plays and musical comedy and, moreover, at the idea that he would want to perform in someone else's work besides his own. Reading the part piques his interest. Still, the encounter ultimately serves up the idea he has been seeking for his own next musical comedy show—which, as it turns out, is this show.

The show's title song comments on the constructed nature of Callahan's Yankee Doodle persona. In the verse, Callahan describes his walks around the city being for the purpose of advertising, adding "That's the way to sell yourself / If you want the folks to buy / That's how mister Yankee Doodle / Caught the public eye." The ensemble sings in the verse's chorus:

> There he goes on his dancing toes
> With that famous American stride
> Full of musical comedy pride
> Traffic holds up when he hits Main Street
> Broadway knows that it's all a pose
> It's a perfect publicity plan
> But they like the pose the dancing toes
> They even go to see his shows
> They've famed him, they've even named him
> The Yankee Doodle—Yankee Doodle
> Musical Comedy Man.[140]

Only the song's words and buoyant, syncopated melody remain, but it has been arranged for use in *George M!*, the 1968 musical about Cohan (discussed in the book's epilogue), and in concerts (▶ Example 5.6). As he did in the song "F-A-M-E," Cohan implicates the public in the process of creating celebrity, and here it is specifically *his* celebrity. "They" are aware that "it's all a pose"—and in fact it is the public who has named and famed him—but they are all too happy to participate in the scheme in return for the joy they receive.

The Musical Comedy Man was structurally and conceptually innovative, taking the metatheatricality Cohan had been using for years to the utmost. The first act, consisting of the encounter between Callahan and the playwright and his conversation afterward with leading lady Julie, is presented "straight," culminating in Callahan's decision to musicalize the event. The second act consists of the rehearsal played to help Callahan find a second act, with various personnel expressing their confusion about what the second act of the show will be. The third act continues the backstage setting but ends with a lengthy musicalized satire of the first act. With pre-postmodern flair (although Cohan certainly would have disliked such a descriptor), the show blurs the line between the real and the staged in a show-becoming-a-show that comments upon the differences, in both genre and cultural register, between drama and musical comedy, in order to ultimately recommit to the latter. Had it been staged, would *The Musical Comedy Man* have been seen as a genre-expanding work along the lines of *A Chorus Line* (1975) or as an oddity? Its existence complicates the notion that Cohan's musical works were simple and stagnant, or that he had given up on the stage, even if they did not fit the "growing sophistication" of the day.[141] Like many of his earlier shows, it was also created to be a vehicle for Cohan's celebrity, even as it commented self-reflexively on it, pulling out many of his favorite tricks.

* * *

As Cohan grasped well, fame was part of the theatrical game. He understood that when he was selling his shows—whether as a playwright/songwriter, star actor, or both—he was also selling himself, and he savvily navigated the exploding popular print media and celebrity journalism of his day to gain national fame. Through his writings, from the *Spot Light* to nationally syndicated columns, as well as through interviews and public engagements, he was highly involved in crafting his public image, in close partnership with the new, important figure of the theatrical press agent. He became known for his personality but also as an emblem of patriotism and of Broadway. He linked them to one another and linked his persona to each, and in selling them, he also sold himself.

Just as his position in theater was unique, so too was his celebrity, leveraging his multiple roles as an artist—playwright, songwriter, producer, and star. The multifaceted nature of his career helped grow his public stature and sustain his presence in the national media. Cohan's celebrity also, however, went beyond his official professional work and is worth examining in itself. Indeed, when Cohan and his work were less in vogue in New York in the wake of the actors' strike of 1919 and Cohan's battle against Equity, it became even more important to leverage his national celebrity, in ways that went beyond producing, writing, or starring in new shows, and he maintained relevance through nostalgia and through the reputations he had established as an emblem of patriotism and of Broadway. His celebrity was such that he was an appealing subject for a film, and despite his misgivings about Hollywood, by 1941 *Yankee Doodle Dandy*—the Warner Bros. film that would define the public image of George M. Cohan for generations to come—was underway.

THE "GREAT AMERICAN SERVICE" OF *YANKEE DOODLE DANDY*

My God, what an act to follow.

—George M. Cohan after seeing *Yankee Doodle Dandy*,
as told by John McCabe

Upon George M. Cohan's death in 1942, only months after the release of the film *Yankee Doodle Dandy*, the *New York Times* declared that "he was patriotism on the stage" and that he "almost represented the American flag."[1] Cohan was well known, especially at the height of his career, for his early, patriotic songs and shows, and the film solidified and made immortal—through the permanent fixity of recording technology—this image of him. Indeed, in the decades since its release, it has become the primary vehicle for his legacy: when most Americans picture Cohan, they likely see a tap-dancing James ("Jimmy") Cagney, for whom playing Cohan was a career-defining role.

Yankee Doodle Dandy, a Warner Bros. film produced by Hal Wallis and associate producer William Cagney and directed by Michael Curtiz, is one of the most long-lived and critically acclaimed twentieth-century "musical biopics." A hybrid subgenre at the intersection of the popular film genres of the film musical and the biopic (short for biographical motion picture), musical biopics dramatize the life and works of musical figures like composers, performers, or music industry professionals. The success of *The Great Ziegfeld* in 1936 (about producer Florenz Ziegfeld Jr.) set off a craze for these films in the 1930s and 1940s, and figures from American show business were a favorite subject, capitalizing on a ready-made story, natural "backstage musical" set-up, and already popular songs and shows.[2]

Yankee Doodle Dandy. Elizabeth T. Craft, Oxford University Press.
DOI: 10.1093/oso/9780197550403.003.0007

The goals of a biopic, a backstage musical, and wartime propaganda intersect in *Yankee Doodle Dandy* in ways that would not have been possible with any other protagonist. Cohan's story offered Warner Bros. and audiences the advantages of a showbiz biopic about one of the most famous showmen in the United States. Moreover, the themes of American identity and patriotism emphasized in Cohan's shows and his self-constructed personal narrative were particularly timely in the early 1940s as World War II loomed. However, other musical biopic subjects like Ziegfeld Jr. (portrayed in *Harmony Lane* of 1935) or Stephen Foster (in *Swanee River* of 1939) were long deceased when their biopics hit the screens, while Cohan was still living at the time of *Yankee Doodle Dandy*'s writing and premiere. Cohan was a skilled self-promoter with a distinct interest in telling his own story, as we saw in Chapter 5, and the film's contract stipulated that he would be an active participant in its development and have final approval of the product.[3] The film's screenwriters and producers struggled to meet Cohan's stipulations while telling an entertaining story that also fit the historical moment as the United States went to war. In the end, the film strategically elided three simultaneous histories—those of Cohan, the musical, and the nation—and harnessed Cohan's story and songs to unify and glorify the United States in wartime. By depicting a rich theatrical history aligned with US history and Cohan's personal story, *Yankee Doodle Dandy* also helped to position the musical as the nation's own, homespun art form, and it solidified Cohan's reputation as patriot extraordinaire.

"THE PICTURIZATION OF HIS LIFE STORY"

Cohan did his best to shape the storyline of *Yankee Doodle Dandy*, even offering his own screenplay at one point. The film's first screenwriter Robert Buckner wrote in a memo to the executive producer, "the picturization of his life story is an extremely serious matter with [Cohan]. He is independent as hell about it."[4] Because of his assertive involvement in the film and because he had already so deliberately shaped his public image, it is unsurprising that the film echoes similar themes to those he had propagated in his own writings and interviews. The film presents his life story as an extended flashback during his visit to President Franklin D. Roosevelt's office, where he expects to be upbraided for his portrayal of the president in the musical *I'd Rather Be Right* (1937) but instead receives a Congressional Gold Medal.[5] As the flashback to the year of his birth begins, the scene shows a banner with the year 1878, and the film character Cohan, in voiceover, describes the period as "the beginning of the Horatio Alger age," setting the scene for his own ascendance from immigrant to preeminent American, poor vaudevillian to famous actor and wealthy impresario.[6]

In keeping with Cohan's autobiographical writings, *Yankee Doodle Dandy* focuses largely on Cohan's childhood and relationships with his parents and sister and glosses over aspects that Cohan did not want included. His father Jerry, mother Helen, and sister Josephine (called Josie) are central characters. As film historian Patrick McGilligan notes in his introduction to the published screenplay, many of "Cohan's anecdotes about his childhood and youth were adopted wholesale."[7] In addition, the film ignored aspects of Cohan's life that were uncomplimentary to him or that he found objectionable for the big screen. He famously insisted, for example, that there be no mention of his first wife Ethel Levey and no love scenes. Levey was, indeed, omitted, as were his children by both his first and second marriages, though Cohan eventually agreed to the film portraying a fictionalized love interest named Mary.[8] The film also avoided any mention of Cohan's infamous hard-line stance against the Actor's Equity Union, despite its major ramifications for his life and career. According to contemporaneous biographer Ward Morehouse, Cohan's daughter Georgette said of the film, "That's the kind of a life daddy would have liked to have lived."[9]

Furthering the messages of his Irish American shows of the late 1910s and 1920s, the film helped to solidify cultural acceptance of a dual, patriotic Irish American identity at a time when the Irish had only relatively recently been accepted as bona fide Americans.[10] Two sequential scenes early in the film establish Cohan's "Yankee Doodle Dandy" patriotic persona: his meeting with the president and his birth, related as a flashback. In both scenes, his Americanness is linked to his Irishness. The scene with President Roosevelt introduces the theme of Cohan's Irish-tinged patriotism: remembering his youth, Cohan tells the president, "I was a pretty cocky kid in those days—a regular Yankee Doodle Dandy. Always *in* a parade or following one." The president comments, "That's one thing I've always admired about you Irish-Americans. You carry your love of country like a flag, right out in the open. It's a great quality." As historian Meaghan Dwyer-Ryan notes, this "oft-repeated quote" from the film "became an acknowledgement of Irish contributions to the country."[11]

As in his own writings, Cohan's purported July 4 birthdate is critical to his historiography. The birth scene in *Yankee Doodle Dandy* forcefully establishes both George's Irish heritage and his complementary fate as a patriotic American through closely intertwined aural and visual signifiers of Irish and US national identity. Initiating the extended flashback after the early scene with President Roosevelt, an image of Cohan in the president's study slowly dissolves to an American flag, then the camera pans downward to Providence, Rhode Island, amidst Independence Day celebrations. We hear, then see, a marching band playing the nineteenth-century patriotic tune "Columbia, the Gem of the Ocean," then we see a sign for the Colony Opera House showing "Week of July 1, 1878 / Mr. and Mrs. Jerry Cohan / 'The Irish Darlings.'" On the stage inside, Jerry sings and dances as Irish dancing master Larry O'Leary, costumed in breeches, a cape, and a "jaunty Irish hat," with shamrock appliqués on his hat and lapels, and carrying a shillelagh (a wooden walking stick or cudgel).[12] (His song, "The Dancing Master," was one that had been performed by the real-life Jerry.[13]) He dashes off the stage as soon as his performance ends, and a Civil War veteran with an Irish brogue rushes him through the parade to his destination—the bedroom where his wife Nellie has just given birth to George. As they consider what to call the newborn, the doctor suggests George Washington Cohan, since he was born on the Fourth of July, but Nellie replies that "Washington" is too long to fit on a billboard. They instead combine George with the "nice short Irish [middle] name" Michael. When the veterans outside fire a cannon in George's honor and the baby breaks into a wail, Jerry exclaims, "He's crying with a brogue!" and hands him an American flag (Figure 6.1).[14] In continued voiceover, Cohan says, "I guess the first thing I ever had my fist on was

Figure 6.1 George M. Cohan at birth in Yankee Doodle Dandy *(1942).*

the American flag. I hitched my wagon to thirty-eight stars. And thirteen stripes." Fulfilling the biopic's generic expectation of establishing its hero's "sense of destiny," the scene introduces the themes of patriotism and life in show business as well as the literal symbol of the flag, one of many to be seen in *Yankee Doodle Dandy*.[15]

THE STAGE AND THE NATION

In its celebration of American theater, *Yankee Doodle Dandy* exemplifies the stage and screen's "intertwining of intimately shared histories," as musicologists Raymond Knapp and Mitchell Morris have put it.[16] The film is at once a chronicle of US theatrical history and a sort of backstage musical, with its attendant tropes. While Cohan wrote plays as well as musicals, *Yankee Doodle Dandy* focuses almost exclusively on the latter. Occasionally musical and dramatic performances serve to advance the plot or develop a character, as when Mary plays and sings the song George has written for her ("Mary's a Grand Old Name") at the piano in her home. More often, however, songs—both snippets heard in montages and complete numbers—mark the passing of time or highlight key moments in Cohan's career. Dressing room scenes, backstage shots, and stage performances abound, and, with the notable exception of "Over There," the songs are part and parcel of show business, whether the characters are performing onstage, auditioning for a producer, or singing a newly written number at a living room piano.[17]

In tracing Cohan's journey through his theatrical experiences, from the touring circuits of vaudeville in small town America to the "legit" stages in the heart of Broadway, *Yankee Doodle Dandy* connects Cohan's biography with the histories of the musical and of the nation. Cohan's voiceover narration at the start of his flashback—with his quip, "There weren't so many stars then, in the flag or on the stage, but folks knew that more were coming"—reveals the story's central metaphor while capturing the Gilded Age sense of optimism, confidence, and growth. After the scene of his birth, we see images of a family photo album, with Cohan's sister Josie (who was, in fact, the elder sibling) added to an empty frame (Figure 6.2), and a series of theatrical scenes. The imagery and narration continue to link the Cohans' experiences to American history. Cohan describes playing a Daniel Boone show on the "kerosene circuit," the term denoting low-budget companies performing a series of one-night engagements in very small towns.[18] We see a train traversing the countryside as Cohan, extending his use of flag symbolism, declares, "They kept putting

Figure 6.2 Images of familial and theatrical documents in Yankee Doodle Dandy *(1942).*

new stars in the flag, and the Cohans kept rushing out to meet them." We see a young George playing the Irish "Dancing Master" as his father did, but with a novelty twist, playing (quite badly) the violin above his head. He also adds a patriotic flourish, shooting an American flag out of his shillelagh at the number's conclusion. In another scene, Josie sings and performs a dance to "The Fountain in the Park," a popular late nineteenth-century tune by Edward Haley, and in yet another, difficult to watch today, we see the Cohan family performing a blackface minstrel number with tambourines. Cohan's narration continues, "We trouped through depression and inflation. Part of the country's growing pains." Throughout the film, the Cohans' history touring the nation as performers is paralleled with the growth of the United States; their ups and downs are aligned with the nation's.

While *Yankee Doodle Dandy*, more than many Hollywood musicals, treats theatrical performance unabashedly as a commercial business, the film also partakes of certain generic mythologies, described by film studies scholar

Jane Feuer. It valorizes entertainment, for instance, and presents a "vision of musical performance originating in the folk."[19] Show business is business, but it's also bound up with family ties (among the Four Cohans), romantic love (between George and Mary), and national sentiment. In one critical scene, the prominent producer Abe Erlanger tells the petulant star Fay Templeton, who has refused a role in a Cohan show, that she should reconsider.

> ERLANGER. You're making a mistake, Fay. He's the most original thing that's ever hit Broadway. And do you know why? Because he's the whole darn country, squeezed into one pair of pants! His writing—his songs—why even his walk and his talk—they all touch something way down here in people! (*He lays a hand over his heart.*) Now don't ask me why it is—but it happens every time the curtain goes up. It's pure magic! . . . George M. Cohan has invented the success story. And every American loves it because it happens to be his own private dream. He's found the mainspring in the Yankee clock—ambition, pride, patriotism. That's why they call him the Yankee Doodle Boy.[20]

Cohan, *Yankee Doodle Dandy* insists, not only creates show business magic but also embodies it. He becomes the epitome of Broadway because he's the epitome of America.

Within *Yankee Doodle Dandy*, even as great liberties are taken with the major events of George's life, considerable care is taken with the details of the Cohans' theatrical history. The film's original screenwriter Robert Buckner did extensive research using Cohan's autobiography, the scrapbooks of the Robinson Locke Collection housed in the New York Public Library, articles in newspapers and magazines, interviews with Cohan's acquaintances, and conversations with Cohan himself.[21] As one montage depicts, the family did indeed tour together: with Jerry's hibernicon company, as "The Cohan Mirth Makers," and later as the famous Four Cohans act. The film's iconography conveys a sense of authenticity: we see signs, playbills, and other documents, frequently used to introduce theatrical scenes (Figure 6.2). The performance scenes are fairly true to life as well. George M. Cohan did play the violin in his boyhood, Josie was known for her dancing, and members of the Cohans did play "Daniel Boone," "Peck's Bad Boy," and other skits and shows referenced in the film. The plethora of seemingly historical images, evocative of a visual archive, serves both to commemorate theatrical history and to deflect from the film's many biographical falsities.

Musical and choreographic decisions, too, were made with the goal of authenticity as well as capitalizing on the popularity of Cohan's songs. Heinz Roemheld and Ray Heindorf were responsible for the film's musical scoring (for which they won an Academy Award), but in the contract, Cohan had agreed to provide music and piano arrangements for the film. He was even to provide three new songs, though that did not happen. He was quite concerned with the accuracy of the film's musical staging of his numbers, however, and his assistance was appreciated more in this realm than others.[22] The final version of the film had a few non-Cohan songs, but the majority were his, including "The Warmest Baby in the Bunch" (1897), "Mary's a Grand Old Name" (1905), "I Was Born in Virginia" (1906, originally published as "Ethel Levey's Virginia Song"), "Harrigan" (1907), and others. The screenwriters took liberties with chronology and also with the arrangement of some numbers, like "The Yankee Doodle Boy" (1904) and "You're a Grand Old Flag" (1906)—the first in order to explain the song's role within the plot and the second to evoke national pride in wartime.[23] Overall, however, fidelity was the byword in the treatment of Cohan's musical oeuvre and the staging of musical numbers. James Cagney also took great care to capture Cohan's renowned, distinctive dancing style; his instructor Johnny Boyle had even performed in Cohan shows and staged dances for Cohan.[24]

The numerous special features on the 2003 DVD release, including a second disc of "bonus material," extend the film's approach to theatrical authenticity while also historicizing the film itself. These include feature-length commentary by film historian Rudy Behlmer; a short documentary chronicling *Yankee Doodle Dandy*'s making; *Warner Night at the Movies 1942*, a recreation of the various features (trailer, newsreel, and more) in a typical evening at the movie theater during the period; and the Looney Tunes cartoons *Yankee Doodle Daffy* (1943) and *Yankee Doodle Bugs* (1954). Numerous features are directly related to James Cagney, including a wartime short he starred in called *You, John Jones*. There are listings of the film's cast, crew, and awards; an "audio vault" including prerecording session outtakes and rehearsals; and the "Waving the Flag Galleries" containing images of sheet music, set and scene stills, and publicity materials. These supplementary features impart a similar veneer of authenticity to the film, as historical object, as the documents and performances do within the film's story, furthering *Yankee Doodle Dandy*'s almost archival aura and masking its notable departures from the facts.

"WITH THE AMERICAN SPIRIT AT A CRISIS"

The film's nostalgia for the late nineteenth and early twentieth centuries and its emphasis on the Americanness of the theater were perfectly suited to the historical moment of its release during World War II. War was underway abroad when discussions about the film began, and Warner Bros. was already showing its keen interest in wartime intervention through anti-Nazi films like *Sergeant York* (1941). During a 1941 congressional hearing to investigate purported "Moving Picture Screen and Radio Propaganda," initiated by the isolationist North Dakotan Senator Gerald Nye, Harry M. Warner gave a speech declaring outright, "I am opposed to nazi-ism. I abhor and detest every principle and practice of the Nazi movement."[25]

For Cohan and Cagney, however, the initial attraction of the project lay elsewhere. Cohan saw in the film a chance to preserve his legacy now that he was no longer so widely known. "Four-fifths of the people who remember me are dead," Buckner recounted Cohan telling him.[26] The film's opening, with Cohan's name in lights on a marquee, was designed in part to "establish the importance of George M. Cohan for today's generation," according to a letter from director Michael Curtiz to Hal Wallis.[27] Cagney, on the other hand, sought a chance to distance himself from recent charges of communism as well as the opportunity to escape his "tough guy" typecasting and to return to the film musical, a genre in which he had established himself several years earlier, with *Footlight Parade* (1933).[28] William Cagney, associate producer of *Yankee Doodle Dandy* and James Cagney's brother, explained later that he told Warner Bros. studio head Jack L. Warner, "We should make a movie with Jim playing the damnedest patriotic man in the country," George M. Cohan.[29]

The wartime climate and William Cagney's comment notwithstanding, patriotism was not initially to be *Yankee Doodle Dandy*'s primary theme. Rather, during the film's development, its writers struggled to choose their focus. In May 1941, Buckner and William Cagney despaired to executive producer Hal B. Wallis that "we needed a romantic personal story," but Cohan refused to let his "private domestic life [be] a major element of [the] picture." Buckner and Cagney explained a number of different approaches they had tried, like keeping the focus on the Four Cohans and developing a fictitious romance. Another tactic they tried, but—incredibly now—found lacking, was "develop[ing] the patriotic theme, George M. Cohan as the symbol of a dynamic and sincere American." "We gave this angle a tremendous workout," they explained, "But it spreads too thin." Cohan, they acknowledged, was a good citizen, but they felt "the evidence is neither complete enough or dramatic enough to ask any intelligent person to accept [it] as the key to his character." Moreover, this theme failed as entertainment as well as biography; they thought it "dangerous as a bore to a modern audience, for today Cohan's flashy type of patriotism sounds as cornily theatrical as it was in 1910."[30] This was a kiss of death for a motion picture with Warner Bros., which marketed itself as "all-out . . . on the entertainment front."[31] Finally, they were concerned about the implications of opportunism: "Accidentally or not," they wrote, "the fact still blares at you that he made several million dollars with this act—*during the War*," presumably referring to the way Cohan profited from patriotism during World War I.[32] The criticism of flag-waving as a cheap trick pandering to the masses to make a buck that plagued Cohan during his career clearly troubled the makers of the film as well.

By the end of *Yankee Doodle Dandy*'s production, however, the Japanese had attacked Pearl Harbor, the United States had formally entered World War II, and Warner Bros. had decided to sell Cohan and the world on the picture's patriotism. In part, when tensions between the recalcitrant Cohan and the studio came to a head in August 1941, stressing *Yankee Doodle Dandy*'s patriotism was a compelling way to persuade Cohan to allow the studio more liberties with the film's storytelling. In a lengthy letter to Cohan dated August 29, Hal Wallis, William Cagney, and Robert Buckner made a forceful, last-ditch effort to get approval for their script, including the plea: "The dramatization of your life, Mr. Cohan, has a great timely importance. It is the story of a typical American boy, who grew up with a strong love of his country, its ways and institutions. His life was spent in expressing and defending an American way of life." By now, the team had settled on its through line; they stated, "We believe that the deep-dyed Americanism of your life is a much greater theme than the success story." The letter concluded, "We have worked for six months because all of us here have an unshaken faith that this picture should be made—and today more than ever, with the American spirit at a crisis. It is our hope that perhaps you, too, will see this story of your life in its broader implications and give us your trust."[33] Had the filmmakers been swept up in patriotism as war loomed? Or was this a ploy to get Cohan onboard? It seems likely that both were true to some extent. Indeed, a memo from a couple of days prior confirms the coercive intention of their pitch. William Cagney reported to Wallis that an outside party close to Cohan "agrees with my point that Cohan should be made to realize that this is a great American message at the most crucial period in American history and he should patriotically bow to our efforts to dramatically present the story of this great American spirit."[34] Whatever the degree of their sincerity, Wallis, Cagney, and Buckner's appeal to Cohan's sense of patriotic duty was successful, and work on the film proceeded.[35]

Several elements of the film and its distribution bear witness to its wartime roots and the ways in which the theme of patriotism came to dominate the story. The emphasis on Americanism is legible from the opening credits, which use a stars-and-stripes pattern for the lettering of the names. (Warner Bros. had recently done the same for *Sergeant York*, released in July 1941.[36]) The film's propagandistic tinge is most glaringly obvious, though, in the treatment of "You're a Grand Old Flag."

The screenplay contained little of the elaborate scene that ended up on the screen; in its version, the Cohans would sing a verse and chorus, and then the company would perform an ensemble dance number. The scene was to show *George Washington, Jr.* as another stop on Cohan and Harris's road to success as well as to emphasize the Cohans' love for one another and Mary's for George. "The happiness on the Cohans' faces as they work together and smile at each other is something to see," and Mary watches George from the chorus "with much affection," the screenplay notes.[37] The number was also marked for spectacle early on—Buckner wrote in an earlier version of the screenplay that there should be "flags all over the stage. This is an excellent opportunity for special trick effects."[38] Still, the emphasis in earlier versions was the characters at least as much as it was the nation.

The final version of "You're a Grand Old Flag" was wholly divorced from both the screenplay and, unlike the film's earlier "Yankee Doodle Boy" number, from the plot and setting of its source. In *George Washington, Jr.*, the song is prefaced by the hero encountering veterans who have come to Mount Vernon to decorate George Washington's tomb.[39] While the scene in the film likewise opens with a group of men in uniform (some with instruments, serving as the "military band" mentioned in the song's verse), and Cagney, as Cohan, singing a verse and chorus, the similarities end there.

In the final number as filmed, the Cohan song is intercut with various scenes representing key moments in United States history with correspondent interpolated or newly composed tunes, creating a sort of historical pageant of wartime scenes. Describing his plans for the number in a memo to William Cagney in January 1942, LeRoy Prinz, one of directors of the musical numbers, cited as inspiration radio programs like *Cavalcade of America*, which dramatized the nation's history in glowing terms.[40] The scene shows Betsy Ross sewing the flag. Revolutionary soldiers with fife and drums play

"Yankee Doodle," visually referencing the iconic painting *The Spirit of '76*, as musicologist Holley Replogle-Wong has noted.[41] An African American soloist and chorus sing "The Battle Hymn of the Republic," and the Lincoln Memorial appears behind them; we hear Lincoln's voice deliver a line from the Gettysburg Address: "And that government of the people, by the people, for the people, shall not perish from the earth." Soldiers of the Spanish–American War led by Theodore Roosevelt march to "When Johnny Comes Marching Home" (in fact a Civil War–era song). We then seem to leave the musical's historical moment as we hear a group of citizens—described by Prinz as the farmer, laborer, banker, and so on—sing a rallying cry for the then-current conflict: "We're one for all and all for one, / . . . / And now that we're in it, / We're going to win it." The closing musical phrase, "We'll fight as we did before," segues directly into "for 'my country, 'tis of thee,'" quoting musically and lyrically from the well-known patriotic song by the same title. "All the tableaux," Prinz wrote to William Cagney, "are to have a spiritual effect."[42] The camera intersperses close-ups—for example, of the African American soloist's face and soldiers' bayonets—with long shots of the stage, moving between the "real-world" framing of the stage, as the theater audience would see it, and a more abstract, cinematic approach that invites film audiences to extrapolate to the present historical moment.

The finale of the number returns to the stage mode and the song "You're a Grand Old Flag," with Jerry Cohan costumed as Uncle Sam and Nellie Cohan as Lady Liberty, but replete with spectacular visual effects along the lines Buckner had suggested early on. We see, as Prinz described it, an "ensemble of flags—entire group on treadmill across entire stage, walking towards audience" to create "a finale of apparently hundreds of flags" (Figure 6.3 and ▶ Example 6.1). For this closing, he sought to evoke the theatrical rather than cinematic: "This will not be a [Busby] Berkeley effect," he said, referring to the famed film musical choreographer, "but all legitimate stagecraft that could have been developed at this period." The flag that appears on a scrim on the number's final bars, he notes, "could have been done by Lantern projection."[43] While he may have aimed to transport the film viewers back to the historical narrative through technological accuracy, the razzle-dazzle, sequined costumes and setting of the number's finale, with the US Capitol Building appearing in the background, make it as anachronistic as the prior sequence. The choice of staging marks the Cohans and the theater itself, however, as emblematic of wartime patriotism. As the song's final chord rings out, the camera shows audience members jumping to their feet and applauding enthusiastically.

Figure 6.3 "You're a Grand Old Flag" finale in Yankee Doodle Dandy *(1942).*

The scenes about Cohan's World War I hit "Over There" are likewise written with pointed reference to current affairs. Upon learning about the sinking of the Lusitania by the Germans in 1915, Cohan says, in voiceover narration, "It seems it always happens. Whenever we get too high-hat and too sophisticated for flag-waving, some thug nation decides we're a push-over all ready to be blackjacked. And it isn't long before we're looking up, mighty anxiously, to be sure the flag's still waving over us." The clear implication is that Cohan's type of exuberant patriotism not only defined and celebrated the nation but also kept it safe, and the universal tone made its then present-day applications patently obvious as well. In another scene, we see Cohan and singer Nora Bayes, played by radio performer and film star Frances Langford, performing "Over There" for the US troops. Langford's casting drew a connection to the contemporary conflict, since she also performed for military forces in real life.[44] As they perform, the lights go out, and Cagney, as Cohan, runs out into the crowd to ask vehicles to turn on their headlights to light the stage—this borrowed from Cohan's own anecdotes.[45] Returning to the stage, Cagney conducts the audience for a few bars and calls out, "Everybody sing!" (▶ Example 6.2). The troops join in heartily, a powerful scene of communal singing that engenders a sense of national pride and civic duty, inviting the film's audience, whether symbolically or literally, to join in.

The filmmakers did not need to manufacture a connection; the officials in the US government had already recognized that "Over There" carried strong associations that reverberated into World War II. A memo from the Office of the Coordinator of Information (which became the Office of Strategic Services and was one predecessor of the CIA) to the president in 1941, as *Yankee Doodle Dandy* was being filmed, stated that "some of our people in London" recommended using "Over There" to open and close all shortwave radio broadcasts to Europe. "Better than any other song showing America's power in last war," the memo declared in clipped speech. "A grim reminder of American invincibility and arouses terror that former doom may be repeated. In France especially the song causes a hope that they will be released eventually from bondage of Germany."[46] With its treatment of "Over There," the film conveyed this sense of invincibility and hope to audiences at home as well.

The scenes with Cohan and President Roosevelt that bookend the film bring the action to the present day. As Patrick McGilligan writes, "History was manipulated so the president's summoning George directly from a performance of *I'd Rather Be Right* [which in reality opened in 1937] coincides with the outbreak of World War II."[47] Lyrics referencing Hitler and the war were added for the performance of "Off the Record" in the *I'd Rather Be Right* scene. When the president gives Cohan the Congressional Gold Medal, Cohan protests that he's undeserving as he's "just a song-and-dance man," but the president insists, "A man may give his life to his country in many different ways, Mr. Cohan. . . . Your songs were a symbol of the American spirit. 'Over There' was just as powerful a weapon as any cannon, as any battleship we had in the First World War. Today, we're all soldiers, we're all on the front. We need more songs to express America. I know you and your comrades will give them to us." (The real-life Cohan had indeed been giving the US more patriotic songs oriented toward the Second World War, though none were as popular as "Over There.") Cohan's response to the fictional FDR ties the Horatio Alger narrative of the film back to the nation's greatness and readiness for war: "I wouldn't worry about this country if I were you," he says. "We've got this thing licked. Where else in the world could a plain guy like me come in and talk things over with the head man?" The president concurs, "Well, that's about as good a definition of America as any I've ever heard."

As Cohan leaves the White House, the soldiers and crowd outside are singing "Over There." He joins the troops, and a soldier asks him, "What's the matter, old-timer, don't you remember this song?" Cagney, as Cohan, then joins in the singing, tears visible on his face. The real-life Cohan had indicated a scene of troops marching in his script, noting that "this shot of the boys marching away might possibly be a delicate thing to do considering world conditions today, but if it is strongly planted that it is June 1917, and *not* 1941, you might get away with it."[48] By the time of *Yankee Doodle Dandy*'s filming and release, however, a marching scene set in the present was no longer risky but apropos.

Another indication of the war's impact on the film's creation is a notable absence—that of Cohan's real-life Japanese American valets Yoshin Sakurai (who Cohan also cast in his 1910 play *Get Rich Quick Wallingford*) and Michio "Mike" Hirano (who had a small part in Cohan's 1936 play *Dear Old Darling*) (Figure 6.4).[49] On December 18, 1941, only days after Pearl Harbor and during the filming of *Yankee Doodle Dandy*, Cohan telegraphed Attorney General Francis Biddle to request permission to travel with Hirano in the wake of the presidential proclamation making the Japanese in the United States who were not naturalized "alien enemies." Cohan wrote that he would "personally vouch" for Hirano.[50] Recounting this story in an article for the magazine *Cabinet*, historian Scott A. Sandage points out that despite Hirano's importance to the Cohan family, "the film did not portray Michio Hirano, not even for one line."[51] We see instead an African American, whom Cohan calls Eddie, assisting Cohan in a mid-film dressing room scene. Japanese Americans were expelled from US society just as they were the film: President Roosevelt signed Executive Order 9066 and the government began its forced "relocation" of Japanese American citizens shortly before *Yankee Doodle Dandy* premiered. Cohan's son later shared with Sandage that his father felt very bad about Mike Hirano, who disappeared during the war. Perhaps Cohan "finally made the connection," as Sandage put it, "between jingoism and prejudice."[52]

"IT'S MORE THAN A PICTURE": THE RELEASE AND LEGACY OF *YANKEE DOODLE DANDY*

In the end, Warner Bros. and Cohan alike viewed the film as more than a commercial product or even a biopic: rather, it was their patriotic contribution to their nation. Hungarian-born Curtiz found the film's subject matter particularly meaningful. As his biographer Alan Rode put it, "The flag-waving jingoism and the overt sentimentality that future critics would characterize as maudlin were, to him, the picture's most appealing aspects."[53] The cast,

Figure 6.4 George M. Cohan and Michio "Mike" Hirano in Hollywood in 1932. From the collection of Scott A. Sandage.

too, sensed the film's timely importance. Rosemary DeCamp, who played George's mother Helen, recalled "work[ing] in a kind of patriotic frenzy, as though we feared we might be sending a last message from a free world because the news was very bad indeed during those months in the winter of '41 and '42."[54]

The film's premiere was a war bonds benefit held in Times Square on May 29, 1942. The date had been moved up from the originally planned release of July 4 in recognition of Cohan's failing health—he had begun feeling the effects of intestinal cancer the prior summer and learned in January that it had spread.[55] Tickets were available for the price of bonds ranging from $25 to $25,000, and a second war bonds benefit called the "Build Ships" premiere followed in Hollywood on August 12.[56] The reception at both was encouraging, and the day after the Hollywood premiere Jack Warner wrote to the heads of advertising and publicity at Warner Bros. that they should put forth "a real campaign, telling not only the Exhibitors but America and the world that we are 'first in the hearts of our countrymen,' and 'YANKEE DOODLE DANDY' is one picture every man, woman and child should see."[57]

Jack Warner telegraphed Cohan on the day of the film's premiere, "Dear George: I want to thank you from the bottom of my heart for permitting me to produce the story of your grand and glorious career. . . . It's more than a picture. It's the whole spirit of America rolled into one and by your permitting me to produce this picture you have done a great American service."[58] Cohan's response echoed these hopes that the film "may aid the theatre to contribute its share towards the realization of peace and civilization to follow the present tragic experiences. . . . With that thought I trust your statement in your telegram that *Yankee Doodle Dandy* is a great patriotic service will be true."[59] He was reportedly quite pleased with the film, which he first screened at his home in Monroe, New York, in October 1941.[60]

Individual responses and reviews alike attest to *Yankee Doodle Dandy*'s impact at a pivotal time in United States history. One enthusiastic viewer wrote to Jack Warner, "This picture will undoubtedly receive all its praise from the Box Office, and what is more important to us all, from the uplift in the morale of the American public." The letter closes, "Viva J. L. Warner! A true (many words could be used here, but only one would do you justice) AMERICAN!!!"[61] Another wrote to Warner, "*Yankee Doodle Dandy* just makes you feel like being a better American."[62] Critic Edwin Schallert described the film in the *Los Angeles Times* as "patriotic, with plenty of flag waving, yet not too much for the present." He further appreciated the film's interweaving of national and theatrical history, complimenting its "delightful nostalgia attaching to the depiction of the old show days" and noting that the film "brings to mind the passing pageant of American history through its chronicle of one man's huge success in the show business."[63] The film also secured a permanent place in Hollywood film history. It won three Academy Awards: for Actor in a Leading Role, Music (Scoring of a Musical Picture), and Sound Recording. In 1993, it was inducted into the National Film Registry of the Library of Congress.

In adapting Cohan's life and works, the makers of *Yankee Doodle Dandy* depicted a rich theatrical history that corresponded with the nation's history. Drawing heavily upon nostalgia for a mythologized past, they sought to show the nation's merit and resilience through its depth of historical experience—both cultural and military—and its national pride, exemplified by the rose-tinted character of one of its homegrown citizens. Demonstrating the Americanness of musico-theatrical entertainment, *Yankee Doodle Dandy* helped establish "the American musical" as a national art form, only a few months before *Oklahoma!* burst onto Broadway. It rejuvenated Cohan's legacy, which had begun to fade. And, furthering the project Cohan had already undertaken in his own public relations, it contributed mightily to his lasting image as a symbol and embodiment of the nation—as *the* Yankee Doodle Dandy.

EPILOGUE

COHAN'S LEGACIES

A throng of people stood outside a theater on a slightly chilly May day in New York City when an energetic and charismatic young man greeted them. He seemed to epitomize the American dream in the new century: family members had come seeking a better life, and now he had achieved astronomical success as a playwright, songwriter, and star. An adept self-publicist, he had also established himself as a celebrity and favorite of the press, who marveled at his fresh approach and ability to do it all. His new show was taking Broadway by storm, joining an African American popular music style and fast-paced comedic drama with a quintessentially American story. He introduced a more established Broadway star who began to sing, unaccompanied, "Give my regards to Broadway, / remember me to Herald Square." A few in the crowd, recognizing the tune, started to sing along.

It was May 18, 2016, just another day at #Ham4Ham, a series of mini-performances for fans gathered outside the Richard Rodgers Theatre, hoping to win $10 lottery tickets to the smash hit *Hamilton*. The host was the show's creator and star Lin-Manuel Miranda, a second-generation Puerto Rican American whose multifaceted career is reminiscent of Cohan's.[1] A century after Cohan's career, it was hip hop rather than ragtime that was perceived to be reinvigorating the American musical. Miranda was joined that spring day by superstar Patti LuPone, who sang Cohan's old love song to Broadway (▶ Example E.1).

• • •

The legacies of George M. Cohan—the mythologization of Broadway, the Americanization of the musical, the songs epitomizing patriotism—live on in powerful ways. They have been shaped by the discourses explicated in this book: of celebrity, of business and labor, of entertainment, and of American identity and patriotism. Like Cohan himself and the place he occupied in US

Yankee Doodle Dandy. Elizabeth T. Craft, Oxford University Press. © Oxford University Press 2024.
DOI: 10.1093/oso/9780197550403.003.0008

society, they are also filled with contradictions. One is that Cohan's songs and ideas have lived on largely without his name attached. Many in the United States grow up singing "You're a Grand Old Flag" and have heard "Give My Regards to Broadway" but do not know who wrote them or anything about their creator, for that matter. His statue stands in Times Square, yet it is so dwarfed by the flashing billboards around him—iconic evidence of the commercialism that he embraced as part of Broadway entertainment—that his likeness is easily overlooked.

In many ways, the Broadway that Cohan helped shape is our Broadway, contradictions and all. One can see traces of the Cohanesque in musicals as diverse as *Oklahoma!* (1943), *The Music Man* (1957), and *Urinetown* (2001), to recall a few mentioned in this book, as well as *Hamilton* (2015). Broadway continues to be a potent site for constructing the nation, and the nature of the American identity it depicts is as debated a century later as it was in Cohan's day. It continues to be both a vehicle for "outsiders" to claim American identity and a realm of exclusion; while the storytellers of putative "true Americans" have shifted over time, the fact that boundaries are drawn around them has not. Broadway has also continued to occupy an iconic place in American culture while maintaining its unapologetically commercial stance.

Yet Cohan's bid to determine the future of the business side of Broadway failed, and his opposition to the Actors' Equity Association had enduring effects for his legacy. In the late teens, Equity was like David taking on Goliath, but it later became a Goliath in its own right, and many among the leadership and members were not quick to forgive or forget. In the 1950s, when Oscar Hammerstein II led a committee to establish a George M. Cohan memorial statue in Times Square and asked for donations, Equity sent an amount "equal to the cost of a life membership"—a membership Cohan had always adamantly refused. Hammerstein noted "that a few stray grains of bitterness remain" and returned the check, refusing to cooperate "in pinpricking George's ghost."[2] In the 1970s, the American Guild of Variety Actors was criticized for naming its annual award, the "Georgie," after Cohan because of his opposition to actors' unionism.[3]

Even as he is sometimes faulted for fighting against Equity and more often forgotten entirely, Cohan the larger-than-life figure, the celebrity, has also lived on in entertainment about his life. In addition to the 1942 musical biopic *Yankee Doodle Dandy*, he is celebrated in the 1968 Broadway show *George M!* and in many other biographical musicals (or bio-musicals) that have circulated throughout the country.[4] Small enough to be easily staged and with music old enough to be largely in the public domain, these shows are affordable and manageable for small companies. These bio-musicals perpetuate Cohan's public persona, but they also draw upon it: they are possible *because* Cohan had already broadcast his appealing personality and neatly packaged the story of his life for public consumption, time and time again. They also have the advantage of using Cohan's name and presenting his songs without having to address the problems inherent in restaging the dated shows they came from.

Cohan's songs and shows as they have circulated in the decades since his death have been largely unmoored from their original productions and defy neat cultural classification. Indeed, very few of Cohan's shows have continued to circulate as shows, and his musicals only as adaptations, with "wax museum" treatment like that of the 1982 Broadway revival of *Little Johnny Jones* or an adaptation of *45 Minutes from Broadway* that uses the device of a school drama club looking for a show to do, a dilemma "solved by the appearance of an old theatrical trunk filled with the memorabilia of early show business days."[5]

What is best remembered about Cohan are his songs, and, given the way he constructed his Yankee Doodle public persona, it is fitting that his patriotic songs are foremost among them. While the last few decades of the twentieth century arguably saw a breakdown between highbrow/lowbrow taste distinctions, Cohan's songs continue to sit in an uneasy place in the cultural categories and hierarchies that still tacitly shape our performed repertoires and scholarly canons.[6] They move between the realms of popular song, occasionally performed within theatrical contexts but more often not, and folksong, songs circulating without their composer or original notation. They are popular as band music, another genre without a clear cultural domain. "You're a Grand Old Flag" has lived on in classrooms, an eminently singable vehicle for teaching patriotism (▶ Example E.2). It has also been elevated as part of the cherished music of the "great American songbook," as when sung by opera singer Marilyn Horne in a shimmering, grandiose, and quite un-Cohan–like arrangement on her album *Beautiful Dreamer* (1986) (▶ Example E.3).

Cohan's patriotic shows and songs may be seen as Americana and the kind of "evocation of a common past" that, as historian Michael Kammen has noted, can cut across cultural registers.[7] Or they may be seen as kitsch, or propaganda, spurned by even the most devoted cultural pluralists. Much depends on context: when patriotism appears to be used for commercial or political benefit, it becomes flag-waving, suggesting a cheapness of the patriotic sentiment. Where genuine, tasteful patriotism ends and flag-waving begins, of course, is in the ear of the beholder.

With their early twentieth-century sound and World War II associations, Cohan's songs have become symbolic of patriotism and also of a nostalgia for a time perceived to be simpler, more unified, and, sometimes, Whiter. Paradoxically, Cohan seemed to have a revival moment in the late 1960s through the 1980s, even as historians were abandoning the study of the nation and patriotism and many citizens were wary of it as well.[8] In 1968, a year so politically and socially tumultuous that *Smithsonian Magazine* later dubbed it "the year that shattered America," *George M!* premiered on Broadway, packing Cohan's songs into a story about his life starring Joel Grey.[9] It opened on the day that Martin Luther King Jr. was buried in Atlanta, having been shot and killed just days earlier. Riots were still underway across the country. Whether critics found it odd or refreshing, they generally agreed that *George M!* was out of step with the times. "A study in nostalgic anachronism," one reviewer wrote, riffing on the early twentieth-century trope of the "tired businessman" to describe the show as "just the thing for the tired super-patriot."[10] Cohan's songs, the *Time* magazine review stated, "hold up remarkably well" but "celebrate the memory of a simple, ardent and unskeptical U.S. that no longer exists."[11] On the other hand, designer and writer William Pahlmann, who was born in 1900 and may well have remembered Cohan during his lifetime, raved about the show, commenting on its bootstraps narrative of a man who became a millionaire despite never having had "a Federal grant or help from a foundation." He recommended the show to anyone with "a feeling that American and exuberance go together and the dream is still worth dreaming."[12] Humor columnist Erma Bombeck discussed the show as part of a surprising reemergence of patriotism, wittily commenting upon the ways region, cultural status, and patriotism intersect: "A few subversives in the audience" who were humming along to "I'm a Yankee Doodle Dandy," she wrote, were "probably just a few of the people from the midwest who are behind the times and don't know patriotism is out." Bombeck reported that by the end of the show, however, "there wasn't a throat in the hall without a lump in it."[13] The *George M!* reviews get at how the potent blend of nostalgia and patriotism Cohan epitomizes—and moreover, helped concoct—continued to have both its detractors and its appeal. The show ran a solid 433 performances.[14]

When a revival of *Little Johnny Jones* transferred from the Connecticut regional theater Goodspeed Opera House to Broadway in 1982, its fortunes were again perceived to rise or fall on Americans' feelings about patriotism. Goodspeed's executive director Michael Price told an interviewer while it was playing in Boston, in the run-up to the show's Broadway opening, "We've certainly found that in the atmosphere of our country today, the show is at the right time and the right place. We're proud to be Americans. We've gone through that whole questioning period of the Vietnam War . . . and the pride of America has come back full strength." Price mentioned the Iran hostage crisis as an event that had unified the country.[15] The *Little Johnny Jones* revival began every performance by singing the national anthem, and "the flags [kept] unfurling right through the curtain call."[16] It may not have been the flag-waving that killed the show, which had done well at Goodspeed and on tour, but it certainly did not save the Broadway production, which closed the same night it opened. "One wonders how sophisticated audiences are reacting to this Old Glory stuff," wrote one critic after seeing it, before its closure was announced.[17] Yet again, the tastefulness of flag-waving was called into question.

Since *George M!* and the *Little Johnny Jones* revival, patriotism has become even more closely associated with conservatism and nationalism, and the "grand old flag" has become one of the nation's most fraught visual emblems. Patriotic songs, including "God Bless America" and the national anthem "The Star-Spangled Banner" as well as Cohan's, have been recontextualized or reinterpreted, heralded or protested in patriotism's rightward turn.[18] At a 2016 rally for then-presidential candidate Donald Trump, for instance, a trio of girls called the USA Freedom Kids, attired in satiny stars-and-stripes dresses, performed a jingoistic number they dubbed "Freedom's Call" to the tune of Cohan's "Over There" (▶ Example E.4). Online responses to videos of the "You're a Grand Old Flag" performance and final scenes from *Yankee Doodle Dandy* similarly bring Cohan's songs and story into the throes of unbridled political debate, most frequently in the service of conservatism, invoking a nativist nostalgia for "the good old days." One such YouTube commenter adds, "Heaven forbid that we actually show pride in our country, because we might offend someone who wasn't born here!"[19] The irony of leveraging the songs of a third-generation immigrant American from one of the most despised groups of his day to promote a nativist nationalism is lost. These performances of and reactions to Cohan's songs speak to their symbolic aural power.[20] As the "Yankee Doodle comedian" knew well, the "patriotic something that no one can understand" that he describes in "You're a Grand Old Flag" does tend to set folks "off [their] noodle[s]," and he set it to music in a catchy and endearing way.[21]

Cohan the Irish American lives on alongside Cohan the flag-waving patriot. Given his celebrity at the height of his career, Cohan's Yankee Doodle reputation intertwined with his Irish American pride contributed to the process of the Irish being written into cultural belonging as Americans. By 1980, when the US census first asked respondents to share their ethnic ancestry, more listed Irish than could be explained by demographic factors alone.[22] Being Irish had become popular. Cohan's legacy has also continued to be intertwined with Irish American identity and pride in the United States, reemerging with Irish Americans' renewed interest and embrace of their heritage beginning in the 1970s.[23] Cohan has been featured in shows premiered at the Irish Repertory Theatre that opened in New York City in 1988, like *The Irish . . . and How They Got That Way* (off-Broadway, 1997) about the history of the Irish in America, and the bio-musical *George M. Cohan Tonight!* (off-Broadway, 2006). Much of Cohan's sheet music, including his more obscure pieces, can be found at the Ward Irish Music Archives, part of the organization CelticMKE celebrating Irish, Irish American, and Celtic culture from its base in Milwaukee, Wisconsin. And Cohan has continued to be a symbol of Irish American patriotism and culture, as he is described in Irish American politician Sen. Daniel Patrick Moynihan's 1985 *Reader's Digest* essay "The Irish Among Us."[24] In many corners, the Cohan of the twentieth and twenty-first centuries is as Irish as he was in the days of *Little Nellie Kelly* and *The Merry Malones*. Yet the Irish have now been so absorbed into the perceived mainstream of US culture that the importance of Cohan's immigrant identity has been largely erased outside of the groups dedicated to celebrating it.

The Cohan of the later twentieth and twenty-first centuries is often fractured into the various roles he embodied, with any given portrayal capturing only one or two. They are often decidedly ahistorical, deployed—as invocations of the past often are—to meet the aims of the contemporary moment. Perhaps most strikingly, though, they tend to miss so much: they miss Cohan the inimitable entertainer, his levity and style, the Cohanesque wink, or as critic Walter Kerr put it, "the undercut that put a slippery floor beneath all the braggadocio, the out-of-kilter smile that seemed to mock the demands he was making of an audience even while he went on making them."[25] They miss the breadth of Cohan's impact on our artistic and cultural life. And they miss what studying him shows us about the actual, rather than imaginary, "good old days": how national identity has long been contested and how national culture has been created through that contestation.

* * *

When Patti LuPone sang "Give My Regards to Broadway" on that afternoon in 2016, Lin-Manuel Miranda and members of the audience looked on raptly. It was the singer and the performance, yes—she is a Broadway star of the highest order and she was right there on the sidewalk, no orchestra, no stage lights, just voice and affect. But it was also the song, with its snappy, affable optimism, and the powerful sense of nostalgia behind it, embedded in the song since its premiere in 1904 and intensified, with new resonances, over the decades. It evokes the Broadway that Cohan helped make a powerful, even mystical symbol of American theatrical entertainment, simultaneously deeply, self-indulgently of New York and yet also of "the road" far beyond it. It was a Broadway he claimed, he shaped, and he personified, as the nation's Yankee Doodle Dandy.

NOTE ON SHEET MUSIC

Sheet music from this period is often available in digitized sheet music collections as well as within physical archival collections. Many of Cohan's published songs circulated widely and are easy to locate; others are rather challenging to find. Where possible, I have indicated the availability of a digitized copy.

ABBREVIATIONS

APC	American Play Company collection, University of Miami Special Collections, Coral Gables, FL
Cohan Collection	Edward B. Marks Co. Collection on George M. Cohan, 1901–1968, Museum of the City of New York, New York
Falk Papers	Sawyer Falk Papers, Special Collections Research Center, Syracuse University Libraries
Harris Papers	Sam Harris Papers, The Shubert Archive, New York
HBTL	Hampden-Booth Theatre Library of the Players Foundation for Theatre Education, New York
HRC	Theater Biography Collection, Harry Ransom Center, University of Texas at Austin
HTC	Harvard Theatre Collection, Houghton Library, Harvard University, Cambridge, MA
Levy Collection	Lester S. Levy Collection of Sheet Music, https://levysheetmusic.mse.jhu.edu/ Sheridan Libraries, Johns Hopkins University, Baltimore, MD
LoC	Library of Congress, Washington, DC
MMB	Vocal Popular Sheet Music Collection (Bagaduce Music Lending Library), Maine Music Box, https://digitalcommons.library.umaine.edu/mmb/, DigitalCommons@UMaine, Fogler Library, University of Maine, Orono, ME
NYPL	New York Public Library for the Performing Arts, Lincoln Center, New York
K&E Collection	Klaw & Erlanger Collection, The Shubert Archive, New York
Radio Scripts LC	George M. Cohan Radio Scripts, 1933–1934, Miscellaneous Manuscripts Collection, Manuscript Division, Library of Congress, Washington, DC
Shubert Correspondence	General Correspondence, 1910–1926, #1400, The Shubert Archive, New York
TOFT	Theatre on Film and Tape Archive, New York Public Library for the Performing Arts, Lincoln Center, New York
UCLA Film	UCLA Film and Television Archive, UCLA Library, University of California, Los Angeles
Ward Archives	Irish Sheet Music Archives, https://irishsheetmusicarchives.com/, Ward Irish Music Archives, Milwaukee, WI

WBA Warner Bros. Archives, School of Cinematic Arts, University of Southern California, Los Angeles

WBS Warner Bros. Scripts: United Artists Corporation, Series 1.2, Wisconsin Center for Film and Theatre Research, Wisconsin Historical Society, Madison, WI

NOTES

INTRODUCTION

1. References to Cohan as the father of musical comedy include Rick Benjamin, liner notes to *You're a Grand Old Rag: The Music of George M. Cohan*, The Paragon Ragtime Orchestra, New World Records 80685-2, compact disc; David Ewen, *The Story of America's Musical Theater* (Philadelphia: Chilton, 1961), 65; and Sheldon Patinkin, *"No Legs, No Jokes, No Chance": A History of the American Musical Theater* (Evanston, IL: Northwestern University Press, 2008), 73.
2. John McCabe, *George M. Cohan: The Man Who Owned Broadway* (Garden City, NY: Doubleday, 1973), xi.
3. For Cohan and in this book, "American" describes the United States rather than the continents of America. On the complexities and power dynamics of American music, with great applicability to Cohan's American entertainment, see Charles Hiroshi Garrett, *Struggling to Define a Nation: American Music and the Twentieth Century* (Berkeley: University of California Press, 2008), 3–8.
4. Oscar Hammerstein II, "Tribute to Yankee Doodle Dandy," *New York Times*, May 5, 1957.
5. On these three as "distinctly American and widely influential" twentieth-century forms, see Raymond Knapp, *The American Musical and the Formation of National Identity* (Princeton, NJ: Princeton University Press, 2005), 3.
6. On usages of the term "legitimate" in nineteenth- and early twentieth-century theater, see Elizabeth L. Wollman, *A Critical Companion to the American Stage Musical* (London: Bloomsbury, 2017), 37–38; Benjamin McArthur, *Actors and American Culture, 1880–1920* (Philadelphia: Temple University Press, 1984), x–xi; and David Savran, *Highbrow/Lowdown: Theater, Jazz, and the Making of the New Middle Class* (Ann Arbor: University of Michigan Press, 2009), 42–43.
7. "Music and the Stage," *Los Angeles Times*, November 23, 1909.
8. Edward B. Marks as told to Abbott J. Liebling, *They All Sang: From Tony Pastor to Rudy Vallée* (New York: Viking, 1934), 131.
9. Sunny Stalter-Pace, *Imitation Artist: Gertrude Hoffmann's Life in Vaudeville and Dance* (Chicago: Northwestern University Press, 2020), 3.
10. Cohan contributed significantly to many shows for which he is not officially credited. An article from his lifetime says he would not take credit for shows on which he collaborated (Garrett D. Byrnes, "A Man Named George M. Cohan," *Providence Journal*, December 25, 1932), but he did share authorship credit, as McCabe explains, when he was responsible for over half the work. McCabe, *George M. Cohan*, 280.
11. "George M. Cohan and His Work," *Washington Post*, January 8, 1905.
12. Sam Forrest, "Three Decades with George M. Cohan," *New York Herald Tribune*, May 24, 1942, George M. Cohan clippings file, Music Division, NYPL.

13. Stacy Wolf, introduction to *The Oxford Handbook of the American Musical*, ed. Raymond Knapp, Mitchell Morris, and Stacy Wolf (New York: Oxford University Press, 2011), 3; Knapp, *The American Musical*; Benedict Anderson, *Imagined Communities: Reflections on the Origin and Spread of Nationalism* (London: Verso, 1983).
14. John McCabe's *George M. Cohan: The Man Who Owned Broadway* (1973) is a valuable and well-researched work on Cohan's career and dramatic work but does not include citations. For a biography published just after Cohan's death, see Ward Morehouse, *George M. Cohan: Prince of the American Theater* (Philadelphia: J. B. Lippincott, 1943). Major dissertations on Cohan include Frank W. Glann, "An Historical and Critical Evaluation of the Plays of George M. Cohan, 1901–1920" (PhD diss., Bowling Green State University, 1976); and Stephen M. Vallillo, "George M. Cohan, Director" (PhD diss., New York University, 1986).
15. Alec Wilder, *American Popular Song: The Great Innovators, 1900–1950* (New York: University Press, 1972) and Wilder, *American Popular Song*, 3rd ed., rev. and ed. Robert Rawlins (New York: Oxford University Press, 2022). Lawrence Thelen's *The Show Makers: Great Directors of the American Musical Theatre* (New York: Routledge, 2002) profiles then-living directors but does not mention Cohan in its list of earlier influential directors (p. ix). There are, of course, counterexamples as well; he makes it in as a "great lyricist," for example, to Philip Furia's *The Poets of Tin Pan Alley: A History of America's Great Lyricists* (New York: Oxford University Press, 1992).
16. Issues in accessing materials are a challenge for popular entertainment in this period, and I suspect they are yet another reason for the dearth of Cohan scholarship. Although I was able to conduct research in the primary Cohan collection, with help from curators at the Museum of the City of New York, access has been limited. When I began researching there in 2010, there were per-session research fees. The COVID-19 pandemic has shuttered onsite research to this day. They are currently working on providing a useable digital platform for accessing some materials from the collection, available at https://collections.mcny.org/.
17. Especially for Cohan's earlier shows, the conductor's score might consist of melody and bass line for some numbers alternating with first violin or cello part for others: see, for example, director's score of *The American Idea*, Cohan Collection 68.123.64A.
18. Michel Mok, "George M. Cohan Is Still Stage-Struck at Sixty," *Camden Courier-Post*, July 5, 1938. There are also sometimes differences in various scripts of the same show: typescript copies of *The Little Millionaire* and *The Talk of New York*, for instance, differ. On the authority of extant typescripts, see also Glann, "Plays of George M. Cohan," 8; Vallillo, "Cohan, Director," x.
19. On The Players, see McArthur, *Actors and American Culture*, 76–84.
20. On the insufficiency of the theatrical text alone and the open, fluid nature of musical theater, see Bruce Kirle, *Unfinished Show Business: Broadway Musicals as Works-in-Process* (Carbondale: Southern Illinois University Press, 2005). "Beyond Broadway" comes from Stacy Wolf, *Beyond Broadway: The Pleasure and Promise of Musical Theatre across America* (New York: Oxford University Press, 2020); see also

Jake Johnson, *Lying in the Middle: Musical Theater and Belief at the Heart of America* (Urbana: University of Illinois Press, 2021).

21. The 1880 census record of the Cohan family shows that the parents of both Jeremiah and Helen (listed as "Ellen") were born in Ireland: 1880 US Census, Suffolk County, Massachusetts, Boston, Roll 559, Page 263C, Enumeration District 726; digital image, Ancestry.com.
22. "Jere J. Cohan Dead; George at His Side," *New York Times*, August 2, 1917; "Mid-Week in the Theaters," *Pittsburgh Post*, September 14, 1905; McCabe, *George M. Cohan*, 2.
23. Jerry J. Cohan, "A Little Talk with Jerry J. Cohan," in *Poems and Sketches* (privately printed, Physioc Press, 1911), 116; George M. Cohan Jr., interview by Scott A. Sandage, October 28, 1988; Elisha Cook Jr., interview by Scott A. Sandage, July 9, 1985. Interviews shared with author by Sandage. Cohan Jr. directly contradicted biographer John McCabe's assertion that Cohan pronounced his name "CO-en, as in 'Cohen,'" *George M. Cohan*, 3.
24. Marriage record for Jeremiah Cohan and Ellen Costigan, September 12, 1874, Rhode Island, Marriage Index 1851–1920; digital record, Ancestry.com.
25. On variety, see Gillian M. Rodger, *Champagne Charlie and Pretty Jemima: Variety Theater in the Nineteenth Century* (Urbana: University of Illinois Press, 2010). On the range of activity by the Four Cohans, see McCabe, *George M. Cohan*, esp. 11–13, 22.
26. Matthew Frye Jacobson, *Whiteness of a Different Color: European Immigrants and the Alchemy of Race* (Cambridge, MA: Harvard University Press, 1998), quotations from 5–8. On the historiography of scholarship on immigrant Whiteness, and the complexities of the Irish's role within it, see also David R. Roediger, "Whiteness and Race," in *The Oxford Handbook of American Immigration and Ethnicity*, ed. Ronald H. Bayor (New York: Oxford University Press, 2016), 197–212; and Michelle Granshaw, *Irish on the Move: Performing Mobility in American Variety Theatre* (Iowa City: University of Iowa Press, 2019), 15–20. This book attends to Whiteness as a historically constructed, contested, and privileged racial category, thus I have chosen to capitalize White as well as Black. For further discussion, see Nell Irvin Painter, "Why 'White' Should Be Capitalized, Too," Washington Post, July 22, 2020, https://www.washingtonpost.com/opinions/2020/07/22/why-white-should-be-capitalized/.
27. Several scholars have used the "century of immigration" framing to describe the period from 1820 to 1924, including Roger Daniels, *Coming to America: A History of Immigration and Ethnicity in American Life*, 2nd ed. (New York: Perennial, 2002). On nativism, see, for example, John Higham's classic book *Strangers in the Land: Patterns of American Nativism, 1860–1925* (1955; repr., New Brunswick, NJ: Rutgers University Press, 1998), 5–11.
28. I have been unable to find verification of this exact event. However, there are reports of an annual Pilgrims Fathers' outing to a spot near Revere, with some accounts of music and dancing: see "Bass Point," *Boston Globe*, July 29, 1894; "Pilgrim Fathers' Outing," *Boston Globe*, September 12, 1895. The Cohans were in Boston the week of July 23, 1894, performing a program including the Doll Dance, so it is possible the event to which Jerry referred was the Pilgrim Fathers' outing that year (see advertisement for B. F. Keith's Amusement Enterprises, *Boston Post*, July 22, 1894).
29. This version of the story is taken from the newspaper article "The Stage" in the *Anaconda Standard*, May 27, 1906. It likely came from the Cohan and Harris

newsletter the *Spot Light*, but the Cohan Collection does not have every issue and is missing those from May and June 1906. See also Cohan, *Poems and Sketches*, 120.

30. Higham discusses this counter set of beliefs, the "cosmopolitan traditions," alongside his treatment of nativism; see *Strangers in the Land*, esp. 19–23, 33–34, 63.
31. Werner Sollors, *Beyond Ethnicity: Consent and Descent in American Culture* (New York: Oxford University Press, 1986), 96.
32. Jerry J. Cohan, Cohan Family Repertoire-Book, MS Thr 226, HTC; Cohan, *Poems and Sketches*, see esp. "Booze," "Half and Half," "Two Mixed Ales," and "Me Ould Friend," 69–70, 74–75, and 91–92. On the Cohan Family Repertoire-Book, see Laurence Senelick, "Variety into Vaudeville: The Process Observed in Two Manuscript Gagbooks," *Theatre Survey* 19, no. 1 (May 1978): 1–15.
33. On the role of Irish-themed entertainment for Irish and Irish American artists including the Cohans, see Granshaw, *Irish on the Move*, 101–45, quotations from 103 and 145. On the Cohans' hibernicon work, see also Michelle Granshaw, "The Hibernicon and Visions of Returning Home: Popular Entertainment in Irish America from the Civil War to World War I" (PhD diss., University of Washington, 2012), 87–137.
34. Quotations are from Eric Lott, *Love and Theft: Blackface Minstrelsy and the American Working Class* (New York: Oxford University Press, 1993), 100; and Michael Rogin, *Blackface, White Noise: Jewish Immigrants in the Hollywood Melting Pot* (Berkeley: University of California Press, 1996), 56. On blackface minstrelsy, including the unequal nature of its racial exchange, see also Matthew D. Morrison, "Race, Blacksound, and the (Re)Making of Musicological Discourse," *Journal of the American Musicological Society* 72, no. 3 (December 1, 2019): esp. 800–801. On stage stereotypes of Irish and African Americans, see William H. A. Williams, *'Twas Only an Irishman's Dream: The Image of Ireland and the Irish in American Popular Song Lyrics, 1800–1920* (Urbana: University of Illinois Press, 1996), 83–86; Lott, *Love and Theft*, esp. 4. Accounts of Jerry Cohan's Irish performances in minstrel shows include "La Rue's Carnival Minstrels," *Buffalo Courier*, April 3, 1869; and Frank Dumont, "The Younger Generation in Minstrelsy and Reminiscences of the Past," *New York Clipper*, March 27, 1915.
35. J. Cohan, *Poems and Sketches*, 85–87.
36. George Ross, "George M. Cohan, 60, Discusses Old Days," clipping dated January 15, 1938, HRC box 86; Cohan, *Twenty Years on Broadway and the Years It Took to Get There: The True Story of a Trouper's Life from the Cradle to the "Closed Shop"* (New York: Harper and Brothers, 1925), 215. On Irving Berlin and minstrelsy, see Jeffrey Magee, *Irving Berlin's American Musical Theater* (New York: Oxford University Press, 2012), esp. 25–28.
37. Larry Stempel, *Showtime: A History of the Broadway Musical Theater* (New York: Norton, 2010), 56–57.
38. Nicholas Gebhardt, *Vaudeville Melodies: Popular Musicians and Mass Entertainment in American Culture, 1870–1929* (Chicago: University of Chicago Press, 2017), 51–56.
39. George M. Cohan, "Theatre Going as a Kid," bound typescript, Cohan Collection 68.123.480.
40. Cohan, "Theatre Going," Cohan Collection; George M. Cohan as told to Charles Washburn, "Back to the Old, Old Days," chap. 7 of "Broadway as It Once Was, Is

and Will Be: As Seen and Foreseen by George M. Cohan," *New York Evening World*, June 30, 1930, clipping in scrapbook, Cohan Collection 31.167. While John McCabe wrote that the character Harrigan and song by that name in *Fifty Miles from Boston* came from Ned Harrigan, I have found no evidence to support that, and in the screenplay Cohan wrote for *Yankee Doodle Dandy*, he describes it as coming from an encounter with a New York policeman. See McCabe, *George M. Cohan*, 86–87; and Cohan, *Yankee Doodle Dandy* Screenplay, WBS box 445, folder 5, pages 59–61 and 100. All dates given for shows are the year of their opening on Broadway unless otherwise noted.

41. Cohan's son George M. Cohan Jr. told Scott A. Sandage that the paperweight "had 'always' been on his father's writing desk at home," letter to author, July 21, 2021. Descriptions of Cohan's work as Hoyt-like include Michael B. Leavitt, *Fifty Years in Theatrical Management, 1859–1909* (New York: Broadway Publishing, 1912), 297; "Channing Pollock's Review of the New Plays: 'Peace at Any Price,'" *Green Book Magazine*, December 1915, 981. On Hoyt's persona, see Hillary Miller, "Marching Off-Beat and On-Screen: New York City's Reform Movements and Charles Hale Hoyt's *A Milk White Flag*," in *Performing the Progressive Era: Immigration, Urban Life, and Nationalism on Stage*, ed. Max Shulman and J. Chris Westgate (Iowa City: University of Iowa Press, 2019), 36.

CHAPTER 1

1. Epigraphs: *Yankee Doodle Dandy* (1942; Burbank, CA: Warner Home Video, 2003) and Patrick McGilligan, ed., *Yankee Doodle Dandy* (Madison: University of Wisconsin Press, 2005), 157; George M. Cohan in collaboration with Verne Hardin Porter, "The Stage as I Have Seen It," *Green Book Magazine*, February 1915, 253.
2. Edwin Booth (1833–1893) and Lawrence Barrett (1838–1891) were well-respected American actors known especially for their performances of Shakespearean tragedy.
3. Extant lyrics to this song, with considerable variance, can be found in booklets of song lyrics from *Hello, Broadway!*, in a *Green Book Magazine* review, and in Cohan's 1930s Radio Reviews. In the version above, I draw on these sources in an attempt to reconstruct the original text as delivered onstage in *Hello, Broadway!* Song lyric booklets for *Hello, Broadway!*, Cohan Collection 68.123.358A and 68.123.358B; "Channing Pollock's Monthly Review: 'Shoes for the Cobbler's Children," *Green Book Magazine*, March 1915, 477; Cohan, "Radio Reviews Six to Ten by George M. Cohan, of Series Commencing December 3, 1933: Sixth Review," p. 3, Cohan Collection 68.123.495. The music can be found, in parts, in the folder "*Hello Broadway* by G. M. Cohan, Assorted Music Sheets," Cohan Collection 68.123.354.
4. John McCabe, *George M. Cohan: The Man Who Owned Broadway* (Garden City, NY: Doubleday, 1973), 132.
5. The closely related, often ambiguous terms "patriotism" and "nationalism" appear throughout this chapter. I use "patriotism" to refer to personal "love of or devotion to one's country" (*Oxford English Dictionary* definition) and "nationalism" to refer to a broader political ideology "based on the assertion by some bounded social group . . . of its right to its own state or sphere of autonomy" (Stuart McConnell's

definition). This ideology tends to place national loyalty and interests above other group and individual ties and privilege one's own nation over others. *Oxford English Dictionary*, 3rd ed., March 2008, http://www.oed.com (accessed June 2022), s.v. "patriotism"; Stuart McConnell, "Nationalism," in *The Oxford Companion to United States History*, ed. Paul S. Boyer (New York: Oxford University Press, 2001), 537. See also Jill Lepore, *This America: The Case for the Nation* (New York: Liveright, 2019).

6. On Cohan's improvements, see "Little Johnny Jones," *New Haven Morning Journal and Courier*, February 2, 1905; and Peter Clark Macfarlane, "George M. Cohan," *Everybody's Magazine*, January 1914, 108. Gerald Bordman makes this point about the show's run being substantial once one considers its total time in New York from 1904–1905, but he, and other sources including past studies of Cohan and Internet Broadway Database (IBDB.com), do not include a two-week run at the New York Theatre in January 1905; the show's presence and number of performances in New York were thus greater than previously realized. Gerald Bordman and Richard Norton, *American Musical Theatre: A Chronicle*, 4th ed. (New York: Oxford University Press, 2010), 240.
7. Macfarlane, "George M. Cohan," 108–109.
8. Journalists frequently mentioned or discussed Cohan's "flag-waving," both implicitly and explicitly. See, for example: "A Few Dates from the Career of George M. Cohan, Actor," *Boston Herald*, February 8, 1936, George M. Cohan clippings file, HTC; and Stephen Rathbun, "'Merry Malones': George M. Cohan Opens New Theater With Own Show," *New York Sun*, September 27, 1927, *The Merry Malones* clippings file, HTC.
9. John Bush Jones, *Our Musicals, Ourselves: A Social History of the American Musical Theater* (Hanover, NH: Brandeis University Press, 2003), 15–23.
10. Gary Gerstle, *American Crucible: Race and Nation in the Twentieth Century*, rev. ed. (Princeton, NJ: Princeton University Press, 2017), 8.
11. Matthew Frye Jacobson, *Barbarian Virtues: The United States Encounters Foreign Peoples at Home and Abroad, 1876–1917* (New York: Hill and Wang, 2000), 3–4.
12. Gerstle, *American Crucible*, 3–6.
13. On Kallen and Bourne's foundations, see Gary Gerstle, "The Protean Character of American Liberalism," *American Historical Review* 99, no. 4 (October 1994): 1051; and Jonathan Hansen, "True Americanism: Progressive Era Intellectuals and the Problem of Liberal Nationalism," in *Americanism: New Perspectives on the History of an Ideal*, ed. Michael Kazin and Joseph A. McCartin (Chapel Hill: University of North Carolina Press, 2006), 73–79.
14. Theodore Roosevelt, "What 'Americanism' Means" [a.k.a. "True Americanism"], *The Forum*, April 1894, 198, 203.
15. On Roosevelt and Zangwill, see Gerstle, *American Crucible*, 50–51; and Aviva Taubenfeld, *Rough Writing: Ethnic Authorship in Theodore Roosevelt's America* (New York: NYU Press, 2008), 13–39.
16. On Roosevelt's coexisting racial and civic nationalism, see Gerstle, *American Crucible*, 14–80. On the racial underpinnings of Roosevelt's thought, see Nell Irvin Painter, *The History of White People* (New York: Norton, 2010), 245–55.
17. Roosevelt, "What 'Americanism' Means," 204–205.

18. Gail Bederman, *Manliness and Civilization: A Cultural History of Gender and Race in the United States, 1880–1917* (Chicago: University of Chicago Press, 1995), 170–215; Andrew M. Johnston, "Sex and Gender in Roosevelt's America," in *A Companion to Theodore Roosevelt*, ed. Serge Ricard (Malden, MA: Wiley-Blackwell, 2012), 112–34; Sarah Watts, *Rough Rider in the White House: Theodore Roosevelt and the Politics of Desire* (Chicago: University of Chicago Press, 2003). See also Roosevelt's essay "The Manly Virtues and Practical Politics," *The Forum*, July 1894, published only a few months after "What 'Americanism' Means" in the same magazine.
19. Johnston, "Sex and Gender," 120.
20. Roosevelt, "Nationalism in Literature and Art," address at the American Academy and the National Institute of Arts and Letters, New York, November 16, 1916, in *The Works of Theodore Roosevelt*, ed. Hermann Hagedorn, vol. 12, *Literary Essays* (New York: Scribner's Sons, 1926), 336. See also Taubenfeld, *Rough Writing*, 2–4.
21. Taubenfeld, *Rough Writing*, 10.
22. The song was initially titled "You're a Grand Old Rag." As Cohan told the story, he was inspired to write the song after hearing the phrase delivered fondly from a Civil War veteran and member of the GAR [Grand Army of the Republic]. He changed the name, however, after some (and according to him, the government) objected. "George Washington, Jr.," *Boston Globe*, December 25, 1906; Franklin Fyles, "Gotham Cheers 'The Duel' Because Paris Liked It," *Chicago Tribune*, February 18, 1906; George Cohan, "Cohan Tells of Row on Famous Flag Song," *Boston Globe*, July 1, 1928.
23. On Roosevelt and Cohan's celebrity statuses and personalities as represented in the press, see Charles L. Ponce de Leon, *Self-Exposure: Human-Interest Journalism and the Emergence of Celebrity in America, 1890–1940* (Chapel Hill: University of North Carolina Press, 2002), esp. 55, 58, 65–66, 91–92, 116.
24. Roosevelt, interestingly, differentiated between Anglomania in the social spheres of the United States and Anglophobia in politics. Theodore Roosevelt to Finley Peter Dunne, November 23, 1904, Theodore Roosevelt Papers, LoC Manuscript Division, online at Theodore Roosevelt Digital Library, Dickinson State University, https://www.theodorerooseveltcenter.org/Research/Digital-Library/Record?libID=0190204.
25. On international marriages and their representation in American literature and culture, see Maureen E. Montgomery, *"Gilded Prostitution": Status, Money, and Transatlantic Marriages, 1870–1914* (London: Routledge, 1989); Richard W. Davis, "'We Are All Americans Now!' Anglo-American Marriages in the Later Nineteenth Century," *Proceedings of the American Philosophical Society* 135, no. 2 (June 1991): 140–99; and Paul Jonathan Woolf, "Special Relationships: Anglo-American Love Affairs, Courtships and Marriages in Fiction, 1821–1914" (PhD diss., University of Birmingham, 2007).
26. Among the literature addressing the issue were Henry James's *The Golden Bowl* and Edith Wharton's short story "The Last Asset," both published in the year in which *Little Johnny Jones* premiered; several other works by James and Wharton; Constance Cary Harrison's *The Anglomaniacs* (1890); Gertrude Atherton's *His Fortunate Grace* (1897); and stage works like playwright Winston Churchhill's *The*

Title-Mart (1905) and Harry B. Smith and Victor Herbert's musical comedy *Miss Dolly Dollars* (1905).

27. Advertisement for Rogers Peet and Co. clothiers in a program for *The American Idea*, New Montauk Theatre (week of February 22, 1909), Cohan Collection box 36.
28. Theodore Roosevelt, "Special Message," April 27, 1908, reproduced in *The American Presidency Project*, by Gerhard Peters and John T. Woolley, University of California at Santa Barbara, http://www.presidency.ucsb.edu/node/206689; see also John Callan O'Laughlin, "Roosevelt Censures Foreign Marriages," *New York Times*, May 3, 1908.
29. Montgomery, *Gilded Prostitution*, esp. 30–31.
30. In *The Yankee Prince*, one character says, "I'm speaking of an Earl—an English Earl," and another responds, "Well, I'm speaking of a Prince—a Yankee prince. . . . That's what they call a good fellow where I come from." "The Yankee Prince," bound typescript (Act I, 37), TS 4756.458.530, HTC.
31. Constance Rourke, *American Humor: A Study of the National Character*, with an introduction by Greil Marcus (New York: New York Review Books, 2004), 23–26.
32. Satire revolving around Yankees touring abroad was another vibrant literary tradition. Since (as mentioned in Chapter 2) Cohan claimed that three books by Twain were all he ever read, one wonders whether Mark Twain's *The Innocents Abroad* (1869) was among them.
33. "The Yankee Prince" (Act I, 10), HTC.
34. "Little Johnny Jones," typescript (Act I, 7), Cohan Collection 68.123.208. All *Little Johnny Jones* quotations are from this script.
35. "George Washington, Jr.," typescript (Act I, 11–11A), Cohan Collection 68.123.330. All *George Washington, Jr.* quotations are from this script.
36. This is most true of McFadden in *George Washington, Jr.*, a bit part tourist character who serves primarily as a comic foil for the trickster Eaton Ham, a minstrel show–descendent. McFadden, clearly intended to be no more than an ethnic type, is referred to in the script's text only as "the Irishman." He is an exception among Cohan's Irish characters, which are usually more fully drawn and positively depicted.
37. *Little Johnny Jones* Liberty Theatre playbill clipping, "Week Beginning . . . Nov. 14, 1904," Cohan Collection box 819.
38. "Drama: Things That Bloom in the Spring," *Life*, May 2, 1907, 618.
39. "No Race Suicide There," *Washington Post*, July 1, 1907.
40. On Roosevelt, "race suicide," and women, see Bederman, *Manliness and Civilization*, 200–208; Gerstle, *American Crucible*, 57–59; and Johnston, "Sex and Gender," 112–34.
41. "Little Johnny Jones" (Act II, 5–6; Act III, 5).
42. A review of a 1906 San Francisco production remarked, "The newspaper woman will be rather gratefully greeted by the lady journalists, because she is a pretty and well-dressed girl, and the nearest approach to even journalistic slang she gets is 'scoop.'" "The Playbills New Last Night," *San Francisco Chronicle*, March 13, 1906.
43. "Little Johnny Jones" (Act I, 10; Act II, 4). The next quotation comes from Act III, 3.

44. John Dizikes, *Yankee Doodle Dandy: The Life and Times of Tod Sloan* (New Haven, CT: Yale University Press, 2000), 183–89.
45. Rick Benjamin, liner notes to *You're a Grand Old Rag: The Music of George M. Cohan*, The Paragon Ragtime Orchestra, New World Records 80685-2, 2008, compact disc, 13.
46. J. Peter Burkholder, *All Made of Tunes: Charles Ives and the Uses of Musical Borrowing* (New Haven, CT: Yale University Press, 1995), 300–301.
47. Burkholder, *All Made of Tunes*, 322–27.
48. On "The Yankee Doodle Boy" within the context of the various uses of "Yankee Doodle" from the late eighteenth to the early twentieth centuries, see William Gibbons, "'Yankee Doodle' and Nationalism, 1780–1920," *American Music* 26, no. 2 (Summer 2008): 265–66. Gibbons also lists the song verse's melodic borrowings in a chart similar to the one in this text; mine was made independently and also includes the refrain and indicates specific textual borrowings.
49. Raymond Knapp, *The American Musical and the Formation of National Identity* (Princeton, NJ: Princeton University Press, 2005), 104–105.
50. "An Especially Awful Example," *Life*, March 1, 1906, 278.
51. Burkholder, *All Made of Tunes*, 325–26.
52. Roosevelt, "What 'Americanism' Means," 196.
53. On the Othering of the show's Chinese characters, including through music, dance, costume, and casting, see Brynn Shiovitz, "Queue the Music: Cohan's Yellowface Substitution in *Little Johnny Jones*," *Theatre Survey* 59, no. 2 (May 2018): 194–97, 202–205, 210–12.
54. When McGee asks Wilson, "You're an American, aren't you?" he replies, "I don't look like a Dago, do I?" "Little Johnny Jones" (Act I, 17). "Dago," an ethnic slur, was a disparaging term for a person from Spain, Portugal, South America, or Italy, primarily the latter by the early twentieth century.
55. While some have argued that Roosevelt intended to exclude southern and eastern Europeans, Gary Gerstle has challenged this view, *American Crucible*, 50–53.
56. *Little Johnny Jones* Liberty Theatre playbill clipping, Cohan Collection; Colgate Baker, "'Little Johnny Jones' Gala Opening Bill," *San Francisco Chronicle*, October 7, 1907; "Liberty—Little Johnny Jones," clipping marked 1904, *Little Johnny Jones* clippings file, HTC.
57. Gerstle, *American Crucible*, 48.
58. "Chinese newspaper man—funniest thing I ever heard," Florabelle Fly declares, and she and McGee laugh at the idea. "Little Johnny Jones" (Act I, 5).
59. "Little Johnny Jones" (Act III, 3).
60. *The American Idea* shared resemblances with *Reilly and the Four Hundred* (1891) as well. Cohan's character Hustleford would seem to take after the Harrigan and Hart plot of an "Irish pawnbroker who hoodwinks (and in the process betrays the shallowness of) a group of high-society individuals." Katherine K. Preston, ed., *Irish American Theater: The Mulligan Guard Ball (1879) and Reilly and the 400 (1891)*, scripts by Edward Harrigan, music by David Braham (New York: Garland, 1994), xvii.

61. The reference to "Brooklyn's 400" comes from the character Sullivan. George M. Cohan, *The American Idea* (New York: Pusey and Company, 1909), Act II, 24, Cohan Collection 68.123.65A. All *American Idea* quotations are from this script.
62. Cohan, *The American Idea* (Act I, 6 and 9).
63. Cohan, *The American Idea* (Act III, 30).
64. Cohan, *The American Idea* (Act I, 2).
65. Cohan, "What the American Flag Has Done For Me," *Theatre Magazine*, June 1914, 288.
66. Cohan, "Too Long from Long Acre Square" (New York: Cohan and Harris, 1908), available online at Levy Collection.
67. Cohan, "The American Rag Time" [a.k.a. "The American Ragtime"] (New York: Cohan and Harris, 1908), available online at Levy Collection.
68. "Drama and Music," *Boston Globe*, September 19, 1908. Another article in the *Globe* reported on the extraordinary popularity of the number, noting that it had "never had less than 10 curtain calls" during its Boston run. "Farewell to 'The American Idea,'" *Boston Globe*, September 27, 1908.
69. "The American Idea," *Boston Globe*, September 29, 1908.
70. As Brynn Shiovitz discusses in her analysis of *Little Johnny Jones* in her excellent article "Queue the Music," Africanist aesthetic traits already underlay Cohan's ragtime-influenced songs and dances, though they were presented as (White) American. We differ, however, in our assessment of the extent to which "Africanisms" pervaded the show's libretto and score, which had several non-ragtime-influenced numbers as well. On the sonic legacy of blackface minstrelsy as an underpinning for popular music, see also Matthew D. Morrison, "Race, Blacksound, and the (Re)Making of Musicological Discourse," *Journal of the American Musicological Society* 72, no. 3 (December 2019): 781–823.
71. Larry Hamberlin, *Tin Pan Opera: Operatic Novelty Songs in the Ragtime Era* (New York: Oxford University Press, 2011), 231.
72. Michael G. Garber, "Eepha-Soffa-Dill and Eephing: Found in Ragtime, Jazz, and Country Music, from Broadway to a Texas Plantation," *American Music* 35, no. 3 (2017): 343–74. This is perhaps the strongest racial referent in "The American Ragtime," though Hamberlin also cites the lines "Now honey" and "Listen baby, ain't it simply grand" as examples of language "associated with Negro dialect song," *Tin Pan Opera*, 231.
73. Cohan, *The American Idea* (Act II, 25).
74. "President Says Negro Makes American Music," *New York Times*, February 15, 1906. Three years before Roosevelt's remarks, W.E.B. Du Bois made the case for Black music, specifically the slave or "sorrow songs," as "the sole American music" and "spiritual heritage of the nation." W. E. B. Du Bois, *The Souls of Black Folk*, with an introduction and chronology by Jonathan Scott Holloway (1903; New Haven, CT: Yale University Press, 2015), 189.
75. Edward A. Berlin, *Ragtime: A Musical and Cultural History* (Berkeley: University of California Press, 1980), 32. On the ragtime debate, see also Charles Hiroshi Garrett's chapter on Ives's *Four Ragtime Dances* in *Struggling to Define a*

Nation: American Music and the Twentieth Century (Berkeley: University of California Press, 2008), 17–25.

76. Hiram K. Moderwell, "Ragtime," *New Republic*, October 16, 1915, 286; cited in Garrett, *Struggling to Define a Nation*, 17.
77. Hamberlin, *Tin Pan Opera*, 231.
78. George M. Cohan, "The Patriotic Coon" (New York: Spaulding, 1898), Historic Sheet Music Collection, University of Oregon Libraries. *The New York Dramatic Mirror* reported the "new song," being performed by minstrel star Lew Dockstader and others, in May 1898. "Vaudeville Jottings," May 14, 1898, 18.
79. Shiovitz, "Queue the Music," 207–208; Brynn Wein Shiovitz, "Red, White, and Blue: Finding the Black Behind George M. Cohan's Patriotic Success," *Congress on Research in Dance Conference Proceedings* (2012): 146–53.
80. In addition to the obvious pun, the character's name may have referenced the Bert Williams and George Walker show *Sons of Ham* (1900) or, more generally, the once-widespread notion that Africans were the cursed descendants of Noah's son Ham, a belief that was used to rationalize slavery in the United States and that, as David M. Goldenberg notes, carried on into the twentieth century. David M. Goldenberg, *The Curse of Ham: Race and Slavery in Early Judaism, Christianity, and Islam* (Princeton, NJ: Princeton University Press, 2003), 141–43.
81. "George Washington, Jr." (Act I, 1).
82. Lester A. Walton, ed., "Music and the Stage," *New York Age*, March 5, 1908.
83. Mabel Rowland, ed., *Bert Williams, Son of Laughter: A Symposium of Tribute to the Man and to His Work* (New York: English Crafters, 1923), 175–77.
84. Wendell Phillips Dodge, "The Actor in the Street," *Theatre Magazine*, February 1911, vii.
85. Cohan, *The American Idea* (Act I, 4). The next quotations come from Act II, 15 and 24–25.
86. James H. Dormon, "Ethnic Cultures of the Mind: The Harrigan-Hart Mosaic," *American Studies* 33, no. 2 (Fall 1992): 24.
87. Cohan, "Sullivan" (New York: Cohan and Harris, 1908), available online at Levy Collection.
88. Cohan, *The American Idea* (Act I, 3).
89. "Sullivans There, All but John L.," *New York Times*, November 12, 1908.
90. *The American Idea* opened on September 7 in Buffalo, New York, before heading to Boston for a three-week run and then to New York for an October 5 opening at the New York Theatre. *The Melting Pot* opened October 5, 1908, in Washington, DC, at the Columbia Theater, and did not play in New York until almost a year later, in September 1909. "Theatrical News," *New York Tribune*, August 18, 1908.
91. William M. Newman, *American Pluralism: A Study of Minority Groups and Social Theory* (New York: Harper and Row, 1973), 63; see also Werner Sollors, "Foreword: Theories of American Ethnicity," in *Theories of Ethnicity: A Classical Reader*, ed. Sollors (New York: NYU Press, 1996), xxvii.
92. Theodore Roosevelt, *The Winning of the West*, vol. 1, *From the Alleghanies to the Mississippi, 1769–1776* (New York: G. P. Putnum's Sons, 1896), 108–109; Gary

Gerstle, "Theodore Roosevelt and the Divided Character of American Nationalism," *Journal of American History* 86, no. 3 (December 1999): 1282–85.

93. In this speech, Roosevelt also invoked those Irish Americans who had contributed to the country's founding and its wars, tapping into the filiopietistic discourse commonly used to establish immigrant groups' worth. He also noted that the Irish were "doing their full share toward the artistic and literary development of the country." "Roosevelt Praises the Hardy Irish," *New York Times*, March 18, 1905.
94. Taubenfeld, *Rough Writing*, 21–27; Werner Sollors, *Beyond Ethnicity: Consent and Descent in American Culture* (New York: Oxford University Press, 1986), 5–6, 66–75.
95. Cohan, *The American Idea* (Act I, 6 and Act II, 20). The next quotation comes from Act III, 30.
96. See, for examples, *Little Johnny Jones* Liberty Theatre playbill clipping, Cohan Collection; *Little Johnny Jones* advertisement, *New York Times*, November 6, 1904; Cohan, "They're All My Friends" (New York: F. A. Mills, 1904), Cohan Collection 68.127.141, available online at Ward Archives. The descriptor "America's Favorite Family of Fun-Makers" comes from a program for *The Governor's Son*. Both shows billed the Four Cohans. *The Governor's Son* playbill clipping from The Savoy, week of March 11, 1901, Cohan Collection box 573.
97. Souvenir program for *The Yankee Prince*, Dana T. Bennett Co., Cohan Collection box 1604; "Rehearsing 'A Yankee Prince,'" *New York Tribune*, February 28, 1908; "The American Idea," *Boston Globe*, September 10, 1908.
98. "Life's Confidential Guide to the Theatres," *Life*, April 25, 1907, 583; untitled article, *Life*, October 12, 1911, 618; "An Especially Awful Example," 278. I am presuming that all of the *Life* theater articles are by Metcalfe, although most are unsigned. They seem to be in one voice, with similar language and opinions, and to build upon one another.
99. "George Washington, Jr.," *New York Tribune*, February 13, 1906; Macfarlane, "George M. Cohan," 109.
100. "Drama: A New Apostle of Stage Righteousness," *Life*, May 4, 1911, 886; "Bounders and Rounders," *Life*, December 19, 1907, 753; "Things That Bloom," 618. On the increasing highbrow/lowbrow divide and the concerns of turn-of-the-century critics about the "legitimate" theater, see Lawrence W. Levine, *Highbrow/Lowbrow: The Emergence of Cultural Hierarchy in America* (Cambridge, MA: Harvard University Press, 1988), esp. 75–79.
101. Theodore Roosevelt, "Citizenship in a Republic" speech delivered at the Sorbonne, Paris, April 23, 1910, in *History as Literature and Other Essays* (New York: Scribner's Sons, 1913), 143.
102. "The Week's Novelties: A Theatrical Primer," *New York Times*, January 7, 1906.
103. The Davis and Dale to whom Cohan refers are likely Acton Davies and Alan Dale. Untitled article, *Life*, March 26, 1908, 323. See also Cohan, "Popular Player Has Many Critics," *Chicago Tribune*, October 21, 1906.
104. "An intellectual aloofness which will not accept contact with life's realities" was among the traits that Roosevelt criticized in his speech "Citizenship in a Republic," 143. For a similar analysis of a composer's connection to contemporary gender ideology, albeit in a different cultural realm, see Judith Tick, "Charles Ives and Gender Ideology," in *Musicology and Difference: Gender and Sexuality in Music*

Scholarship, ed. Ruth A. Solie (Berkeley: University of California Press, 1993), 83–106.

105. For one mention of "Cohanians," see Fyles, "Gotham Cheers"; see also *Life*'s description of "the fractionally educated multitude" that "supports the Cohan cult": untitled article, *Life*, October 12, 1911, 618. For examples of positive reviews not focused on edification, see "News of the Theaters: Little Johnny Jones," *Chicago Tribune*, March 13, 1905; and "Drama and Music: Attractive Offerings at the Various Boston Theatres," *Boston Globe*, April 25, 1905. On Cohan as having "strictly American" talent and being an American dramatist, see "Cohan's Summer Show in Aerial Gardens," *New York Times*, June 5, 1906; "Playbills for the Warm Weather," *New York Times*, July 22, 1906; Montrose J. Moses, "The American Dramatists," *The Independent . . . Devoted to the Consideration of Politics [. . .]*, September 27, 1906, 737. "Exploiter": Walter Anthony, "A Japanese Invasion," *San Francisco Call*, January 28, 1912. George Jean Nathan quotation: "The Puppet Shop," *Puck*, January 9, 1915.
106. S. J. Woolf, "Four Decades on the Great White Way," *New York Times*, October 1, 1933.

CHAPTER 2

1. Epigraphs: *Actorviews: Intimate Portraits by Ashton Stevens* (Chicago: Covici-McGee, 1923), 93; George M. Cohan to Alexander Woollcott, n.d., MS Am 1449, Houghton Library, Harvard College Library, Harvard University. Critics included H. T. P. [Henry Taylor Parker], "Hollis Street: The American Idea," *Boston Transcript*, September 15, 1908.
2. "Cohan Show Is Seen at Mason," *Los Angeles Herald*, December 3, 1909; Frank Ward O'Malley, "Cohan's Consuming Ambition to Write the Great American Play," *New York Sun*, April 27, 1919.
3. "Cohanism Heard Abroad," *Spokesman-Review* (Spokane, WA), October 17, 1909; "Quotations from Cohan's Play," *Philadelphia Inquirer*, March 4, 1906; "Colonial Theatre," *Mattoon (IL) Morning Star*, July 30, 1908. Cohan's fans were described as "Cohanians," as Chapter 1 mentions, and sometimes with cases of "Cohanitis." "Quartette of Clever Cohans are in Buffalo This Week," *Buffalo Express*, September 13, 1907.
4. These personal neologisms appear, for instance, in advertisements for *The Yankee Prince* (1908) including "'The Yankee Prince' Number" of the *Spot Light*, May 23, 1908, p. 3, Cohan Collection 68.123.615.
5. "Holiday Entertainments: George Cohan as a Junior Washington," *Boston Transcript*, December 26, 1906. The review is unsigned.
6. His unfinished, highly autobiographical show *The Musical Comedy Man* is discussed in Chapter 5.
7. To cite one appearance: "The Difference Between a High Brow, a Low High Brow, a High Low Brow, and Just a Plain Low Brow," *Birmingham News*, July 12, 1911.
8. Franklin Fyles, "Gotham Cheers 'The Duel' Because Paris Liked It," *Chicago Tribune*, February 18, 1906.

9. Doug Reside, "Musical of the Month: A Trip to Chinatown," Musical of the Month blog, New York Public Library, June 30, 2012, https://www.nypl.org/blog/2012/06/30/musical-month-trip-chinatown.
10. "George Washington, Jr.," *New York Tribune*, February 13, 1906; Providence review of *Little Johnny Jones* as reprinted in Ward Morehouse, *George M. Cohan: Prince of the American Theater* (Philadelphia, J. B. Lippincott, 1943), 69–70. It was not the last time a critic censured him for giving such a speech; see Walter Pritchard Eaton's "On Taking Cohan Seriously," about *Fifty Miles from Boston*, in *The American Stage of To-Day* (Boston: Small, Maynard, 1908), 236.
11. Peter Clark Macfarlane, "George M. Cohan," *Everybody's Magazine*, January 1914, 107.
12. "News of the Theaters," *Chicago Tribune*, September 17, 1906; Cohan, "Musical Comedy," *Saturday Evening Post*, April 10, 1909, 7; O'Malley, "Cohan's Consuming Ambition to Write the Great American Play"; Cohan, "H. L. Highbrow Meets G. M. Hoakum: A Stage Fright," *Chicago Tribune*, November 30, 1924.
13. George M. Cohan, "My Beginnings," *Theatre Magazine*, January 1907, 52; MacFarlane, "George M. Cohan," 114; George M. Cohan, *Twenty Years on Broadway and the Years It Took to Get There: The True Story of a Trouper's Life from the Cradle to the "Closed Shop"* (New York: Harper and Brothers, 1925), 103. By 1915, Cohan had added "the livest [*sic*] parts of Dickens, and about ten thousand plays" to the list of things he had read, though he mentioned wanting to read Shakespeare, whose plays he had only seen. Cohan with Verne Hardin Porter, "The Stage as I Have Seen It," *Green Book Magazine*, January 1915, 39.
14. On children in the nineteenth-century theater, see Shauna Vey, *Childhood and Nineteenth-Century American Theatre: The Work of the Marsh Troupe of Juvenile Actors* (Carbondale: Southern Illinois University Press, 2015).
15. "Stories of the Players Who Appeared Last Week," *Pittsburgh Daily Post*, April 28, 1912.
16. O'Malley, "Cohan's Consuming Ambition."
17. As shared by John McCabe in *George M. Cohan: The Man Who Owned Broadway* (Garden City, NY: Doubleday, 1973), 134.
18. "Stories of the Players."
19. Clipping of article, *College Magazine*, Cohan Collection box 3 (1719); "Stories of the Players."
20. George M. Cohan, "The Actor as a Business Man," *Saturday Evening Post*, September 3, 1910, 6; Cohan, "Musical Comedy," 7, 66–67. All quotations in the remainder of this paragraph are from the latter article.
21. *The Governor's Son* program clipping, The Savoy, week of March 11, 1901, Cohan Collection box 573; *Running for Office* program clipping, Grand Opera House, week of September 28, [1903], Cohan Collection 34.79.51; *George Washington, Jr.* program, Grand Opera House, March 18, [1907], Cohan Collection box 519; *George Washington, Jr.* program, Herald Square Theatre, week of February 19, 1906, Cohan Collection box 519; *Little Johnny Jones* program clipping, Liberty Theatre, Week of November 19, 1904, Cohan Collection box 819.

22. Frank W. Glann, "An Historical and Critical Evaluation of the Plays of George M. Cohan" (PhD diss., Bowling Green State University, 1976), 304; Stephen M. Vallillo, "George M. Cohan, Director" (PhD diss., New York University, 1987), 222.
23. On the style and structure of Cohan's shows up to 1920 and musical numbers throughout his career, see Glann, "Plays of George M. Cohan," 221–383 and Vallillo, "George M. Cohan, Director," 220–92.
24. "Little Johnny Jones," *Chicago Tribune*, March 13, 1905.
25. Cohan and Porter, "The Stage as I Have Seen It," April 1915, 787.
26. "Sam H. Harris Realizes His Ambition to Become a Broadway Manager," *New York Telegraph*, October 22, 1905.
27. Scott McMillin, *The Musical as Drama* (Princeton, NJ: Princeton University Press, 2006), esp. 15–35; Geoffrey Block, "Integration," in *The Oxford Handbook of the American Musical*, ed. Raymond Knapp, Mitchell Morris, and Stacy Wolf (Oxford: Oxford University Press, 2011), 97–110; Bradley Rogers, "The Emergence of the Integrated Musical: Otto Harbach, Oratorical Theory, and the Cinema," *Theatre Survey* 63, no. 2 (2022): 160–82.
28. James O'Leary, "Oklahoma!, 'Lousy Publicity,' and the Politics of Formal Integration in the American Musical Theater," *Journal of Musicology* 31, no. 1 (2014): 139–82.
29. Examples include "Common Sense in Musical Comedy," *Pine Bluff Daily Graphic*, March 4, 1906 and "A Few Words about George M. Cohan," *Des Moines Register and Leader*, May 6, 1906.
30. "Common Sense in Musical Comedy."
31. Block, "Integration," 99.
32. Mayhew "Mike" Lake, *Great Guys: Laughs and Gripes of Fifty Years of Show-Music Business* (Grosse Pointe Woods, MI: Bovaco Press, 1983), 88; Dan Dietz, *The Complete Book of 1920s Broadway Musicals* (Lanham, MD: Rowman and Littlefield, 2019), 132.
33. Cohan, "Musical Comedy," 7.
34. On Cohan as a director, see Vallillo, "George M. Cohan, Director."
35. Cohan, *Twenty Years on Broadway*, 184–85.
36. Janet M. Davis, "Cultural Watersheds in Fin de Siècle America," in *A Companion to American Cultural History*, ed. Karen Halttunen (Malden, MA: Blackwell, 2008), 173; Caren Irr, *The Suburb of Dissent: Cultural Politics in the United States and Canada During the 1930s* (Durham, NC: Duke University Press, 1998), 46.
37. Cohan, *Twenty Years on Broadway*, 201. Cohan tells the story differently in a 1939 magazine article, with Erlanger's comment coming later and the shows written in response beginning with *Seven Keys from Baldpate* (1913). Cohan as told to Henry Albert Phillips, "I Like Small-Town Audiences," *Rotarian*, September 1939, 60.
38. Clipping of article, *College Magazine*, Cohan Collection; Cohan and Porter, "The Stage as I Have Seen It," January 1915, 45.
39. "Fay Templeton Afield in Sight of Broadway," *New York Times*, January 2, 1906.
40. "Forty-Five Minutes from Broadway," typescript (Act I, 3–4 and 5), APC box 55. All *Forty-Five Minutes from Broadway* quotations are from this script unless otherwise noted.

41. “Forty-Five Minutes from Broadway” (Act I, 8 and 37).
42. Cohan, “Musical Comedy,” 7.
43. “Forty-Five Minutes from Broadway (Act I, 28 and 34). The language is very similar in a different version of the script in the MCNY: Cohan Collection 68.123.131.
44. *Life*, December 15, 1904, 625.
45. “Fay Templeton Afield.” The review is unsigned.
46. George M. Cohan and George J. Nathan, “The Mechanics of Emotion,” *McClure's*, November 1913, 71.
47. “Cohan's New Show a Good Anomaly,” *Indianapolis Star*, October 1, 1905.
48. Reviews of the production “on the road” and the list of songs on published sheet music indicate that early incarnations of the show had seven musical numbers. By the time the show reached New York, however, programs listed only five, with “Retiring from the Stage” and “Stand Up and Fight Like Hell” dropped.
49. “In Stageland,” *Dayton (OH) Herald*, September 27, 1905.
50. There is some variance in how the song reappears: in most if not all versions I have consulted, it is played as underscoring at the pivotal moment of Burns reading the will. That page is missing from one of my copies of the script, from the Cohan Collection, in which annotations suggest that the song was sung offstage and possibly onstage as well: Cohan, “Forty-Five Minutes from Broadway,” typescript with handwritten annotations (Act I, 38), Cohan Collection 68.123.131. Other versions consulted are the previously cited copy of the APC collection and other copies at the MCNY.
51. Dennis Loranger, “Women, Nature and Appearance: Themes in Popular Song Texts from the Turn of the Century,” *American Music Research Center Journal* 2 (1992): 68–85; Erin Sweeney Smith, “Popular Music and the New Woman in the Progressive Era, 1895–1916” (PhD diss., Case Western Reserve University, 2016).
52. Frank Cullen with Florence Hackman and Donald McNeilly, *Vaudeville, Old & New: An Encyclopedia of Variety Performers in America*, vol. 1 (New York: Routledge, 2007), 1096–98. Articles from Templeton's lifetime also give a sense of her personality and reputation. See, for example, Gove Hambidge, “50 Years of Stardom,” *Billings Gazette*, March 18, 1934.
53. “Cohan's Skill,” unidentified clipping in Cohan scrapbook, Chamberlain and Lyman Brown Papers box 317, *T-Mss 1961-002, Billy Rose Theatre Division, NYPL.
54. Alan Preston, “Plays and Players,” *Passaic Daily News*, January 13, 1906.
55. “Railroad Trains on the Stage,” *Chicago Tribune*, November 4, 1906.
56. “Forty-Five Minutes from Broadway” (Act I, 5).
57. This exchange appears in multiple versions of the script with slightly different phrasing and punctuation: “Forty-Five Minutes from Broadway” (Act I, 19–20), Cohan Collection 68.123.131; “Forty-Five Minutes from Broadway” (Act I, 23), APC.
58. “Cohan's New Show.”
59. George M. Cohan as told to Charles Washburn, “Give My Regards to Broadway,” chap. 18 of “Broadway as It Once Was, Is, and Will be; As Seen and Foreseen by George M. Cohan,” *New York Evening World*, July 14, 1930; also recounted in Morehouse, *George M. Cohan*, 78.

60. Adam Christopher Rush, "Recycled Culture: The Significance of Intertextuality in Twenty-First Century Musical Theatre" (PhD diss., University of Lincoln, 2017), esp. 87–125, 197–231; Elizabeth L. Wollman, *A Critical Companion to the American Stage Musical* (London: Bloomsbury, 2017), 182.
61. Greg Kotis and Mark Hollmann, *Urinetown, the Musical* (New York: Faber and Faber, 2003), Act I, Scene 1, p. 9.
62. Anne Beggs, "'For Urinetown Is Your Town . . .': The Fringes of Broadway," *Theatre Journal* 62, no. 1 (2010): 41–56; Scott Miller, "Inside the Bowels of *Urinetown*," New Line Theatre, accessed January 2022, http://www.newlinetheatre.com/urinechapter.html. On the place of Brecht in the show's critical reception, see Kathryn A. Edney, "A New Brechtian Musical? An Analysis of *Urinetown* (2001)," in *Brecht, Broadway and United States Theater*, ed. J. Chris Westgate (Newcastle-upon-Tyne: Cambridge Scholars, 2007), 101, 114–19.
63. George M. Cohan, *The American Idea* (New York: Pusey and Company, 1909), Act II, 14, Cohan Collection 68.123.65A; "The Royal Vagabond," bound typescript (Act II, 7), Cohan Collection 68.123.497. On Cohan's rewriting of *The Royal Vagabond*, which remained credited largely to original authors William Carey Duncan, Anselm Goetzl, and Stephen Ivor-Szinney, see McCabe, *George M. Cohan*, 143–46.
64. Wilma Soss, "George M. Cohan—Man of Many Talents," *Brooklyn Daily Times*, November 20, 1927.
65. McCabe, *George M. Cohan*, 88.
66. My thanks to Hannah Lewis for this observation.
67. See, for example, Jane Feuer, *The Hollywood Musical*, 2nd ed. (Bloomington: Indiana University Press, 1993); Michael G. Garber, "Songs about Entertainment: Self-Praise and Self-Mockery in the American Musical," *Studies in Musical Theatre* 1, no. 3 (2007), 227–30; Millie Taylor, *Musical Theatre, Realism and Entertainment* (Farnham, UK: Ashgate, 2012), esp. 6; Jeffrey Magee, *Irving Berlin's American Musical Theater* (New York: Oxford University Press, 2012), 32; Rush, "Recycled Culture," esp. 6–8, 47. On theater itself as intertextual, "deeply involved with memory and haunted by repetition," see Marvin Carlson, *The Haunted Stage: The Theatre as Memory Machine* (Ann Arbor: University of Michigan Press, 2001), quotation p. 11.
68. "The Royal Vagabond" (Act I, 18), Cohan Collection.
69. Rush, "Recycled Culture," 16, 210–13.
70. *A Chorus Line* is described and classified as a metamusical in Larry Stempel, *Showtime: A History of the Broadway Musical Theater* (New York: Norton, 2010), 606.
71. Rush, "Recycled Culture," 198. The use of this concept is similar to Richard Hornby's "self-reference," for him a subtype of metadrama but one typically found in drama by "serious" playwrights. Hornby, *Drama, Metadrama, and Perception* (Lewisburg, PA: Bucknell University Press, 1986), 103–104, 114–17. Cohan biographer John McCabe uses "intratheatricality." McCabe, *George M. Cohan*, 88.
72. On the Shuberts' shows, see Jonas Westover, *The Shuberts and Their Passing Shows: The Untold Tale of Ziegfeld's Rivals* (New York: Oxford University Press, 2016).
73. Stempel, *Showtime*, 208.
74. "'*Hello, Broadway* at the Colonial," *Boston Globe*, April 27, 1915.

75. Robert Baral credited Cohan with creating the "personality revue," one that is the sole work of and centers on one creator, though this term was not used at the time. Baral, *Revue: The Great Broadway Period*, rev. ed. (New York: Fleet Press, 1970), 29–30. On Cohan's revues, especially *The Cohan Revue of 1918*, see also Jane Katherine Mathieu, "Out of Many, One: Tin Pan Alley and American Popular Song, 1890–1920" (PhD diss., University of Texas at Austin, 2014), 170–203.
76. Program for *Hello, Broadway!*, Astor Theatre (New York), week beginning February 15, 1915, Cohan Collection box 633.
77. "Hello, Broadway!," typescript (Act I, Scene 1), Cohan Collection 68.123.357. All *Hello, Broadway!* quotations are from this script unless otherwise noted. The next quotations come from Act I, Scene 1 and Act I, Scene 3.
78. "Hello, Broadway!" (Act I, Scene 7 and Act II, Scene 6). Sinclair Lewis biographer Richard R. Lingeman notes that Lewis may have "unconsciously" recalled Cohan's Babbit in creating the title character of *Babbitt* (1922). Lingeman, *Sinclair Lewis: Rebel from Main Street* (St. Paul, MN: Borealis Books, 2002), 171–72.
79. Channing Pollock, "Shoes for the Cobbler's Children," *Green Book Magazine*, March 1915, 476; see also Gilbert Seldes, *The Seven Lively Arts* (New York: Harper and Brothers, 1924), 137.
80. "Hello, Broadway!" (Act I, Scene 3). The next quotation comes from Act II, Scene 6.
81. Stanley Fish, *Is There a Text in This Class? The Authority of Interpretive Communities* (Cambridge, MA: Harvard University Press, 1980), 14. Marvin Carlson notes that in relation to theater audiences, interpretive communities are built around overlapping memory. Carlson, *The Haunted Stage*, 5.
82. Pollock, "Shoes for the Cobbler's Children," 476.
83. Untitled article in *Life*, January 7, 1915; "'Hello Broadway,' Says George Cohan," *New York Sun*, December 26, 1914; "Cohan's Confessions of Broadway," *Philadelphia Evening Public Ledger*, April 13, 1915; "*Hello, Broadway* at the Colonial"; Mathieu, "Out of Many," 172–73.
84. The lyric is "The ushers applaud and they shout for more, / They resort to the trick of the gallery 'clique' / So the encores will not miss." George M. Cohan, "Down by the Erie Canal" (New York: Cohan and Harris, 1915), available online at MMB. Presumably, the meaning of *clique* is the same as *claque*, which the *Oxford English Dictionary* defines as "an organized body of hired applauders in a theatre."
85. Pollock, "Shoes for the Cobbler's Children," 476.
86. Garber, "Songs about Entertainment," 234.
87. Cohan, "Hello, Broadway!" (Act I, Scene 6).
88. This song was not published as sheet music but lyrics can be found in the show's script. The lines about song and dance at Tony Pastor's do not appear in all versions of the script and may have been a revision; they appear in the bound typescript copy of *Hello, Broadway!* at the HBTL (Act I, Scene 4). I'm grateful to Michel Garber for sharing his observations about this number and show. This book's introduction contains a fuller discussion of Cohan and minstrelsy.
89. Dongshin Chang, *Representing China on the Historical London Stage: From Orientalism to Intercultural Performance* (New York: Routledge, 2015), 161–67; on Whiteside's orientalist performances, see Robert Charles Lancefield, "Hearing

Orientality in (White) America, 1900–1930" (PhD diss., Wesleyan University, 2004), 371–81.

90. George M. Cohan, "Hello, Broadway!" (Act I, Scene 2).
91. Cohan, "Hello, Broadway!" (Act I, Scene 3). On Martin Brown's yellowface performance in the musical comedy *Up and Down Broadway* (1910), see Charles Hiroshi Garrett, *Struggling to Define a Nation: American Music and the Twentieth Century* (Berkeley: University of California Press, 2008), 131.
92. Lyrics are taken from Cohan's rendition of "I Want to Hear a Yankee Doodle Tune," Victor 60045, recorded 1911; this recording is Example 2.2 on the book's companion website.
93. Contemporaneous author E. M. Wickes described many of these in his manual *Writing the Popular Song* (Springfield, MA: Home Correspondence School, 1916), 6–35.
94. "George M. Cohan and Company at the Opera House," *Providence Journal*, April 11, 1905; Walter Pritchard Eaton, "On Taking Cohan Seriously," in *The American Stage of To-day* (Boston: Small, Maynard and Co., 1908), 237; H. T. P. [Henry Taylor Parker], "Mr. Cohan Entertains: Capital Fooling in His New Review," *Boston Transcript*, April 27, 1915. See also Gilbert Seldes's description of Cohan as a disappointment as a songwriter in *The Seven Lively Arts*, 70.
95. *Being the Ricardos*, written and directed by Aaron Sorkin, Amazon Studios, 2021.
96. Michael Lasser, *City Songs and American Life* (Rochester, NY: University of Rochester Press, 2019), 42.
97. "George M. Cohan Dinner," bound typescript signed by secretary, p. 34, Lotos Club, New York City, November 9, 1930, "Misc. Manuscripts, Typescripts" folder, Cohan Collection box 3 (1719).
98. Elliott Carter, "Films and Theatre," *Modern Music* 20, no. 3 (March–April 1943), 206.
99. Don Walker, *Men of Notes* (Pittsburgh, PA: Dorrance, 2013), 73.
100. Cohan, *Twenty Years on Broadway*, 9.
101. An article as early as 1899 credits Von Olker with helping George develop his reputation as "the wonderful boy violinist." Articles about Cohan give his name as Herman von Olker, but it is likely that someone misremembered or misconstrued the name (perhaps from "Herr Von Olker") and that the teacher was Ferdinand Von Olker, a violinist, composer, and music director who immigrated from Belgium and worked in New York City and New Orleans before his two-decade stint as musical director of the Opera House in Providence. Von Olker advertised for violin students in the *Providence Journal* ca. 1888–1890. He died in 1892, when George was 13. Garrett D. Byrnes, "A Man Named George M. Cohan," *Providence Journal*, December 25, 1932; "Cohans Have Friends Here," *Pawtucket Evening Times*, May 2, 1899; John Franceschina, *Incidental and Dance Music in the American Theatre from 1786 to 1923*, vol. 3, *Biographical and Critical Commentary: Alphabetical Listings from Edgar Stillman Kelley to Charles Zimmerman* (Albany, GA: BearManor Media, 2018), 454–55.
102. As quoted in McCabe, *George M. Cohan*, 8.
103. According to one account, he and Josephine were good enough to play violin and piano at hotels when they were not performing onstage with the Four Cohans.

Footage from a 1934 newsreel shows him playing the piano to accompany himself as he performs at what appears to be a hospital. Byrnes, "A Man Named George M. Cohan"; Hearst Newsreels Collection Inventory number VA13969 M, UCLA Film.

104. Dominic McHugh, "'I'll Never Know Exactly Who Did What': Broadway Composers as Musical Collaborators," *Journal of the American Musicological Society* 68, no. 3 (2015): 605–52.
105. Cohan and Porter, "The Stage as I Have Seen It," February 1915, 252.
106. Mary B. Mullett, "George Cohan's Definition of One Who Is 'On the Level,'" *American Magazine*, August 1919, 20.
107. Franceschina, *Incidental and Dance Music in the American Theatre*, vol. 2, *Biographical and Critical Commentary*, 234.
108. Walker, *Men of Notes*, 70–76.
109. Lake, *Great Guys*, 99–100.
110. Cohan, *Twenty Years on Broadway*, 103.
111. Cohan, *Twenty Years on Broadway*, 104. On trends in courtship-themed songs in the post–Civil War period, including the "lascivious waltz" popular in the 1890s, see Jon W. Finson, *The Voices That Are Gone: Themes in Nineteenth-Century American Popular Song* (New York: Oxford University Press, 1994), 43–82.
112. George M. Cohan, "Venus, My Shining Love" (New York: Spaulding and Gray, 1894), available online at Americana Sheet Music Collection, University of Wisconsin–Madison Libraries, https://digital.library.wisc.edu/1711.dl/7V2NFFASAGA7I8N.
113. George M. Cohan, "My Little Polly's a Peach" (New York: Spaulding and Gray, 1896), available online at Levy Collection.
114. Wickes, *Writing the Popular Song*, 31.
115. "Cohan Sells 'Over There,'" *Variety*, November 9, 1917; "Over There" (New York: Leo Feist, 1917), Harry and Sara Lepman Collection Box 2/Folder 3, Music Division, LoC.
116. As told by John McCabe, for whom Mary was a principal source: *George M. Cohan*, 137, 283.
117. "Walter Winchell," syndicated column, *Wilkes-Barre Times Leader, The Evening News*, September 10, 1959.
118. F. Belasco (Monroe H. Rosenfeld), "Johnny Get Your Gun" (New York: T. B. Harms, 1886), available online at Representations of Blackness in Music of the United States (1830–1920), Brown University Library, https://repository.library.brown.edu/studio/item/bdr:23667/.
119. Morehouse, *George M. Cohan*, 126.
120. It also appears in the orchestral parts for the 1914 show *Hello, Broadway!* in the Cohan Collection 68.123.354, but it is not listed on the show's program or, to my knowledge, in any reviews.
121. Rick Benjamin, liner notes to *You're a Grand Old Rag: The Music of George M. Cohan*, The Paragon Ragtime Orchestra, New World Records 80685-2, 2008, compact disc; Gillian M. Rodger, "When Singing Was Acting: Song and Character in Variety Theater," *The Musical Quarterly* 98, no. 1–2 (2015): 57–80.

122. Cohan, *Twenty Years on Broadway*, 215, 221, 228–29, 260–61.
123. Glann, "Plays of George M. Cohan," 31. Percy Hammond seems to be the first to bestow the "America's first actor" title, in 1929. He also urged him to "try to get a play [sufficient] for [his] talents": Percy Hammond review of *Gambling* under headline "George Cohan Named First Player by Critic," *Atlanta Constitution*, October 6, 1929; McCabe, *George M. Cohan*, 212–13.
124. Stephen Rathbun, "'The Song and Dance Man': George M. Cohan Stars in Enjoyable Revival of His Comedy at the Fulton," [*New York Sun*?], clipping dated 1930, HRC box 86.
125. Brooks Atkinson, "The Play: In Which Eugene O'Neill Recaptures the Past in a Comedy with George M. Cohan," *New York Times*, October 3, 1933.
126. "Shea's Garden Theater," *Buffalo Review*, May 5, 1900.
127. George M. Cohan, "Theatre Going as a Kid," bound typescript, 2–3, Cohan Collection 68.123.480.
128. John McCabe, *George M. Cohan*, 53.
129. Burns Mantle, "Eleven New Plays on Broadway, Including New Triumph by George Miracle Cohan," *Chicago Tribune*, January 3, 1915; "A Few Dates from the Career of George M. Cohan, Actor," *Boston Herald*, clipping dated February 8, 1936, George M. Cohan clippings file, HTC; "The Theatre of George Jean Nathan," *Life*, May 1936, 20.
130. Tim Gracyk with Frank Hoffmann, *Popular American Recording Pioneers, 1895–1925* (New York: Haworth Press, 2000), 18.
131. George M. Cohan, "The Practical Side of Dancing," *Saturday Evening Post*, May 21, 1910.
132. Cohan, "Practical Side of Dancing," 12; Cullen with Hackman and McNeilly, *Vaudeville, Old and New*, vol. 1, 346.
133. "George M. Cohan, 64, Dies at Home Here," *New York Times*, November 6, 1942.
134. "Cohan Fills a House; Pickets Play Comedy," *New York Times*, August 9, 1919; George M. Cohan as interviewed by H. G. Robison, "Why I Do—What I Do," *Dance Magazine*, May 1928, 12, clipping in Cohan Collection Box 3 (1719); Constance Valis Hill, *Tap Dancing America: A Cultural History* (New York: Oxford University Press, 2010), 30–31.
135. Dorothy Rodgers, interview by Scott A. Sandage, November 18, 1987, shared with author by Sandage.
136. *I'd Rather Be Right* home movie footage, NCOV 31, TOFT.

CHAPTER 3

1. Epigraph: Wendell Phillips Dodge, "The Actor in the Street," *Theatre Magazine*, February 1911, vii.
2. "Then I'd Be Satisfied with Life" (New York: F. A. Mills, 1902), available online at MMB; and "If I Were Only Mister Morgan" (New York: Cohan, Niblo and Cohan, 1903), available online at Levy Collection. 1902 was when Teddy Roosevelt got involved in trust-busting by bringing a lawsuit against the railroad trust the Northern Securities Company; it is possible this spurred the change of approach

in Cohan's lyrics from "If I only stood in with the steel trust rake-off" in "Then I'd Be Satisfied with Life," which was published in 1902 but possibly written earlier, to "ev'ry trust I'd surely bust" in "If I Were Only Mister Morgan," published in 1903.

3. The show's review in the *New York Times* reported that the number received vigorous applause, despite its obvious indebtedness to the "Women" number in *The Merry Widow*, which was still running a few blocks away. "Yankee Prince is Amusing," *New York Times*, April 21, 1908.
4. George M. Cohan, "M-O-N-E-Y," arr. Charles J. Gebest (New York: Cohan and Harris, 1908), available online at MMB.
5. "George M. Cohan, 64, Dies at Home Here," *New York Times*, November 6, 1942; George M. Cohan, "Why My Office Is in My Hat," *World Magazine*, October 24, 1926, clipping in Cohan folder, Shubert Archive; George M. Cohan as told to Charles Washburn, "An Office in My Hat," chap. 17 in "Broadway as It Once Was, Is and Will Be as Seen and Foreseen by George M. Cohan," *New York Evening World*, July 12, 1930.
6. As quoted in John McCabe, *George M. Cohan: The Man Who Owned Broadway* (Garden City, NY: Doubleday, 1973), 101.
7. Richard Hofstadter, *The Age of Reform* (New York: Vintage Books, 1955); Robert H. Wiebe, *The Search for Order, 1877–1920* (New York: Hill and Wang, 1967); Alan Dawley, "The Abortive Rule of Big Money," in *Ruling America: A History of Wealth and Power in a Democracy*, ed. Steve Fraser and Gary Gerstle (Cambridge, MA: Harvard University Press, 2005), 149; Nell Irvin Painter, *Standing at Armageddon: The United States, 1877–1919* (New York: Norton, 1987).
8. Painter, *Standing at Armageddon*, ix–xiii, xvii–xliv (quotation from p. xliii).
9. On the railway system, see Leon Fink, *The Long Gilded Age: American Capitalism and the Lessons of a New World Order* (Philadelphia: University of Pennsylvania Press, 2015), 3.
10. "New-style businessmen": Sean P. Holmes, *Weavers of Dreams, Unite!: Actors' Unionism in Early Twentieth-Century America* (Urbana: University of Illinois Press, 2013), 15. On the Theatrical Syndicate, see also John Frick, "A Changing Theater: New York and Beyond," in *The Cambridge History of American Theatre*, vol. 2: 1870–1945, ed. Don B. Wilmeth and Christopher Bigsby (Cambridge: Cambridge University Press, 1999), 212–18.
11. As quoted in McCabe, *George M. Cohan*, 6–7. Nellie's recollections are very similar in "The Story of George M. Cohan," by Verne Hardin Porter, *Green Book Magazine*, December 1914, 968.
12. George M. Cohan, *Twenty Years on Broadway and the Years It Took to Get There: The True Story of a Trouper's Life from the Cradle to the "Closed Shop"* (New York: Harper and Brothers, 1924), 163–68; Ward Morehouse, *George M. Cohan: Prince of the American Theater* (New York: J. B. Lippincott, 1943), 42.
13. "Cohan Gets Mother's Estate," *New York Times*, March 10, 1931. Cohan had made a curtain speech in 1913 in which he promised 50 percent of his interests to his parents. Morehouse, *George M. Cohan*, 116.
14. Letter from Josephine Cohan to her parents as published in *Green Book Magazine*, February 1913, 336; Robert Grau, "Remarkable Earnings in Theatredom," *Business*

America, September 1912, 16; "George M. Cohan's Estate $827,384," *Los Angeles Times*, April 11, 1946; calculation made using US Bureau of Labor Statistics inflation calculator (https://www.bls.gov/data/inflation_calculator.htm).

15. George M. Cohan with Verne Hardin Porter, "The Stage as I Have Seen It," *Green Book Magazine*, February 1915, 246–47.
16. Garrett D. Byrnes, "A Man Named George M. Cohan," *Providence Journal*, December 25, 1932; Cohan and Porter, "The Stage as I Have Seen It," February 1915, 253.
17. Cohan, *Twenty Years on Broadway*, 174–85.
18. Cohan and Porter, "The Stage as I Have Seen It," February 1915, 250.
19. Howard Barnes, "A Man Who Won't Be Standardzied [*sic*]," *New York Herald Tribune*, September 1, 1929, clipping in Cohan folder, Shubert Archive.
20. "Mr. Cohan Talks," *Mexican Herald* (Mexico City), March 3, 1912.
21. Alisa Roost, "Sam Harris: A Producing Patron of Innovation," in *The Palgrave Handbook of Musical Theatre Producers*, ed. Laura MacDonald and William A. Everett (New York: Palgrave Macmillan, 2017), 83.
22. "Sam H. Harris, 69, Theatrical Producer, Dies," *New York Herald Tribune*, July 4, 1941.
23. Cohan, *Twenty Years on Broadway*, 178.
24. Roost, "Sam Harris," 86–87.
25. Edward B. Marks as told to Abbott J. Liebling, *They All Sang: From Tony Pastor to Rudy Vallée* (New York: Viking, 1934), 84. Both the sheet music cover and the song itself fit the promotion strategies described by Daniel Goldmark in "Creating Desire on Tin Pan Alley," *Musical Quarterly* 90, no. 2 (2007): 208, 220–22.
26. Cohan and Porter, "The Stage as I Have Seen It," January 1915, 49.
27. Warren A. Patrick, "Chicago Amusements," *Billboard*, May 25, 1907. Dunn is described as "energetic" in "What?," *Green Book Magazine*, December 1913, 1012; and "ubiquitous" in "Enveloped in Christmastide are Cincinnati Playhouses," *Billboard*, December 29, 1906.
28. The *Spot Light*, March 24, 1906, p. 1; all issues cited are from Cohan Collection 68.123.615.
29. Cohan credits Walter Kingsley in his autobiography, but Dunn's name is given as associate editor and general press representative in the newsletter itself, which reports Kingsley's being hired in 1908. *Spot Light*, July 4, 1908, p. 4. A report of the new publication appears in the *New York Clipper* on October 21, 1905, under the "Notes" for Philadelphia.
30. Cohan, *Twenty Years on Broadway*, 199.
31. "Theatrical Newspapers," *Variety*, December 11, 1909. On the "Keith News," see "Rhode Island: Providence," *New York Clipper*, September 17, 1904; and M. Alison Kibler, *Rank Ladies: Gender and Cultural Hierarchy in American Vaudeville* (Chapel Hill: University of North Carolina Press, 1999), 26.
32. Cohan, *Twenty Years on Broadway*, 200.
33. James Fisher, "The Man Who Owned Broadway: George M. Cohan's Triumph in Eugene O'Neill's *Ah, Wilderness!*" *Eugene O'Neill Review* 23, no. 1/2 (Spring/Fall 1999), 112.
34. George M. Cohan, "Musical Comedy," *Saturday Evening Post*, April 10, 1909, 67.

35. A 1913 article reported that the show had made over $250,000 in profits and that Cohan had made $35,000 in music royalties. Rennold Wolf, "George Michaels [*sic*] Cohan," *Green Book Magazine*, January 1913, 45. See also Cohan and Porter, "The Stage as I Have Seen It," January 1915, 45; and Wilma Soss, "George M. Cohan: Man of Many Talents," *Brooklyn Daily Times*, November 20, 1927.
36. Cohan, *Twenty Years on Broadway*, 208.
37. Frick, "A Changing Theater," 218.
38. Cohan and Porter, "The Stage as I Have Seen It," February 1915, 257.
39. Cohan and Porter, "The Stage as I Have Seen It," March 1915, 426.
40. "Theater: *Little Johnny Jones*," *Lexington Leader*, September 24, 1905.
41. Advertisement for *It Pays to Advertise* by Roi Cooper Megrue and Walter Hackett, produced by Cohan and Harris, in the *Anaconda Standard*, March 12, 1916.
42. See, for example, *The Yankee Prince* advertisement, *Birmingham Age-Herald*, October 4, 1909; *Broadway Jones* advertisement, *Detroit Free Press*, January 30, 1914.
43. Frick, "A Changing Theater," 199–218.
44. "Obituary: George M. Cohan," *Stage* (London), November 12, 1942; and "The New Oxford: *Little Nellie Kelly*," *Stage* (London), July 5, 1923.
45. "The Letters of Josephine Cohan," *Green Book Magazine*, February 1913.
46. Advertisement, *Panama Star and Herald* (Panama City), October 17, 1913; "The Girl from Nowhere," *Port-of-Spain Gazette*, November 14, 1913.
47. Cohan, "De 'Yankee Doodle Boy'" (Amsterdam: Bureau T.A.V.E.N.U.: Abrahamson and Van Straaten, n.d.), in author's possession.
48. John Graziano, "Music in William Randolph Hearst's *New York Journal*," *Notes* 48, no. 2 (December 1991), 422.
49. Michael B. Leavitt includes both Cohan and Harris on a set of photographs of "The Theatrical Syndicate and Several of Its Allies," in *Fifty Years in Theatrical Management, 1859–1909* (New York: Broadway Publishing, 1912), illustration plate facing p. 284.
50. This and the following quotation are from McCabe, *George M. Cohan*, 101.
51. Various correspondence, K&E Collection box 33, folder 8.
52. George M. Cohan, "Spot Lights," *Spot Light*, October 20, 1906.
53. Cohan and Harris's stationary reflected the changes. "New Theatrical Circuit Formed," *New York Clipper*, November 23, 1907; correspondence in K&E Collection box 33, folders 8 and 9.
54. "George M. Cohan, Petitioner, v. Commissioner of Internal Revenue, Respondent," in *Reports of the United States Board of Tax Appeals*, vol. 11, "March 16, 1928 to May 16, 1928" (Washington, DC: United States Government Printing Office," 1928), 746.
55. Unsigned letters from A. L. Erlanger to Marc Klaw, March 30, 1908–April 17, 1908, K&E Collection box 90, folder 7.
56. A. L. Erlanger to Samuel H. Harris, September 3, 1907, Harris Papers box 2, folder 2.1.
57. Invitation, K&E Collection box 33, folder 8; "A Loving Cup for an Actor: Theatrical Folk of a Banquet Honored George M. Cohan's Companies," *Kansas City Times*, January 13, 1906.

58. Lee Shubert to J. J. Shubert, December 18, 1917, in response to letter from Sam Harris raising funds for a hospitalized fellow producer, Frederic W. Thompson, Shubert Correspondence.
59. "Cohan & Harris Hustling Executives," image in the *Spot Light*, July 4, 1908, p. 5.
60. Cohan had waded into music publishing with the songs from *Running for Office* (1903), published by Cohan, Niblo, and Cohan, but the songs from *Little Johnny Jones* the following year were published with F. A. Mills. Cohan & Harris Music Publishing was launched in 1908 and disbanded in the mid-1910s, whereupon Cohan joined with William Jerome in a firm in 1916. He left it, however, only a year later. Songs from Cohan's musicals of the 1920s were published with M. Witmark and Sons, and in the 1930s, Vogel Music reissued some of his older songs and published several new ones. "Cohan & Harris as Music Publishers," *New York Clipper*, February 29, 1908; "Popular Songs Sold," *Variety*, April 18, 1908; "Some Knockout Songs," *Billboard*, October 21, 1916; "William Jerome Going It Alone," *Billboard*, December 15, 1917; "Geo. M. Cohan Standards to Vogel," *Variety*, January 23, 1934. On their acquisition of theaters, see: theater listings in *Julius Cahn's Official Theatrical Guide*, vol. 13 (New York: Publication Office, Empire Theatre Building, 1908) and other volumes; "George M. Cohan's Career at a Glance," *Green Book Magazine*, May 1913, 854; "Klaw & Erlanger's Plans for the Coming Season," *Billboard*, July 11, 1908; "New Cohan Theatre's Play," *New York Times*, January 29, 1911; "Cohan and Harris in Chicago," *Variety*, November 4, 1911; McCabe, *George M. Cohan*, 109.
61. "Deal About Completed," *Variety*, May 27, 1911.
62. Cohan and Porter, "The Stage as I Have Seen It," March 1915, 431.
63. *The Cahn-Leighton Official Theatrical Guide*, vol. 17 (New York: Publication Office, New Amsterdam Theatre Building, 1913), 419–21.
64. Telegram from George M. Cohan and Sam H. Harris to Lee Shubert, February 19, 1918, Shubert Correspondence.
65. "Green Room Club Regulars Win," *New York Clipper*, June 10, 1911; "Cohan Now Friars' Abbot," *Brooklyn Times*, June 6, 1914; correspondence ca. 1915, Shubert Correspondence; "Managers to Have Lunch Club," *New York Clipper*, May 30, 1917.
66. Frank W. Glann, "A Historical and Critical Evaluation of the Plays of George M. Cohan 1901–1920" (PhD diss., Bowling Green State University, 1976), 114. Glann's analysis focuses on the shows from 1901–1920, but wealth continues to be a frequent theme in Cohan's later shows as well.
67. "Cohan & Harris Hustling Executives," *Spot Light*.
68. "Little Johnny Jones," typescript (Act I, 15, and Act II, 9), Cohan Collection 68.123.208.
69. Arthur Ruhl, "From Falstaff to Cohan," *Collier's*, December 24, 1910, 17; reprinted in Ruhl, "A Minor Poet of Broadway," in *Second Nights: People and Ideas of the Theatre To-Day* (New York: Charles Scribner's Sons, 1914), 87–88.
70. On the "doctoring" of the shows by other authors, see Michael Schwartz, "Signed on the Dotted Line: George Kelly's *The Show-Off* and the Fall and Rise of the Can-Do Hero," in *Texts and Presentation, 2013*, ed. Graley Herren (Jefferson, NC: McFarland, 2014), 112; and McCabe, *George M. Cohan*, 280.

71. John Corbin, "Among the New Plays," *New York Times*, February 17, 1924; Schwartz, "Signed on the Dotted Line," 111; Michael Schwartz, *Broadway and Corporate Capitalism: The Rise of the Professional-Managerial Class, 1900–1920* (New York: Palgrave Macmillan, 2009), 2. Other scholars, too, have noted the shift; see, for example, Glann, "Plays of George M. Cohan," 145, 422.
72. Charles L. Ponce de Leon, *Self-Exposure: Human-Interest Journalism and the Emergence of Celebrity in America, 1890–1940* (Chapel Hill: University of North Carolina Press, 2002), 27.
73. Scrapbook pages on *The Molly Maguires*, Cohan Collection box 25 (1739). On this and other dramatizations of the Molly Maguires, see Michelle Granshaw, *Irish on the Move: Performing Mobility in American Variety Theatre* (Iowa City: University of Iowa Press, 2019), 70–74, 83–99.
74. "At the Theatres," *Theatre Magazine*, November 1909, xiv.
75. Richard Butsch, *The Making of American Audiences: From Stage to Television, 1750–1990* (Cambridge: Cambridge University Press, 2000), 115; "American Chorus Girls Plan Beauty Invasion of London," *New York Sun*, April 27, 1919.
76. "Seven Keys to Baldpate Here Thursday Night," *Eugene Guard*, April 3, 1915.
77. *Broadway Jones* was later musicalized as *Billie* (1928), with the emphasis changed to the female heroine in keeping with Cohan's "Cinderella" musicals of the 1920s.
78. Painter, *Standing at Armageddon*, xxxix–xli.
79. George M. Cohan, *Broadway Jones: A Comedy in Four Acts* (New York: Samuel French, 1923), 54.
80. Gail Bederman, *Manliness and Civilization: A Cultural History of Gender and Race in the United States, 1880–1917* (Chicago: University of Chicago Press, 1995), esp. 16–20.
81. The non-chorus roles of Cohan's shows from 1901–1920 were 70 percent male. Glann, "Plays of George M. Cohan," 148.
82. Schwartz, *Broadway and Corporate Capitalism*, 38–39.
83. Cohan and Porter, "The Stage As I Have Seen It," January 1915, 49.
84. "A Few Dates from the Career of George M. Cohan, Actor," clipping marked *Boston Herald*, February 8, 1936), George M. Cohan clippings file, HTC; Kasper Monahan, "George M. Cohan Is Voted Stage's 'Most Regular Guy,'" *Pittsburgh Press*, May 10, 1933.
85. Cohan and Porter, "The Stage As I Have Seen It," July 1915, 30.
86. Cohan and Porter, "The Stage As I Have Seen It," January 1915, 48.
87. Bederman, *Manliness and Civilization*, 16–17; Glann, "Plays of George M. Cohan," 198.
88. Chester's stories were published in book form in 1908. Cohan's play makes several notable changes, including many of the aspects highlighted here: he adds a Japanese valet character and a love interest (Chester's Wallingford is married), and the company song. He amplifies Wallingford's associations with and use of patriotism. Most significant, he changes the ending; in Chester's version, Wallingford is given another chance but does not truly change ("Upon thistles grow no roses," he concludes) whereas Cohan's Wallingford experiences a true change of heart and goes straight. George Randolph Chester, *Get-Rich-Quick Wallingford* (New York: A. L. Burt, 1908), 448.

89. Ruhl, "From Falstaff to Cohan," 17.
90. George M. Cohan, "Get-Rich-Quick Wallingford," typescript (Act I, 10), APC box 55. Subsequent *Get-Rich-Quick Wallingford* quotations are also from this version of the script. The other quotation in this paragraph comes from Act I, 14.
91. Cohan, "Get-Rich-Quick Wallingford" (Act I, 16). The remaining quotations in this paragraph come from Act I, 30; Act II, 2 and 20; and Act I, 23.
92. Some accounts have Gold arriving in the United States in 1904, and others in 1905. "The Theater: Korean Prince an Actor," *Washington Evening Star*, September 11, 1910; "Theatrical," *Anaconda Standard*, December 4, 1910; Charles Darnton, "In and Out of the Theatres," *New York Evening World*, April 5, 1912. A photograph of Gold can be found in " 'Dandy' Daniel Gold: He's Now a Real Actor," *Hartford Courant*, October 22, 1912.
93. *Japanese American History: An A-to-Z Reference from 1868 to the Present*, ed. Brian Niiya (New York: Facts on File, 1993), 40; Esther Kim Lee, *A History of Asian American Theatre* (Cambridge: Cambridge University Press, 2006), 14. This also corrects my past chapter "'A Great American Service': George M. Cohan, the Stage, and the Nation in *Yankee Doodle Dandy*," in *The Oxford Handbook of Musical Theatre Screen Adaptations*, ed. Dominic McHugh (New York: Oxford University Press, 2019), 325. Sakurai may, however, have been the first Japanese actor on Broadway, as asserted in Tooru Kanazawa, "Issei on Broadway," *Scene: The International East–West Magazine* 5, no. 10 (February 1954).
94. O. O. McIntyre, "New York Day by Day," *Nashville Banner*, November 2, 1937.
95. Cohan, "Get-Rich-Quick Wallingford" (Act I, 28).
96. Cohan, *Twenty Years on Broadway*, 217.
97. Cohan, "Get-Rich-Quick Wallingford" (Act II, 29). The next quotation comes from Act III, 17.
98. The 4/4 version shown in Figure 3.6 differs from an undated copy that appears to be a reprint of the original, in which this chorus is in a "tempo di valse" 3/8, but it is likely that Cohan was emulating the song as it circulated in community settings or singing manuals like this one; compare G. W. Hunt, *Dear Old Pals* (New York and Chicago: S. Brainard's Sons, n.d.), Historic Sheet Music Collection, 1800–1922, LoC, https://www.loc.gov/item/ihas.100006752/.
99. Sheryl Kaskowitz, *God Bless America: The Surprising History of an Iconic Song* (New York: Oxford University Press, 2013), 4.
100. Benedict Anderson, *Imagined Communities: Reflections on the Origin and Spread of Nationalism* (London: Verso, 1991), 145.
101. Esther M. Morgan-Ellis, *Everybody Sing!: Community Singing in the American Picture Palace* (Athens: University of Georgia Press, 2018), 52–79.
102. Cohan, "Get-Rich-Quick Wallingford" (Act III, 37).
103. Interestingly, details of a tax case state that Jerry Cohan wrote the fourth act of the play. "George M. Cohan, Petitioner, v. Commissioner of Internal Revenue, Respondent," 747.
104. Cohan, "Get-Rich-Quick Wallingford" (Act IV, 8). The next quotation comes from Act IV, 6.

105. The APC copy of the script says "Right out of Frohman's office," but "Frohman's" is crossed out and "Shuberts" is handwritten there. Cohan, "Get-Rich-Quick Wallingford" (Act IV), 15. The next quotation comes from Act IV, 25.
106. "Leading Players Go Out, Closing Big Attractions," *New York Times*, August 8, 1919.
107. The *Stage* newspaper reported in June 1916 that they were among the managers expected to agree to Equity's demands, in contrast with the Shuberts: "The American Stage" and "Chit Chat," *Stage* (London), June 22, 1916.
108. George M. Cohan, "The Actor as a Business Man," *Saturday Evening Post*, September 3, 1910, 7.
109. I have not found music for this number. "Hitchy-Koo," *Variety*, June 15, 1917; "The American Stage: Hitchy Koo," *Stage* (London), September 13, 1917.
110. Holmes, *Weavers of Dreams*, 6–7, McArthur, *Actors and American Culture*, 220.
111. McArthur, *Actors and American Culture*, 104–105, 218.
112. Holmes, *Weavers of Dreams*, 6–7.
113. Holmes, *Weavers of Dreams*, 54. On the formation of Equity and the lead-up to the strike, see Holmes, *Weavers of Dreams*, 11–57; Frick, "A Changing Theatre," 218–22; and McArthur, *Actors and American Culture*, 213–28.
114. Craig Timberlake, *The Life and Work of David Belasco: The Bishop of Broadway* (New York: Library Publishers, 1954), 338.
115. "Cohan Kids Actors," *New York Clipper*, May 7, 1919; "Lambs Gambol and Frisk on $30,000 of B'dway's Green," *New York Clipper*, June 11, 1919.
116. George M. Cohan, "Actors and Manager's [*sic*] Dinner," typescript, 13–14, Cohan Collection 68.123.616.
117. Cohan, "Actors and Manager's Dinner," 7–8.
118. Holmes, *Weavers of Dreams*, 58–86.
119. "Cohan Fills a House; Pickets Play Comedy," *New York Times*, August 9, 1919.
120. Cohan, *Twenty Years on Broadway*, 242.
121. "Actors May Call Out Mechanics in Strike," *New York Tribune*, August 1, 1919.
122. Harris and Lambart took one another to court thereafter for assault and trespassing. "Harris Struck Actor?" *New York Daily News*, August 9, 1919; "Theatrical Bout, Staged in Court, Goes to a Draw," *New York Evening World*, August 20, 1919.
123. "Twelve Theatres Closed in N.Y. by Actors' Strike," *Montreal Gazette*, August 9, 1919.
124. Cohan, *Twenty Years on Broadway*, 247.
125. "Cohan Fills a House."
126. "Echoes of the Strike," *New York Times*, August 17, 1919.
127. "Fight to Death On In Strike of Actors," *Philadelphia Inquirer*, August 13, 1919.
128. "A Wonderful Actors' Meeting," *Billboard*, August 9, 1919, iv, vii.
129. Holmes, *Weavers of Dreams*, 70.
130. Timberlake, *Life and Work of David Belasco*, 338. Details of this anecdote vary: in Timberlake's telling, the sign is hung from the window of an Equity partisan; in other accounts, it is hung from the window of Equity's office. In still other versions, the sign says Cohan "need not apply." See, for example, Robert Simonson, "When Actors' Equity Staged Its First Strike," *American Theatre*, March

1, 2013, https://www.americantheatre.org/2013/03/01/when-actors-equity-staged-its-first-strike/.

131. Eddie Cantor, *"My Life Is in Your Hands" and "Take My Life": The Autobiographies of Eddie Cantor*, with David Freedman and Jane Kesner Ardmore (1928 and 1957; New York: Cooper Square Press, 2000), *"Take My Life,"* 169.
132. "Official Statements: Actors' Equity: Letter to George M. Cohan from Francis Wilson," *Variety*, August 22, 1919.
133. See, for example, "The Actors as a Labor Organization," *Literary Digest*, September 13, 1919, 29.
134. Cohan's sister and Niblo's wife Josephine had died in 1916. "Actors' Strike to Be Discussed at Meeting," *Los Angeles Evening Express*, August 18, 1919; Holmes, *Weavers of Dreams*, 45–46.
135. It was reported but also then denied that a telegram accusing Cohan of making his father turn over in his grave with his treatment of actors was sent to Cohan from the son of Ned Harrigan. McCabe, *George M. Cohan*, 151; "Chorus Forms Union to Back Actors' Strike," *New York Tribune*, August 13, 1919; "Actors' Strike Closes Follies, Also '39 East," *New York Sun*, August 14, 1919.
136. Johnnie O'Connor (Wynn), "George M. Cohan and the Strike," *Variety*, August 15, 1919.
137. Accounts of Cohan's positive reputation and dealings with actors and other employees include O'Connor (Wynn), "Cohan and the Strike"; Mayhew ("Mike") Lake, *Great Guys: Laughs and Gripes of Fifty Years of Show-Music Business* (Grosse Pointe Woods, MI: Bovaco Press, 1983), 98; Charles Foster, *Donald Brian: The King of Broadway* (St. John's, NL: Breakwater Books, 2005), 30–47, 64. Fair treatment was relative. *Variety* reported, for instance, that theater professionals had taken note when rehearsal time, which was typically unpaid, was notably less for *The Cohan Revue of 1916* than other productions. "Actors Equity Assn. Meets to Discuss W.R.A.U. Affiliation," March 17, 1916. Accounts of Cohan's personal generosity in supporting "down-and-out" actors abound but are difficult to verify.
138. *New York Review*, August 30, 1919, in Robinson Locke Scrapbook, series 2, vol. 78, p. 329, Billy Rose Theatre Division, NYPL, as quoted in Holmes, *Weavers of Dreams*, 80–81; George M. Cohan, "To All Members of the Acting Profession," *Variety*, December 3, 1920.
139. Cohan, *Twenty Years on Broadway*, 186–91; McCabe, *George M. Cohan*, 151. An anecdote about Cohan helping former White Rats president George Fuller Golden, on the other hand, would suggest that Cohan did not carry too much of a grudge. Walter Anthony, "Tom Lewis Cohan's Friend," *San Francisco Call*, December 5, 1909.
140. Statement to the *New York Sun* as quoted in "The Actors as a Labor Organization," *Literary Digest*, 29.
141. "Statement from George M. Cohan, 1st Vice President, December 17, 1920," in "Theatrical 'Closed Shop' a Vain Threat," Cohan Collection box 3 (1719).
142. George M. Cohan, "To the members of the acting profession," autograph draft of open letter referenced above, Cohan Collection box 3 (1719). My thanks to Scott A. Sandage for sharing this document with me. In the version published in *Variety*,

"the rules and regulations laid down by a few 'radicals'" was changed to "certain rules and regulations." Cohan, "To All Members of the Acting Profession."

143. "Statement from George M. Cohan," Cohan Collection.
144. "Statement from George M. Cohan," Cohan Collection; see also Cohan, *Twenty Years*, 247–48.
145. Camille F. Forbes, *Introducing Bert Williams: Burnt Cork, Broadway, and the Story of America's First Black Star* (New York: Basic Books, 2008), 297.
146. See, for one example, "Actor Strike Spreading to Other Cities," *Brooklyn Daily Times*, August 13, 1919.
147. Morehouse, *George M. Cohan*, 143.
148. See, for example, the summary in Stephen M. Archer, "*E Pluribus Unum*: Bernhardt's 1905–1906 Farewell Tour," in *The American Stage: Social and Economic Issues from the Colonial Period to the Present*, ed. Ron Engle and Tice L. Miller (Cambridge: Cambridge University Press, 1993), 159–60.
149. Harris intervened, for example, when the Shuberts refused to pay the men of the chorus what they paid the women. Correspondence between Sam Harris and the Shuberts, September–October 1919, Shubert Correspondence. On actors' unionism during this period, see Holmes, *Weavers of Dreams*, 87–118.
150. "Annual Meeting Echoes," *Fidelity*, June 1920, Cohan Collection box 3 (1719).

CHAPTER 4

1. Epigraph: Leonard Lyons, "The Lyons Den," syndicated column, *New York Post*, October 28, 1948.
2. George M. Cohan, "You Can Tell That I'm Irish" (New York: George M. Cohan Music, 1916), available online at Ward Archives; Cohan, "You Can't Deny You're Irish" (New York: George M. Cohan Music, 1918), available online at Francis G. Spencer Collection of American Popular Sheet Music, Baylor University Libraries, https://digitalcollections-baylor.quartexcollections.com/Documents/Detail/you-cant-deny-youre-irish/16212.
3. George M. Cohan, *Twenty Years on Broadway and the Years It Took to Get There: The True Story of a Trouper's Life from the Cradle to the "Closed Shop"* (New York: Harper and Brothers, 1925), 61, 68; Ward Morehouse, *George M. Cohan: Prince of the American Theater* (Philadelphia: J. B. Lippincott, 1943), 32; Michelle Granshaw, *Irish on the Move: Performing Mobility in American Variety Theatre* (Iowa City: University of Iowa Press, 2019), 145–46.
4. Dates are of first performances. On Irish stereotypes in vaudeville, see Jennifer Mooney's book by that name (New York: Palgrave Macmillan, 2015). The sheet music for "Hugh McCue" (New York: Spaulding and Gray, 1896) is available online at Ward Archives. On "The Dangerous Mrs. Delaney," see M. Alison Kibler, *Rank Ladies: Gender and Cultural Hierarchy in American Vaudeville* (Chapel Hill: University of North Carolina Press, 1999), 55, 63–64. On "Hogan of the Hansom," see "Some Vaudeville Laughs," *New York Times*, December 17, 1902. Cohan's earliest efforts at songs, as he describes them in the *Green Book Magazine* feature "The Stage as I Have Seen It," were also Irish themed. Cohan comments that one called "The First Floor

Front" "establishes [his] ancestry and [his] loyalty," February 1915, 252. Interestingly, the article is from around the time he turned back to Irish themes in his work.

5. See, for example, Thomas S. Hischak, *Word Crazy: Broadway Lyricists from Cohan to Sondheim* (New York: Praeger, 1991), 3–4.
6. William H. A. Williams, *'Twas Only an Irishman's Dream: The Image of Ireland and the Irish in American Popular Song Lyrics, 1800–1920* (Urbana: University of Illinois Press, 1996), 209.
7. The 1900 census counted 1,615,459 Irish-born and 3,375,546 second-generation Irish Americans according to J. J. Lee, "Introduction: Interpreting Irish America," in *Making the Irish American: History and Heritage of the Irish in the United States*, ed. J. J. Lee and Marion R. Casey (New York: NYU Press, 2006), 41. For the total US population, see Frank Hobbs and Nicole Stoops, US Census Bureau, *Demographic Trends in the 20th Century*, Census 2000 Special Reports, Series CENSR-4 (Washington, DC: US Government Printing Office, 2002), 11.
8. On Irish Americans' continued sense of being in "figurative, if not literal, 'exile'" in the late nineteenth through early twentieth centuries, see Kerby A. Miller, *Emigrants and Exiles: Ireland and the Irish Exodus to North America* (New York: Oxford University Press, 1985), 3–8, 492–555, quotation on 493.
9. Thomas J. Rowland, "Irish-American Catholics and the Quest for Respectability in the Coming of the Great War, 1900–1917," *Journal of American Ethnic History* 15, no. 2 (Winter 1996): 3–31. Oral tradition had it that the term came from the lace curtains that this emerging middle-class group could afford to hang on their windows. Francis Walsh, "Lace Curtain Literature: Changing Perceptions of Irish American Success," *Journal of American Culture* 2, no. 1 (Spring 1979): 139.
10. "Irish Comedian Must Go," *Chicago Tribune*, May 7, 1902. See also Williams, *'Twas Only an Irishman's Dream*, 4, 200–201.
11. On the term "old stock," see Russell A. Kazal, *Becoming Old Stock: The Paradox of German-American Identity* (Princeton, NJ: Princeton University Press, 2021), 120–26.
12. Liam Stack, "1916 Easter Rising in Ireland, a Milestone of Foreign Reporting," *New York Times*, April 25, 2016, https://www.nytimes.com/2016/04/26/world/europe/easter-rising-archival-coverage.html.
13. Kevin Kenny, "American-Irish Nationalism," in *Making the Irish American: History and Heritage of the Irish in the United States*, ed. J. J. Lee and Marion R. Casey (New York: NYU Press, 2006), 295.
14. American involvement was highly charged in Ireland and Great Britain as well: Lindsey Flewelling, *Two Irelands Beyond the Sea: Ulster Unionism and America, 1880–1920* (Liverpool: Liverpool University Press, 2018), 56.
15. Rowland, "Irish-American Catholics," 22.
16. Arthur S. Link, ed., *The Papers of Woodrow Wilson*, vol. 35 (Princeton, NJ: Princeton University Press, 1966), 306.
17. These comments by Joseph Smith and Matthew Cummings are reported in "Hours of Oration for Irish Freedom," *New York Times*, March 6, 1916; and "Redmond Is Hissed: Wilson's Policy Is Attached. England Scored as Robber," *Boston Globe*, March 6, 1916.

18. Rowland, "Irish-American Catholics," 25–26.
19. Selected news accounts include "Stars of Stage Aid Salvation Army," *New York Times*, May 12, 1919; "Open 'Hut' in Times Square," *New York Times*, February 2, 1919; United War Work Campaign ad, *Atlanta Constitution*, November 6, 1918; "How 'Out There' Started," *New York Times*, July 14, 1918.
20. See, for example, Edward Cuddy, "The Irish Question and the Revival of Anti-Catholicism in the 1920's," *Catholic Historical Review* 67, no. 2 (April 1981): 236–55; Matthew J. O'Brien, "Transatlantic Connections and the Sharp Edge of the Great Depression," in *New Directions in Irish-American History*, ed. Kevin Kenny (Madison: University of Wisconsin Press, 2003), 81–83.
21. Calvin Coolidge: "First Annual Message," December 6, 1923, reproduced in The American Presidency Project, by Gerhard Peters and John T. Woolley, University of California at Santa Barbara, https://www.presidency.ucsb.edu/node/206712. On the Johnson-Reed Act, see Mae Ngai, *Impossible Subjects: Illegal Aliens and the Making of Modern America* (Princeton, NJ: Princeton University Press, 2004), 15–55; and Desmond King, *Making Americans: Immigration, Race, and the Origins of the Diverse Democracy* (Cambridge, MA: Harvard University Press, 2000), 199–228.
22. Rowland, "Irish-American Catholics," 22.
23. Keith Fitzgerald, *The Face of the Nation: Immigration, the State, and the National Identity* (Stanford, CA: Stanford University Press, 1996), 151–52; Ngai, *Impossible Subjects*, 32.
24. Lynn Dumenil, "The Tribal Twenties: 'Assimilated' Catholics' Response to Anti-Catholicism in the 1920s," *Journal of American Ethnic History* 11, no. 1 (October 1991): 30, 42.
25. This fit broader trends, especially among Irish Americans striving to enter the middle classes; see O'Brien, "Transatlantic Connections," 83; Marion R. Casey, "Ireland, New York and the Irish Image in American Popular Culture, 1890–1960" (PhD diss., New York University, 1998), esp. 372–74.
26. "Catholic Actors Unite," *New York Tribune*, June 9, 1914; "Meeting of Catholic Actors' Guild," *New York Tribune*, December 8, 1918.
27. Herbert's 1917 operetta *Eileen*, which told the story of an Irish revolutionary in 1798, was also viewed as supporting the nationalist cause. On Herbert's Irish ties, see also Neil Gould, *Victor Herbert: A Theatrical Life* (New York: Fordham University Press, 2008), esp. 433–43; and Marion R. Casey, "Was Victor Herbert Irish?," *History Ireland* 25, no. 1 (2017): 20–23.
28. William M. Leary Jr., "Woodrow Wilson, Irish Americans, and the Election of 1916," *Journal of American History* 54, no. 1 (June 1967): 66. See also Miller, *Emigrants and Exiles*, 535–55.
29. "Cohan to Quit," *Chicago Defender*, June 18, 1921.
30. "Hours of Oration for Irish Freedom," *New York Times*, March 6, 1916; "Irishmen Uphold Revolt in Dublin," *New York Times*, May 1, 1916; "Meeting of Irish Today in Memory of Men Shot," *Chicago Tribune*, May 21, 1916.
31. The George M. Cohan Theatre in New York was put under the management of A. L. Erlanger and Marcus Klaw in 1913 as Cohan and Harris prioritized their work as producers, but Cohan did retain control of the Chicago theater, among others. At

some point the New York theater was sold—many sources state 1915, but news sources suggest 1919. Either way, as of 1919, Cohan and Harris along with Klaw, Erlanger, and Frank Tate were reportedly still lessees. Erlanger took over the lease in 1920. "Klaw and Erlanger Take Cohan Houses," *New York Times*, July 4, 1913; "Cohan Theatre Change Denied," *New York Times*, November 3, 1919; "Erlanger Gets Cohan," *Variety*, August 27, 1920.

32. "George M. Cohan," *Gaelic American*, November 14, 1942.
33. *Report of American Committee for Relief in Ireland* (New York: Treasurer and Secretary's Office, 1922), 6; "Business Men Act to Save the Irish," *New York Times*, December 30, 1920; "Stage Stars Raise $57,000 for Irish," *New York Times*, April 4, 1921; "Callahan for Kentucky," *Kentucky Irish American*, January 1, 1921; "N.Y. Has Big Benefit for Irish Relief," *Irish Press*, April 9, 1921.
34. The Society passed a resolution urging repeal of a section of the immigration law, criticizing national origins as a basis for quotas and the "misleading" quotas established. "Immigration Law," *Recorder: Bulletin of the American Irish Historical Society* 3, no. 6 (September 1926): 9. Cohan became a life member of the American Irish Historical Society in 1941.
35. Miles Hoffman, "Irish Tenor John McCormack, Revisited: A St. Patrick's Day Tribute to a World-Famous Voice," March 17, 2004, https://www.npr.org/2004/03/17/1770553/. On McCormack's life, see: Raymond Foxall, *John McCormack* (London: Robert Hale, 1963); Gordon Ledbetter, *The Great Irish Tenor: John McCormack* (Dublin: Town House, 2003).
36. On Olcott's audiences, see Mari Kathleen Fielder, "Chauncey Olcott: Irish-American Mother-Love, Romance, and Nationalism," *Éire-Ireland* 22, no. 2 (Summer 1987), 7; and Gerald Bordman and Richard Norton, *American Musical Theatre: A Chronicle*, 4th ed. (New York: Oxford University Press, 2010), 154, 332.
37. Due to conflicting source materials, the exact number and placement of the show's songs are difficult to determine. Based on my consultation of a script, program, sheet music, reviews, and advertisements for the show, I surmise that it included four or five numbers: the three numbers newly composed by Cohan ("Ireland, My Land of Dreams," "You Can't Deny You're Irish," and "When I Look In Your Eyes, Mavourneen"), which appear consistently in the various materials; the interpolated number "Mother Machree"; and probably also "That Tumble Down Shack in Athlone" with music by Monte Carlo and Alma M. Sanders and lyrics by Richard W. Pascoe. See George M. Cohan, "The Voice of McConnell," bound typescript, Cohan Collection 68.123.476; Manhattan Opera House program for *The Voice of McConnell*, week of January 13, 1919, Cohan Collection box 1535; "That Tumble Down Shack in Athlone" (New York: Waterson, Berlin, and Snyder, 1918), available online at Ward Archives; and reviews including "Theater Bills for Next Week," *Philadelphia Evening Public Ledger*, March 15, 1919.
38. Cohan, "Voice of McConnell" (Act I, 7). All *Voice of McConnell* quotations are from this script. The next quotation in this paragraph is from Act I, 12.
39. Cohan, "Voice of McConnell" (Act I, 38). The remaining quotations in this paragraph are from Act I, 20 and 27.
40. Cohan, "Voice of McConnell" (Act I, 13).

41. Cohan, "Voice of McConnell" (Act I, 35A–36).
42. Theo Mortimer, "John Count McCormack: Freeman of Dublin," *Dublin Historical Record* 48, no. 2 (Autumn 1995), 102. *Wings of Song: The Story of Caruso* (New York: Minton, Balch, 1928), by Enrico's wife Dorothy Caruso and Torrance Goddard, reports that Caruso and McCormack were "devoted companions" and "always amused at stories of any rivalry between them," 175. The press seemed to relish the semblance of competition, however. In March 1918, for example, *The New York Times* reported that "M'Cormack Turns in $75,000 Income Tax: Famous Concert and Phonograph Tenor Tops Caruso's Payment by $16,000," March 7, 1918.
43. Many contemporary sources refer to the "brow level" of musical performances by McCormack and the Irish tenor generally, usually in their defense. See, for example, Allison Gray, "The Most Popular Singer in the World: John McCormack as He Really Is," *American Magazine*, April 1919, 78.
44. Cohan, "Voice of McConnell" (Act I, 49, 53–54). The remaining quotations in this paragraph are from Act II, 24–25.
45. Cohan, "Voice of McConnell" (Act I, 2 and 6). The next quotation is from Act II, 6.
46. Cohan, "Voice of McConnell" (Act I, 22–23). The remaining quotations in this paragraph are from Act I, 40 and 3.
47. Cohan, "Voice of McConnell" (Act I, 17).
48. Manhattan Opera House program for *The Voice of McConnell*, Cohan Collection.
49. The pseudo-exception is "When I Look in Your Eyes, Mavourneen," which is sung diegetically but not with a concert performance in mind; rather, it is a gift for McConnell's beloved, Evelyn. On diegetic song in the musical, see Stephen Banfield, *Sondheim's Broadway Musicals* (Ann Arbor: University of Michigan Press, 1993), 184.
50. Cohan, "The Voice of McConnell" (Act I, 57–58). Not all of the songs discussed in this scene are actually performed in the show.
51. George M. Cohan, "Ireland, My Land of Dreams" (New York: M. Witmark and Sons, 1918), available online at Levy Collection.
52. On the use of pentatonicism in Irish song tradition, Moore's *Irish Melodies*, and subsequent American song, in particular in Stephen Foster's tunes, see Charles Hamm, *Yesterdays: Popular Song in America* (New York: Norton, 1979), 55, 174, 215–19. Note that it is the third, rather than the fourth, that is missing in this "Mixolydian pentatonic" scale, as it is sometimes characterized. See, for example, Jeremy Day-O'Connell, *Pentatonicism from the Eighteenth Century to Debussy* (Rochester, NY: University of Rochester Press, 2007), 5.
53. Williams, *'Twas Only an Irishman's Dream*, 230.
54. John H. Raftery, "Olcott Appears in Cohan Comedy," *New York Telegraph*, December 27, 1918, *The Voice of McConnell* clippings file, HTC.
55. Cohan, "You Can't Deny You're Irish," 2–4.
56. Cohan, "The Voice of McConnell" (Act II, 44–45).
57. "Chauncey Olcott in Chicago," *Music Trade*, December 7, 1918, 32.
58. Cohan, "The Voice of McConnell" (Act I, 56); Cohan, "When I Look in Your Eyes, Mavourneen" (New York: M. Witmark and Sons, 1918), available online at Ward Archives.

59. On romance and marriage as a way of reconciling difference in musicals, see Rick Altman, *The American Film Musical* (Bloomington: Indiana University Press, 1987), esp. chap. 2 "The American Film Musical as Dual-Focus Narrative" and pp. 45–58; and Raymond Knapp, *The American Musical and the Formation of National Identity* (Princeton, NJ: Princeton University Press, 2005), 9.
60. "Cohan's Play Fits Olcott: 'The Voice of McConnell' Is Brisk and Rich in Humor, Not All Irish," *New York Times*, December 26, 1918.
61. "New Cohan Play Another Success," *New York Sun*, December 26, 1918.
62. Review of "The Voice of McConnell," *Theatre Magazine*, February 1919, 79.
63. Raftery, "Olcott Appears in Cohan Comedy"; "Chauncey Olcott in George M. Cohan Play," *New York Tribune*, December 27, 1918.
64. "New Cohan Play Another Success."
65. "Cohan, McCormack, Olcott," unidentified clipping marked November 22, 1918, *The Voice of McConnell* clippings file, HTC.
66. Raftery, "Olcott Appears in Cohan Comedy."
67. "New Cohan Play Another Success."
68. Bordman and Norton, *American Musical Theatre*, 395.
69. Bordman and Norton, *American Musical Theatre*, 413. On the Cinderella trope on stage and Irish American Cinderellas on screen, see also Maya Cantu, *American Cinderellas on the Broadway Musical Stage: Imagining the Working Girl from "Irene" to "Gypsy"* (New York: Palgrave Macmillan, 2015); and Christopher Shannon, *Bowery to Broadway: The American Irish in Classic Hollywood Cinema* (Scranton, PA: University of Scranton Press, 2010), 65–99.
70. George M. Cohan and George Jean Nathan, "Plotting Against the Public," *New York Tribune*, July 19, 1914.
71. Timothy J. Meagher, *The Columbia Guide to Irish American History* (New York: Columbia University Press, 2005), 115–16.
72. Williams, *'Twas Only an Irishman's Dream*, esp. 106–108, 207.
73. "Little Nellie Kelly" flyer, HRC box 488/folder L-1.
74. *Little Nellie Kelly* ad, *New York Times*, November 22, 1922; *Little Nellie Kelly* ad, *New York Times*, December 24, 1922.
75. *The Rise of Rosie O'Reilly* ad, *New York Times*, January 1, 1924 (emphasis mine).
76. "The Hinky Dee" is described in a song by that title (the sheet music cover spells it "Hinkey Dee"). "The Brooklyn" is described in the song "Keep A-Countin' Eight." *The Rise of Rosie O'Reilly*, a particularly dance-heavy show, also included a number that was "a travesty on the marathon dance fad." "The Rise of Rosie O'Reilly," *Christian Science Monitor*, May 23, 1923.
77. George M. Cohan, "Little Nellie Kelly," typescript (Act II, 55), Cohan Collection 68.123.216; George M. Cohan, "The Rise of Rosie O'Reilly," bound typescript (p. 1-3-85), Miscellaneous Screen, Stage, and Radio Scripts Collection Box 43, HTC. All *Little Nellie Kelly* and *Rise of Rosie O'Reilly* quotations are from these respective scripts.
78. Williams, *'Twas Only an Irishman's Dream*, 208.
79. "'Little Nellie Kelly' Hums," *New York Times*, November 14, 1922.
80. See Williams, *'Twas Only an Irishman's Dream*, 206–207. For additional discussion of the lace curtain Irish as represented onstage, see Walsh, "Lace Curtain Literature,"

and William H. A. Williams, "Green Again: Irish-American Lace-Curtain Satire," *New Hibernia Review* 6, no. 2 (2002): 9–24.

81. This assertion is based primarily on the scripts, which do tend to indicate "Irishisms" and brogue for certain characters but do not for Rosie or Nellie. For the reference to "deep slums," see Cohan, "The Rise of Rosie O'Reilly" (p. 1-44).
82. Cohan, "Nellie Kelly I Love You."
83. This was true especially in New York City. See, for example, Hasia R. Diner, "'The Most Irish City in the Union': The Era of the Great Migration, 1844–1877," in *The New York Irish*, ed. Ronald H. Bayor and Timothy J. Meagher (Baltimore: Johns Hopkins University Press, 1996), 96–97, 105; Tyler Anbinder, *Five Points: The 19th-Century New York City Neighborhood that Invented Tap Dance, Stole Elections, and Became the World's Most Notorious Slum* (New York: Free Press, 2001); 146–47.
84. Cohan, "Little Nellie Kelly" (Act I, 46).
85. George M. Cohan, "The Name of Kelly" (New York: M. Witmark and Sons, 1922), 4, available online at Levy Collection. The lyrics as written in the script contain minor differences: the Kellys came "*with* their ermine *wraps* and things," and "It's the name was known to own *the* throne." Cohan, "Little Nellie Kelly" (Act I, 65).
86. The former had words by Sam M. Lewis and Joe Young and music by Bert Grant; the latter had words by E. Steinhaeufel and music by Robert E. Miller.
87. "Little Nellie Kelly," *Christian Science Monitor*, November 13, 1923, *Little Nellie Kelly* clippings file, HTC.
88. Cohan, "Little Nellie Kelly" (Act II, 20–22).
89. Chad Heap, *Slumming: Sexual and Racial Encounters in American Nightlife, 1885–1940* (Chicago: University of Chicago Press, 2009), 7.
90. Cohan, "The Rise of Rosie O'Reilly" (p. 1-5).
91. Heap, *Slumming*, 7.
92. Cohan, "Little Nellie Kelly" (Act I, 9).
93. Cohan, "Little Nellie Kelly" (Act II, 55–56).
94. John Bush Jones, *Our Musicals, Ourselves: A Social History of the American Musical Theater* (Hanover, NH: Brandeis University Press, 2003), 58.
95. Cohan, "Little Nellie Kelly" (Act I, 54). The remaining quotations in this paragraph are from Act II, 18 and 24.
96. Cohan, "Little Nellie Kelly" (Act II, 25–26).
97. Hasia R. Diner, *Erin's Daughters in America: Irish Immigrant Women in the Nineteenth Century* (Baltimore: John Hopkins University Press, 1983), 67.
98. Cohan, "Little Nellie Kelly" (Act II, 50). Past theater historians have read this as Cohan upholding more traditional values. "In the glittering twenties, when prosperity made material acquisitions more readily obtainable and clever advertising made them more universally desired, Cohan often held to the earlier American dream that love outweighed riches," writes Gerald Bordman. John Bush Jones similarly calls *Little Nellie Kelly* a "throwback." Bordman and Norton, *American Musical Theatre*, 428; Jones, *Our Musicals, Ourselves*, 59.
99. Mrs. Langford says that she bought the shop and gives it to Nellie as a gift, adding by way of explanation, "Remember, your father saved my life once—a long time ago." Cohan, "Little Nellie Kelly" (Act II, 52–53).

100. Cohan, "The Rise of Rosie O'Reilly" (2-1-23).
101. Cohan, "The Rise of Rosie O'Reilly" (1-38).
102. The policemen identify themselves, in a Gilbert and Sullivan-like chorus, as "six little Micks . . . six little coppers." Cohan, "The Rise of Rosie O'Reilly" ("Cast of Characters," p. 1-3, pp. 2-3-52–2-3-53).
103. There were plans to keep several of the musical numbers from the original, but the final version had only one. "'Nellie Kelly' and 'Follow Thru' Cue Filmusical Trend," *Variety*, March 6, 1940. See also Thomas S. Hischak, *Through the Screen Door: What Happened to the Broadway Musical When It Went to Hollywood* (Lanham, MD: Scarecrow Press, 2004), 21–22.
104. "'Little Nellie Kelly,' New Cohan Show, Full of Zest," *New York Tribune*, November 14, 1922.
105. W. R., "At the Liberty Theatre 'The Rise of Rosie O'Reilly,'" unidentified clipping marked December 27, 1923, *The Rise of Rosie O'Reilly* clippings file, HTC.
106. "Cohan's New Play, Here from Boston, Sparkles with Fun," *New York Herald*, November 14, 1922; "'Merton of Movies' Makes New Hit In 'Legitimate,'" *Atlanta Constitution*, November 17, 1922.
107. A Yiddish ballad is presumably considered another authentic expression of the city, given its significant Jewish population. John Farrar, "To See or Not to See: Plays and Motion Pictures of the Month," *Bookman: A Review of Books and Life*, August 1923.
108. "Stories of the Stage," *Boston Globe*, September 4, 1927; "Comedian Drops Dead at Rehearsal," *Boston Globe*, September 5, 1927.
109. Richard Watts Jr., "George M. Cohan's 'Merry Malones' Opens New House," *New York Herald Tribune*, September 27, 1927, *The Merry Malones* clippings file, HTC.
110. George M. Cohan, "The Merry Malones," typescript (Act I, 37), Cohan Collection 68.23.284. All *Merry Malones* quotations are from this script.
111. Cohan, "The Merry Malones" (Act I, 39).
112. George M. Cohan, "Molly Malone" (New York: M. Witmark and Sons, 1927), available online at MMB.
113. "Cockles and Mussels," or "Molly Malone," has become a famed folk tune. On the discovery of an eighteenth-century songbook with lyrics featuring Molly Malone, see Maev Kennedy, "Tart with a Cart? Older Song Shows Dublin's Molly Malone in New Light," *Guardian*, July 18, 2010, https://www.theguardian.com/world/2010/jul/18/molly-malone-earliest-version-hay. Late nineteenth- and early twentieth-century Molly Malone songs in the US included "Sweet Little Mollie Malone" by W. H. Brockway (1885); "Molly Malone (My Own)" by Hale N. Byers and Chris Schonberg (1919); and "Sweet Molly Malone" by Arthur E. Behim, Frank J. Gillen, and Walter Hirsch (1921).
114. George M. Cohan, "Charming" (New York: M. Witmark and Sons, 1927), Cohan Collection Box 950.
115. W. H. Grattan Flood, "Historical Notes on the 'Adeste Fideles,'" *Irish Ecclesiastical Record* 24, no. 492 (December 1908), 601, 603, 606. "Great Throng Views St. Patrick's Parade," *New York Times*, March 18, 1926; "Famous Stars Sing First Time by Radio to 6,000,000 People," *New York Times*, January 2, 1925. According to

the online Discography of American Historical Recordings (DAHR), McCormack recorded "Adeste Fideles" in 1915 and 1926: DAHR, s.v. "McCormack, John," https://adp.library.ucsb.edu/names/101915.

116. Cohan, "The Merry Malones" (Act I, 24).
117. Cohan, "The Merry Malones" (Act II, 83 and Act I, 6). The remaining quotations in this paragraph are from Act I, 53–54.
118. Cohan and Harris voiced their strong support for Smith, describing him as a "personal friend," in a letter addressed "Dear Sir," to the Shubert brothers and presumably others with "theatrical interests," dated October 26, 1918, during his gubernatorial run, Shubert Correspondence.
119. Cohan, "The Merry Malones" (Act I, 89). The next quotations are from Act II, 97.
120. On this rhyme, see Grace Neville, "'Tous Les Jours Fête': Games and Pastimes in Irish Folklore," *Cycnos* 10, no. 2 (1993, put online in 2008), http://revel.unice.fr/cycnos/index.html?id=1334.
121. Cohan, "The Merry Malones" (Act II, 97). Another version of the script indicates that Mr. and Mrs. Malone sing the nursery rhyme together: "The Merry Malones," annotated typescript (Act II, 7), Cohan Collection 68.123.278.
122. Cohan, "The Merry Malones" (Act II, 97); George M. Cohan, "God Is Good to The Irish" (New York: M. Witmark and Sons, 1927), Cohan Collection box 950. The song's verse, with the line that the Irish are "dancing and singing and happiness bringing," appears only in the sheet music.
123. Irving Berlin, for instance, would move from minor to the relative or parallel major in his early "ethnic songs." Charles Hamm, ed., *Irving Berlin: Early Songs*, vol. 1, *1907–1911* (Madison, WI: A-R Editions, 1994), xxvi. On African American songwriters' use of verse and refrain to speak to in-group and out-group audiences, see Karen Sotiropoulos, *Staging Race: Black Performers in Turn of the Century America* (Cambridge, MA: Harvard University Press, 2009), 94–97
124. George M. Cohan, "The Yankee Father in The Yankee Home" (New York: M. Witmark and Sons, 1927), Cohan Collection box 950.
125. Cohan, "The Merry Malones" (Act I, 51). The remaining quotations in this paragraph are from Act I, 53 and Act II, 101.
126. Cohan, "The Merry Malones" (Act II, 75).
127. "[']The Merry Malones' Are a Cheerful Family," *Melbourne Star*, June 25, 1934, clipping in Cohan Collection box 950.
128. "Theatre: New Plays: Jan. 7, 1924," *Time*, January 7, 1924.
129. Brooks Atkinson, "Wasting an Actress," *New York Times*, November 20, 1927.

CHAPTER 5

1. Epigraphs: Michael B. Leavitt, *Fifty Years in Theatrical Management, 1859–1909* (New York: Broadway Publishing, 1912), 296–97; Cohan, "What I Think of Myself," *Green Book Album*, February 1909, 341.
2. See the song's first violin part within the director's score of *The American Idea*, Cohan Collection 68.123.64A.

3. David Collins's informative website on "George M. Cohan in America's Theater" describes him as "the American Theater's first mega star," accessed April 2022, https://www.members.tripod.com/davecol8/.
4. As reported by Garrett D. Byrnes in "A Man Named George M. Cohan," *Providence Journal*, December 25, 1932.
5. Sharon Marcus, *The Drama of Celebrity* (Princeton, NJ: Princeton University Press, 2019), 3–4.
6. Edward B. Marks as told to Abbott J. Liebling, *They All Sang: From Tony Pastor to Rudy Vallée* (New York: Viking, 1934), 84.
7. George M. Cohan in collaboration with Verne Hardin Porter, "The Stage as I Have Seen It," *Green Book Magazine*, April 1915, 713.
8. "Noted Theatrical Man Talks on Advertising," *Sumner (IA) Gazette*, May 12, 1932. This also appears in George M. Cohan as told to Harold Boyce, "The Yankee Doodle Boy's Good Time," typescript, Cohan Collection box 3 (1719).
9. Cohan and Porter, "The Stage as I Have Seen It," *Green Book Magazine*, April 1915, 713.
10. On these figures as agents in their own celebrity, see Marcus, *Drama of Celebrity*, 16, 29, 31, 39–40, 57–58; Susan A. Glenn, *Female Spectacle: The Theatrical Roots of Modern Feminism* (Cambridge, MA: Harvard University Press, 2000), 9–39; Bluford Adams, *E Pluribus Barnum: The Great Showman and the Making of U.S. Popular Culture* (Minneapolis: University of Minnesota Press, 1997), 1–40; Patrick Warfield, "The March as Musical Drama and the Spectacle of John Philip Sousa," *Journal of the American Musicological Society* 64, no. 2 (Summer 2011): 289–318.
11. On the history of celebrity and its development in the United States during this period, see Leo Braudy, *The Frenzy of Renown: Fame and Its History* (1986; New York: Vintage Books, 1997), 476, 491–583; Joshua Gamson, *Claims to Fame: Celebrity in Contemporary America* (Berkeley: University of California Press, 1994), 15–39; Charles L. Ponce de Leon, *Self-Exposure: Human-Interest Journalism and the Emergence of Celebrity in America, 1890–1940* (Chapel Hill: University of North Carolina Press, 2002), esp. 6, 11–41; Robert van Krieken, "Celebrity's Histories," in *Routledge Handbook of Celebrity Studies*, ed. Anthony Elliott (London: Routledge, 2018), 26–43; Sharon Marcus, *Drama of Celebrity*, esp. 9–14. For one discussion of the impact of changes in journalism during this time on reporters, see Marianne Salcetti, "The Emergence of the Reporter: Mechanization and the Devaluation of Editorial Workers," in *Newsworkers: Toward a History of the Rank and File*, ed. Hanno Hardt and Bonnie Brennen (Minneapolis: University of Minnesota Press, 1995), 48–74.
12. Braudy, *Frenzy of Renown*, 508–509.
13. Leavitt, *Fifty Years in Theatrical Management*, 611.
14. Leavitt, *Fifty Years in Theatrical Management*, 611; Anthony Slide, *Inside the Hollywood Fan Magazine: A History of Star Makers, Fabricators, and Gossip Mongers* (Jackson: University Press of Mississippi, 2010), 11.
15. Marcus, *Drama of Celebrity*, 130; "The Birthday Green Book" page in front matter, *Green Book Album*, January 1910, 2.

16. On scrapbooks as a "precious but overlooked resource for historians of theater and of celebrity" and the power of multiplication, see Marcus, *Drama of Celebrity*, 17–18, 120–47.
17. On theatrical press agentry in this period, see Leavitt, *Fifty Years in Theatrical Management*, 272–77; Mark A. Luescher, "What Becomes of the Press Agent," *Billboard*, July 3, 1920; Charles Washburn, *Press Agentry* (New York: National Library Press, 1937); Glenn, *Female Spectacle*, 35–36.
18. Byrnes, "A Man Named George M. Cohan."
19. The *Spot Light*, July 4, 1908, pp. 4 and 5, Cohan Collection 68.123.615.
20. Dunn and Kingsley worked with Cohan and Harris before they split, and Dunn continued on as Cohan's "personal representative" afterward ("Press and Advance Agents," *Billboard*, September 4, 1920). On Washburn's work with Cohan and others, see Washburn, *Press Agentry*.
21. Walter J. Kingsley, "Lo, the Press Agent," in *The Broadway Anthology*, ed. Edward L. Bernays, Samuel Hoffenstein, Walter J. Kingsley, and Murdock Pemberton (New York: Duffield, 1917), 27–29.
22. Laurette Taylor, *"The Greatest of These": A Diary with Portraits of the Patriotic All-Star Tour of "Out There"* (New York: George H. Doran, 1918), 17.
23. Washburn, *Press Agentry*, 11, 18, 24–32.
24. Whitney Bolton, "George M. Cohan Books Himself to Play in Bryant's Showboat," *New York Herald Tribune*, January 29, 1928.
25. Whitney Bolton, "Cast a Play Upon the Waters," *New York Herald Tribune*, September 30, 1928. Articles about Bryant that draw upon his connection to Cohan include "Another Cohan Comedy for Bryant Showboat," *Billboard*, December 7, 1929; "Bryant Players Return to Boat," *Billboard*, September 12, 1936; "Billy Bryant Looks to a 4F Crew and Cast for His 41st Showboat Year" [letter to the editor from Billy Bryant], *Variety*, October 27, 1943. See also Philip Graham, *Showboats: The History of an American Institution* (Austin: University of Texas Press, 1951), 147, 154.
26. Joseph Mitchell, *My Ears Are Bent*, rev. ed., foreword by Sheila McGrath and Dan Frank (1938; repr. New York, Pantheon Books, 2001), 299. The story appears in multiple papers; see, for example, "George M. Cohan Seeks Job as Song and Dance Man on Showboat," *Springfield (OH) News*, September 11, 1936.
27. Bolton, "George M. Cohan Books Himself to Play in Bryant's Showboat."
28. "Cohan's Plays for Showboat," *Billboard*, January 28, 1928.
29. Kasper Monahan, "George M. Cohan Is Voted Stage's 'Most Regular Guy,'" *Pittsburgh Press*, May 10, 1933. Cohan's charm and understated humor with the press, later in his life, is evident in the 1937 newsreel clip "Fireside! Off the Record with Mr. Cohan," RKO Pathé newsreel, 3:16, https://youtu.be/fGLnuqfCgFU.
30. Byrnes, "A Man Named George M. Cohan."
31. "De heer George M. Cohan is erg gesteld op reclame en doet al het mogelijke om minstens iederen dag in het een of ander dagblad te worden genoemd." "De millionair voor één dag," *Bredasche courant*, February 17, 1912; my thanks to Esther Viola Kurtz for her assistance with this translation. Many newspapers reported the original story; see, for example, "'Butch' M'Devitt Reaches Gotham," *Washington Herald*, January 13, 1912.

32. George M. Cohan, "Am I an Egotist?" in the *Spot Light*, July 4, 1906, p. 1, Eda Kuhn Loeb Music Library, Harvard University, available online at https://nrs.lib.harvard.edu/urn-3:fhcl.loeb:102838772; John McCabe, *George M. Cohan: The Man Who Owned Broadway* (Garden City, NY: Doubleday, 1973), 78–79.
33. George M. Cohan, "Personality" (New York: M. Witmark, 1928), Cohan Collection 68.123.46D; George M. Cohan, "Billie," bound typescript (pp. 2-11–2-13), Cohan Collection 68.123.53; cut second verse: George M. Cohan, "Billie," bound typescript (Act II, between p. 10 and p. 11), Cohan Collection 68.123.56.
34. For example, George Spink's "Personality" (1909) performed by vaudeville star Eva Tanguay, and Victor Herbert and Henry Blossom's "Personality" (1914) from *The Only Girl* preceded Cohan's version.
35. Ponce de Leon, *Self-Exposure*, 37; see also Glenn, *Female Spectacle*, 88.
36. Mary B. Mullett, "George M. Cohan's Definition of One Who Is 'On the Level,'" *American Magazine*, August 1919, 20; see also Ponce de Leon, *Self-Exposure*, 116.
37. "George M. Cohan's Personality Real Star in 'Yankee Doodle Dandy,'" *Rochester Democrat and Chronicle*, June 21, 1942.
38. "Drama," *Life*, October 12, 1911, 618.
39. Oscar Hammerstein II, "Tribute to Yankee Doodle Dandy," *New York Times*, May 5, 1957.
40. Michael Schwartz, *Broadway and Corporate Capitalism: The Rise of the Professional-Managerial Class, 1900–1920* (New York: Palgrave Macmillan, 2009), 133.
41. On Broadway and fashion during this period, see Marlis Schweitzer, *When Broadway Was the Runway: Theater, Fashion, and American Culture* (Philadelphia: University of Pennsylvania Press, 2011).
42. "How Actors Dress Off the Stage," *Chicago Tribune*, March 10, 1907.
43. Images, descriptions, or the items themselves appear in HRC box 83/folder A-1p-12; the personal collections of David Collins and Scott A. Sandage; and "George M. Cohan, Jr., Prize Doll Wins Bail," *Chicago Examiner*, January 14, 1913.
44. Glenn, *Female Spectacle*, 74–95.
45. Taylor, *Diary with Portraits of the Patriotic All-Star Tour of "Out There,"* 31.
46. "Trade Mark of 'George M.,'" *Chicago Tribune*, October 3, 1909.
47. I suspect this statement, which appeared in newspapers, was first published in the *Spot Light*, but I have been unable to locate issues before December 1905. "Plays and Players," *Chicago Tribune*, August 20, 1905; see also Glenn, *Female Spectacle*, 85; for advertisements of both acts, see the *New York Sun*, July 23, 1905, p. 26.
48. Faith Baldwin to George M. Cohan, *Spot Light*, July 4, 1908, p. 4, Cohan Collection 68.123.615.
49. Sunny Stalter-Pace, *Imitation Artist: Gertrude Hoffman's Life in Vaudeville and Dance* (Evanston, IL: Northwestern University Press, 2020), 41–42; "Another Cohan Roof Play," *New York Tribune*, June 4, 1907.
50. "Great Music Hall Planned for Gotham," *Minneapolis Journal*, July 14, 1907; H. T. P. [Henry Taylor Parker], "The Cohanic Drama," *Boston Transcript*, October 7, 1911; see also Schwartz, *Broadway and Corporate Capitalism*, 131–32.
51. H. T. P., "Cohanic Drama."
52. Cohan is pictured waving "the grand old rag" from the original lyrics of "You're a Grand Old Flag."

53. "The Biggest Hits of the Old Days: The Most Popular Plays and Musical Comedies of the American Stage," clipping marked *Boston Post*, February 17, 1934, *Little Johnny Jones* clippings file, HTC.
54. William Collier, "Save the U.S. Actor," ed. George M. Cohan, *San Francisco Call*, April 20, 1913.
55. Ward Morehouse, *George M. Cohan: Prince of the American Theater* (Philadelphia: J. B. Lippincott, 1943), 24–25; McCabe, *George M. Cohan*, 1–2.
56. "Massachusetts Births, 1841–1915," database with images, *FamilySearch* (https://familysearch.org/ark:/61903/3:1:S3HY-DC67-XT2); "George M. Cohan's Fathers Show-Bizz Diary 1883," *Collector's Weekly*, accessed May 2022, https://www.collectorsweekly.com/stories/28256-george-m-cohans-fathers-show-bizz-diar. I am grateful to Scott A. Sandage for bringing this documentation to my attention.
57. "Vaudeville and Minstrel," *New York Clipper*, November 20, 1897; "Gossip of Stageland," *Scranton Times*, July 18, 1899; "Birthday of George M. Cohan," *New York Tribune*, July 4, 1906.
58. See, for example, "The Theater: The Remarkable Versatility and Success of George M. Cohan as Author, Composer, Promoter and Star," *Town and Country*, July 28, 1906, 23; and "Yankee Doodle Comedian is Nephew of Uncle Sam," *Billboard*, November 3, 1906. On the use of handouts, see Washburn, *Press Agentry*, 18.
59. George M. Cohan, "My Beginnings," *Theatre Magazine*, January 1907, 52.
60. Plans changed, and his wedding to Agnes Nolan actually occurred on June 29, 1907. Cohan, "What the American Flag Has Done For Me," *Theatre Magazine*, June 1914, 286; "Agnes Nolan of Brookline to Become Mrs. George M. Cohan," *Boston Globe*, April 15, 1907; "George M. Cohan Weds," *New York Times*, June 30, 1907.
61. George Michael Cohan, World War I draft registration card, New York, no. 3710, September 11, 1918, in "United States World War I Draft Registration Cards, 1917–1918," database with images, *FamilySearch* (https://familysearch.org/ark:/61903/3:1:33SQ-G1X3-998N); citing NARA microfilm publication M1509 (Washington, DC: National Archives and Records Administration, n.d.).]
62. Ponce de Leon, *Self-Exposure*, 19–21.
63. Wendell Phillips Dodge, "The Actor in the Street," *Theatre Magazine*, February 1911, 60.
64. Cohan and Porter, "The Stage as I Have Seen It," January 1915, 48.
65. Franklin Fyles, "Gotham Cheers 'The Duel' Because Paris Liked It," *Chicago Tribune*, February 18, 1906.
66. John McCabe, for example, discusses the "self-created mystique, in which [Cohan] identified himself indelibly with everything elemental to American life," *George M. Cohan*, 2.
67. H. T. P. [Henry Taylor Parker], "The 'American Idea': As Mr. Cohan Makes It in His Own Image," *Boston Transcript*, September 15, 1908, *The American Idea* clippings file, HTC.
68. On nonconformity and "defiance" as a feature of celebrity, see Marcus, *Drama of Celebrity*, 21–44.
69. "Drama: An Especially Awful Example," *Life*, March 1, 1906, 278.

70. Martha Banta, *Barbaric Intercourse: Caricature and the Culture of Conduct, 1841–1936* (Chicago: University of Chicago Press, 2003), 152; Steven Alan Carr, *Hollywood and Anti-Semitism: A Cultural History up to World War II* (Cambridge: Cambridge University Press, 2001), 42–44.
71. Morehouse, *George M. Cohan*, 89; "Caught in the Act," *Indianapolis Star*, May 25, 1919, also appears in "Abusing the Name of Cohan," unidentified clipping, n.d., Chamberlain and Lyman Brown Papers, Billy Rose Theatre Division, NYPL; "A Bulletin of Current Stage Gossip," *Spot Light*, July 4, 1908, p. 4. The version reprinted in the *Spot Light*, attributed to Joe Humphreys, also included African Americans, using the offensive racial terminology of the day.
72. Hammerstein, "Tribute to Yankee Doodle Dandy."
73. George M. Cohan, "Actors and Manager's [*sic*] Dinner," typescript, 6, Cohan Collection 68.123.616.
74. On the development of midtown Manhattan and Times Square, see *Inventing Times Square: Commerce and Culture at the Crossroads of the World*, ed. William R. Taylor (New York: Russell Sage, 1991), although it neglects Cohan's critical role in "br[inging] Broadway national and international fame," xvi; and Jane Mathieu, "Midtown, 1906: The Case for an Alternate Tin Pan Alley," *American Music* 35, no. 2 (Summer 2017): 197–236.
75. Cohan and Porter, "The Stage as I Have Seen It," January 1915, 39.
76. George M. Cohan, "Give My Regards to Broadway" (New York: F. A. Mills, 1904), available online at Levy Collection.
77. Cohan performed the song at a program at Carnegie Hall in 1939, which was broadcast by radio, and at a concert as part of San Francisco's world fair in 1940; both were celebrations for the American Society of Composers, Authors, and Publishers (ASCAP). Recordings of these performances are, to my knowledge, the only extant recordings of Cohan singing "Give My Regards to Broadway." The 1940 recording is featured on the book's companion website.
78. George M. Cohan as told to Henry Albert Phillips, "I Like Small-Town Audiences," *Rotarian*, September 1939, 60.
79. James Fisher, "The Man Who Owned Broadway: George M. Cohan's Triumph in Eugene O'Neill's *Ah, Wilderness!*" *Eugene O'Neill Review* 23, no. 1/2 (Spring/Fall 1999), 112.
80. Cohan's "Dear Old Friend Broadway" letter was printed in many newspapers; see, for example, "George Cohan Says So Long to His 'Old Pal' Broadway with a Thousand Thanks," *Lima Republican-Gazette*, July 3, 1921.
81. George M. Cohan, *Broadway Jones: A Comedy in Four Acts* (New York: Samuel French, 1923), Act IV, 110; McCabe, *George M. Cohan*, 120–21.
82. Cohan and Porter, "The Stage as I Have Seen It," *Green Book Magazine*, January 1915, 39.
83. See, for example, Sidney Skolsky, "Behind the News," *New York Daily News*, October 29, 1931; "George M. Cohan, 'Yankee Doodle' of Theater, Dead," *Pittsburgh Sun-Telegraph*, November 5, 1942; and "George M. Cohan," unidentified clipping marked June 1946, George M. Cohan clippings file, Music Division, NYPL.

84. George M. Cohan, "Musical Comedy," *Saturday Evening Post*, April 10, 1909; Cohan, "The Actor as a Business Man," *Saturday Evening Post*, September 3, 1910; Cohan, "Stage Traditions," *New York Tribune*, February 18, 1912; Cohan and George Jean Nathan, "Plotting Against the Public," *New York Tribune*, July 19, 1914; Cohan, "Plotting Against the Producer," *New York Tribune*, November 8, 1914; Cohan, "Murderers of the Stage," *New York Tribune*, November 10, 1912.
85. Cohan and Porter, "The Stage as I Have Seen It," *Green Book Magazine*, January 1915, 39, 3.
86. Cohan, "George M. Cohan Settles Everything," *New York Times*, January 29, 1933; Cohan as told to Charles Washburn, "'Hello, Broadway!': In Which a Favorite Son Sees the Dawn of a New and Better Era," *New York Times*, December 10, 1933.
87. George M. Cohan, "Rhapsody of Broadway," *New York Times*, March 1, 1936.
88. *George M. Cohan's Songs of Yesteryear* (New York: Richmond-Robbins, 1924).
89. "George M. Cohan Leaves Broadway," *Philadelphia Inquirer*, June 26, 1921; "George Cohan Says So Long"; Cohan sang a goodbye to Broadway at a benefit in 1922, as reported in "St. Joseph's Hospital Ladies Raise $1,400 for the Maternity Ward," *Yonkers Statesman and News*, January 4, 1922.
90. "George M. Cohan Wants to Raise Beets and Turnips," *Boston Post*, July 3, 1921. Reports of his baseball and London plans abounded.
91. "George M. Cohan Is a Fiend for Free Publicity," *Vancouver Daily World*, July 2, 1921.
92. Rennold Wolf, "'Hello Broadway' Makes a Hit of the Season," clipping marked *New York Telegraph*, December 26, 1914, in scrapbook, Press Notices of Ned Wayburn, 1906–1932, MWEZ + n. c. 21060, Billy Rose Theatre Collection, NYPL.
93. McCabe, *George M. Cohan*, 161.
94. Biographer John McCabe notes that Cohan continued to work on *The Musical Comedy Man* after he began experiencing cancer symptoms in 1941 and even after a second operation in January 1942. McCabe, *George M. Cohan*, 260–66.
95. On the pivotal changes to musical culture of 1917 in particular, see Douglas Bomberger, *Making Music American: 1917 and the Transformation of Culture* (New York: Oxford University Press, 2018).
96. McCabe, *George M. Cohan*, 254.
97. George M. Cohan, letter to the editor, *Forum*, September 1928, 471.
98. Cohan subsequently appeared in one other talking picture, *Gambling* (1934), which was based on his 1929 play and was filmed on Long Island.
99. Harrison Carroll, "Behind the Scenes in Hollywood," *Atlanta Daily World*, June 7, 1932.
100. Lee Shippey, "The Lee Side o'L-A," *Los Angeles Times*, September 4, 1932.
101. Shippey, "Lee Side o'L-A."
102. Gilbert Seldes, "Song and Dance Man–I," *New Yorker*, March 17, 1934, 31; Sara M. Benson, *The Prison of Democracy: Race, Leavenworth, and the Culture of Law* (Oakland: University of California Press, 2019), 4.
103. George M. Cohan, "George M. Cohan Radio Review: Second Series No. 4," typescript, n.d., p. 14, Radio Scripts LC. Typescripts of Cohan's radio programs can also be found in the Cohan Collection box 3 (1719). I have decided to use quotations from the radio scripts even though I have been unable, in most cases, to hear the programs themselves. Based on the programs I have heard,

the scripts, reviews, the fact that the scripts were copyrighted and preserved, and Cohan's treatment of texts elsewhere, significant changes in the performed versions seem unlikely. Cohan's concerns about radio reflect broader debates about its commercial versus civic functions and the "struggles between rampant commercialism and a loathing of that commercialism" discussed in David Goodman, *Radio's Civic Ambition: American Broadcasting and Democracy in the 1930s* (New York: Oxford University Press, 2011), xiii–xv; see also Susan J. Douglas, *Listening In: Radio and the American Imagination* (Minneapolis: University of Minnesota Press, 2004), 17.

104. Henry Albert Phillips, "It's Like Playing with the Curtain Down," *Radioland*, June 1934, 67; see also Tom Meany, "Am I Wrong About Radio?" *Radio Stars*, April 1936, 24–25, 89–90.
105. George M. Cohan, "Radio Review, Third Series #4," typescript, stamped April 10, 1933, p. 6, Radio Scripts LC. On nostalgia in radio, see Douglas, *Listening In*, esp. 7, 25. On nostalgia in American musical theater, and also its role in national mythologies, see Rebecca Ann Rugg, "What It Used to Be: Nostalgia and the State of the Broadway Musical," *Theater* 32, no. 2 (Summer 2002): 44–55; Kathryn Ann Tremper Edney, "'Gliding Through Our Memories': The Performance of Nostalgia in American Musical Theater" (Ph.D. diss., Michigan State University, 2009); Phoebe Rumsey, "Embodied Nostalgia: Early Twentieth Century Social Dance and U.S. Musical Theatre" (Ph.D. diss, City University of New York, 2019); and Raymond Knapp, *The American Musical and the Formation of National Identity* (Princeton, NJ: Princeton University Press, 2005), esp. 120–21, 127, 138, 146.
106. "Cohan and Harris Reunion," *Variety*, February 10, 1937. This article is about a 1937 program, but the same sentiment applies to his earlier programs in 1933 and 1934.
107. George M. Cohan, "George M. Cohan Radio Review: Second Series #1," typescript, broadcast December 3, 1933, Radio Scripts LC.
108. Cohan, "Second Series #1," and Cohan, "Second Series No. 4," 10–11, Radio Scripts LC; Karen L. Cox, *Dreaming of Dixie: How the South Was Created in American Popular Culture* (Chapel Hill: University of North Carolina Press, 2013), 16.
109. Cohan, "Radio Review, Third Series #2," typescript, stamped April 10, 1934, p. 2, Radio Scripts LC.
110. "The Good Gulf Broadcast," September 17, 1933, *L (Special 91-11), Irving Berlin Collection of Noncommercial Sound Recordings, Rodgers and Hammerstein Archives of Recorded Sound, NYPL.
111. George M. Cohan, "George M. Cohan Radio Review: Second Series #3," typescript, broadcast December 17, 1933, pp. 1–3, Radio Scripts LC; Cohan, "Radio Review, Third Series #1," typescript, stamped April 10, 1934, 1–3, Radio Scripts LC.
112. Cohan, "Second Series No. 4," Radio Scripts LC.
113. Cohan, "Radio Review, Third Series #3," typescript, stamped April 10, 1934, Radio Scripts LC.
114. Cohan, "Second Series #3," 7–8, Radio Scripts LC.
115. "Santa Claus of the U.S.A." was in Cohan, "Second Series No. 4," 16, Radio Scripts LC. Gerald Bordman and Richard Norton use the term "spelling song" in *American Musical Theatre: A Chronicle*, 4th ed. (New York: Oxford University Press, 2010), 289.

116. "Many Radio Stars Pledge Aid to NRA," *Brooklyn Times Union*, September 17, 1933; "Cohan to Sing 'New Deal' Song on Radio Tonight," *Philadelphia Inquirer*, August 20, 1933.
117. Goodman, *Radio's Civic Ambition*, 3–6.
118. "'We Must Be Ready,' Cohan Warns in Song: Publishers Applaud His 'Sung Editorial,'" *New York Times*, April 28, 1939.
119. On the use of the song in Smith's campaign, see Janet I. Nicoll and G. Douglas Nicoll, "Political Campaign Songs from Tippecanoe to '72," *Popular Music & Society* 1, no. 4 (1972): 203–204.
120. Charles B. Lawlor and James W. Blake, "Sidewalks of New York," arranged by Charles Miller (New York: Howley, Haviland, 1894), available online at Levy Collection.
121. Printed in many newspapers, see, for example, O. O. McIntyre, "New York Day by Day," *Indianapolis Star*, November 7, 1924.
122. George M. Cohan, "When New York Was New York (New York Was a Wonderful Town)" (New York: Jerry Vogel Music, 1937), Brigham Young University Special Collections, available online at Internet Archive, https://archive.org/details/whennewyorkwasneoocoha.
123. The serial version appeared in *Liberty* magazine. Personal autobiographies, memoirs, and accounts of American theater and popular music published from in the 1910s to early 1920s include Leavitt, *Fifty Years in Theatrical Management*; Taylor, *Diary with Portraits of the Patriotic All-Star Tour of "Out There"*; Marie Dressler, *The Eminent American Comedienne Marie Dressler in The Life Story of an Ugly Duckling: An Autobiographical Fragment in Seven Parts* (New York: McBride, 1924). Charles K. Harris's *After the Ball: Forty Years of Melody; An Autobiography* (New York, Frank-Maurice, 1926) was published soon after Cohan's book.
124. It appeared in the *New York Evening World* from June to July, 1930. Scrapbook, Cohan Collection 31.167.
125. Thomas F. Ford, "Mr. George M. Cohan Presents," *Los Angeles Times*, June 7, 1925.
126. George M. Cohan, *Twenty Years on Broadway and the Years It Took to Get There: The True Story of a Trouper's Life from the Cradle to the "Closed Shop"* (New York: Harper and Brothers, 1925), 7.
127. Hunter Stagg, "Cohan Writes of Stage Life," *Richmond Times-Dispatch*, April 12, 1925.
128. Brooks Atkinson, "In Which Eugene O'Neill Recaptures the Past in a Comedy with George M. Cohan," *New York Times*, October 3, 1933.
129. Richard Watts Jr., "O'Neill Is Eager to See Cohan in 'Ah, Wilderness,'" *New York Herald Tribune*, September 9, 1933; see also Fisher, "The Man Who Owned Broadway," 115.
130. "Personality": George S. Kaufman and Moss Hart, *I'd Rather Be Right: A Musical Revue*, lyrics and music by Lorenz Hart and Richard Rodgers (New York: Random House, 1937), 41. Examples of this response to Cohan's performance include: Burns Mantle, "'I'd Rather Be Right' Sweeps George Cohan Into Third Term," *New York Daily News*, November 4, 1937; Edgar Price, "The Premiere," *Brooklyn Citizen*,

November 3, 1937; "One Hoofer to Another, Regards and Felicitations," *New York Herald Tribune*, March 6, 1938; Morehouse, *George M. Cohan*, 215.

131. George M. Cohan, *The Man Who Owns Broadway* (1910), 34 and 25, Cohan Collection 68.123.236. All *Man Who Owns Broadway* quotations are from this script.
132. Benjamin McArthur, *Actors and American Culture, 1880–1920* (Philadelphia: Temple University Press, 1984), 140.
133. Cohan, *Man Who Owns Broadway*, 13. The other quotations from the show in this paragraph are from pages 37 and 38.
134. Margherita Arlina Hamm, *Eminent Actors in Their Homes* (New York: James Pott, 1909), 5–6.
135. Cohan, *Man Who Owns Broadway*, Appendix, 10. The next quotations in this paragraph are from pages 6 and 9.
136. Marcus, *Drama of Celebrity*, 95.
137. On fans and sexual intimacy, see Marcus, *Drama of Celebrity*, 109–16.
138. Walter Winchell's syndicated column mentioned *The Musical Comedy Man* in August 1939; see, for one appearance, "Walter Winchell on Broadway," *Waterbury Evening Democrat*, August 21, 1939. Biographer John McCabe notes that Cohan started writing the show in 1940. McCabe, *George M. Cohan*, 254.
139. George M. Cohan, "The Musical Comedy Man," typescript (Act II, 18), Falk Papers. All *Musical Comedy Man* quotations are from this script.
140. Cohan, "Musical Comedy Man" (Act II, 27), Falk Papers. The script designates "Cohan" rather than "Callahan" in this song, suggesting the extent to which Cohan considered them one and the same.
141. "Growing sophistication": Fisher, "The Man Who Owned Broadway," 122. Frank W. Glann makes a similar observation about *The Musical Comedy Man* in "An Historical and Critical Evaluation of the Plays of George M. Cohan" (PhD diss., Bowling Green State University, 1976), 301.

CHAPTER 6

1. Epigraph: John McCabe writes that Cohan said this, in admiration of Cagney's performance, to his son George Jr. after screening the film at his home in October 1941. *George M. Cohan: The Man Who Owned Broadway* (Garden City, NY: Doubleday, 1973), 265. In the *New York Times*, see Russell Owen, "Yankee Doodle Dandy," March 1, 1942.
2. Rick Altman, *The American Film Musical* (Bloomington: Indiana University Press, 1987), 235. On the musical biopic, see also John C. Tibbetts, *Composers in the Movies* (New Haven, CT: Yale University Press, 2005), 102–54.
3. For an excellent account of the film's creation, see Patrick McGilligan's introduction to the published screenplay: "The Life Daddy Would Have Liked to Live," in *Yankee Doodle Dandy*, Wisconsin/Warner Bros. Screenplay Series (Madison: University of Wisconsin Press, 1981), 11–64. The contract with Cohan is discussed on pp. 16–17.
4. James and William Cagney were not happy with the versions of the script that Buckner submitted in October 1941, and Edmund Joseph, then Julius J. and Philip G. Epstein, were brought in to "doctor" the script. The final production credits

state that the screenplay is by Robert Buckner and Edmund Joseph; despite their significant contributions, the Epsteins agreed not to be listed. McGilligan, *Yankee Doodle Dandy*, 39–45, 54. "The picturization": Buckner to Hal Wallis, November 25, 1941, folder 2375 " 'Yankee Doodle Dandy' Story—Memos and Correspondence (hereafter 'Correspondence'), 11/1/41–11/28/41," WBA. Buckner described Cohan's script as an "egotistical epic," see Buckner to Wallis, September 27, 1941, folder 2375 "Correspondence, 9/8/41–10/30/41," WBA.

5. Although Cohan's real-life Congressional Gold Medal was authorized by Congress in 1936, Cohan did not receive it from President Roosevelt until 1940. Cohan may have delayed the meeting for political reasons. See McCabe, *George M. Cohan*, 234; and Garrett Eisler, "Kidding on the Level: The Reactionary Project of *I'd Rather Be Right*," *Studies in Musical Theatre* 1, no. 1 (2007): 19–20.
6. All film quotations are from *Yankee Doodle Dandy*, based on the story of George M. Cohan, directed by Michael Curtiz, starring James Cagney (1942; Burbank, CA: Warner Home Video, 2003), DVD, unless otherwise noted.
7. McGilligan, *Yankee Doodle Dandy*, 21.
8. McGilligan, *Yankee Doodle Dandy*, 20. Levey nonetheless sued Warner Bros. for invasion of her right to privacy; her complaint was ultimately dismissed. As legal historian Jessica Lake writes, the film's injury actually lay in failing to capture Levey's significance and contribution. Buckner's testimony in the court case bears out that Cohan did not want Levey or his private life mentioned. Levey v. Warner Bros Pictures, Civil Case File 20-438, US District Court for the Southern District of New York, pp. 316–22; Records of the District Courts, Record Group 21; copied at the National Archives at Kansas City, MO; Jessica Lake, *The Face That Launched a Thousand Lawsuits: The American Women Who Forged a Right to Privacy* (New Haven, CT: Yale University Press, 2016), 208–13.
9. Ward Morehouse, *George M. Cohan: Prince of the American Theater* (Philadelphia: J. B. Lippincott, 1943), 229.
10. On the film's portrayal of Irish Americanness, see Meaghan Dwyer-Ryan, "'Yankee Doodle Paddy': Themes of Ethnic Acculturation in *Yankee Doodle Dandy*," *Journal of American Ethnic History* 30, no. 4 (Summer 2011): 57–62; and Christopher Shannon, *Bowery to Broadway: The American Irish in Classic Hollywood Cinema* (Scranton, PA: University of Scranton Press, 2010), 153–69.
11. Dwyer-Ryan, " 'Yankee Doodle Paddy,' " 61. The ability for Irish American characters in film to easily maintain both identities stands in notable contrast to other ethnic groups as portrayed by Hollywood, for instance the Jewish American protagonist Jakie Rabinowitz in *The Jazz Singer*. See Shannon, *Bowery to Broadway*, xxxi–xxxii, 161–62.
12. McGilligan, *Yankee Doodle Dandy*, 92.
13. Jerry Cohan's Irish-themed sketches and performances are discussed in this book's introduction.
14. When they filmed this scene, the war had recently begun and tensions were high, so director Michael Curtiz had to get permission from both Warner Bros. and the city of Burbank to fire the cannon. Behlmer commentary on *Yankee Doodle Dandy*, DVD.

15. Richard Gustafson describes a "sense of destiny" as one of the archetypes of the early- to mid-century biopic in "The Vogue of the Screen Biography," *Film & History* 7, no. 3 (September 1977): 36. On the use of flags in American cinema, including *Yankee Doodle Dandy* and this scene, see Robert Eberwein, "Following the Flag in American Film," in *Eastwood's Iwo Jima: Critical Engagements with Flags of Our Fathers and Letters from Iwo Jima*, ed. Anne Gjelsvik and Rikke Schubart (New York: Columbia University Press, 2013), esp. 85–86; and William H. Epstein, "Introduction: Biopics and American National Identity—Invented Lives, Imagined Communities," *a/b: Auto/Biography Studies* 26, no. 1 (Summer 2011), 12, 15–17.
16. Raymond Knapp and Mitchell Morris, "The Filmed Musical," in *The Oxford Handbook of the American Musical*, ed. Raymond Knapp, Mitchell Morris, and Stacy Wolf (New York: Oxford University Press, 2011), 136.
17. On the use of the framing of the stage as part of LeRoy Prinz's style, see Allen L. Woll, *The Hollywood Musical Goes to War* (Chicago: Nelson-Hall, 1983), 55.
18. James Fisher, *Historical Dictionary of American Theater: Beginnings* (Lanham, MD: Rowman and Littlefield, 2015), 252.
19. Jane Feuer, "The Self-Reflective Musical and the Myth of Entertainment," in *Genre: The Musical*, ed. Rick Altman (London: Routledge and Kegan Paul, 1981), 159–74, esp. 168. On the musical's mythologies, see also Feuer, *The Hollywood Musical*, 2nd ed. (Bloomington: Indiana University Press, 1993), esp. 15–22 and 90–97.
20. Quotation from the film with the parenthetical direction from the screenplay in McGilligan, *Yankee Doodle Dandy*, 157.
21. Research ("Material on the life of George M. Cohan") by Robert Buckner, April 4, 1941, WBS box 445/folder 2; Robert Buckner to Hal Wallis, April 15, 1941, folder 2375 "Correspondence, 1/16/41–4/28/41," WBA.
22. McGilligan, *Yankee Doodle Dandy*, 16–17, 30, 38, 54.
23. Seymour Felix, who staged the production numbers along with Leroy Prinz, wrote to Hal Wallis about going outside the bounds of the contract to interpolate small bits of music for dramatic purposes; for example, he proposed adding music and lyrics to "The Yankee Doodle Boy" to explain that Little Johnny Jones will be racing in the Derby. The additions "Good Luck Johnny" and "All Aboard for Broadway" were written by Jack Scholl and M. K. Jerome. Felix to Wallis, November 12, 1941, folder 2375 "Correspondence, 11/1/41–11/28/41," WBA; George Feltenstein, liner notes to *Original Warner Bros. Motion Picture Soundtrack: Yankee Doodle Dandy*, R2 78210, 2002, cd.
24. McGilligan, *Yankee Doodle Dandy*, 47.
25. On Warner Bros. politically oriented pre-war films, see Woll, *Hollywood Musical*, 3–11, 33–44, quotation on 7; Michael E. Birdwell, *Celluloid Soldiers: The Warner Bros. Campaign against Nazism, 1934–1941* (New York: NYU Press, 1999); Thomas Doherty, *Projections of War: Hollywood, American Culture, and World War II* (New York: Columbia University Press, 1993), 39–42.
26. McGilligan, *Yankee Doodle Dandy*, 14–15; Buckner to Wallis, April 15, 1941, folder 2375 "Correspondence, 1/16/41–4/28/41," WBA.
27. Curtiz to Wallis, November 14, 1941, folder 2375 "Correspondence, 11/1/41–11/28/41," WBA.

28. McGilligan, *Yankee Doodle Dandy*, 15–16, 46.
29. Thomas F. Brady, "Facts Behind 'Yankee Doodle Dandy,'" *New York Times*, January 10, 1943. The anecdote is related similarly on the *James Cagney: Top of the World* feature hosted by Michael J. Fox on the *Yankee Doodle Dandy* special edition DVD set.
30. William Cagney and Robert Buckner to Hal Wallis, May 5, 1941, folder 2375 "Correspondence, 5/2/41–6/30/41," WBA. The last quotation in this paragraph is from the same source.
31. *Yankee Doodle Dandy* advertisement, undated, folder 2883 "Yankee Doodle Dandy—Picture File," WBA.
32. The notion that he would appear to be profiting from the war may have been a concern at the time as well. Newspapers and, in the case of "Their Hearts Are Over Here," sheet music reported that Cohan was donating proceeds from his World War I patriotic songs, which also included "Over There" and "When You Come Back: And You Will Come Back, There's the Whole World Waiting for You." See, for example, "Their Hearts Are Over Here" (New York: Waterson, Berlin, and Snyder, 1918), available online at Levy Collection; "Little Stories of Stage and Screen," *Wichita Eagle*, February 2, 1919; Frank Ward O'Malley, "Cohan's Consuming Ambition to Write the Great American Play," *New York Sun*, April 27, 1919.
33. Hal B. Wallis, William Cagney, and Robert Buckner to George M. Cohan, copying [story editor] Jacob Wilk, August 29, 1941, folder 2375 "Correspondence, 7/1/41–9/5/41," WBA.
34. Cagney to Wallis, August 27, 1941, folder 2375 "Correspondence, 7/1/41–9/5/41," WBA.
35. In response to this letter Cohan agreed to compromise according to September 8 correspondence from Buckner to Wilk. An October 6 telegraph from Buckner to Hal Wallis reported a "very encouraging conference with Cohan today" in which he "assure[d] general approval of new script" with minimal changes. Robert Buckner to Jake Wilk, September 8, 1941, and Robert Buckner to Hal B. Wallis, October 6, 1941, folder 2375 "Correspondence, 9/8/41–10/30/41," WBA.
36. Eberwein, "Following the Flag," 85.
37. McGilligan, *Yankee Doodle Dandy*, 169.
38. McGilligan, *Yankee Doodle Dandy*, 219n42.
39. "George Washington, Jr.," typescript (Act I, 37–40), Cohan Collection 68.123.330.
40. Prinz to Cagney, January 7, 1942, folder 2375 "Correspondence, 7/1/42–1/31/44" [filed out of date?], WBA.
41. Replogle-Wong's analysis of this scene demonstrates how it presents "an idealistic version of the American model of national inclusiveness, in which past offenses are absorbed by the spirit of unification." Holley Replogle-Wong, "Coming-Of-Age in Wartime: American Propaganda and Patriotic Nationalism in *Yankee Doodle Dandy*," *Echo: A Music-Centered Journal* 8, no. 1 (Fall 2006): paragraphs 9–16.
42. Prinz to Cagney, January 7, 1942, WBA. Seymour Felix had been taken off the project in December 1941: Seymour Felix to Hal Wallis, December 26, 1941, folder 2375 "Correspondence, 12/1/41–1/30/42," WBA; Rudy Behlmer commentary on *Yankee Doodle Dandy*, DVD.

43. Prinz to Cagney, January 7, 1942, WBA.
44. She later said that entertaining the troops was "the greatest thing in [her] life." Richard Severo, "Frances Langford, Trouper on Bob Hope Tours, Dies at 92," *New York Times*, July 12, 2005.
45. McGilligan, *Yankee Doodle Dandy*, 221n52.
46. "Memorandum for the President," December 16, 1941, Office of Strategic Services Reports, December 12–17, 1941 folder, President's Secretary's File, Franklin D. Roosevelt Library, https://catalog.archives.gov/id/16620496.
47. McGilligan, *Yankee Doodle Dandy*, 24.
48. George M. Cohan, "Yankee Doodle Dandy" screenplay, typescript, 107, WBS box 445, folder 5.
49. Cohen, "Dear Old Darling," *Variety*, January 8, 1936.
50. George M. Cohan to Hon. Francis Biddle, December 16, 1941, Cohan Collection. My thanks to Scott A. Sandage and Morgen Stevens-Garmon for their assistance in locating this document.
51. Scott A. Sandage, "Old Rags, Some Grand," *Cabinet* 7 (Summer 2002), http://www.cabinetmagazine.org/issues/7/oldrags.php.
52. Sandage, "Old Rags, Some Grand."
53. Alan K. Rode, *Michael Curtiz: A Life in Film* (Lexington: University Press of Kentucky, 2017), 299.
54. Rosemary DeCamp, *Tigers in My Lap* (Baltimore: Midnight Marquee Press, 2000), 106.
55. McCabe, *George M. Cohan*, 260, 265.
56. "Exploitation: Treasury Dept Cued WB's $25,000 'Tickets' for 'Yankee Doodle,'" *Variety*, May 6, 1942. On the premiere and publicity, see also McGilligan, *Yankee Doodle Dandy*, 58.
57. Jack Warner [to "Messrs. Einfeld and Blumenstock"], August 13, 1942, folder 2375 "Correspondence, 7/1/41–9/5/41," WBA. The document is filed with the July–September 1941 documents. However, the 1942 date is probably correct given that it was common during the period for a film to move gradually to different theaters and that the press reported that the national merchandising campaign would be rolled out following the film's premiere: "Exploitation: Nat'l Campaign on 'Yankee' Rests on Preem Results," *Variety*, May 27, 1942.
58. Warner to Cohan, May 29, 1942, folder 2375 "Correspondence, 2/2/42–6/20/42," WBA.
59. Cohan to Warner, August 17, 1942, folder 2375 "Correspondence, 7/1/42–1/31/44," WBA.
60. McCabe, *George M. Cohan*, 265–66; McGilligan, *Yankee Doodle Dandy*, 62.
61. Donald A. Sardinas to [Jack] Warner, May 29, 1942, folder 2375 "Correspondence, 2/2/42–6/20/42," WBA.
62. Lydia Wilbur to Jack L. Warner, July 21, 1942, folder 2375 "Correspondence, 7/1/42–1/31/44," WBA.
63. Edwin Schallert, "'Yankee Doodle Dandy' Registers Super Success," *Los Angeles Times*, August 13, 1942.

EPILOGUE

1. Ivor Novello (1893–1951) and Noël Coward (1899–1973) were similarly multitalented figures in British theater.
2. Angus Duncan (Executive Secretary, Actors' Equity Association) to Max Gordon, January 24, 1958; Max Gordon to Oscar Hammerstein II, January 28, 1958; and unsigned letter [presumably from Oscar Hammerstein II] to Angus Duncan, February 3, 1958, Oscar Hammerstein II Collection, Music Division, LoC. Other responses mentioned bad feelings about Cohan, likely at least in part because of his stance against Equity; see Mark Eden Horowitz, comp. and ed., *The Letters of Oscar Hammerstein II* (New York: Oxford University Press, 2022), 850–51, 973. My thanks to Mark for consulting with me about this correspondence.
3. "'Georgie' Award Stirs AGVA Discord over Honor to Cohan, Enemy of Equity," *Variety*, October 20, 1971.
4. These began during Cohan's lifetime, with the 1939 Catholic University of America production *Yankee Doodle Boy*, which Cohan consulted on and attended, and continue through the present. On *Yankee Doodle Boy*, see Mary Jo Santo Pietro, *Father Hartke: His Life and Legacy to the American Theater* (Washington, DC: Catholic University of America Press, 2002), 77–90.
5. "Wax museum" comes from Frank Rich's review of the 1982 Broadway revival of *Little Johnny Jones* in the *New York Times*, March 22, 1982; "45 Minutes from Broadway," Dramatic Publishing, https://www.dramaticpublishing.com/45-minutes-from-broadway, accessed June 2022.
6. On breakdowns of taste distinctions, see Michael Kammen, *American Culture, American Tastes* (New York: Knopf, 1999), 121–25. On the critique and persistence of elitist ideologies in musicology, see Christopher Chowrimootoo and Kate Guthrie, introduction to "Colloquy: Musicology and the Middlebrow," *Journal of the American Musicological Society* 72, no. 2 (Summer 2020): 327–34.
7. Kammen, *American Culture, American Tastes*, 104–105, 118–19.
8. David Glassberg, "Patriotism from the Ground Up," review of *Sacred Ground: Americans and their Battlefields* by Edward Tabor Linenthal and *Remaking America: Public Memory, Commemoration, and Patriotism in the Twentieth Century* by John Bodnar, *Reviews in American History* 21, no. 1 (1993), 1; Jill Lepore, *This America: The Case for the Nation* (New York: Liveright, 2019), 15–20.
9. "A Timeline of 1968: The Year That Shattered America," by Matthew Twombly, research by Kendrick McDonald, *Smithsonian Magazine*, January 2018, https://www.smithsonianmag.com/history/timeline-seismic-180967503/.
10. Stephen Allen, "George M! Sentimental," *Camden Courier-Post*, March 14, 1968.
11. "George M!," *Time*, April 19, 1968. On *George M!* as nostalgic, see also Clive Barnes, "The Theater: 'George M!'" *New York Times*, April 11, 1968.
12. William Pahlmann, "Patriotic Show," *Baltimore Sun*, July 5, 1968.
13. Erma Bombeck, "And That Grand Old Flag Still Waves," *Tampa Tribune*, November 5, 1968.
14. Theater critic Peter Filichia has speculated that the show may have run longer had it been eligible for the Tony Awards shortly after it opened in 1968; instead, a changed

cut-off date for the awards meant that the show could not be considered until the following year. Filichia, "*George M!*: The Musical that NBC Sabotaged," Masterworks Broadway Blog, April 25, 2018, https://www.masterworksbroadway.com/blog/george-m-the-musical-that-nbc-sabotaged-by-peter-filichia/.

15. *Elliot Norton Reviews: Little Johnny Jones*, directed by Joanna Lu and Elliot Norton. Boston, MA: WGBH Boston, 1982, https://search.alexanderstreet.com/view/work/bibliographic_entity%7Cvideo_work%7C2180383.
16. Frank Rich, "Stage: Cohan Revival, 'Little Johnny Jones," *New York Times*, March 22, 1982.
17. Evelyn Renold, "Donny Doodle Dandy," *New York Daily News*, March 21, 1982.
18. On the "rightward ideological shift" of "God Bless America," see Sheryl Kaskowitz, *God Bless America: The Surprising History of an Iconic Song* (New York: Oxford University Press, 2013), 68–92; on the "The Star-Spangled Banner," see Mark Clague, *O Say Can You Hear? A Cultural Biography of "The Star-Spangled Banner"* (New York: Norton, 2022).
19. Comments on "The Grand Old Flag," YouTube, November 23, 2016, https://www.youtube.com/watch?v=56qQYwOmkXw&lc=Ugx5JEOJrZghGKpK2MF4AaABAg (quotations from comments by JoMarieM [July 5, 2021] and 000 Responses [August 10, 2019]); and comments on "Yankee Doodle Dandy Finale," YouTube, August 30, 2010, https://www.youtube.com/watch?v=v1rkzUIL8oc.
20. Cohan himself has also been a powerful symbol for political co-option. A historically inept but attention-grabbing 2019 *Wall Street Journal* editorial by writer and prominent Republican William McGurn likened then-President Donald Trump's "ordinary guy" appeal and performative patriotism to Cohan's. July 8, 2019 online and July 9, 2019 in print, https://www.wsj.com/articles/yankee-doodle-donald-11562626189.
21. Calls to reclaim patriotism—a constructive patriotism, one animated by love and committed to a "clear-eyed reckoning with American history"—abound and have been an inspiration behind this book. On these patriotisms, see Clague, *O Say Can You See*, xv; and Lepore, *This America*, quotation on 137.
22. Michael Hout and Joshua R. Goldstein, "How 4.5 Million Irish Immigrants Became 40 Million Irish Americans: Demographic and Subjective Aspects of the Ethnic Composition of White Americans," *American Sociological Review* 59, no. 1 (1994): 64–82.
23. Marilyn Halter, *Shopping for Identity: The Marketing of Ethnicity* (New York: Schocken Books, 2000), 161–69.
24. Sen. Daniel Patrick Moynihan, "The Irish Among Us," *Reader's Digest*, January 1985, 63–64.
25. Walter Kerr, "Yankee Doodle's Out of Breath," *New York Times*, April 21, 1968.

SELECTED BIBLIOGRAPHY

Books, Articles, and Scholarly Editions

Adams, Bluford. *E Pluribus Barnum: The Great Showman and the Making of U.S. Popular Culture*. Minneapolis: University of Minnesota Press, 1997.

Altman, Rick. *The American Film Musical*. Bloomington: Indiana University Press, 1987.

Anbinder, Tyler. *Five Points: The 19th-Century New York City Neighborhood that Invented Tap Dance, Stole Elections, and Became the World's Most Notorious Slum*. New York: Free Press, 2001.

Anderson, Benedict. *Imagined Communities: Reflections on the Origin and Spread of Nationalism*. London: Verso, 1991.

Archer, Stephen M. "*E pluribus unum*: Bernhardt's 1905–1906 Farewell Tour." In *The American Stage: Social and Economic Issues from the Colonial Period to the Present*, edited by Ron Engle and Tice L. Miller, 159–74. Cambridge: Cambridge University Press, 1993.

Banfield, Stephen. *Sondheim's Broadway Musicals*. Ann Arbor: University of Michigan Press, 1993.

Banta, Martha. *Barbaric Intercourse: Caricature and the Culture of Conduct, 1841–1936*. Chicago: University of Chicago Press, 2003.

Baral, Robert. *Revue: The Great Broadway Period*. Rev. ed. New York: Fleet Press, 1970.

Bederman, Gail. *Manliness and Civilization: A Cultural History of Gender and Race in the United States, 1880–1917*. Chicago: University of Chicago Press, 1995.

Beggs, Anne. "'For Urinetown Is Your Town . . .': The Fringes of Broadway." *Theatre Journal* 62, no. 1 (2010): 41–56.

Benjamin, Rick. Liner notes to *You're a Grand Old Rag: The Music of George M. Cohan*. The Paragon Ragtime Orchestra. New World Records 80685-2, 2008, compact disc.

Benson, Sarah M. *The Prison of Democracy: Race, Leavenworth, and the Culture of Law*. Berkeley: University of California Press, 2019.

Berlin, Edward A. *Ragtime: A Musical and Cultural History*. Berkeley: University of California Press, 1980.

Birdwell, Michael E. *Celluloid Soldiers: The Warner Bros. Campaign Against Nazism, 1934–1941*. New York: NYU Press, 1999.

Block, Geoffrey. "Integration." In Knapp, Morris, and Wolf, *Oxford Handbook of the American Musical*, 97–110.

Bomberger, Douglas. *Making Music American: 1917 and the Transformation of Culture*. New York: Oxford University Press, 2018.

Bordman, Gerald, and Richard Norton. *American Musical Theatre: A Chronicle*. 4th ed. New York: Oxford University Press, 2010.

Braudy, Leo. *The Frenzy of Renown: Fame and Its History*. New York: Vintage Books, 1997.

Brooks, Van Wyck. *America's Coming-of-Age*. New York: B. W. Huebsch, 1915.

Burkholder, J. Peter. *All Made of Tunes: Charles Ives and the Uses of Musical Borrowing.* New Haven, CT: Yale University Press, 1995.

Butsch, Richard. *The Making of American Audiences: From Stage to Television, 1950–1990.* Cambridge: Cambridge University Press, 2000.

The Cahn-Leighton Official Theatre Guide. Vol. 17. New York: Publication Office, New Amsterdam Theatre Building, 1913.

Cantor, Eddie. *"My Life Is in Your Hands" and "Take My Life": The Autobiographies of Eddie Cantor*. With David Freedman and Jane Kesner Ardmore. New York: Cooper Square Press, 2000.

Cantu, Maya. *American Cinderellas on the Broadway Musical Stage: Imagining the Working Girl from "Irene" to "Gypsy."* New York: Palgrave Macmillan, 2015.

Carlson, Marvin. *The Haunted Stage: The Theatre as Memory Machine*. Ann Arbor: University of Michigan Press, 2001.

Carr, Steven Alan. *Hollywood and Anti-Semitism: A Cultural History up to World War II.* Cambridge: Cambridge University Press, 2001.

Carter, Elliott. "Films and Theatre." *Modern Music* 20, no. 3 (March–April 1943): 205–207.

Caruso, Dorothy, and Torrance Goddard. *Wings of Song: The Story of Caruso*. New York: Minton, Balch, 1928.

Casey, Marion R. "Ireland, New York and the Irish Image in American Popular Culture, 1890–1960." PhD diss., New York University, 1998.

Casey, Marion R. "Was Victor Herbert Irish?" *History Ireland* 25, no. 1 (2017): 20–23.

Chang, Dongshin. *Representing China on the Historical London Stage: From Orientalism to Intercultural Performance*. New York: Routledge, 2015.

Chester, George Randolph. *Get-Rich-Quick Wallingford*. New York: A. L. Burt, 1908.

Chowrimootoo, Christopher, and Kate Guthrie. Introduction to "Colloquy: Musicology and the Middlebrow." *Journal of the American Musicological Society* 72, no. 2 (Summer 2020): 327–34.

Clague, Mark. *O Say Can You Hear?: A Cultural Biography of "The Star-Spangled Banner."* New York: Norton, 2022.

Cohan, George M. *Broadway Jones: A Comedy in Four Acts*. New York: Samuel French, 1923.

Cohan, George M. *Twenty Years on Broadway and the Years It Took to Get There: The True Story of a Trouper's Life from the Cradle to the "Closed Shop."* New York: Harper and Brothers, 1925.

Cohan, Jerry J. *Poems and Sketches*. Privately printed, Physioc Press, 1911.

Cox, Karen L. *Dreaming of Dixie: How the South Was Created in American Popular Culture*. Chapel Hill: University of North Carolina Press, 2013.

Craft, Elizabeth Titrington. "'A Great American Service': George M. Cohan, the Stage, and the Nation in *Yankee Doodle Dandy*." In *The Oxford Handbook of Musical Theatre Screen Adaptations*, edited by Dominic McHugh, 315–36. New York: Oxford University Press, 2019.

Cuddy, Edward. "The Irish Question and the Revival of Anti-Catholicism in the 1920's." *Catholic Historical Review* 67, no. 2 (April 1981): 236–55.

Cullen, Frank, with Florence Hackman and Donald McNeilly. *Vaudeville, Old & New: An Encyclopedia of Variety Performers in America*. Vol. 1. New York: Routledge, 2007.

Daniels, Roger. *Coming to America: A History of Immigration and Ethnicity in American Life*. 2nd ed. New York: Perennial, 2002.
Davis, Janet M. "Cultural Watersheds in Fin de Siècle America." In *A Companion to American Cultural History*, edited by Karen Halttunen, 166–80. Malden, MA: Blackwell, 2008.
Davis, Richard W. "'We Are All Americans Now!' Anglo-American Marriages in the Later Nineteenth Century." *Proceedings of the American Philosophical Society* 135, no. 2 (June 1991): 140–99.
Dawley, Alan. "The Abortive Rule of Big Money." In *Ruling America: A History of Wealth and Power in a Democracy*, edited by Steve Fraser and Gary Gerstle, 149–80. Cambridge, MA: Harvard University Press, 2005.
Day-O'Connell, Jeremy. *Pentatonicism from the Eigtheenth Century to Debussy*. Rochester, NY: University of Rochester Press, 2007.
DeCamp, Rosemary. *Tigers in My Lap*. Baltimore: Midnight Marquee Press, 2000.
Dietz, Dan. *The Complete Book of 1920s Broadway Musicals*. Lanham, MD: Rowman and Littlefield, 2019.
Diner, Hasia R. *Erin's Daughters in America: Irish Immigrant Women in the Nineteenth Century*. Baltimore: Johns Hopkins University Press, 1983.
Diner, Hasia R. "'The Most Irish City in the Union': The Era of the Great Migration, 1844–1877." In *The New York Irish*, edited by Ronald H. Bayor and Timothy J. Meagher, 87–106. Baltimore: Johns Hopkins University Press, 1996.
Dizikes, John. *Yankee Doodle Dandy: The Life and Times of Tod Sloan*. New Haven, CT: Yale University Press, 2000.
Doherty, Thomas. *Projections of War: Hollywood, America Culture, and World War II*. New York: Columbia University Press, 1993.
Dormon, James H. "Ethnic Cultures of the Mind: The Harrigan-Hart Mosaic." *American Studies* 33, no. 2 (Fall 1992): 21–40.
Douglas, Susan J. *Listening In: Radio and the American Imagination*. Minneapolis: University of Minnesota Press, 2004.
Dressler, Marie. *The Eminent American Comedienne Marie Dressler in The Life Story of an Ugly Duckling: An Autobiographical Fragment in Seven Parts*. New York: McBride, 1924.
Du Bois, W. E. B. *The Souls of Black Folk*. With an introduction and chronology by Jonathan Scott Holloway. New Haven: Yale University Press, 2015.
Dumenil, Lynn. "The Tribal Twenties: 'Assimilated' Catholics' Response to Anti-Catholicism in the 1920s." *Journal of American Ethnic History* 11, no. 1 (October 1991): 21–49.
Dwyer-Ryan, Meaghan. "'Yankee Doodle Paddy': Themes of Ethnic Acculturation in *Yankee Doodle Dandy*." *Journal of American Ethnic History* 30, no. 4 (Summer 2011): 57–62.
Eaton, Walter Pritchard. *The American Stage of To-Day*. Boston: Small, Maynard, 1908.
Eberwein, Robert. "Following the Flag in American Film." In *Eastwood's Iwo Jima: Critical Engagements with Flags of Our Fathers and Letters from Iwo Jima*, edited by Anne Gjelsvik and Rikke Schubart, 81–99. New York: Columbia University Press, 2013.
Edney, Kathryn A. "'Gliding Through Our Memories': The Performance of Nostalgia in American Musical Theater." PhD diss., Michigan State University, 2009.
Edney, Kathryn A. "A New Brechtian Musical? An Analysis of *Urinetown* (2001)." In *Brecht, Broadway and United States Theater*, edited by J. Chris Westgate, 100–21. Newcastle-upon-Tyne: Cambridge Scholars Publishing, 2007.

Eisler, Garrett. "Kidding on the Level: The Reactionary Project of *I'd Rather Be Right*." *Studies in Musical Theatre* 1, no. 1 (December 2006): 7–24.
Epstein, William H. "Introduction: Biopics and American National Identity—Invented Lives, Imagined Communities." *a/b: Auto/Biography Studies* 26, no. 1 (Summer 2011): 1–33.
Everett, William A., and Paul R. Laird, eds. *The Cambridge Companion to the Musical*. 2nd ed. Cambridge: Cambridge University Press, 2008.
Ewen, David. *The Story of America's Musical Theater*. Philadelphia: Chilton, 1961.
Feltenstein, George. Liner notes to *Original Warner Bros. Motion Picture Soundtrack: Yankee Doodle Dandy*. R2 78210, 2002, compact disc.
Feuer, Jane. *The Hollywood Musical*. 2nd ed. Bloomington: Indiana University Press, 1993.
Feuer, Jane. "The Self-Reflective Musical and the Myth of Entertainment." In *Genre: The Musical*, edited by Rick Altman, 159–74. London: Routledge and Kegan Paul, 1981.
Fielder, Mari Kathleen. "Chauncey Olcott: Irish-American Mother-Love, Romance, and Nationalism." *Éire-Ireland* 22, no. 2 (Summer 1987): 4–26.
Fink, Leon. *The Long Gilded Age: American Capitalism and the Lessons of a New World Order*. Philadelphia: University of Pennsylvania Press, 2015.
Finson, Jon W. *The Voices That Are Gone: Themes in Nineteenth-Century Popular Song*. New York: Oxford University Press, 1994.
Fish, Stanley. *Is There a Text in This Class? The Authority of Interpretive Communities*. Cambridge, MA: Harvard University Press, 1980.
Fisher, James. *Historical Dictionary of American Theater: Beginnings*. Lanham, MD: Rowman and Littlefield, 2015.
Fisher, James. "The Man Who Owned Broadway: George M. Cohan's Triumph in Eugene O'Neill's *Ah, Wilderness!*" *Eugene O'Neill Review* 23, no. 1/2 (Spring/Fall 1999): 98–126.
Fitzgerald, Keith. *The Face of the Nation: Immigration, the State, and the National Identity*. Stanford, CA: Stanford University Press, 1996.
Flewelling, Lindsey. *Two Irelands Beyond the Sea: Ulster Unionism and America, 1880–1920*. Liverpool: Liverpool University Press, 2018.
Flood, W. H. Grattan. "Historical Notes on the 'Adeste Fideles.'" *Irish Ecclesiastical Record* 24, no. 492 (1908): 601–606.
Forbes, Camille F. *Introducing Bert Williams: Burnt Cork, Broadway, and the Story of America's First Black Star*. New York: Basic Books, 2008.
Foster, Charles. *Donald Brian: The King of Broadway*. St. John's, NL: Breakwater Books, 2005.
Foxall, Raymond. *John McCormack*. London: Robert Hale, 1963.
Franceschina, John. *Biographical and Critical Commentary: Alphabetical Listings from Alfred E. Aarons to Joe Jordan*. Vol. 2 of *Incidental and Dance Music in the American Theatre from 1786 to 1923*. Albany, GA: Bearmanor Media, 2017.
Franceschina, John. *Biographical and Critical Commentary: Alphabetical Listings from Edgar Stillman Kelley to Charles Zimmerman*. Vol. 3 of *Incidental and Dance Music in the American Theatre from 1786 to 1923*. Albany, GA: Bearmanor Media, 2017.
Frick, John. "A Changing Theater: New York and Beyond." In *The Cambridge History of American Theatre*, vol. 2: 1870–1945, edited by Don B. Wilmeth and Christopher Bigsby, 199–218. Cambridge: Cambridge University Press, 1999.

Furia, Philip. *The Poets of Tin Pan Alley: A History of America's Great Lyricists*. New York: Oxford University Press, 1992.

Gamson, Joshua. *Claims to Fame: Celebrity in Contemporary America*. Berkeley: University of California Press, 1994.

Garber, Michael G. "Eepha-Soffa-Dill and Eephing: Found in Ragtime, Jazz, and Country Music, from Broadway to a Texas Plantation." *American Music* 35, no. 3 (2017): 343–74.

Garber, Michael G. "Songs about Entertainment: Self-Praise and Self-Mockery in the American Musical." *Studies in Musical Theatre* 1, no. 3 (2007): 227–44.

Garrett, Charles Hiroshi. *Struggling to Define a Nation: American Music and the Twentieth Century*. Berkeley: University of California Press, 2008.

Gebhardt, Nicholas. *Vaudeville Melodies: Popular Musicians and Mass Entertainment in American Culture, 1870–1929*. Chicago: University of Chicago Press, 2017.

"George M. Cohan, Petitioner, v. Commissioner of Internal Revenue, Respondent." In *Reports of the United States Board of Tax Appeals*, vol. 11, 743–62. Washington, DC: United States Government Printing Office, 1929.

Gerstle, Gary. *American Crucible: Race and Nation in the Twentieth Century*. Rev. ed. Princeton, NJ: Princeton University Press, 2017.

Gerstle, Gary. "The Protean Character of American Liberalism." *American Historical Review* 99, no. 4 (October 1994): 1043–73.

Gerstle, Gary. "Theodore Roosevelt and the Divided Character of American Nationalism." *Journal of American History* 86, no. 3 (December 1999): 1280–1307.

Gibbons, William. "'Yankee Doodle' and Nationalism, 1780–1920." *American Music* 26, no. 2 (Summer 2008): 246–74.

Gier, Christina. "Gender, Politics, and the Fighting Soldier's Song in America during World War I." *Music and Politics* 2, no. 1 (Winter 2008): 1–21.

Glann, Frank W. "A Historical and Critical Evaluation of the Plays of George M. Cohan 1901–1920." PhD diss., Bowling Green State University, 1976.

Glassberg, David. "Patriotism from the Ground Up." Review of *Sacred Ground: Americans and their Battlefields* by Edward Tabor Linenthal and *Remaking America: Public Memory, Commemoration, and Patriotism in the Twentieth Century* by John Bodnar. *Reviews in American History* 21, no. 1 (1993): 1–7.

Glenn, Susan A. *Female Spectacle: The Theatrical Roots of Modern Feminism*. Cambridge, MA: Harvard University Press, 2000.

Goldenberg, David M. *The Curse of Ham: Race and Slavery in Early Judaism, Christianity, and Islam*. Princeton, NJ: Princeton University Press, 2003.

Goldmark, Daniel. "Creating Desire on Tin Pan Alley." *Musical Quarterly* 90, no. 2 (2007): 197–229.

Goodman, David. *Radio's Civic Ambition: American Broadcasting and Democracy in the 1930s*. New York: Oxford University Press, 2011.

Gould, Neil. *Victor Herbert: A Theatrical Life*. New York: Fordham University Press, 2008.

Gracyk, Tim, and Frank Hoffmann. *Popular American Recording Pioneers, 1895–1925*. New York: Haworth Press, 2000.

Graham, Philip. *Showboats: The History of an American Institution*. Austin: University of Texas Press, 1951.

Granshaw, Michelle. "Hibernicon and Visions of Returning Home: Popular Entertainment in Irish America from the Civil War to World War I." PhD diss., University of Washington, 2013.

Granshaw, Michelle. *Irish on the Move: Performing Mobility in American Variety Theatre*. Iowa City: University of Iowa Press, 2019.

Graziano, John. "Music in William Randolph Hearst's *New York Journal*." *Notes* 48, no. 2 (1991): 383–424.

Gustafson, Richard. "The Vogue of the Screen Biography." *Film & History* 7, no. 3 (September 1977): 32–39.

Hagedorn, Hermann, ed. *Literary Essays*. Vol. 12, *The Works of Theodore Roosevelt*. New York: Scribner's Sons, 1926.

Halter, Marilyn. *Shopping for Identity: The Marketing of Ethnicity*. New York: Schocken Books, 2000.

Hamberlin, Larry. *Tin Pan Opera: Operatic Novelty Songs in the Ragtime Era*. New York: Oxford University Press, 2011.

Hamm, Charles, ed. *Irving Berlin: Early Songs*. Vol. 1, *1907–1911*. Madison, WI: A-R Editions, 1994.

Hamm, Charles. *Yesterdays: Popular Song in America*. New York: Norton, 1979.

Hamm, Margherita Arlina. *Eminent Actors in Their Homes*. New York: James Pott, 1909.

Hammerstein, Oscar, II. "Cohan: A Yankee Doodle Dandy." *Music Journal* 16, no. 1 (January 1958): 10.

Hansen, Jonathan. "True Americanism: Progressive Era Intellectuals and the Problem of Liberal Nationalism." In *Americanism: New Perspectives on the History of an Ideal*, edited by Michael Kazin and Joseph A. McCartin, 73–89. Chapel Hill: University of North Carolina Press, 2006.

Harris, Charles K. *After the Ball: Forty Years of Melody; An Autobiography*. New York: Frank-Maurice, 1926.

Heap, Chad. *Slumming: Sexual and Racial Encounters in American Nightlife, 1885–1940*. Chicago: University of Chicago Press, 2009.

Higham, John. *Strangers in the Land: Patterns of American Nativism, 1860–1925*. New Brunswick, NJ: Rutgers University Press, 1998.

Hill, Constance Valis. *Tap Dancing America: A Cultural History*. New York: Oxford University Press, 2009.

Hischak, Thomas S. *Through the Screen Door: What Happened to the Broadway Musical When It Went to Hollywood*. Lanham, MD.: Scarecrow Press, 2004.

Hischak, Thomas S. *Word Crazy: Broadway Lyricists from Cohan to Sondheim*. New York: Praeger, 1991.

Hoffman, Warren. *The Great White Way: Race and the Broadway Musical*. New Brunswick, NJ: Rutgers University Press, 2014.

Hofstadter, Richard. *The Age of Reform*. New York: Vintage Books, 1955.

Holmes, Sean P. *Weavers of Dreams, Unite! Actors' Unionism in Early Twentieth-Century*. Urbana: University of Illinois Press, 2013.

Hornby, Richard. *Drama, Metadrama, and Perception*. Lewisburg, PA: Bucknell University Press, 1986.

Horowitz, Mark Eden, comp. and ed. *The Letters of Oscar Hammerstein II*. New York: Oxford University Press, 2022.

Hout, Michael, and Joshua R. Goldstein. "How 4.5 Million Irish Immigrants Became 40 Million Irish Americans: Demographic and Subjective Aspects of the Ethnic Composition of White Americans." *American Sociological Review* 59, no. 1 (1994): 64–82.

Hyland, William G. *The Song Is Ended: Songwriters and American Music, 1900–1950*. New York: Oxford University Press, 1995.

Irr, Caren. *The Suburb of Dissent: Cultural Politics in the United States and Canada during the 1930s*. Durham, NC: Duke University Press, 1998.

Jacobson, Matthew Frye. *Barbarian Virtues: The United States Encounters Foreign Peoples at Home and Abroad, 1876–1917*. New York: Hill and Wang, 2000.

Jacobson, Matthew Frye. *Whiteness of a Different Color: European Immigrants and the Alchemy of Race*. Cambridge, MA: Harvard University Press, 1998.

Johnson, Jake. *Lying in the Middle: Musical Theater and Belief at the Heart of America*. Urbana: University of Illinois Press, 2021.

Johnston, Andrew M. "Sex and Gender in Roosevelt's America." In *A Companion to Theodore Roosevelt*, edited by Serge Ricard, 112–34. Malden, MA: Wiley-Blackwell, 2012.

Jones, John Bush. *Our Musicals, Ourselves: A Social History of the American Musical Theater*. Hanover, NH: Brandeis University Press, 2003.

Julius Cahn's Official Theatrical Guide. Vol. 13. New York: Publication Office, Empire Theatre Building, 1908.

Kammen, Michael. *American Culture, American Tastes*. New York: Knopf, 1999.

Kanazawa, Tooru. "Issei on Broadway." *Scene: The International East-West Magazine* 5, no. 10 (February 1954): 15–17.

Kaskowitz, Sheryl. *God Bless America: The Surprising History of an Iconic Song*. New York: Oxford University Press, 2013.

Kaufman, George S. and Moss Hart. *I'd Rather Be Right: A Musical Revue*. Lyrics and music by Lorenz Hart and Richard Rodgers. New York: Random House, 1937.

Kazal, Russell A. *Becoming Old Stock: The Paradox of German-American Identity*. Princeton, NJ: Princeton University Press, 2021.

Kenny, Kevin. "American-Irish Nationalism." In Lee and Casey, *Making the Irish American*, 289–301.

Kibler, M. Alison. *Rank Ladies: Gender and Cultural Hierarchy in American Vaudeville*. Chapel Hill: University of North Carolina Press, 1999.

King, Desmond. *Making Americans: Immigration, Race, and the Origins of the Diverse Democracy*. Cambridge, MA: Harvard University Press, 2000.

Kingsley, Walter J. "Lo, the Press Agent." In *The Broadway Anthology*, edited by Edward L. Bernays, Samuel Hoffenstein, Walter J. Kingsley, and Murdock Pemberton, 27–29. New York: Duffield, 1917.

Kirle, Bruce. *Unfinished Show Business: Broadway Musicals as Works-in-Progress*. Carbondale: Southern Illinois University Press, 2005.

Knapp, Raymond. *The American Musical and the Formation of National Identity*. Princeton, NJ: Princeton University Press, 2005.

Knapp, Raymond, and Mitchell Morris. "The Filmed Musical." In Knapp, Morris, and Wolf, *Oxford Handbook of the American Musical*, 137–51.

Knapp, Raymond, Mitchell Morris, and Stacy Wolf, eds. *The Oxford Handbook of the American Musical*. New York: Oxford University Press, 2011.

Kotis, Greg, and Mark Hollmann. *Urinetown, the Musical*. New York: Faber and Faber, 2003.

Krieken, Robert van. "Celebrity's Histories." In *Routledge Handbook of Celebrity Studies*, edited by Anthony Elliott, 26–43. London: Routledge, 2018.

Lake, Jessica. *The Face That Launched a Thousand Lawsuits: The American Women Who Forged a Right to Privacy*. New Haven: Yale University Press, 2016.

Lake, Mayhew. *Great Guys: Laughs and Gripes of Fifty Years of Show-Music Business*. Grosse Pointe Woods, MI: Bovaco Press, 1983.

Lancefield, Robert Charles. "Hearing Orientality in (White) America, 1900–1930." PhD diss., Wesleyan University, 2004.

Lasser, Michael. *City Songs and American Life*. Rochester, NY: University of Rochester Press, 2019.

Leary Jr., William M. "Woodrow Wilson, Irish Americans, and the Election of 1916." *Journal of American History* 54, no. 1 (June 1967): 57–72.

Leavitt, Michael B. *Fifty Years in Theatrical Management, 1859–1909*. New York: Broadway Publishing, 1912.

Ledbetter, Gordon. *The Great Irish Tenor: John McCormack*. Dublin: Town House, 2003.

Lee, Esther Kim. *A History of Asian American Theatre*. Cambridge: Cambridge University Press, 2006.

Lee, J. J. "Introduction: Interpreting Irish America." In Lee and Casey, *Making the Irish American*, 1–62.

Lee, J. J., and Marion R. Casey, eds. *Making the Irish American: History and Heritage of the Irish in the United States*. New York: NYU Press, 2006.

Lepore, Jill. *This America: The Case for the Nation*. New York: Liveright, 2019.

Levine, Lawrence W. *Highbrow/Lowbrow: The Emergence of Cultural Hierarchy in America*. Cambridge, MA: Harvard University Press, 1988.

Lingeman, Richard R. *Sinclair Lewis: Rebel from Main Street*. St. Paul, MN: Borealis Books, 2002.

Link, Arthur S., ed. *The Papers of Woodrow Wilson*. Vol. 35. Princeton, NJ: Princeton University Press, 1966.

Loranger, Dennis. "Women, Nature and Appearance: Themes in Popular Song Texts from the Turn of the Century." *American Music Research Center Journal* 2 (1992): 68–85.

Lott, Eric. *Love and Theft: Blackface Minstrelsy and the American Working Class*. New York: Oxford University Press, 1993.

MacDonald, Laura, and William A. Everett, eds. *The Palgrave Handbook of Musical Theatre Producers*. New York: Palgrave MacMillan, 2017.

Magee, Jeffrey. *Irving Berlin's American Musical Theater*. New York: Oxford University Press, 2012.

Marcus, Sharon. *The Drama of Celebrity*. Princeton, NJ: Princeton University Press, 2019.

Marks, Edward B., as told to Abbott J. Liebling. *They All Sang: From Tony Pastor to Rudy Vallée*. New York: Viking, 1934.

Mathieu, Jane. "Midtown, 1906: The Case for an Alternate Tin Pan Alley." *American Music* 35, no. 2 (Summer 2017): 197–236.

Mathieu, Jane. "Out of Many, One: Tin Pan Alley and American Popular Song, 1890–1920." PhD diss., University of Texas at Austin, 2014.

McArthur, Benjamin. *Actors and American Culture, 1880–1920*. Philadelphia: Temple University Press, 1984.

McCabe, John. *George M. Cohan: The Man Who Owned Broadway*. Garden City, NY: Doubleday, 1973.

McConnell, Stuart. "Nationalism." In *The Oxford Companion to United States History,* edited by Paul S. Boyer, 537. New York: Oxford University Press, 2001.

McGilligan, Patrick. *Yankee Doodle Dandy*. Wisconsin/Warner Bros. Screenplay Series. Madison: University of Wisconsin Press, 1981.

McHugh, Dominic. "'I'll Never Know Exactly Who Did What': Broadway Composers as Musical Collaborators." *Journal of the American Musicological Society* 68, no. 3 (2015): 605–52.

McMillin, Scott. *The Musical as Drama*. Princeton, NJ: Princeton University Press, 2006.

Meagher, Timothy J. *The Columbia Guide to Irish American History*. New York: Columbia University Press, 2005.

Miller, Hillary. "Marching Off-Beat and On-Screen: New York City's Reform Movements and Charles Hale Hoyt's *A Milk White Flag*." In *Performing the Progressive Era: Immigration, Urban Life, and Nationalism on Stage*, ed. Max Shulman and J. Chris Westgate, 35–53 (Iowa City: University of Iowa Press, 2019).

Miller, Kerby A. *Emigrants and Exiles: Ireland and the Irish Exodus to North America*. New York: Oxford University Press, 1985.

Mitchell, Joseph. *My Ears Are Bent*. Rev. ed. Foreword by Sheila McGrath and Dan Frank. New York: Pantheon Books, 2001.

Montgomery, Maureen E. *"Gilded Prostitution": Status, Money, and Transatlantic Marriages, 1870–1914*. London: Routledge, 1989.

Mooney, Jennifer. *Irish Stereotypes in Vaudeville, 1865-1905*. New York: Palgrave Macmillan, 2015.

Mordden, Ethan. *Make Believe: The Broadway Musical in the 1920s*. New York: Oxford University Press, 1997.

Morehouse, Ward. *George M. Cohan: Prince of the American Theater*. Philadelphia: J. B. Lippincott, 1943.

Morgan-Ellis, Esther M. *Everybody Sing! Community Singing in the American Picture Palace*. Athens: University of Georgia Press, 2018.

Morrison, Matthew D. "Race, Blacksound, and the (Re)Making of Musicological Discourse." *Journal of the American Musicological Society* 72, no. 3 (December 2019): 781–823.

Morrison, William. *Broadway Theatres: History and Architecture*. Mineola, NY: Dover Publications, 1999.

Mortimer, Theo. "John Count McCormack: Freeman of Dublin." *Dublin Historical Record* 48, no. 2 (Autumn 1995): 94–110.

Moses, Montrose J. *Representative American Dramas: National and Local*. Boston: Little, Brown, 1925.

Most, Andrea. *Making Americans: Jews and the Broadway Musical*. Cambridge, MA: Harvard University Press, 2004.

Neville, Grace. "'Tous les jours fête': Games and Pastimes in Irish Folklore." *Cycnos* 10, no. 2 (1993). http://revel.unice.fr/cycnos/index.html?id=1334.

Newman, William M. *American Pluralism: A Study of Minority Groups and Social Theory*. New York: Harper and Row, 1973.

Ngai, Mae. *Impossible Subjects: Illegal Aliens and the Making of Modern America*. Princeton, NJ: Princeton University Press, 2004.

Nicoll, Janet I., and G. Douglas Nicoll. "Political Campaign Songs from Tippecanoe to '72." *Popular Music and Society* 1, no. 4 (1972): 193–209.

Niiya, Brian, ed. *Japanese American History: An A-to-Z Reference from 1868 to the Present*. New York: Facts on File, 1993.

O'Brien, Matthew J. "Transatlantic Connections and the Sharp Edge of the Great Depression." In *New Directions in Irish-American History*, edited by Kevin Kenny, 78–98. Madison: University of Wisconsin Press, 2003.

O'Leary, James. "*Oklahoma!*, 'Lousy Publicity,' and the Politics of Formal Integration in the American Musical Theater." *Journal of Musicology* 31, no. 1 (2014): 139–82.

Painter, Nell Irvin. *The History of White People*. New York: Norton, 2010.

Painter, Nell Irvin. *Standing at Armageddon: United States, 1877–1919*. New York: Norton, 1987.

Patinkin, Sheldon. *"No Legs, No Jokes, No Chance": A History of the American Musical Theater*. Evanston, IL: Northwestern University Press, 2008.

Poggi, Jack. *Theater in America: The Impact of Economic Forces, 1870–1967*. Ithaca, NY: Cornell University Press, 1968.

Ponce de Leon, Charles L. *Self-Exposure: Human Interest Journalism and the Emergence of Celebrity in America, 1980–1940*. Chapel Hill: University of North Carolina Press, 2002.

Preston, Katherine K., ed. *Irish American Theater: The Mulligan Guard Ball (1879) and Reilly and the 400 (1891)*. Scripts by Edward Harrigan, music by David Braham. New York: Garland, 1994.

Replogle-Wong, Holley. "Coming-Of-Age in Wartime: American Propaganda and Patriotic Nationalism in *Yankee Doodle Dandy*." *Echo: A Music-Centered Journal* 8, no. 1 (Fall 2006). http://www.echo.ucla.edu/Volume8-Issue1/roundtable/replogle.html.

Reside, Doug. "Musical of the Month: A Trip to Chinatown." Musical of the Month blog. New York Public Library. June 30, 2012. https://www.nypl.org/blog/2012/06/30/musical-month-trip-chinatown.

Rode, Alan K. *Michael Curtiz: A Life in Film*. Lexington: University Press of Kentucky, 2017.

Rodger, Gillian M. *Champagne Charlie and Pretty Jemima: Variety Theater in the Nineteenth Century*. Urbana: University of Illinois Press, 2010.

Rodger, Gillian M. "When Singing Was Acting: Song and Character in Variety Theater." *The Musical Quarterly* 98, no. 1–2 (2015): 57–80.

Roediger, David R. "Whiteness and Race." In *The Oxford Handbook of American Immigration and Ethnicity*, edited by Ronald H. Bayor, 197–212. New York: Oxford University Press, 2016.

Roediger, David R. *Working Towards Whiteness: How America's Immigrants Became White; The Strange Journey from Ellis Island to the Suburbs*. New York: Basic Books, 2005.

Rogers, Bradley. "The Emergence of the Integrated Musical: Otto Harbach, Oratorical Theory, and the Cinema." *Theatre Survey* 63, no. 2 (2022): 160–82.
Rogin, Michael. *Blackface, White Noise: Jewish Immigrants in the Hollywood Melting Pot*. Berkeley: University of California Press, 1996.
Roosevelt, Theodore. *History as Literature and Other Essays*. New York: Scribner's Sons, 1913.
Roosevelt, Theodore. "The Manly Virtues and Practical Politics." *The Forum*, July 1894.
Roosevelt, Theodore. *The Winning of the West*. Vol. 1, *From the Alleghanies to the Mississippi, 1769–1776*. New York: G. P. Putnum's Sons, 1896.
Roosevelt, Theodore. "What 'Americanism' Means [True Americanism]." *The Forum*, April 1894.
Roost, Alisa. "Sam Harris: A Producing Patron of Innovation." In *The Palgrave Handbook of Musical Theatre Producers*, edited by Laura MacDonald and William A. Everett, 83–94. New York: Palgrave MacMillan, 2017.
Rourke, Constance. *American Humor: A Study of the National Character*. Introduction by Greil Marcus. New York: New York Review Books, 2004.
Rowland, Mabel, ed. *Bert Williams, Son of Laughter: A Symposium of Tribute to the Man and to His Work*. New York: English Crafters, 1923.
Rowland, Thomas J. "Irish-American Catholics and the Quest for Respectability in the Coming of the Great War, 1900–1917." *Journal of American Ethnic History* 15, no. 2 (Winter 1996).
Rugg, Rebecca Ann. "What It Used to Be: Nostalgia and the State of the Broadway Musical." *Theater* 32, no. 2 (2002): 44–55.
Ruhl, Arthur. "A Minor Poet of Broadway." In *Second Nights: People and Ideas of the Theatre To-Day*, 83–92. New York: Charles Scribner's Sons, 1914.
Rumsey, Phoebe. "Embodied Nostalgia: Early Twentieth-Century Social Dance and U.S. Musical Theatre." PhD diss., City University of New York, 2019.
Rush, Adam Christopher. "Recycled Culture: The Significance of Intertextuality in Twenty-First Century Musical Theatre." PhD diss., University of Lincoln, 2017.
Salcetti, Marianne. "The Emergence of the Reporter: Mechanization and the Devaluation of Editorial Workers." In *Newsworkers: Toward a History of the Rank and File*, edited by Hanno Hardt and Bonnie Brennen, 48–74. Minneapolis: University of Minnesota Press, 1995.
Sandage, Scott A. "Old Rags, Some Grand." *Cabinet* 7 (Summer 2002). https://www.cabinetmagazine.org/issues/7/sandage.php.
Santo Pietro, Mary Jo. *Father Hartke: His Life and Legacy to the American Theater*. Washington, DC: Catholic University of America Press, 2002.
Savran, David. *Highbrow/Lowdown: Theater, Jazz, and the Making of the New Middle Class*. Ann Arbor: University of Michigan Press, 2009.
Schwartz, Michael. *Broadway and Corporate Capitalism: The Rise of the Professional-Managerial Class, 1900–1920*. New York: Palgrave Macmillan, 2009.
Schwartz, Michael. "Signed on the Dotted Line: George Kelly's *The Show-Off* and the Fall and Rise of the Can-Do Hero." In *Texts and Presentation, 2013*, edited by Graley Herren, 110–122. The Comparative Drama Conference Series, 10. Jefferson, NC: McFarland, 2014.

Schweitzer, Marlis. *When Broadway Was the Runway: Theater, Fashion, and American Culture*. Philadelphia: University of Pennsylvania Press, 2011.

Sears, Benjamin, ed. *The Irving Berlin Reader*. New York: Oxford University Press, 2012.

Seldes, Gilbert. *The Seven Lively Arts*. New York: Harper and Brothers, 1924.

Senelick, Laurence. "Variety into Vaudeville: The Process Observed in Two Manuscript Gagbooks." *Theatre Survey* 19, no. 1 (May 1978): 1–15.

Shannon, Christopher. *Bowery to Broadway: The American Irish in Classic Hollywood Cinema*. Scranton, PA: University of Scranton Press, 2010.

Shiovitz, Brynn. "Queue the Music: Cohan's Yellowface Substitution in *Little Johnny Jones*." *Theatre Survey* 59, no. 2 (May 2018): 190–220.

Shiovitz, Brynn Wein. "Red, White, and Blue: Finding the Black Behind George M. Cohan's Patriotic Success." *Congress on Research in Dance Conference Proceedings* (2012): 146–53.

Shulman, Max, and J. Chris Westgate, eds. *Performing the Progressive Era: Immigration, Urban Life, and Nationalism on Stage*. Iowa City: University of Iowa Press, 2019.

Simonson, Robert. "When Actors' Equity Staged Its First Strike." *American Theatre*, March 1, 2013.

Slide, Anthony. *Inside the Hollywood Fan Magazine: A History of Star Makers, Fabricators, and Gossip Mongers*. Jackson: University Press of Mississippi, 2010.

Smith, Cecil, and Glenn Litton. *Musical Comedy in America*. Rev. ed. New York: Theatre Arts Books, 1981.

Smith, Erin Sweeney. "Popular Music and the New Woman in the Progressive Era, 1895–1916." Ph.D. diss., Case Western Reserve University, 2016.

Sollors, Werner. *Beyond Ethnicity: Consent and Descent in American Culture*. New York: Oxford University Press, 1986.

Sollors, Werner. "Foreword: Theories of American Ethnicity." In *Theories of Ethnicity: A Classical Reader*, edited by Werner Sollors, x–xliv. New York: NYU Press, 1996.

Sotiropoulos, Karen. *Staging Race: Black Performers in Turn of the Century America*. Cambridge, MA: Harvard University Press, 2009.

Stalter-Pace, Sunny. *Imitation Artist: Gertrude Hoffman's Life in Vaudeville and Dance*. Evanston, IL: Northwestern University Press, 2020.

Stempel, Larry. *Showtime: A History of the Broadway Musical Theater*. New York: Norton, 2010.

Stevens, Ashton. *Actorviews: Intimate Portraits by Ashton Stevens*. Chicago: Covici-McGee, 1923.

Taubenfeld, Aviva F. *Rough Writing: Ethnic Authorship in Theodore Roosevelt's America*. New York: NYU Press, 2008.

Taylor, Laurette. *"The Greatest of These": A Diary with Portraits of the Patriotic All-Star Tour of "Out There."* New York: George H. Doran, 1918.

Taylor, Millie. *Musical Theatre, Realism and Entertainment*. Farnham, UK: Ashgate Publishing, 2012.

Taylor, William R., ed. *Inventing Times Square: Commerce and Culture at the Crossroads of the World*. New York: Russell Sage, 1991.

Thelen, Lawrence. *The Show Makers: Great Directors of the American Musical Theatre*. New York: Routledge, 2002.

Tibbetts, John C. *Composers in the Movies*. New Haven, CT: Yale University Press, 2005.

Tick, Judith. “Charles Ives and Gender Ideology.” In *Musicology and Difference: Gender and Sexuality in Music Scholarship*, edited by Ruth A. Solie, 83–106. Berkeley: University of California Press, 1993.
Timberlake, Craig. *The Life and Work of David Belasco: The Bishop of Broadway*. New York: Library Publishers, 1954.
Vallillo, Stephen M. “George M. Cohan, Director.” PhD diss., New York University, 1986.
Vey, Shauna. *Childhood and Nineteenth-Century American Theatre: The Work of the Marsh Troupe of Juvenile Actors*. Carbondale: Southern Illinois University Press, 2015.
Walker, Don. *Men of Notes*. Pittsburgh, PA: Dorrance, 2015.
Walsh, Francis. “Lace Curtain Literature: Changing Perceptions of Irish American Success.” *Journal of American Culture* 2, no. 1 (Spring 1979): 139–46.
Warfield, Patrick. “The March as Musical Drama and the Spectacle of John Philip Sousa.” *Journal of the American Musicological Society* 64, no. 2 (Summer 2011): 289–318.
Washburn, Charles. *Press Agentry*. New York: National Library Press, 1937.
Watts, Sarah. *Rough Rider in the White House: Theodore Roosevelt and the Politics of Desire*. Chicago: University of Chicago Press, 2003.
Westover, Jonas. *The Shuberts and Their Passing Shows: The Untold Tale of Ziegfeld's Rivals*. New York: Oxford University Press, 2016.
Wickes, E. M. *Writing the Popular Song*. Springfield, MA: Home Correspondence School, 1916.
Wiebe, Robert H. *The Search for Order, 1877–1920*. New York: Hill and Wang, 1967.
Wilder, Alec. *American Popular Song: The Great Innovators, 1900–1950*. New York: Oxford University Press, 1972. 3rd edition edited and revised by Robert Rawlins. New York: Oxford University Press, 2022.
Williams, William H. A. “Green Again: Irish-American Lace-Curtain Satire.” *New Hibernia Review* 6, no. 2 (2002): 9–24.
Williams, William H. A. *'Twas Only an Irishman's Dream: The Image of Ireland and the Irish in American Popular Song Lyrics, 1800–1920*. Urbana: University of Illinois Press, 1996.
Wolf, Stacy. *Beyond Broadway: The Pleasure and Promise of Musical Theatre across America*. New York: Oxford University Press, 2020.
Woll, Allen L. *The Hollywood Musical Goes to War*. Chicago: Nelson-Hall, 1983.
Wollman, Elizabeth L. *A Critical Companion to the American Stage Musical*. London: Bloomsbury, 2017.
Woolf, Paul Jonathan. “Special Relationships: Anglo-American Love Affairs, Courtships and Marriages in Fiction, 1821–1914.” PhD diss., University of Birmingham, 2007.

Digital Resources

American Popular Entertainment Collection. University of Illinois Urbana-Champaign Library. https://idnc.library.illinois.edu/?a=p&p=collections&cltn=APE
Ancestry.com.
Chronicling America: Historic American Newspapers. Library of Congress. https://chroniclingamerica.loc.gov/
Discography of American Historical Recordings. University of California, Santa Barbara Library. https://adp.library.ucsb.edu/

Entertainment Industry Magazine Archive. https://about.proquest.com/en/products-services/eima/
Newspapers.com by Ancestry. https://www.newspapers.com/
Proquest Historical Newspapers. https://about.proquest.com/en/products-services/pq-hist-news/
Twentieth Century North American Drama, Second Edition. Alexander Street. https://alexanderstreet.com/products/twentieth-century-north-american-drama-second-edition

INDEX

For the benefit of digital users, indexed terms that span two pages (e.g., 52–53) may, on occasion, appear on only one of those pages.

Tables and figures are indicated by *t* and *f* following the page number